For Willie

Victoria Corby was born and educated in England. She travelled and worked in Australia and Hong Kong before returning to London to work in advertising and PR. She now lives in south west France with her husband and three daughters. Her first novel, *Something Stupid*, is also available from Headline.

Also by Victoria Corby

Something Stupid

Seven-Week Itch

Victoria Corby

HEADLINE

First published in 2000
by HEADLINE BOOK PUBLISHING

First published in paperback in 2000
by HEADLINE BOOK PUBLISHING

10 9 8 7 6 5 4 3

ISBN 0 7472 6337 X

Typeset by Avon Dataset Ltd, Bidford-on-Avon, Warks

Printed and bound in Great Britain by
Mackays of Chatham plc, Chatham, Kent

HEADLINE BOOK PUBLISHING
A division of Hodder Headline
338 Euston Road
London NW1 3BH

www.headline.co.uk
www.hodderheadline.com

I'd like to thank John Saner and John Henniker Major for their advice and Elizabeth Mortimer and Theo Wayte for providing invaluable research material.

CHAPTER 1

Joyce Grenfell, where were you? If I had to say, '*Don't* do that,' one more time I was going to have hysterics. I was a mother hen who'd lost it completely with the control factor. Though, frankly, if I'd been mother to any of this lot milling around restlessly on the steps of the church I would probably have slit my throat by now, that is after I'd done a few things you aren't supposed to do to children in this enlightened age. It's not that I'm lacking in maternal instinct, well not completely. I don't think anyone, not even Supernanny, could have kept control of ten children aged between two and eight in moods varying from (according to sex) extreme overexcitement to excessive stroppiness.

A suspiciously damp hand attached itself to my silk skirts. I trusted it was merely due to thumb-sucking and not to anything less savoury. 'Susie. When's Wose coming?'

That must have made it the fifteenth time in five minutes I'd been asked that particular question. I didn't know the answer now any better than the first time I'd been asked. My hand gripped the stem of my posy hard, better that got mangled than this little darling's neck. Her mother might be watching. I forced my mouth into a semblance of a smile. The bride wouldn't appreciate arriving and finding her bridesmaids in terrified hysterics. 'Soon, I'm sure, um, um . . .' Which one

1

was she? I took a wild stab at it. 'Clemmie.'

A deeply reproachful gaze hit me from all of two and a half feet off the ground. 'I'm Gwace,' she said firmly. 'Clemmie's different. We aren't *dentical*.'

As near as damn it, as far as I was concerned. In my opinion, only a nursery school teacher can tell the difference between blonde four-year-olds, even when they aren't twins, identical or not. And I'm *not* a nursery school teacher.

'No, of course you aren't, you're just a bit taller, aren't you?' I said mechanically, hoping desperately this time I'd got it right. My eyes strayed gloomily amongst my charges. The twins weren't too bad, actually none of the girls were, despite their incessant need to go to the loo due to excitement, but marshalling the four boys, sulky as bears because they'd been forced into satin Gainsborough Blue Boy suits and buckled shoes, needed all my skills as a one-woman law-enforcement service. Naturally, I didn't say so to their proud mothers, but I reckoned the only things that would keep those four in control were heavy-duty handcuffs and a cattle prod. At the rehearsal yesterday one had locked three of the bridesmaids in a cupboard in the vestry and claimed he'd dropped the key down a grating. His sister, well versed in his ways, retrieved it from his sock. Another announced he was bringing his pet stink-bomb to the service, which had resulted in forcible frisking of all the pages as they arrived at the church this afternoon. The haul included the stink bomb, two catapults and a collection of marbles which hadn't done anything for the line of the owner's satin britches, and certainly wouldn't have done anything for the solemnity of the service as they rolled down the aisle one by one.

The erstwhile owners of the catapults, their hell-born skills refined at the very best and most expensive schools, now had

2

their heads together and were whispering excitedly with many smothered giggles. I eyed them uneasily. It didn't take much brainpower to realise this boded ill for the smooth running of the service. Rose must have been absolutely certifiable to have allowed them anywhere near her wedding procession. And I must have been even madder to allow her to shanghai me into being her bridesmaid and chief whipper-in, I thought, racing forward to grab the twins as they were about to sit down in frilly pink skirts on steps still damp from the morning's rain. Thank God none of the pages had worked out that a bottom covered in lichen would almost certainly mean they'd be banned from processing up the aisle.

A smartly dressed woman hurrying to get into the church in front of the bride slowed down to smile indulgently at the children. Her son, I noted with rancour, barely glanced at me before letting his eyes slide right on by to rest on the generous rear of the lady photographer. So much for Rose's promises that being a grown-up bridesmaid meant you were the chief centre of attention after the bride and, even better, it was obvious you were still available. You could virtually have your choice of any single man, she had said, and a lot of the ones who weren't single as well.

On current form, my choice was going to be strictly limited to either Rose's Uncle Julius, who was notorious for making passes at any female over fourteen and under ninety-three, never mind her shape or quantity of teeth, or a fifteen-year-old schoolboy who had made a not quite *sotto voce* enough comment about 'knockers'. Of course, it would have helped if I hadn't been done up like a giant strawberry milk-shake. I had been intending to come to my best friend's wedding in an enormous hat and a very expensive dress (which I couldn't afford, but who cares if it gives you a figure to die for), but

3

Rose's mother had thrown a complete, and probably justified, wobbly at the idea of ten small attendants without a chief marshal, and guess who was chosen for the post? ('Because you're *so* good with children, Susie.' I was? It was news to me.) Unfortunately, by that time Rose had already conceived her vision for her bridal procession, with the bridesmaids wearing dresses in her favourite pink and copied from a portrait of her four-times-great-aunt posed in a charming bucolic fantasy with lambs and puppies frisking around her feet. Painted when four times Great-Aunt Harriet was six. The resulting costumes were absolutely delightful on Clemmie and Grace, considerably less adorable on me. Unlike the little girls, I have a shape which has been compared (not always in a complimentary manner) to a ship's figurehead. But Rose and her mother both thought it would spoil the charm of the ensemble if I had a different outfit, though they graciously made a concession to my age and figure by lowering the neckline on my dress a little and allowing me to have full-length skirts rather than ones brushing the tops of the ankles. They wouldn't do away with any of the frills or draperies, however, not even the muslin apron which fastened around my waist with an enormous bow and drew, in my opinion, far too much attention to my derrière. As my younger brother had gleefully exclaimed while I was modelling my outfit for my mother yesterday, I looked like a demented Hollywood mogul's vision of Bo Peep. All I needed was a couple of lambs. (Luckily for him, he ducked just before my shoe got him on the head. Two brothers and many years helping them practise their batting means that I have a fine overarm bowling action, not usually seen in women.)

I looked down at my sugar-pink skirts and scowled. Why hadn't I stood up to Rose and refused to be a bridesmaid unless

4

I could wear something slightly more suited to an adult? Probably because I hadn't felt it was really the done thing for the chief bridesmaid to throw a tantrum because she didn't like her dress, and I'd allowed Rose to wheedle me into thinking perhaps it wasn't so bad after all. Rose has elevated wheedling to a fine art. Within five minutes of our first meeting at boarding school she'd managed to persuade me that the coveted bed by the window wasn't in nearly such a superior position as the one in the corner and got me to swop with her. Then she realised her new bed was in a freezing draught and got Jasmine to swop, which goes to show that I'm not the only one who's a sucker for Rose's wiles. (A junior matron, who was later dismissed for having an inappropriate sense of humour, made up the dormitory lists. The four Sophies were next door, one corridor had a Lucy and a Camilla in every room, our room had Rose, Fleur, Daisy, Jasmine and me. My surname is Gardener.)

A surreptitious movement of a page's hand caught my eye and I snapped out a command to not even *think* about undoing Polly's sash. It had taken me a good five minutes to retie it in a perfect bow on the last occasion. He eyed me speculatively to see if I meant it, and must have gathered somehow from the set of my jaw that this time it really wasn't worth risking the retribution that was bound to result from what had been a very good joke the first and second times. I looked impatiently up the road, as eager as any of the other bridesmaids to see the bride. The groom's mother, resplendent in designer green, with a very large hat, and the bride's mother, in blue, with a slightly smaller hat but with several feathers, had disappeared into the church a good five minutes ago, so she couldn't be much longer, could she?

There was a flash of pink skirts disappearing around the

corner of the church. Rose's goddaughter, the youngest of the crew, had taken advantage of my momentary lack of concentration to dash off into the graveyard. With a sigh, I gave chase. In my opinion, children shouldn't be allowed to be bridesmaids until they've grown enough for their skirts to cover their nappies. It also helps if their vocabulary extends beyond a very loud 'No!' when asked to do anything. To my relief, she'd been arrested before she could do anything like excavate a molehill and was now safely being held aloft by the best man, a tall, brown-haired man with heavily lidded eyes and a rather tense expression.

He smiled briefly as I rounded the corner, the expression not meeting his eyes. 'One of yours, I believe, Susie.' His tone implied clearly that he was doing his bit and I could at least try to do mine and keep the bridesmaids safely corralled. Maybe I should use the ties of her apron as leading reins, I thought, eyeing my charge sourly. Not one whit abashed, she was busy flirting with her captor and patting his face lovingly. I was still nice enough, just, to hope her chubby hand wasn't sticky. But any words of gratitude that might have been trembling on my lips were abruptly swallowed as his eyebrows rose and he looked me up and down. 'Striking outfit that,' he commented. I could have sworn he was hiding a smile, not that it was likely, since my limited acquaintance of Hamish Laing hadn't done anything to convince me he had a sense of humour. Though, to be fair, the strain of making sure that Jeremy got to the altar on time, or got to the altar at all before he collapsed with alcoholic poisoning as a result of a week's wake for the end of his bachelorhood, was enough to cauterise anybody's funny bone.

'Aren't you two supposed to be in the church, rather than skulking around out here?' I demanded shortly.

Hamish gestured with his head towards where the groom was leaning against the church wall. Jeremy was normally held to be quite good-looking, with the tall, beaky looks that come from hundreds of years of selective breeding amongst the landed gentry, though he had quite enough chin to escape one particular cliché, but right now it was to be doubted if even his mother would find his greeny pale face attractive. Actually, it was bad enough to make me wonder for a moment if Rose would take one appalled look and bolt back down the aisle with a ringing, 'Not on your life!' when she was asked if she would take this man . . . 'Jeremy found the church rather hot,' Hamish said blandly.

Jeremy must have a remarkable internal radiator, since despite the best efforts of the verger, and a heating system installed as recently as the nineteen-fifties, the church still held all the sepulchral chill of its six hundred years. Either they'd had a very good lunch with the ushers, or Jeremy had managed to circumvent Rose's mother's instructions to the owner of the pub where they'd stayed last night that they weren't to have more than a couple of pints each. 'Susie, when's Rose arriving?' he asked, keeping his eyes tight shut against the pallid glare of the April sun.

That made sixteen times. 'Soon, I hope,' I said fervently. 'When we left she was calling for a needle and cotton because she was worried one of her suspenders was going to give way.'

'Suspenders,' he repeated slowly, as if he was unsure what the word meant. He opened a bloodshot eye. 'Suspenders, as in suspenders and stockings?'

'As in white silk stockings,' I confirmed. 'With seams.'

'Ah, seams,' he said thoughtfully, in the manner of a man who has decided there might be some reason to live after all.

A large black Daimler was turning the corner at the top of

the road. 'She's here at last!' I said, glancing at my watch, and was surprised to see she was only five minutes late. It felt more like five hours.

'Bloody hell!' exclaimed Jeremy, jerking into ambulant life. 'If I'm not there ready and waiting at the altar when Rose reaches the church it'll be a locked-door situation for the whole bloody honeymoon!' He started patting his pockets. 'The ring! The ring! Where's the bloody ring?'

'I've got it,' said Hamish in a patient tone, thrusting young Amelia at me. 'Don't panic! We've got plenty of time. If she's anything like my sister she'll spend ages on the steps, titivating for her grand entrance.' He straightened the carnation button-hole Jeremy had dislodged in his panic, and said, 'Come on, we can go back in via the vestry door.'

Someone upstairs must have been looking after me, for my flock didn't appear to have caused any more mayhem during my brief absence. They were even still clean and everyone had their shoes on. 'Look, children! Here comes Rose!' I called in an overly bright voice as I put Amelia down quickly. I don't care to come in too close a contact with nappies. The boys' scowls deepened even further, the girls squealed and, as the car swept into the drive and came to a stop, stood with desperate seriousness, gripping their flower-decorated hoops for dear life. At least I'd stuck to my guns and refused absolutely to carry one of those.

Even the blasé little male monsters' eyes widened a little as Rose stepped carefully out of the car, holding her train up to avoid letting it drag in a small puddle. In the softest and finest white silk trimmed with lace, her dark hair held back by her godmother's tiara, she was tall, slim and ravishing, the epitome of modest English maidenhood. It was a true tribute to her dressmaker's art, since Rose and virginal were not two words that came together naturally. I couldn't remember anyone ever calling her modest either.

'You look absolutely gorgeous!' I said sincerely. I hadn't seen her completely rigged out before. When I'd left her house half an hour ago she'd actually still been racing around in basque and suspenders, swearing in a most unmaidenly manner as she tried to find her blue garter. (There are some things it is best to conceal from the groom.)

I noticed that she didn't return the compliment. I can't say that I blamed her. It was just the smallest consolation that she looked slightly conscience-stricken as she took in the full impact of my outfit, muslin apron and all, down to the absurd topknot of pink roses on top of my head. Not frightfully conscience-stricken though. She grinned at me from behind her veil. 'This corset thing is killing me! It had better have the effect that it's supposed to on Jeremy tonight. I want him beside himself with passion and devastatingly grateful he's managed to persuade someone as stunning as me to take him on. Otherwise I'm going to complain to the shop. I'm not going to be able to eat or drink a thing! And I was really looking forward to the champagne. Pa's splashed out on vintage.'

'Surely you'll be able to sip a glass or two.'

'I was intending to do a lot more than just *sip* at a couple of glasses!' she said indignantly.

It sounded as if she meant it. 'I don't think you're supposed to get plastered at your own wedding reception,' I said.

'Why not?' she retorted. 'I bet Jeremy's still paralytic from last night.'

Thinking of the groom's pale-green face, I had a feeling if he wasn't still blotto he was sincerely wishing he was. The vicar, a shy soul who lived in mortal terror of Rose's father, the

9

bully of the Parish Council, was hopping around in an agitated manner to indicate we ought to start lining up to process into the church. The organist pre-empted us all and began to play the opening bars of the Wedding March. I marshalled my charges, smallest in front, gingerly wiped a runny nose and hoped desperately no one was going to decide they had to go to the loo again. The Hell's Cherubs took their places as train carriers, still smirking in an ominous fashion. I nudged Rose. 'I don't want to spoil your wedding, but those two are up to something.'

They were both her nephews, so she had good reason to know the depths they could sink to. She turned around and eyed them thoughtfully. 'Understand this, you two!' she said. After a moment they started to shift their feet uneasily. 'If either of you is even thinking of a trick like holding up my train so everyone can see my knickers –' the sudden wide-eyed innocent look on their faces showed that she had hit the nail right on the head – 'you can forget it! Now!' She waved a finger with its tip painted a very unvirginal scarlet in their faces, and turned to the one on the right. 'If you do *anything* to annoy me, Alexander, I'll make you carry my flowers back down the aisle. And, Barnaby, I'm coming to see you star in your school play. If you put even one foot wrong I'm going to wear A Very Large Hat. With a decoration of *plastic fruit*. Got it?'

Two of Satan's finest reneged and went speedily over to the other side. Their behavior transformed in front of our eyes into that of the very nicest sort of choir boy, and they picked up Rose's train with the most discreet gestures, their halos almost dazzling.

Out of the corner of my eye, I saw a bright-red sports car slew to a halt outside the gate and two men half fell out, faces falling as they realised they were about to compete with the bride for who got through the door first. The driver dithered for a moment, then shrugged helplessly, evidently deciding in favour of leaving the car half blocking the road and a chance of getting to the finish line in front. They both sprinted for the church, the passenger still buttoning his waistcoat, as if he'd only just started getting dressed at the top of the lane. Muttering apologies, they vanished into the body of the church.

Rose swayed slightly on her perilously high heels and grabbed my arm for balance. 'Susie, did you see that?' she croaked, her face so pale that her expertly applied 'natural' make-up stood out like a child's face-paints. 'The man with the blue eyes.'

'Yes, he was cutting it a bit fine, wasn't he?' I said.

'I don't mean that!' she said impatiently. 'It was Nigel. *Nigel Flaxman,*' she repeated as I looked at her blankly. 'What's he doing here? *I* certainly didn't invite him.'

'Haven't got a clue,' I said lightly. 'I never met him, remember? But why does it matter? The church must be packed with old boyfriends of yours. What's one more?'

'He was a bit more than just a boyfriend,' she muttered, as she stared into the church with an absent expression. 'I thought he was living in the States. Why's he come? I haven't heard from him for at least three years. And to come with . . .' I clasped her hand, to stop it from shredding any more of the white bud-roses in her bouquet. One had already been reduced to confetti around her feet. 'Oh, Susie. I don't know . . .'

Her face was a mask of indecision. What on earth was going on? So Rose is notorious for the way that she changes her mind, but surely not even she would back out on the steps of the church, would she? I mean, I felt I'd do almost anything

11

not to have to parade up the aisle behind her looking like a right prat in this ridiculous dress, but there were limits. And making a scandal like this was one of them. I took a deep breath. 'Rose, you're about to walk into this church and marry *Jeremy*, remember? It's hardly the time to start considering lost opportunities!'

'I'm not! Not in the way you think,' she protested. 'You don't understand.' She was right, I didn't. She shook her head in a bewildered manner. 'But what's Nigel *doing* here?'

The organist had already run through the Wedding March once. I thought the vicar would have an apoplexy if he didn't get Rose's attention soon. I shrugged. 'If you can't wait until after the ceremony, you'd better go in the church now and ask him yourself, because I'm not doing it for you! And afterwards – ' I gestured towards six expectant and eager milkmaids – '*you* can escort six little girls to the loo because they can't hold out any more through nervous tension! In fact –' I looked at them consideringly – 'if you keep them hanging around any longer they'll all have to go anyway.'

Rose looked appalled. She bit her lip uncertainly, sending the work of a no doubt extortionately expensive make-up artiste west. Her father looked at us with the uncertain air of a man who fears he's about to be subjected to a display of female temperament. He knew his daughter well, and cleared his throat. 'Rose, I think this vicar chappie wants to get on. You never know, he might have another do afterwards, funeral or something.' He held out his arm for her. To the vicar's, and my, immense relief, she hesitated for a minute, then took it. The vicar took off at army marching pace. I barely had time to take my place at the end of the procession before we were halfway up the aisle.

I have to admit I fell down a bit in my role as Universal

Aunt. I was so preoccupied wondering about what lay behind that strange little scene outside the church, and exactly what it was about this Nigel Flaxman that sent Rose up the aisle looking as if she were about to be forcibly wed to Dracula, that I failed to notice our frisking hadn't revealed that the third page was secreting a packet of extra-powerful bubble gum until a dangerously large sphere appeared in front of his face. Fortunately, when it inevitably burst it splattered over a pew end and a decorative little flower-ball hanging off it, and not over Clemmie or the woman in the Chanel suit at the end of the pew. The page spent the rest of the service peacefully occupied in trying to dig as much gum as he could out of the cracks in the wood and off the leaves of the posy. I left one of the mothers to deal with the somewhat precocious five-year-old who invited the youngest page to inspect what she had on under her skirts. To his disappointment, he'd only got to the top of her mother's pop socks (mid-thigh in her case) before he was rapped smartly on the head with a hymn sheet and told to *stop it!* So he did, and then went on to amuse himself by slowly and methodically taking off all his clothes. But the girls had had plenty of practice with Barbie and speedily and efficiently re-dressed him even if all the buttons didn't match perfectly.

I missed that, since I was doing my chief-bridesmaid bit and standing out front, holding Rose's extremely heavy bouquet. Judging by the rigid tension in her back, she was suffering from more than the normal wedding nerves. When we got to the 'just cause and impediment' bit the vicar paused meaningfully for what seemed like an agonisingly weighted second. Rose's head quivered, as if she were willing herself not to turn around and look at the congregation, and I heard an audible sigh of relief as the vicar moved on to the next bit. She

13

was asked if she would take this man Jeremy and she hesitated long enough for my heart to plummet sickeningly before she replied with a confidence-inspiringly firm, 'Yes.' She'd probably been momentarily unsure exactly who this 'Primrose' the vicar was talking to was. Rose claims she was about two when everyone realised that to call her 'Prim' anything was a ludicrous misnomer. She's been simply Rose ever since.

I was trying to examine the guests without making it too obvious that I was rubbernecking, not easy when you're supposed to be standing with eyes to the front. I too was intensely curious about the man with blue eyes, but not for the same reasons as Rose, though naturally I was dying to find out just what it was about this Nigel that had alarmed her so much. For it hadn't just been shock, it was fright as well. I was sure of it. As far as I knew, he was just someone she'd had a fling with during the year I'd spent in France as part of my history degree. It had been long over by the time I returned and she'd never mentioned his name since, except in passing, so I'd assumed he was simply one of her long list of loved, left and forgotten. It seemed that I'd been wrong. But I knew Rose well enough to be aware that the beans would be spilt eventually. In the meantime, it was this Nigel's friend that I was interested in. The one who looked as if he'd only just got out of bed in time to dress on the way to a wedding at three-thirty in the afternoon. The one who could have modelled for my adolescent fantasies of what a man should look like, and sometimes I didn't feel that I'd grown up so very much. Not that someone with the face, and I was prepared to bet the pulling power, of a fallen angel was going to take a second look at an oversized shepherdess, apart from to have another laugh. As we charged up the aisle I'd caught a glimpse of them, tucked away in one of those dark corners with a limited

14

view of the bride given as a punishment to late arrivals. They had their heads together and were whispering. Golden-haired Lucifer was directing his friend's attention to the front. He certainly hadn't been bothering to look at me. Still, it didn't do any harm to dream and I was pleasantly occupied whiling away the service, which was going on a bit. Rose's mother was determined to get her money's worth, so she'd insisted on including all the extra bits most people usually cut so they can get down to some serious drinking and guzzling all the quicker. It wasn't until I heard some indignant throat-clearing that I realised I'd been so lost in my thoughts I'd missed my cue when Rose turned around to take her bouquet back. She held out her hand with an expression promising explanations were going to be expected, and had better be given, later. I smiled sheepishly, handed it over, and tried to get the circulation back into my hands. Well, there'd have to be explanations on both sides, wouldn't there?

CHAPTER 2

I was glad to see that Rose had given up her imitation of the spectral bride. It's not really the done thing for a bride to walk back down the aisle looking as if she's just received a death sentence, certainly not very flattering for her new husband. Actually, he probably wouldn't have noticed, Jeremy isn't long on observation even when not suffering from a crippling hangover, but his mother would have had great pleasure in pointing it out.

I gathered my flock together, noticing in a slightly conscience-stricken way that the contents of the bags of jelly beans I'd slipped into everyone's pockets just before we came in seemed to have been transferred to several faces. I'd thought I'd been so clever in choosing something that wasn't sticky too. Still, we could always suspend the pages from the ceiling of the marquee and use them instead of fly papers, I thought hopefully as, avoiding any actual physical contact, I sent them off down the aisle. Luckily, a super-efficient mother had placed her nanny at the door with an extra-large packet of baby wipes, just in case, and she deftly cleaned the worst off each reluctant face as it passed to go and line up for the photographs. But even she had to admit defeat with some of the bubble gum.

Rose's mother, who was having a field day getting her only

17

daughter married off, and so well too (a thousand-acre estate and a large house), was eking out every enjoyable moment and insisted on even more photographs as soon as we got back to the Nicholls' house, much to the annoyance of the bride, who was saying in a loud voice she needed a drink and a cigarette or she'd pass out. The groom looked as if he heartily agreed with the first part of her demands. The photographer attempted to compromise by having an ever-so-romantic shot of them lifting a glass to each other in a toast. By the time he got his focus right both glasses were empty.

As soon as we finished being recorded for posterity I dashed upstairs and made what improvements I could to my outfit. There wasn't much I could do without scissors and a total dye job, but at least without the topknot of pink roses and the wretched apron I merely looked as if I was wearing a grossly unflattering dress of quite the wrong colour rather than resembling an ageing Shirley Temple manqué who'd never really made it in the cute stakes. Then I ripped the muslin fichu thing off from around the neckline and began to feel a bit happier. The neckline was cut unexpectedly low under its frilly covering and now you could see my cleavage (one of my better points) rather than me looking as if I was supporting a lace-trimmed bolster. The colour was still hell. Have I mentioned that my hair is red? Well, my mother likes to call it strawberry blonde, but truthfully it's more of a pale carrot, which can be quite an attractive colour. Just not when combined with pink. Never mind, a few – a lot of glasses of champagne and my face would probably be a pleasing match. I hoped I'd be beyond caring by that stage.

A queue had already built up to congratulate the happy couple and observe at close quarters who out of the two mothers had won the competition for the largest and most spectacular hat. One of Rose's brothers had opened a book to see how long his mother could keep on smiling while her new in-law kept on repeating to the guests, supposedly *sotto voce*, 'Yes, *such* a pity they insisted on having the reception here. At Moor End Hall there wouldn't have been a need for a marquee at all. The ballroom holds five hundred.' I nipped into the drawing room where the reception line was holding court, waved at Rose, whipped a glass of champagne off a tray held by a middle-aged woman dressed in severe black, and went out through the French windows to the large marquee set out on the tennis lawn. A covered passageway, complete with heaters, had been erected to protect the guests from any inclement weather on their way from house to marquee, but it was unused as, with Rose's usual luck, the sun shone down out of a cloudless blue sky on to a garden where every bloom was absolutely at the height of its perfection. Helped, of course, by a dash to the garden centre yesterday and the purchase of what seemed like hundreds of pot plants to fill in the gaps in the flowerbeds and the orchard where the family mutt had been busily boring for bunnies. Rose's mother would have preferred the wedding to take place in June, when the roses were at their best, but Jeremy, who as the possessor of a degree from Cirencester takes his responsibilities to the workers on his estate very seriously, flatly refused to get married when he should be supervising the haymaking. The result was what looked almost like indecent haste for the pair of them to get married in time to fit in what Rose called a decent honeymoon. In spite of this perfectly reasonable explanation for engagement to marriage in under two months, Rose complained that a lot of people were taking a keen interest in her waistline, hence her eye-wateringly small corseted waist today.

I'd been too busy coping with Rose to attend to lunch and

was starving, so I wandered into the pink-and-cream tent to see if I could snaffle some of the eats before the rush started. Unfortunately, the huge silver salvers of little sandwiches, vol-au-vents, smoked-salmon pinwheels and asparagus rolls laid out on the bank of white-covered tables down one side of the tent were still covered up with cling film and the only waitress apparently on food duty was wearing a grim air that suggested she wasn't prepared to have her immaculate arrangements of nibbles disturbed just yet. A posse of well-covered elderly men, looking as if they were probably major-generals of industry, came in with their smartly dressed wives and began waving their empty glasses around in a hopeful way. The waitress sighed slightly, picked up a napkin-covered bottle and bustled up towards them. I backed up to a table and, trying to look as if I was gazing admiringly at the huge arrangements of pink roses and gypsophila in front of each ribbon-decked tent pole, reached behind me and eased up the corner of some cling film. That egg sandwich was delicious. And so was the next one.

'Here, Susie, you might find it easier if you pile them on this.'

I jumped and swore in embarrassment as I dropped the third sandwich, tomato this time I saw regretfully. I'm very fond of tomato sandwiches. Hamish Laing was standing next to me, holding out a plate, and looking rather odiously amused. 'No thank you,' I said stiffly, horribly aware my face was now probably the same colour as my dress. I don't think I'd been caught sneaking food since I was in single figures. 'I'm not hungry any more.'

'You must have a very small appetite,' he said calmly, helping himself to several sandwiches. It's one of the great unfairnesses of life that it never seems to matter when men are

20

seen grazing on anything edible that comes within their reach, in fact, it's accepted as being quite normal to continually feed the male appetite. Whereas females doing the same thing tend to provoke remarks along the lines of, 'It's no surprise *she* strips a bit burly these days, is it?' Certainly, the middle-aged waitress, who had been distantly pretending not to notice my ham-fisted pilfering, instantly raced forward and with a distinctly soapy smile said, 'Is there anything else you would like, sir? The hot sausages will be here in a moment if you'd like to wait for them.'

'These will do just fine, thank you very much,' Hamish said with a smile.

The waitress's well-upholstered bosom swelled with pleasure as she beamed back. I glanced at him curiously, wondering what had produced this effect. I supposed that his sort of rumpled, slept-in face was attractive if you liked that sort of thing. The waitress certainly seemed to, I thought with amusement, as she began to pick out some tiny stuffed quails' eggs, saying she was sure Hamish would like these. He glanced down and one thick eyebrow rose as he caught my eyes still fixed speculatively on his face. Damn! I thought crossly. He wouldn't be human if he didn't take that to signify some form of interest. Oh, hell! I couldn't be colouring up *again*, that would really make it seem as if I was in the midst of some inarticulate maidenly attraction. I was about to put him right, just in case he was harbouring any delusions along those lines, but he'd lost interest in me, and was looking down the length of the tent, a distinct frown between his brows.

'Sorry, Susie,' he muttered, straightening himself up. 'I think that might be someone I know. I'll just go and see. No doubt we'll bump into each other later.'

If we did, it wouldn't be at his instigation, I thought, as I watched him stride purposefully away.

Rose had made several decidedly bolshy remarks over lunch about the prospect of being stuck in the reception line offering platitudes to elderly relations she'd never seen before when she could be having fun socialising in the tent, so I wasn't surprised to see she'd escaped rather sooner than was usual and was belting over the grass with scant regard to yards of veil and train waving around behind her. She hardly paused to say 'hello' and 'speak to you later' to various people who were trying to buttonhole her, and purposefully beckoned me over into a corner. 'Have you seen Nigel anywhere?' she hissed with an anxious expression.

I shook my head. 'No,' I said truthfully, though I thought I'd caught a glimpse of the fallen angel's burnished hair a minute ago. But Rose wasn't asking about him.

'He didn't come down the line – I thought he might have skipped it. It'd be typical of him. As the car was parked right outside the church, he'd have been one of the first to arrive, but if he isn't in here it probably means he and Luke decided not to come to the reception.'

So his name was Luke, I thought dreamily. Luke. It suited him. I'd always liked the name.

Rose was almost visibly relaxing in front of me, then tensed back into full rigidity as she said, 'But perhaps he's here after all and is in the gents.'

'There must be an extremely long queue if he is. If he came straight from the church he'll have been in there for half an hour,' I pointed out and asked curiously, 'What is it with you and this Nigel to get the wind up you so much?'

She shrugged in a way that struck me as being distinctly evasive. 'He's just an old boyfriend. I was a bit worried he might make a fuss or something. We didn't part good friends, as they say.'

There was a whole lot more to this. You don't share a dormitory with someone for five years without sensing when they're covering something up. Especially as I'd have said Rose and I knew all about each other's affaires (more of hers than mine) and I'd hardly ever heard her mention Nigel Flaxman, and never anything about a sticky break-up. But it's not done to conduct a full-blown interrogation of the bride about one of her former lovers, especially not when two aunts are within hearing distance, so I shrugged and said, 'It's been a long time, Rose. He's had plenty of time to embarrass you if he wanted to and, what's more, he doesn't look like the sort of person who thinks it good form to make a fuss at weddings. So even if he's here –' though a gap in the tent I'd just caught a glimpse of his profile in an animated group about twenty feet away on the lawn – 'I'm sure all he'll do is show what a good sort he is by handing over a socking big wedding present and wishing you all the very best.'

To my surprise, my soothing platitudes had a real effect. Rose began to brighten like a flower given water. 'You're right! Clever Susie! Of course, he wouldn't have waited until now . . . There's nothing to worry about!' She smiled brilliantly. 'You can't think how it was hanging over me, not much, but just a bit, but now I can really enjoy myself!' And picking up her train in one hand she launched herself into the fray, looking every inch the radiant bride.

I puzzled about what exactly was going on, then forgot it as, fuelled by ample quantities of Rose's father's excellent champagne, the reception got into full noisy swing. To my pleasure, I discovered Rose had been right after all in saying that as a bridesmaid I'd come in for a fair amount of masculine

23

attention. Whilst I can't say that I was exactly flattened in the rush for my favours, I will admit I ended up with a modest stream of men of the right age (over the age of consent and under the age of Zimmerframes), if not always the right height (tall women seem to have a fatal attraction for men whose eyelines are at bust level – but perhaps that's the attraction), who appeared to be happy to chat, fetch me glasses of champagne and even pay me the odd compliment or two.

Sadly, the real object of my desire wasn't amongst my admirers. He wasn't even anywhere near me, but right down the other end of the tent with Nigel Flaxman, talking to a crowd of people I'd never seen before. That could be because he didn't fancy talking to Bo Peep; on the other hand, the explanation I preferred, it could simply be that he hadn't felt able to push through the throng to get down to this end of the tent. Though I daresay the two of them would have cut through a Welsh rugby scrum if it had been Cameron Diaz or Sophie Marceau standing here dressed up to the nines in sugar-pink silk. Those two ladies would even have looked quite nice in it too. On the mountain and Lucifer principle (not that I really enjoyed comparing myself to a mountain, it was too close to home) I started sort of edging my way up the tent, hoping if I got close enough the old bridesmaid magic would start working. It did, but not in the way I'd intended. I kept on being buttonholed by friends of Rose's parents who have known me since I first started coming here at the age of eleven and wanted to tell me how charming I looked, how sweet the bridal procession had looked, though only a couple with very thick glasses mentioned what a lovely colour the dress was on me. When I got a chance to do a quick shufty, the two men had wandered out into the garden.

'Soddit!' I said crossly. It was one thing to linger alluringly near them in the tent, pursuing them outside was altogether too blatant.

'Is that a wude word, Susie?' asked a reproachful voice from about hip level.

I bent down towards my small shadow. 'It's certainly a very satisfying word, Grace,' I said confidentially. She gazed at me wide-eyed and opened her mouth to repeat it. I remembered, too late, that Clemmie and Grace had developed an absolute passion for me and had been following me around, copying my speech. It had been rather amusing to hear them saying in my voice, 'If you *dare* do that again . . .' but I doubted their parents would be quite so thrilled if their four-year-old daughters picked up my vocabulary of swear-words as well. I said quickly, 'But you have to be an aunt before it's all right to say it.'

She nodded solemnly. 'That's all wight then. I'm a narnt now.' Oh God! I'd forgotten that her mother was the second wife and was younger than her stepdaughters. Grace added experimentally, 'Soddit! Soddit!'

I shushed her before the volume level reached every corner of the tent. 'You've got to be a *married* aunt,' I said firmly, in what I thought was a brilliant piece of improvisation, and before the little horror could inform me that she'd been married by proxy in her cradle like some fifteenth-century princess (or point out that I was neither an aunt nor married) I said cunningly, 'Shall we go and see if they've got any more of those little eclairs? They're your favourite, aren't they?'

Grace looked up, impressed by this unusual adult perspicacity. Sherlock Gardener doesn't give out her secrets to four-year-olds, but since the remains of Grace's last two eclairs still adorned her mouth liberally and added an interesting pattern to her white muslin apron, the deduction wasn't

25

particularly difficult. Fortunately, I discovered as she took my hand, she had licked her fingers clean.

I settled her down with a loaded plate of eclairs and meringues, hoping a good sugar fix would erase any memory of naughty words. I was just glad I hadn't used my full vocabulary. I contemplated whether I should inform the mothers of the two elder pages that their dearly beloved boys were knocking back Buck's fizz as if there was no tomorrow. But I wasn't in charge any longer; besides, it would serve the two hell-born imps right if they suffered their first hangovers at the age of eight. I was still sore about the plastic spider Barnaby had put in my cup of coffee this morning when I really wasn't awake enough to be given that sort of shock.

'Hi there, how ya doing?' asked Rose from behind me. She grinned at me, leaning back against a flower-bedecked pillar in a most unbride-like fashion, with her veil hoiked up over one arm, holding a cigarette, and taking a hearty swig from the glass of champagne she held in her other hand. It took more than a tight corset to keep Rose away from a decent drop to drink. From the way that her new mother-in-law was glaring at her from a few feet away, you would have thought she'd just discovered that her darling son was united with an alcoholic. Or perhaps it was fear for the veil, a family heirloom which she had pressed on Rose, much to her annoyance, that most concerned her. I have to say that I thought Rose's cigarette was waving a bit too close to hundreds of pounds' worth of antique Brussels lace for comfort. Rose glanced over towards me and whispered, 'Terrible old bat, isn't she? And can you believe she's going to be living with us? Well, in a separate wing actually, and I know that Moor End is a big house –' about the size of a small village from what I'd heard – 'but that won't stop her dropping in uninvited to check that I'm cooking her

26

darling boy wholesome meals.' It was highly unlikely Mrs Ashton would ever see any such thing. I didn't think Rose had ever cooked anything wholesome in her life, unless it came from the chiller cabinet. And I knew quite well she had no intention of nipping off to the nearest cookery school and doing a course in advanced pudding techniques. As she said often, Rose reckoned there were better things to do with your time than cook – such as lie on the sofa and read a book, or go to bed with someone. She'd always had plenty of eager takers for this latter option, though as a result she'd had to learn how to do a rudimentary breakfast. Most men, no matter how besotted, eventually get to the point where they need to be refuelled by regular infusions of things like bacon and eggs.

Rose emptied her glass and looked around for a waitress with a bottle to refill it. 'I'm really enjoying myself,' she informed me unnecessarily. It was quite obvious to all and sundry that Rose was simply having a ball as the centre of attention. Well, she was used to that, but even by her standards today was something special. 'It's about time you settled down, Susie,' she informed me with staggering nerve. Compared to her, I had always been positively sedate. 'Find someone nice, I really recommend it. Forget all about that slimy frog—'

'He's not slimy,' I interrupted, cheeks burning. Rose had had an ambition to be an actress at one stage, until she realised it would interfere with her social life, and she could still project to the back of a theatre without difficulty. Or, as I feared in this case, around a marquee (large size).

'OK, he's not,' she said amiably, squinting down into her glass. I've never been absolutely sure whether Arnaud and Rose really disliked each other or if they both just enjoyed being rude about each other. I suspected the latter. 'But you've been going out with him for years and he's spoilt you for

27

anyone else. It's so annoying! You should have hordes of people after you, yet you walk around with a sort of "already taken" sign on you –' I do? I thought in astonishment – 'so, of course, you're putting out the wrong vibes. I happen to know Edward Fairley has been keen on you for ages and you won't even look at him.' Like the best of us, Rose has a tendency to get woefully indiscreet when drink taken. But in her case, as I've said, she's indiscreet in a carryingly clear voice with faultless enunciation. If only that corset had been as tight as she said. In fact, if she didn't shut up, I'd go and tighten it for her myself, I thought vengefully.

'He's got hairy hands,' I said coldly.

'Has he?' she asked, surprised. 'I've never got close enough to notice. Yuk! No wonder you won't let him touch you! I wonder if he's got a hairy back too. That's even worse. I've got a thing about thick ankles and red beards as well, but what really makes my skin crawl is men with spots on their b—'

'Rose!' I hissed, belatedly aware it probably wasn't the done thing for the bride to be loudly proclaiming her least favourite male body parts.

She looked at me and giggled. 'Still, Susie, we really should find you a decent man,' she said, with all the generosity of the newly married. With rare tact she lowered her voice as she added, 'But not one that comes with a mother-in-law like mine! I'm sure Jeremy's got some friends who'd suit you perfectly.'

I doubted it somehow. Jeremy's friends were much like him as far as I could see, hearty country types who were all nice enough in their way, but hardly likely to set the heart strings singing. Unlike the fallen angel, I thought wistfully. Even my great-aunt, who proudly proclaims that she's never found a man she's liked better than her King Charles spaniels, which is

28

why she's never married, would find him worth a second look. But I had a fairly certain feeling that even if Rose did get around to setting up the Northampton and Rutland branch of FindadateforSusie she wouldn't be including him on her list.

'Frankly, Rose, unless he's a sugar daddy willing to pay my rent, you'd be doing me a far greater service by finding me a job,' I said, in a weak effort to stop her loudly proclaiming to all three hundred and fifty guests that Susie Gardener needed a date.

Rose raised her eyebrows. 'I'll see what I can do,' she said, as her attention was claimed by one of Jeremy's relations.

There wasn't anything she *could* do, unless it was to offer me the cleaning of the pile she was moving to, and I expected there was an army of women from the village already in place to do that. At least I had got her off the subject of my love life, which was not something I wanted aired in front of the two women who were approaching me with expectant smiles and 'Susie, we would hardly have recognised you!'

Thanks, girls. I hadn't seen either of them since my last day at school, so we spent the next twenty minutes engaged in one-upmanship, or catching up, as it's known in popular parlance. We started off with a fairly even distribution of points. One better degree was equalled by a lesser plus travelling to India etc., then I fell sharply back into third place – Lucy was on the fast track in the Civil Service and one day would be a PPS, and Sophie already owned her own PR agency with a rising turnover, though she admitted she wasn't making much money yet. I said I was a Food and Drink Distribution Executive earmarked for promotion in the near future, which was acceptable, if not quite the high-flying career expected of a St Peter's girl. I didn't care to mention that my brand of food-and-drink distribution consisted of pushing packets

29

of peanuts and crisps over a bar and pulling pints, and I'd been promised I'd shortly be allowed to serve chicken in a basket at the tables, which meant I'd get tips. However, I did regain a few pips when it came to the discreet nosing around about boyfriends (not that any of the three of us were prepared to openly admit that we were quite as interested in love lives as careers). A French boyfriend, even a part-time one, is one hell of a lot more prestigious than nothing at all or a tax inspector.

After we'd sized each other up to see who was ageing the best, who'd got slimmer/fatter and who was wearing the most glamorous outfit (I was definitely the one with 'nul points' there) we made insincere noises about meeting for lunch soon and drifted our separate ways.

Rose came tearing down the tent, skirts hitched up in a most unladylike fashion, and displaying a rather natty design on her silk stockings. 'Susie, I've had the most brilliant idea! It could solve all your problems!' she exclaimed, grabbing my wrist and beginning to tow me back again. 'Come on, hurry! We're going to have to cut the cake soon so the oldies have a reasonable chance of getting home for the news and a cup of Ovaltine, and then there's all the speeches. I might not have a chance to get his attention again.'

I obediently followed, wondering uneasily exactly what it was that Rose had a 'brilliant idea' about. I've been the recipient of them before, and though to be fair Rose isn't malicious and always means well, her judgment can become a bit slewed at times. Especially after quite a lot of champagne. Had she taken me seriously about needing a sugar daddy? Oh God! I'd never live it down! 'Rose,' I began as she slowed down a little, 'I don't think . . .'

'Good!' she said, looking towards two men making desultory conversation, both looking more than a little apprehensive.

'He's still there. I was afraid that he might have gone off to practise his speech.'

It seemed safe to assume that by 'he' she wasn't referring to her new husband, so by brilliant deduction I worked out she meant the best man. 'Rose, you aren't trying to set me up with *Hamish*, are you?' I asked with the deepest foreboding. I had a nasty feeling it was what she'd call a nice tying up of the ends.

'Oh, no,' she said airily. 'It wouldn't be any use. You aren't his type. Jeremy says his last three girlfriends were small and dark, so you, being tall and fair, wouldn't stand a chance.' I wasn't at all keen on her assumption that the decision was entirely up to him. Because he wasn't my type either. I'd known that before I even met him. Every Hamish I'd come across before (a grand total of three at university) had an unfortunate predilection for wearing a kilt at every possible opportunity, thus displaying unpleasantly hairy knees, had red hair (bad enough on me, worse on a man) and a mystifying liking for haggis and salt on porridge. Which they tried to make me eat as well. So I'd reckoned it was inevitable this Hamish would be a chip off the auld block too. Actually, when I met him for the first time yesterday, he was a pleasant surprise. His hair was sort of peaty-coloured, if a bit too short and disciplined for my tastes, his knees were decently covered by chinos, and he didn't display any unusual culinary appetites. And even without the positive contrast to what I'd been expecting, I'd had to admit that, while not being tall, dark and handsome, he was certainly tall, quite dark and would definitely be attractive to some. Quite a few actually. But not to me. He still wasn't my type.

He looked up with a faintly unwelcoming expression as we approached. In fairness, I knew I ought to put it down to nerves about the speech rather than anything more personal. I wouldn't be exactly acting normal either if I were about to

31

stand up in front of over three hundred people and had to make a speech that didn't offend the oldies, didn't contain anything which might later be used in a divorce action, didn't imply that the bride was the good time that was had by all but at the same time emphasised how all the single men there were broken-hearted that they no longer had the chance to have her, didn't have any smutty jokes and still managed to amuse everybody. The last wedding I went to the best man got so paralytic as a result of trying to quell his nerves he had to sit down after thirty seconds of trying, and failing, to enunciate the first word. Everyone agreed it was the best speech of the whole wedding.

'Hamish!' Rose said brightly. 'Susie needs a job.'

Not surprisingly, Hamish didn't immediately leap in with, 'Well, she shall have one. In fact, she shall have two.' Instead, he stepped back, looking at me with the air of a man who can't think why on earth he is being involved in this. 'I hope she finds one soon,' he said politely after a pause.

Most people would regard this as a set-down, a stand-off, a bucket of cold water, etc. Not Rose. She smiled at him sunnily. 'Weren't you saying at lunch the other day that er ... er Stephen Bailey-Stewart was in desperate need of someone to help him? Susie'd be brilliant at that.' Her ringing vote of confidence in my abilities was only slightly marred by her addition of, 'Whatever it is he needs someone to do for him.'

Hamish's eyes flickered over to rest on me thoughtfully. 'I'd like to be able to help you out, Susie,' he said at last. Did I detect a trace of insincerity there? 'But Stephen needs someone to organise him, not pull him a pint every so often.'

'Idiot!' exclaimed Rose. 'Susie isn't really a barmaid, that's just to pay the rent while she's looking for a proper job. She used to work in the City, but you know what it's like, it's a

32

man's world and it's so difficult for a woman to get anywhere. To be even considered women have to be twice as good as the male applicants . . .'

I was sure the last thing Hamish felt he needed just then was a feminist rant and that was why he cut in quickly with a promise to ring me the next day at my flat to discuss the job. Rose shut her mouth with a satisfied air. She'd just about reached the end of her list of feminist polemic anyway. Typically, she refused to see Hamish's cool response as a face-saving stand-off and insisted on him finding a discarded service sheet so he could write down my telephone number at once.

I grabbed her arm and towed her away out of earshot. 'Rose, what is this?' I hissed. 'Who is this Stephen whatsit? What's he do? Where's the job?' It wasn't that I was ungrateful for Rose's efforts in setting herself up as a one-woman employment agency, but I had a horrid feeling this might end up with embarrassment all round if, when, I was deemed to be thoroughly unsuitable for this job. That's why I hate asking friends for favours, because of the aftermath. Some people, notably my brothers, call it wimpy; I call it sensitive.

Rose shrugged blithely. 'Dunno exactly. He's a schoolfriend of Hamish's elder brother, that I do know. Actually, Jeremy must know him as well.'

I looked at her sharply. It sounded to me as if she was being deliberately vague, but any questions were forgotten with her next statement. 'I should imagine it's some kind of assistant's job, PA maybe.'

'Rose, I can't be someone's PA!' I said, horrified. 'That would be a real career step backwards, you know that!'

Rose slowly and deliberately took out a cigarette, and lit it while staring at me loftily down her nose. 'A step backwards from being a *barmaid*?' she enquired coldly, looking extremely offended that I was treating her sterling efforts in such a cavalier fashion.

'I've only been a barmaid for a couple of months,' I said reasonably. 'I didn't intend it as a genuine career move.'

She smiled at me and blew a smoke ring (one of her most admired tricks at school). 'Point taken. I'm sorry. But the job market's really hard at the moment, and I think this is to cover some sort of maternity leave, so it's not as if you'd be committing yourself. It'd give you a chance to do something a bit different, look around a bit, decide what you want to do.'

I didn't want to do something different. I wanted to go back to being a money broker. But I knew better than to say so, Rose had never understood the fascination of working in the City; in fact, Rose didn't understand the fascination of working, full stop, so she wasn't the ideal person to dispense careers advice. Besides, her mother was upon us, instructing her to present herself at the cake for cutting duties and to look besottedly at Jeremy while he told all of us how very lucky he was to catch a girl who looked just like her mother (or something along those lines if he wanted a harmonious relationship with the in-laws).

I was hovering near the edge of the crowd, determinedly not pushing myself forward in case I got collared by the maniacal photographer, who was taking pictures of Rose and Jeremy posing with the cake – pretending to cut it, smiling at each other over the top of it, standing with the bridesmaids while they gazed open-mouthed at it, not smiling at the youngest page as he broke off a piece of icing – enough, in fact, for them to completely paper their downstairs loo in cake pics if the fancy took them. 'Your glass is empty,' said a man from beside me, handing me a full one. 'You, of all people, must be able to drink the bride and groom's health.'

I turned to thank him and almost spilt my drink down my detested skirts. It was him, Luke. He didn't seem in the least surprised at my reaction, but then perhaps someone who looks like that is quite used to women being reduced to open-mouthed imbecility in his presence. 'Shall I take your empty glass for you?' he asked with a charming smile, though I was so temporarily dazzled that just then I'd have found it charming if he'd sat down to file his fingernails.

I handed it over, almost expecting, as in the best romantic trash, a bolt of electricity to shoot up my arm at his touch. Disappointingly, I didn't get it; but more satisfying than any electrical discharge, he came back to talk to me once he'd dumped the glass on a table. Close-up he was just as good-looking as I'd thought, bright blond hair falling in an unruly fashion over his forehead, grey-green eyes heavily fringed with brown lashes, and a full mouth that would have been the envy of many a top model. His physique looked like it fully matched up to his face too, I thought, making a surreptitious survey. To my intense irritation, they started all the speech business before we'd had time to do more than exchange a few pleasantries of the where-do-you-live kind, and in all honesty the chief bridesmaid couldn't be seen to be chatting all the way through, even if that was exactly what she wanted to do. Rose's godfather droned on for ages and he hadn't even started winding up when Luke was tapped on the shoulder by Nigel Flaxman, who smiled apologetically at me and made urgent signalling gestures towards his watch. I watched them slip out quietly, my disappointment at seeing Luke leave only slightly mollified by the way he had kissed my cheek and murmured, 'I hope we meet again, Susie.' I wanted to believe he'd meant it.

An hour later, Rose was being shooed upstairs by her mother to go and get changed into her going-away outfit. 'Yes, darling,

I know you're enjoying yourself,' her mother said patiently, 'but if the bride and groom don't show any signs of being keen to be alone it does make one wonder about what's been going on before . . .'

Rose rolled her eyes up to heaven and with a 'Really, Mum!' obediently went upstairs, signalling that I was to come with her and undo the ninety-four covered buttons down her back. At least it gave us a chance to natter, something we're both very good at. Rose was parading about in her white basque and silk stockings like some Victorian pin-up while she was excitedly telling me all about whom she'd been talking to, and her *immense* satisfaction that Jamie Willis, who'd dumped her a couple of years ago, was now shacked up with a vegetarian poet who had made him give up everything that he felt made his life worth living; alcohol, cigarettes, meat, naturally, and any tome that had a joke or words of less than six syllables in it. 'And sex too, judging by the frantic way he was trying to touch up Lucy Strang. And you'd need to be pretty desperate to do that,' commented Rose as she wriggled her way into the most divine Karen Millen suit I'd ever seen. It would even look good on me, I thought, gazing at it enviously, a couple of sizes larger, of course, since Rose is built on racehorse lines and I am not.

She smoothed the asymmetric lines of the jacket over her hips and leant forward to make a minute adjustment to her lipstick. 'And you, young Susie. Did you have any successes?' she asked idly.

I settled back comfortably on the bed, leaning against the pillows and flexing feet that were suffering from spending too long in the pink satin shoes that matched my outfit. I had a distinct feeling that Rose wasn't really interested in any successes of mine, she wanted to talk about hers, so I said vaguely, 'Not really.'

She swivelled around to look at me properly, 'I despair of you!' she exclaimed in exasperation. 'There were three hundred and fifty people there today, at least fifty of whom were male, single and eligible! Some of them were even passable. Are you really telling me you're so hung up on Arnaud, who incidentally isn't even as tall as you are—'

'Yes, he is!' I interrupted indignantly. 'We're exactly the same height.'

'Only when you're barefoot and he's wearing lifts!' she retorted and turned back to the mirror. I let this piece of blatant sizeism go. There was no point in stopping Rose when she got into her stride. 'As I was saying,' she went on loftily, then stopped. 'You've made me lose track,' she said reproachfully. 'Oh yes, that even after three years –' actually, it was getting on for five years, but maths has never been Rose's strong point – 'you don't even find other men attractive, let alone *do* anything with them. I despair of you sometimes, Susie, you're wasting all these lovely opportunities! Haven't you ever heard of when the cat's away . . .?'

'Of course I have and I do find other men attractive,' I said, a touch defensively.

'Like who?' she demanded derisively. Then, as I didn't answer, 'Someone today? I don't believe it!'

'Don't believe it, then!' I retorted childishly.

She swung around again with a grin. 'You did! Come on! Tell me! Who was it?'

I sighed, knowing that I wouldn't be allowed a minute's peace until I confessed all. 'Your Nigel's friend, Luke,' I said quickly. 'And you don't have to tell me that I'm one of a long line either! I know that perfectly well.'

Her bouncy vivacity seemed to leak out of her like a punctured balloon. 'Luke?' she queried slowly. 'What were you doing with Luke?' Her elbow jerked, knocking her lipstick over. It rolled off the dressing table unheeded, making a thin red line down her cream skirt as it fell to the floor.

I'd been expecting her to say something along the lines of Wheyhey, nice one girl! or, I hope you manage to score there! so it took me a couple of seconds to register her sudden mood change. 'He brought me a glass of champagne to drink your health with and we started chatting, that's all.'

'I hope that was all,' she said. 'Because let me assure you, Susie, Luke Dillon isn't for you.'

I propped myself up on one elbow, staring at her, hardly able to believe what I had just heard coming from the mouth of someone who'd promised to 'forsake all others' only a few hours ago. That was our code for, 'I saw him first, lay off.'

Just to emphasise the point, she looked at me hard and stated flatly, 'Stay away from him, Susie. Stay away.' She wasn't joking either.

What the hell was going on?

CHAPTER 3

The signs of spring were everywhere, from the houses in our street with their bright windowboxes carefully padlocked to security grilles, to the yellow swathes of daffodils in the parks, to the bright light clothes that everyone had optimistically changed into because they'd forgotten how perishingly cold April usually is.

I stumped along on my way to work, hands in my pockets, victim of the same delusion that a sky the brilliant blue of June automatically means a similar temperature. I was restless and edgy, with the same sort of feeling which had afflicted me every spring when I was a teenager, that fizzy sense that everything is waking up around you and now *something* is really going to happen. Rose and I had spent many intense and moody hours discussing exactly what it might be, when we would probably have been better occupied learning German verbs. But I hadn't felt like this for ages, and the rational part of me pointed out it had nothing to do with the season, but a lot to do with a general feeling of dissatisfaction that had been afflicting me since Rose's wedding, ten days ago.

Meeting all those old classmates, and hearing the apparently exciting things that they were doing, had left me with the uncomfortable feeling that I was the only one stuck in a rut and not going anywhere. I knew perfectly well they'd been putting as much of a glamorous gloss on what they were doing as I'd been, and that they were probably quite as fed up with what they were doing, but since when has knowing that other people are in the same boat ever actually made you feel better?

It didn't help that, not entirely unexpectedly, I had heard precisely zilch from Hamish and his friend about this supposedly wonderful job. Well, Hamish had rung to take down the barest details of my CV, but he hadn't vouchsafed any information in return, merely saying in a discouraging voice that his friend would ring me if he was interested. The 'don't hold your breath' was clearly implied, even if not enunciated. Even if Hamish hadn't, as I suspected he had, pigeonholed me as one of those girls who flit around from job to job whilst waiting to get married and thankfully give up all paid work, my performance as chief whipper-in of ten children at the wedding can't have given him a very good idea of my organisational abilities. (I have yet to meet a man, no matter how New, who doesn't believe deep-down inside that the ability to cope with children and operate the washing machine comes automatically with the possession of a pair of ovaries. I daresay the incident with the penknives at the wedding rehearsal hadn't helped. But it hadn't been *me* who'd been stupid enough to give them to the pages in the first place.) It would have been nice to have a sniff at a proper job again, though, even if it turned out not to be right for me, I thought gloomily as I turned into the little road where the Bull and Bush hid itself from the more fashionable elements of Camden. I hadn't been up for a place on a long list, let alone a short list, for three months; unemployed graduates are two a penny, and ones who have been asked to resign are about as welcome as a fox in a chicken coop at your average interview. The one temp agency which had been prepared to give my rather dubious secretarial skills a try had now ceased to offer me even the real dregs, ever since I was returned for having the wrong attitude. The patronising little twerp for whom I was working told me just once too often in the space of an hour not to worry about all the anomalies in the report I was compiling for him and to get on with the typing, leaving the brain work to the expert. This accompanied by a lingering look at my chest. I'd only pointed out, in a very polite voice, that a woman's IQ isn't necessarily in exact inversion to her bust measurement.

My thoughts weren't running along any more cheerful lines as I stomped around the saloon bar, wiping spilt beer off the tables at the end of the lunchtime rush. My mood hadn't been improved by a lunchtime full of demanding and exhausting customers who hadn't been quite rude enough for me to be able to let off steam by getting angry. I dumped a tray-load of dirty glasses on the end of the bar and turned to smile mechanically at a man who'd just come in, but Lauren, my lunchtime co-worker, pushed past me, hissing, '*I'll* do this one.' She advanced on him, tightly bejeaned hips swinging from side to side provocatively, shoulders back to make the most of what she'd got. The Bull and Bush doesn't do table service outside the lunch hour, and normally Lauren reserved the right to refuse to carry a half around the bar with all the passion of a trade-union convenor. She must have broken up with Saul again, I thought, watching her go into action. Lauren had an extremely volatile relationship with her boyfriend, who was in 'trading' (exactly what sort unspecified) in the East End. Their frequent bust-ups, due to his habit of chasing blondes, had developed into the Bull and Bush's own soap opera. I'd been too busy this morning clearing up the debris from two hen parties last night to catch up on the latest instalment, but it was normally only when Saul had been up to something that Lauren got her own back by changing from perky Lauren from Lewisham into a smouldering sex goddess. Watching her run her tongue around her scarlet mouth and then pout seductively at the man who was staring up at her with the bemused stare of a rabbit caught in headlights, I decided that Saul must have been caught in full *flagrante delicto* for her to come on like this, especially as he wasn't even present to witness what she was doing. Usually, she restored her self-respect with a few mild 'Hello Handsomes' or a bit of suggestive looking in the eyes, while glancing pointedly at Saul to make it clear if he chose to play away from home then so could she. There would be a flaming row, much appreciated by the regulars, who took bets on how long it was going to last, before Lauren and Saul made up and disappeared into the stock room. I usually finished the shift on my own.

I started getting the clean glasses out of the washer and drying them, glancing over to see how she was getting on. I'd have thought he was a bit old for her, he looked to be in his mid-thirties at least, though he was fairly good-looking, with well-cut but not cutting-edge hair. His glasses were surprisingly fashionable for someone wearing his sort of classic grey suit, which looked as if it had come from a seriously upmarket tailor rather than a seriously stylish and infinitely more expensive men's designer clothing emporium. The Bull and Bush, to be frank, was not accustomed to punters of either type patronising it, which was probably why he was getting the full treatment from Lauren. So far, we'd escaped all the gentrification that had been showered on this area in the last thirty years or so. Not for us any theming or a wine list full of 'interesting little discoveries' or Mexican beer. The landlord even flatly refused to have a non-smoking area, saying they were only for pansies. (Though to do him credit he refused to have a cigar area either.) Lauren sashayed back, giving the customer ample opportunity to admire the fine shape of her rear, and leant with her elbows on the bar, thus stretching her back (and the other bits) out elegantly. 'Be a love, Susie, and do us a half of Special and a roast-beef sarnie, with mustard.'

'I, in case you haven't noticed, am already busy,' I grumbled not very seriously, putting the tea towel down. You can get very tired of drying two hundred glasses. I poured out the half and pushed it over, saying, 'The sandwich'll be ready in a couple of mos. I'll leave it on the bar for you to serve him with your own fair hands.' I had a distinct feeling she was wasting her time. Unlike my best friend, I'm not capable of summing up a man at a hundred paces, but I reckoned this one bore the air of someone who was afraid molestation was imminent and, what's more, didn't believe in the old adage that when rape's inevitable you should lie back and enjoy it. True to my fears, when I came back with the sandwich, which, if I say so myself, was immaculately made with a particularly fetching garnish of lettuce and tomato on the side (not that men notice little details like that), Lauren was muttering under her breath that he must be a poof or something.

'He didn't even look at me properly!' she said indignantly, and it has to be admitted that most men with the normal number of hormones look at Lauren – several times. She almost snatched the plate from me, scattering my handiwork around, and stumped over, hurling the plate on the table as if she were playing Shove Ha'penny. To add insult to her injury, the man didn't appear to notice he'd caused offence, for his eyes were fixed on a small notebook as he reached one hand out for the sandwich. To my relief, as when Lauren's in a sulk because she's feeling unattractive everyone suffers, a group of journalists from the local paper came in for a swift half and a bag of crisps. She'd said before that one of them could pass (in a dim light, a very dim light indeed in my opinion) for Brad Pitt's younger brother and she was off like a terrier after a bone, the man with the sandwich completely forgotten. He looked relieved.

I went back to polishing glasses, letting my mind wander, which is about the only way of dealing with the tedium of the job; inevitably, it drifted back to Rose's oblique comments as she was getting changed. Even more than a week later I still couldn't work out what she thought she was up to. She'd clammed up completely, shaking her head and looking mysterious when I pressed her, just saying in a maddeningly superior voice, 'You've got to trust me on this one, Susie. You don't want to go near Luke Dillon.' But I had the feeling that I might like to go very near Luke Dillon indeed, at the very least go and have a closer look, and this sounded suspiciously like the advice she'd doled out when we were sixteen and I was eyeing up the hero of the sixth form from St Anselm's Boys' School at our school dance. I suspected that now, as then, her advice wasn't strictly dispassionate. (She'd ended up wound around the hero of the sixth form herself and we didn't speak for nearly two weeks.)

The most I'd got out of her was she'd explain to me later (that I *really* believed) and then, in a masterly shutting up manoeuvre, she'd opened her door and called to her mother to come and help fix the jaunty little hat that completed her going-away outfit.

I'd been so distracted by it all I wasn't concentrating when Rose lobbed her bouquet in my direction and it was caught instead by one of Jeremy's maiden aunts (who undoubtedly needed it a lot more than I did. She's been waiting for her lover to pop the question for fifteen years now). Secretly, I'd wondered before if Rose wasn't a bit more in love with Jeremy's house and the idea of being the mistress of Moor End Hall than with the man himself. I didn't mean to imply she was merely motivated by things mercenary, since, unlike men, women are capable of thinking about two things at once; we tend to assess both the sex appeal and the quality of the future nest when making our decisions. Look at Elizabeth Bennett; no one would accuse her of being mercenary, but she didn't start to seriously fancy Darcy until she got a look at his house, did she? And I knew Rose had started to worry about heading for twenty-eight without a ring on her finger. The dreaded thirtieth wasn't so far away either, and the last year had seen a positive rash of her friends racing for the altar. Had she panicked and decided she had to grab the next available man because, unlike buses, she couldn't be sure there'd be another coming along to save her from a life on the shelf?

I liked Jeremy, it would have been difficult not to, for he was full of good nature and bonhomie, but it has to be said, while it wouldn't bother Rose that he wasn't exactly brimming over in the brains department, he was also singularly lacking in the street-cred glamour which she'd always insisted on in her boyfriends before. Jeremy would rather have died than have an earring, or have any other part of his anatomy pierced for that matter. I'd presumed that her tastes had changed, matured a bit, for her previous men were definitely not what you'd call good husband material, or even husband material at all, but it seemed I might be wrong. She'd better have realised now she was married it was strictly a question of look, don't touch, or I could see real trouble ahead.

And why hadn't I ever heard of Luke before? Had she ever had an affair with him? I frowned, searching my memory for his name. When she was going out with Nigel Flaxman, and

45

had presumably met Luke, I hadn't, for once, been paying much attention to what she was up to. I was far too absorbed in my own belated discovery of the delights of the flesh. I'd had boyfriends before, of course, and experienced a certain degree of the delights, but it wasn't until I went to Montpellier for the third year of my degree that I really discovered what it was all about. And being someone who doesn't understand moderation, as my mother is always complaining, I became totally immersed in my new-found pleasures.

I suppose I must have done some of the normal things in that year, explored, made friends, talked a lot of student rubbish, I know I must have gone to my lectures, for my marks were fine, but I can't really remember any of it. All my memories of Montpellier have Arnaud in them. Walking, talking, cooking, driving, swimming with him. Above all, being in bed with him. Wrapped around him, making love, the sheer pleasure of someone's warm skin next to you. And then at the end the sick despair when I realised he didn't have any intention of waiting in solitary state while I finished my degree. He'd always had a thoroughly masculine, French view of our liaison. It had been fun, and he'd be very happy for us to continue having a part-time affair, but that was it.

Back in England that last year at university, I'd been so busy boring my friends rigid about my heartbreak and getting payback for the many hours I'd spent listening to their problems that Rose could have told me she was having simultaneous affairs with the entire judging panel for that year's Booker Prize and it would have gone in one of my ears and winged straight out of the other. So I might have missed Luke's name, though surely if he'd been anything more than her ex-lover's friend I'd have registered his name sometime after I became a functioning member of society again?

I hung on with Arnaud, accepting the situation even if I didn't like it, because I lived in the hope that if I stayed around long enough he'd eventually realise that a rose-tinted future lay in wait for the pair of us. Then, just as I was at last accepting it was unlikely to happen and I'd better cut my losses while I could, the great cosmic joker up there arranged for Arnaud to be transferred to London for a year. Of course, I ditched any vague ideas to chuck him. I decided to live for the moment, grab what I could, and our affair went back into reheat. He had been back in Paris since August and, contrary to what Rose believed, I wasn't living in some sort of nun-like state, waiting for him to call. I was actively, if not on the prowl, at least eyeing up what talent there was on offer. The problem was, I didn't find most of it very enticing. I'd tried branching out a couple of times, but neither man held my interest for very long. But then they hadn't looked like Luke Dillon.

I swore as I pressed too hard and the glass broke under the protective layer of cloth. I shook the bits into the bin and went on drying and putting away.

So was Rose simply being dog-in-the-mangerish when she warned me off him? Did she really expect me to hold off one of the most delicious men I'd ever seen because she was a bit unsure about whether she wanted to keep him in cold storage? Or did she know something about him? Was he a serial killer, or mean to kittens, or didn't pay his parking fines? No, Rose wouldn't care too much about the last. But she was the one who told me I was walking around with a 'noli me tangere' label on my back, so why had she told me to lay off the moment I showed any sign of wanting to rip it off? I frowned. All this pondering was pretty academic. Luke's tongue hadn't exactly been hanging out while he was talking to me, and since he hadn't taken my telephone number I wasn't likely to run into him again even if he had been doing a deft job of concealing almost unbearable lust.

I came back to earth as a throat was cleared noisily in front of me. It was the man Lauren had served, with his cleared plate on the counter and holding his empty glass. I smiled at him broadly. I do like it when a customer is considerate enough to think of the barmaid's feet, besides, in the looks department he was a considerable improvement on the majority of our customers, who tend to have the sort of figures which come from the regular propping up of bars. 'I'm sorry, I was miles away!' I gestured towards his glass, 'Can I get you another?'

His eyes slid sideways towards Lauren, still fully occupied in flirting with Brad Pitt II, and nodded. 'Please.'

'I haven't seen you before,' I said chattily in my best barmaid fashion as I poured the beer. 'Are you from around here?'

'No, I'm just up for the day,' he said in an annoyingly uncommunicative manner, and took the glass from me.

Obviously the best barmaid f. wasn't too effective, so I returned to polishing the hundred and ninety-third glass (well it felt like that) while he seemed to be quite happy to stay where he was, leaning on the bar and watching me work. I smiled at him brightly again, you never knew, he might be from one of the pub guides, though the mind rather boggled at anyone recommending the Bull and Bush. Well, maybe someone who was seriously into 'unspoilt' as in untouched for a hundred years. Our original Victorian decor had been cheap and nasty in the 1890s and looked far, far worse now.

'You're very quick,' he commented. 'Why do you wrap the tea towel around the rim of the glass like that?'

'So I don't cut my hand if the glass breaks,' I replied.

He nodded wisely and glanced down the bar in a hunted

48

fashion to where Lauren was taking her time with the journalists' order. Leaning forward, he asked in a hushed voice, 'Is she always like that?'

'Usually only when she's had a row with the boyfriend.'

'She's got a boyfriend?' he asked. 'I got the impression that—'

He was interrupted by Lauren, who pushed past him almost rudely. As a supposed poof she wasn't going to waste any more of her valuable time on him. 'Hey, Suze! Three Specials, a Guinness, and a Bass, two cheese-and-onion crisps, a salt and vinegar and two peanuts.' This said in such a rapid bartender's drawl I couldn't blame the customer for raising his eyebrows in sheer incomprehension.

I'd filled all the glasses and put them on a battered tin tray for Lauren to take from me with a chirpy 'Thanks, Suze,' before he got around to clearing his throat and saying, 'Suze? Are you Susie? Susie Gardener?'

'Yes,' I said in some surprise. I'd never seen him in my life before. He'd come in here looking for me and mistaken Lauren for me? There are several basic differences between the two of us, starting with about eight inches both horizontally and vertically. I mean the first adjective you'd use to describe Lauren is 'petite', for heaven's sake!

He looked extremely embarrassed. 'I'm sorry, I don't know why I thought . . . well, it's that chain she's wearing around her neck. It's got an S on it. I thought it stood for Susanna.'

'It stands for Saul – her boyfriend. Instead of notches on the bedpost, Lauren collects her boyfriends' initials and then hangs them above her bed when she's broken up with them. She's got a row and a half by now.'

'Really?' he said, casting her a fearful glance. He turned his attention back to me and said, 'Well, I have to say she didn't

49

look like what I thought you'd look like. I began to think it must be me . . .' He broke off and looked at me over the top of his glasses. 'Oh dear, I'm getting a bit tangled up here. I expect first of all you'd like to know why I came in here looking for you.'

I nodded vigorously. 'Mm, I would.'

'I'm Stephen Bailey-Stewart,' he said, putting out his hand across the width of the bar.

I shook it, rather amused at the formality of his greeting after I'd already made him a sandwich and pulled him a pint. 'Err, I heard you were looking for a job,' he said after a silence.

I stared at him incredulously, then exclaimed, 'Oh God! You're him, Hamish's friend!' He nodded. 'I'd given up any hope of hearing from you.'

'Hamish only rang me a couple of days ago,' he said. 'He said it had slipped his mind.'

Oh yeah? It would have been pretty obvious even to a blithering idiot that Hamish had felt that he was being pushed into something. Perhaps he'd been hoping if he left it for long enough this Stephen would have recruited someone else. 'Excuse me if I sound a bit rude, but do you normally go into pubs to search out unknown barmaids on the chance that they might be just what you need?'

Under my fascinated eye, I could have sworn that he actually blushed, but I couldn't be sure as the lighting was a bit dim (according to rumour, so you couldn't see if Jack the landlord was giving short measures). 'Well, actually, I thought I might just nip in here to see what you were like, if you know what I mean, before I decided if I was going to contact you –' I didn't know whether to be annoyed or amused at this preliminary vetting – 'but I was delayed in the traffic so I was late and then I made a mistake about who you were . . .'

'And you're bitterly disappointed about it,' I interrupted, not completely sure if I was joking or not.

He cast a swift glance at Lauren. 'God, no!' he said, so quickly that it was true balm to my spirits, then he dampened them down again by adding, 'You look altogether more practical.' I'm sure he thought he was paying me a real compliment, but I have yet to meet a woman whose heart thrills at being called 'practical'. Well, I suppose it's better than 'well covered' but any stranger who called me that once wouldn't do it again. 'Quite different to what I expected from Hamish's description,' he said thoughtfully.

I would have given my eye teeth to know exactly how Hamish Laing had described me, in none-too-flattering terms, I daresay, since Stephen had thought it necessary to give me the once over before deciding whether to contact me. There was no point in asking though. Stephen looked like someone who was far too gentlemanly and good mannered to come out with the unvarnished truth.

He was looking at me with a degree of approval that made a welcome change from the way that anyone else with a job to offer had eyed me recently. Not that it was going to come to anything, viable jobs that come through saloon-bar doors just don't get offered to people like me. (Though I have had one or two employment offers of the other type over the bar. 'Girls with figures like yours are wasted behind bars. You should be on top of one. With less on. Know what I mean?') 'Would you like to know about the job?' Stephen asked. You bet I would. I was longing to find out exactly why Stephen was so desperate for help that he was forced to ignore the more normal channels of the local recruitment agency, or even an ad in the paper. My mind boggled pleasurably, delving into wild fantasies about *very* unusual working practices. As it had come via Rose and

51

Hamish it couldn't be anything too disreputable, so perhaps it was one of those jobs you can't tell your friends about because they'll crack up laughing. Chicken sexing or putting the holes in Polos maybe?

Three men from the solicitors' opposite, who should have been defending the populace's legal rights, but were bunking off instead, came in. I knew them of old, they tipped, but were bores with an inflated opinion of their wit and repartee (non-existent). 'Look, if we stay around here we won't get a moment's peace,' I said. 'My shift ended ten minutes ago, so why don't we go to the coffee bar around the corner and discuss it there?'

I grabbed my handbag and jacket from the cubby hole at the back and shot out before the legal eagles reached the bar and started demanding service. 'OK, Lauren, I'm off!' I called. 'See you tomorrow. I'm not on tonight.'

She was standing so close to Brad Pitt II she'd virtually grown into him. She looked around with a pout, 'Soooze . . .' she started crossly, then her eyes widened as she saw who I was leaving with. 'Bleeding heck, Suze! That's quick work!' she exclaimed with more respect than she'd ever accorded me before. 'So he's not –' mercifully she dropped her voice a bit 'you-know-what?'

I rolled my eyes. 'Not on the evidence so far!'

'Well, I suppose he is more your age than mine,' she said generously, from the viewpoint of her nineteen years, and looking at me as if I was a candidate for support stockings. 'He's even got a few grey hairs, I noticed.'

'Maybe, but at least he's old enough to hold a driving licence!' I retorted, and on this highly witty note went to join Stephen outside.

All I can say about the coffee at the Astoria Coffee House is it's better than what you can get at the Bull and Bush. This little corner of Camden is singularly lacking in real coffee houses where you can get a cup of just about any coffee in the world for approximately the price of a glass of vintage champagne. Stephen didn't appear to notice. He drank his brown liquid mechanically while, speaking in short, nervy sentences, he described the estate agency he ran (an estate agent? That killed any idea of this job stone-dead. Never in a hundred years would I consider working in an estate agency, but I kept on listening), Frampton, the almost too picturesque market town it was based in, and how his highly competent secretary, who I gathered had organised his life to the extent she virtually chose which ties he'd wear, had unexpectedly become pregnant and had been ordered to bed because of a repeatedly threatened miscarriage. And then, once her sick leave was over and the baby was born, she wanted to spend some time with her surprise packet.

'Frankly, I should think she'll decide she doesn't want to come back at all and I can't really blame her, though it leaves me in a bind,' he said. So now he needed someone to put his life back into order and boss him about for at least the next six months. I gathered that at least two others had tried and failed, he glossed over exactly why, and now, apparently basing his decision on my skill at making roast-beef sandwiches, he'd decided that someone should be me.

'But you don't know anything about me,' I protested. 'I don't have any proper qualifications for a job like this.'

He smiled, the crinkles around his eyes magnified by the thick glasses, 'The last two had qualifications coming out of their ears and I couldn't stand either of them!' He glanced down at the scuffed formica of the table top, looking slightly embarrassed, 'You look like someone I could get on with, which is the most important thing. So are you going to work for me?'

It was out of the question. I belonged to London, not some two-bit little country town. I'd dreamed of living here since I was a teenager, of making a big noise for myself in the City. And those dreams hadn't been too off course. I was one of the few from my year at university to leave with a job already fixed up, not a brilliant one, but a proper job, so perhaps, if not exactly marked out as a high flyer, I was still well above the roof tops. I'd done fine for two years and then I made the mistake of turning the boss down and, worse, believing fondly if I pretended it hadn't happened we could go back to where we were b.p. (before the pass). A month later he reorganised the department and I found all my best clients had been given to someone else, though my targets remained the same. Six weeks after that I was informed my falling figures showed I'd lost interest in the job and I was given the chance to resign before I was sacked. It was too late to say anything about the pass, it would just have looked like sour grapes. I'd been well and truly stitched up. But I did find another job with a really fun, energetic, go-ahead firm. Too go-ahead. It went spectacularly bust in a scandal that rocked the City. That was six months and no job offers ago, but I still entertained hopes that somehow I'd claw myself back into an executive position in the Square Mile. It's all right to be a barmaid while waiting for the golden job to come up, it's so way off beam as to be acceptable, but to accept a job as a PA to a country *estate agent* would announce to the world in fifteen-foot high letters that Susanna Gardener had given up every hope of ever being Someone in the City.

Even if the said PA's salary *was* surprisingly high – I had no idea they earned that much – I didn't want to move to the country. I like the country, heck I was brought up in it and I still liked to escape to it from time to time, but I'd lived in

London for years, all my friends were here. (Actually, when I came to think of it, quite a few had already moved out.) I liked the freedom of the big city, all the things you could do; it was my sort of place.

Being no stranger to amateur personal psychoanalysis, I knew perfectly well my passion for town was founded in a long-extended teenage rebellion. Once I'd discovered my mother's finest hour had been the Summer of Love, I'd speedily worked out the best mother-tease of all was to adopt every single one of the tenets of the material society. But I liked to think I was more grown up now and I could rise above having a mother who still wore bits of *mirror* on her dresses. Just because she'd approve of my doing something was no longer an excuse for automatically rejecting it.

Stephen reminded me rather of a Labrador as he looked at me with big brown eyes and waited hopefully for me to make a positive decision. Though your average Labrador doesn't wear designer horn-rim specs. Country estate agency must be a profitable business. I'm a sucker for Labradors, and I could no more have turned Stephen down brutally than I can refuse my father's Harris a quick titbit when he asks for one (possibly why he resembles an ambulant coffee table). Besides, Stephen was obviously a really nice bloke, if a bit do-lally on the organisation front, so I started to let him down really gently, saying it all sounded fascinating, but . . .

Too gently, because with a skill that made me wonder why he hadn't gone into politics, he demolished every one of my objections, one by one. I'd have a real job to put on my CV, I could give it a trial for just six months to see how I liked it, Rose and Jeremy would be living only about twenty miles away so I'd have a ready-made circle of friends, he knew of a cottage I could have until Christmas at a peppercorn rent in return for caretaking. He didn't mention my overdraft (the result of still living like a City exec on a barmaid's pay), but I'm sure he wouldn't have had any scruples about quoting the very figures if he had known about them. Somehow he seemed to have sensed my restlessness, because every second point was about it being an adventure and how a change would do me good. The guy's fervour made the average Jehovah's Witness look positively restrained. I was wavering (I particularly liked the sound of the peppercorn rent, especially as Stephen talked the cottage up to sound as if it belonged on the front of a heavily tinted postcard) when he inadvertently played his trump card. I was playing for time, afraid that I, who in my opinion am not particularly impulsive, was about to do something very impulsive indeed, so I asked him exactly where Frampton was.

'Well, Jeremy and Rose are to the east, Market Burrough is to the north and it's about ten miles from Wickham –' I didn't hear any more. 'Wickham' blazed into my brain in ten-foot-high letters, winking in neon pinks and oranges with spinning Catherine-wheels and the odd rocket or two flashing all around it. You might say it caught my attention. Surely Wickham was where Luke Dillon had said he had a house? Not that I was intending to go and chase him or anything. What was the point? Even if someone as beautiful as that hadn't already got a stunning supermodel type girlfriend, he'd probably have been irrevocably put off me by the Bo Peep outfit. He might even have thought that I'd chosen it, God forbid! All chances completely blown.

I presumed Rose didn't realise he was living so close to her new home; even she wouldn't think her chances of a happily married life were improved by having an object of desire a mere hand-delivered billet-doux away. But given what I strongly suspected she felt about him, surely in a way it was my duty, as her best friend, to make sure she didn't do anything she might regret later. Which required my presence in the vicinity so I could act as policewoman and general guardian of virtue. And if I was forced to imperil my own virtue in the interests of protecting hers, well, it would be in a good cause, wouldn't it?

'When do you want me to start?' I asked, so abruptly that Stephen carried on with his persuasive spiel for a few seconds, then stopped, his eyes blinking in surprise behind the trendy lenses.

'Monday?' he said at last.

It was my turn to blink. It seemed that despite his vague appearance Stephen was a man who knew what he wanted, and wanted it soon. I made a few token protests about having to give notice at both job and flat and pack up, but I was no proof against his brand of deadly persistence, and I found myself meekly agreeing to present myself for work on Monday morning. I wasn't even allowed to have any doubts about the accommodation; if the fairytale cottage fell through I could always go and stay with his sister, who was a bit of a dragon, but very good-hearted, while Stephen found me somewhere else, which he assured me he would. 'You want to watch her gin and tonics though,' he advised me seriously. 'They smoke.'

For a startled moment I thought of overflowing flasks in chemistry experiments and wondered if Stephen's sister was quite sane, until he added, 'They're all gin and no tonic. Horsy women like them that way, and Carol's extremely horsy.' He folded up the piece of paper on which he'd jotted my phone number, put it in his wallet, and pushed his chair back. 'I'd better get going,' he said, 'I've got a couple of other appointments. I'll ring you later in the week to confirm the arrangements about Number Three, Green Cottages.'

With that he departed, leaving me to stare after him and wonder if he was going to despatch the business of his other meetings in the same vague, but ultimately ruthlessly efficient manner as he'd dealt with me.

I spent the next few days in a frantic whirl that only left me time to wonder if I'd gone stark raving bonkers about a hundred times a day. Some of the tummy-wrenching pangs of fear about uprooting myself to a place I'd never even been before, to take up a job for which I hadn't even seen a description and my only contract was a handshake, and with only the vaguest idea of whether I was going to be force-fed neat gin for the next few weeks were at least partially assuaged by the really genuine pleasure of my bank manager. He came from Rutland himself and knew of the agency. 'Very good reputation, Miss Gardener, very good indeed.' In fact he was so delighted I was moving near the county of his birth he only mentioned my overdraft to say that I probably needed a few new clothes for my new job and with the excellent salary I was going to be earning he had no hesitation in increasing the overdraft by another two hundred and fifty pounds. Was this some bizarre version of *You've Been Framed* and somebody was about to leap through the door, shrieking, 'You've been had!' The door stayed shut, so I decided that Mr Brown, who had just moved straight to the top of my list of favourite people, must have been taking happy pills. It didn't stop me accepting with alacrity. Or going shopping.

Jack at the Bull and Bush was dispiritingly sanguine about my precipitate departure. I'd known he wouldn't have much trouble filling my position, but he needn't have been quite so unfazed by having to replace me; Lauren, on the other hand, was completely gobsmacked, though I suppose that wasn't much of a compliment either, as she was completely unable to get over the fact that Stephen had apparently preferred me, despite my great age, to her. I tried, to no avail, to tell her that his interest in me was only professional. Well, I did at first and then I began to rather enjoy her awed looks towards an unexpected femme fatale, especially as it meant I got treated with a lot more respect and wasn't always left to do the dirty jobs on my own.

My flatmates were also unnervingly cheerful about my leaving them in the lurch like this. OK, so I was going to pay rent until they found a replacement, so they didn't have any money worries, but even so, the four of us had come down from university together and had shared for several years in an atmosphere of remarkable peace and tranquillity considering none of us could exactly be called retiring or unopinionated. Surely it was going to be difficult to find a successor to me who wouldn't upset the balance of relationships in the flat? But the alacrity with which they all said they wouldn't give up the chance to live in a cottage made me wonder if they hadn't been suffering from living with somebody who had Unpleasant Personal Habits. For a couple of days I took to surreptitiously sniffing at my armpits and in the region of my shoes, but the only odours I could detect were Rightguard and Kiwi shoe cream. Finally, I twigged they'd seized on the many advantages of a country cottage lived in by an old, and they hoped hospitable, friend, which were going to amply compensate for the nuisance of finding another congenial flatmate. They were looking forward to long sunny weekends spent in a deckchair on the lawn, sipping Pimms, occasionally getting up to wander along to the cricket field to watch the muscular arms of the local lothario as he bowled to save the match. Actually it didn't sound such a bad idea to me either.

Apart from packing up the truly staggering number of

possessions I'd accumulated through living in the same place for four years, I was making a series of farewell visits to friends and acquaintances who acted as if I was moving to Australia rather than ninety-odd miles up the M1. I was beginning to get used to these previously supportive souls, who for months had assured me I should continue striving for what I really wanted to do, now announcing they thought I'd been flogging a dead horse for much too long and it was high time I did something different. This was usually followed by the announcement they'd be coming to stay. I'd already taken a booking for August. I began to worry that my last night at the pub would be crowned by Jack saying, 'You've got a spare room, haven't you, Susie . . .'.

Stephen had rung to say the owner of 3, Green Cottages was delighted to have the place lived in for about six months, the rent really was bank-balance boostingly minuscule and he was arranging to have it aired and cleaned. He also warned me that it was absolutely tiny (it looked like the house partiests were going to be disappointed) so among all the other things on my list to do I had to fit in a couple of fast trips to my parents' to dump several boxes of things not used now, but too good to throw away.

I dashed back to the flat after the second exercise in breaking the speed limits to Sussex and back to hear the telephone ringing as I fumbled to put my key in the lock. Cursing my flatmates under my breath for not being there to answer it, I flung the door open and made a heroic leap and caught the receiver as the phone rang for what must have been the twentieth time. I stood there catching my breath and rasping heavily in a way that must have surprised the caller very much, 'Ullo, who is that?' demanded a familiar marked French accent.

I took a deep breath, 'Arnaud!' I exclaimed in pleasure.

'How lovely to hear from you. Where are you?'

'Susie, you sound strange. Are you ill?'

'No, I just had to run for the phone.'

'That is all right then.' Arnaud takes great care of his health. For reasons that escape me he believes that he suffers from a particular susceptibility to infection. 'I am in London. We have lunch? Today? My appointment has been cancelled.'

'Now?' I asked blankly, leaning back against the wall. I usually got a little more warning of Arnaud's flying visits to London, enough to wash my hair at least. I investigated my roots gingerly. I supposed they felt clean enough, if not absolutely straight-out-of-the-salon shiny and bright.

'My boss, he rings me at six o'clock this morning to tell me he has *la grippe* and I have to go in his place, then *zut*, when I am here the meeting is cancelled. And then I think, what luck, I can have lunch with Susie.'

He must be missing me, I thought, misty-eyed. Arnaud usually keeps lunchtimes for making contacts and deals, he takes the pursuit of his bonus very seriously. I was about to ask if he was in his normal hotel and jump in a taxi when I remembered the terrifyingly huge amount of packing up I still had to do, and also I'd sworn faithfully I'd have tea with my elderly godmother.

He sounded distinctly put out I was turning him down, his tone getting even frostier when I explained I was moving. I couldn't quite work out whether he disapproved of my taking a non-executive job, of moving to the country (being a true Parisian, Arnaud believes the country is best visited only infrequently, when your liver is in need of a rest), or of my not consulting him, though he did mellow a bit about my godmother. He has an entirely practical, very French attitude to elderly relatives – they deserve respect because they're old

61

and also because they might leave you something.

I suggested to him we meet up later that evening; it was my last shift at the Bull and Bush and after we'd thrown the last of the punters out there'd be a general goodbye drink-up and knees-up with the rest of the staff. Lauren had asked me to bring Stephen, but I'd hastily refused on his behalf. I had a nasty feeling that she wanted to test out whether he really was a poof and I didn't think his nerves were up to it. 'You could meet me there,' I said brightly. I could almost feel his shudder of distaste come down the telephone lines. How could I even think of him coming to a place that served English beer and European wine-lake vin de table? Anyway, he was going to Marlow for the night, where he was entertaining the director of a bank, and he hadn't asked me to come because he'd known I'd be working. I wasn't entirely sure whether I believed this excuse or not. I thought it far more probable Arnaud didn't want the director of a major-league merchant bank to know his girlfriend was a barmaid, but frankly I was so knackered by all my tearing about I could barely summon up the energy to feel more than a pang of regret I wasn't going to see him this time. Especially as he demands full participation and doesn't appreciate someone who lies back thinking of *La Belle France* and lets him get on with it. Still, he did say the deal he was working on probably meant he'd have to come over again soon and next time he'd try and arrange to arrive on a Friday so he could spend the weekend with me in my *petite maison*. I was truly moved by this noble gesture of magnanimity, since tiny cottages are only slightly more Arnaud's style than pubs, and put down the phone thinking in a sentimental fashion that even if it had been about time I'd got myself a new job and a new home, the old boyfriend was absolutely fine, thank you very much.

CHAPTER 4

Two days later I was speeding up the motorway towards my new home, or rather progressing relatively sedately, since several farewell parties seemed to have wreaked havoc with my coordination. The back of my car (a Peugeot 205 convertible, bought when I was in the money and which I'd managed to hang on to, just) was crammed with all that I had deemed absolutely essential and various presents to help me in my new life, including a hand-painted pair of green wellies from Lauren and Saul (who only ever left London for a Spanish beach) and a collective present from the flat, a book called *How to Succeed at Housework*, which I trusted was a joke. Unlike Katie, I knew how to change the bag on the vacuum cleaner.

Stephen had given me a truly lyrical description of 3, Green Cottages, Little Dearsley during his sales spiel. I'd taken it with a mega pinch of salt. He was an estate agent after all, even if they are subject to stringent rules in the trades descriptions area these days. 'Picture postcard' can mean anything, there's one of our local sewage works, and I was quite prepared to find that 'near the pub' meant it overlooked the car park and 'unspoilt' meant no interior plumbing. (In that case I was really going to kick up a fuss. I spent part of my gap year in Australia in a house with an outside dunny. Going to the loo in the middle of the night was not an amusing experience.) So you could have knocked me over with the proverbial feather when I discovered that, if anything, Stephen had been a bit sparing with the superlatives; it also made me wonder exactly how many houses he managed to sell, and if indeed he was an estate agent at all and not masquerading as one to cover something infinitely more sinister.

Number 3 was one of a row of four very venerable work-men's cottages, each with a small pointed porch over a flat, painted front-door and one or two climbing plants to the side of the door. The plants spread and entwined with each other across the width of the terrace, so that in summer the grey stone underneath would be nearly concealed in a mass of honeysuckle, roses, jasmine and, reaching from around the corner of the house on the end, pale-pink cyclamen (according to Stephen, who must know a lot more about horticulture than I do, since they just looked like plants to me). The narrow strips of garden in front of the cottages were bright with patches of daffodils and crocuses and led directly off a genuine, if small, village green; all it needed was a duckpond and it could have been accused of being too perfect. So it was lucky in a way that the middle of the green was occupied by a very ugly Victorian monument to a Sir Thomas Eyre, who had graciously donated sixteen pounds annually for the succour of poor, but respectable, maidens of the parish who had fallen on hard times.

Even the pub was a decent hundred yards away from the front gate; the Dearsley Arms looked very staid from the outside, but I'm not so naive as to believe that seemingly tranquil little places like this aren't just as much a seething mass of iniquity as your average inner-London suburb. Chucking-out time after a hotly disputed quiz night could become quite vicious and it was better not to be within hearing distance of arguments about what really happened at the Defenestration of Prague. And they probably had karaoke nights too. The only disadvantage to the cottage as far as I could see was it had been built in the days when your transport, if you were lucky enough to have it, was a horse who could walk over the grass, and its modern-day equivalent had to be parked on the road and all my suitcases lugged one by one across fifty yards of green. A dark-haired man was leaning against one of the gates, reading a folded-over paperback. It must be Stephen, who'd said he would wait for me with the keys and show me where the important things like the stopcock were. I appreciated the thought, even if it wasn't going to leave me much wiser. I wouldn't know what to do with a stopcock if it leapt up and bit me.

He glanced up as I was parking the car, so I waved, hoping he might have enough of a sense of chivalry to come over and do a bit of suitcase-lugging. He did. At least, I presumed he wasn't just coming over to watch me do all the work. A depressing number of men think that because I'm a good big girl I have the muscles to match. In fact, the only real advantage I have over your average female in the street is that I can lift things down from the top shelf in the supermarket. Stephen looked quite different dressed in jeans and a big green jumper. Not at all the establishment figure he'd seemed in his suit, I thought, as I began to delve in the boot. I wouldn't necessarily have recognised him. I finished easing out a large box and handed it straight into a pair of hands conveniently placed to catch it. They weren't hairy, I noticed irrelevantly. I'd got into the habit of checking hands. As hands go, they were rather nice. But they weren't Stephen's. They belonged to Hamish.

I gaped at him, taken aback in that way you are when you

65

ask for tea and someone gives you coffee and you take your first sip without noticing. For a moment, your taste buds can't adjust. Hamish didn't look particularly thrilled at my reaction. I can't say that I blamed him very much. I'd be fairly teed off myself if I'd given up my Sunday evening to let somebody I didn't even know well into their new house and was greeted for my pains with the sort of look normally reserved for the creature from the Black Lagoon. I'd have started apologising, but I know from experience that when I do I usually put my shapely, but large foot even further in the mire. 'I was expecting Stephen,' I said at last.

Hamish smiled faintly. 'Sorry to disappoint you, Susie.'

'I'm not disappointed, not at all, in fact I'm thrilled to see you . . .' I began, in what sounded even to me like manifestly false gush, and my voice trailed off as his eyebrows rose in a distinctly sarcastic manner. Metaphorical footprints were making splat sounds from all around me. I took a deep breath and started again. 'I'm sorry. I've been rushing around so much my brain doesn't cope well with unexpected changes, but it is kind of you to meet me.'

Ah, that was better. His brown eyes lost their deep-freeze look, and he smiled, properly this time, which made him look a lot more approachable than he did normally. 'Well, it wasn't by my choice.' It was my turn to look surprised. He laughed, but quite nicely. 'Stephen had a family lunch miles away which he'd forgotten about, so he asked me to come and let you in.'

'He seems to be quite good at getting people to do what he wants,' I commented. 'I hope it hasn't put you out too much.' To my annoyance, Hamish didn't make an immediate denial and protest that it had been his pleasure. 'I hope that you didn't have to come too far.'

'Not really.'

'I didn't even know that you lived around here,' I went on chattily.

He shrugged. 'I only moved recently. I had the choice of a job in Bradford or Leicester. Leicester's marginally warmer.' His eyes drifted pointedly to the boot of the car. I gave up being chatty, it would have been obvious even to someone with a lot less sensitivity than me that Hamish reckoned he had better things to do than hang around talking. To me in particular. He needn't make it so glaringly obvious though, I thought crossly. I was working up a fine head of offence when he cut it off at the ankles, saying, 'But Bradford must be positively tropical compared to here. It's perishing!' He hoiked the box under one arm and picked up a suitcase with his other hand. 'Come on, let's get inside and I'll show you round.' He strode off across the road without waiting to see if I was following.

I trotted after him, as usual having overloaded myself thoroughly so that I was wheezing and gasping like a sixty-a-dayer when I reached the gate. Hamish gave me a slightly odd look. Probably because my face must have gone red with effort, which always makes a fetching contrast to my hair, though of course he could have been worried I was about to expire in a dramatic fashion at his feet. The porch had been glassed in to make a tiny vestibule, which was just about big enough for the two of us (providing I held my stomach in or it might have become embarrassingly intimate). Hamish gestured with his head in a somewhat perfunctory manner at the coat hooks and with his hip pushed open a door to the main room, realising just a fraction too late he needed to duck under the low lintel. There was a brief outburst of swearing; I hung tactfully back until he finished, reckoning bandages and stitches probably wouldn't be needed. Anyone who could make

67

that amount of noise wasn't too badly hurt.

As soon as I judged it safe, I began to explore my new home. Stephen was right, it was absolutely charming, but I wasn't altogether surprised that the owner, Preston, an actor who'd landed a six-month contract with a play touring the southern hemisphere, had had difficulty finding someone to rent it. For a start, to say it was small was like describing Thumbelina as a bit on the petite side. If the little brick-floored sitting room had held much more than its two-seater sofa and two chairs it would have been dangerously over-furnished, and to get into the single bed in the spare bedroom it was necessary to shut the door first. But it was all absolutely enchanting, with slightly wobbly whitewashed walls every-where and beamed ceilings downstairs. Hamish had to duck under those as well.

Preston favoured minimalism, so what little furniture there was came in strict neutrals, even the pictures on the walls were grey-and-white abstracts, though he did branch out into a couple of theatre posters in the upstairs bathroom. (He liked his comforts, it was bigger than the spare room, with an incredibly deep-pile carpet and a huge bath in which you could lie back and look at the view across the fields through a tiny window above the taps.) But despite all the cool colours the cottage was anything but cold; the brick floor downstairs glowed a rich varnished red, there was loads of wood every-where and the enormous fireplace cried out to have a huge arrangement of flowers when it wasn't being used for its proper purpose. Apparently, one or two people had expressed interest in looking after it as a weekend cottage, but Preston was, in Stephen's words, something of a green fascist and disapproved strongly of weekenders, saying they did nothing for the village and didn't use the local facilities. Quite why they did less for it than leaving the cottage empty escaped me, but it was my gain. I made a resolve to patronise the village shop at least once a week.

I leant on the sink, looking at the view out of the window, planning long summer evenings spent sitting under the apple tree with a drink and gazing down the length of the narrow garden to the field beyond. By rights, it should have had a meandering stream and black-and-white cows wandering along in the shade. Instead, there was a large prairie expanse of still-green wheat, but there was an admirable view of a church with a pointed steeple on the other side of the valley. There was what looked like a properly dug, but unplanted, vegetable patch at the far end of the garden. My mind drifted in a bucolic manner to lettuces and tomatoes; since my gardening expertise was limited to pots of basil which were usually stripped of all their leaves before they had a chance to die I'd have to call on Mum, the earth-mother incarnate, who adored growing things and would be delighted to give me a few tips on what to do. The only problem was she didn't believe in being mean to slugs or other garden pests, saying that they needed food as much as we did, with the result that she usually had to buy her lettuces from the pick-your-own up the road . . . I spun around at a clatter from behind me. Hamish had just dumped a cardboard box on the pine kitchen table. 'That's the last one,' he said, holding my car keys out. 'Here you are. I've locked it for you.'

I'm not sure if I had the grace to blush at leaving him to do all the work while I wandered around in a dream, but at least I had the decency to offer him a drink as a consolation prize. 'I'd better not,' he said, 'you've got a lot to do. Besides, I bet you can't even find it,' he added, looking around at the boxes and carrier bags which seemed to take up every surface and most of the floor. I could see I was going to have to make another lightning trip to my parents' to dump more stuff next weekend.

'Of course I can,' I said with dignity. I always know where the alcohol is. 'It's in that box over there.' With a flourish I opened a box on the dresser, dumping the pile of books that had been on top of it on the table, and extracted a bottle of wine. I turned around to see his eyes fixed in apparent fascination on the books. Too late, I realised they were the last-minute present from two of my now ex-flatmates; copies of *The Rules*, *How to Get a Man to Marry You*, *How to Catch Your Man*, *What Men Really Want* and about six other titles along the same lines. Trish and Claire claimed that I'd announced rather grandly late one night (very late and equally far down the bottle) while we were sitting around discussing the world and, more specifically, me that it was 'new job, new home, new man' and since in their opinion I was severely out of practice in the getting-a-man stakes they decided I needed some guides. Trish and Claire have always believed that if you're going to play a joke, you should do it properly. The sheer quantity of books smacked of true desperation, of someone who'd already tried car-maintenance classes and found them full of women, who'd hung around Sainsbury's in Nine Elms on a Friday evening and hadn't managed a single meaningful encounter over the chiller cabinet, of being the last desperate step before joining a dating agency for lighthouse keepers and other such professionals who have a natural difficulty in meeting women (so can't afford to be too fussy). If I tried denying it was me who'd bought the wretched things it was going to make me look like even more of a sad act, I thought gloomily. At least the tasselled G-string and matching bra which they'd included as my props for the second stage, i.e. reeling in the man on whom I'd set my sights, were still safely tucked away down the side of the box. Thank heavens for very small mercies.

I hastily bent over and pretended to be looking for glasses in a cupboard while I waved the bottle at shoulder height and asked if he'd like some. I know from experience what the combination of a face tomato-red with embarrassment and my hair is like, and while I certainly wasn't intending to use any of the tips in those get-a-man books on Hamish it'd be preferable if he didn't recoil at the sight of me. After closely examining a half-empty bottle of Fairy Liquid and two dusters for long enough to allow my colour to go back to normal I straightened up and smiled at him brightly.

'Er, yes, just the one,' he said. 'I've got some papers to finish at home before tomorrow morning, so I can't be too late.' Was his slightly hunted expression anything to do with worry that he might be the target of a seduction attempt by a desperate female wearing one of the cheesiest grins ever seen? More likely it was the bottle on offer. With my unerring talent for failing to impress people, I'd pulled out a bottle brought to my farewell party by persons unknown, which had been picked up and examined many times and then returned thoughtfully to the table, unopened. I'd tried to leave it behind in the flat, and failed. I suppose some Algerian reds can be quite good, but somehow the shocking-pink and sky-blue label with an illustration of a bunch of grapes and three camels just didn't inspire much confidence that what was inside was a witty and cheaper version of a St Emilion or even a Bulgarian Cabernet Sauvignon. Oh hell, his estimation of me had never been very high, now he must think I chose to drink stuff like that, I thought gloomily, wondering for a nasty moment if he was a wine merchant. That'd really cap it. Then to my relief I remembered dimly that Rose had described whatever he did as 'dull', and I was sure that in her book a wine merchant would be classified as 'useful' at the very least, if not 'essential', so I was off that particular hook. Or was I? With my luck he was studying to be a Master of Wine in his spare time. I was tempted to brave it out and watch him try and be polite about it, but respect for the lining of my own stomach (to hell with his) made me search out another bottle from the box, merely an Oddbins special, but at least there wasn't any wildlife on the front. I held it up, saying I thought it might be better, and was rewarded with a smile that made me think he could really be quite attractive at times, that is if you went for big-boned, loose-limbed men like that. Personally, I preferred them finer, almost dapper you might say, like Arnaud. Or Luke Dillon.

I unearthed glasses and corkscrew – yes, I could lay my hands on those at once too – and took everything through to the sitting room. 'I haven't thanked you yet for recommending me to Stephen,' I said as we sat down.

A strange grimace spread over Hamish's face. I didn't think the wine was that bad. 'All I did was mention you were looking for a job.'

'Yes, but I thought you weren't even going to do that,' I said, leaning back comfortably. In half an hour I was going to have one hell of a lot of unpacking to do, right now I was going to relax.

'What choice did I have? It was that or find myself barred from the house of one of my oldest friends because I hadn't done what his wife wanted,' he said lightly. 'She even sent me a postcard from the airport to remind me to get on with it.'

I stared at him. I knew Hamish could make jokes, I'd heard his speech at the wedding and unless he'd employed a speech-writer he was nothing like as humourless as I'd initially thought, but despite his tone I had a nasty feeling he wasn't joking right now.

I looked at him thoughtfully, wondering what my chances were of getting him to spill the beans about why he'd thought I'd be about as welcome in Stephen's office as a back-dated tax demand. I decided regretfully they were about nil, that was a particularly clam-like expression he had on his face. But why? He hardly knew me, and he didn't strike me as the sort of man who'd refuse to recommend a woman for a job simply because she wasn't the physical type he fancied. Unless Rose had been telling him some very indiscreet stories . . . I was about to offer to refill his glass when I had a sudden vision of him talking to a woman in a yellow silk suit with a large matching hat and veil. I bounded back upright again, slopping some wine on the arm of the sofa. 'Dammit! First evening too,' I muttered in irritation, rubbing at the stain with the hem of my skirt, forgetting until too late I was giving him an excellent view of the large hole in the top of my tights.

I smoothed the skirt down again quickly and put my elbow over the mark. Maybe my jumper would absorb it all and it would have vanished by the time I lifted my arm again, I thought hopefully. 'You were talking to Gabrielle Nicholls, weren't you?' I demanded accusingly. 'No wonder you were afraid to let me loose on Stephen!' Rose's sister-in-law has the looks of a flower fairy and a tongue that drips the sweetest venom. She has a particular line in flaying alive people she doesn't like with compliments. She doesn't like me. The sentiment is entirely returned. She particularly didn't like me on the afternoon of Rose's wedding, due to the strong line I'd had to take with her beloved son, Alexander, over the stories he'd been telling the smaller bridesmaids about the skeletal hands that came out of the grating and grabbed your ankles as

73

you walked up the aisle. I'd thought Alexander enjoyed my threat to hang, draw and quarter him if I heard one more word, he certainly enjoyed the details of how I'd actually do it and we had a lengthy argument about whether I'd use ponies or horses to pull him apart, but his mother had acted as if I'd been caught in first-degree child abuse.

Hamish looked startled, as well he might. I don't have supernatural powers of recollection or anything, it's just that my feelings about Gabrielle are such that I prefer to know where she is, just in case I ever have the need to be made to feel really bad about myself, in which case I go and stand within earshot of Gabrielle and listen. I smiled coldly. 'So what did she tell you about? How I've been sacked from every job since I was six? I'm chronically unreliable? My filthy temper? I spilt tea in the computer and made the whole system crash, costing the company hundreds of thousands of pounds? I vandalised the coffee machine? I was caught reading a dirty book when I should have been working? I gave a complete presentation without realising I had pigeon's mess in my hair? I misplaced the decimal point working out a sale price and lost millions? I wrote a rude limerick about the chairman and accidentally left it on my desk for him to see? I streaked at the office dinner dance . . .'

My diatribe came to an end as I heard him murmur, 'Now, that must have shaken a few tail feathers!'

I stared at him crossly. This was no laughing matter. My mood of righteous indignation wasn't improved when he added with a glint in his eyes, 'I had no idea you'd had such a . . . varied career. What were you when you were six? Lollipop taster in the sweet factory?'

'None of that was true!' I yelped, then amended more honestly, 'Well hardly any. Actually, I *was* sacked when I was six. I was modelling children's wear for a catalogue being put together by a friend of my mother's. At the time, I thought yellow net was the ultimate in fashion statements so I strongly objected to being forced into all this boring home-spun, organic, *natural* stuff. Finally, I struck over a jumper.' I looked at him and shrugged. 'It itched and it smelt revolting, goat probably. I told Charity so too. She said I was an obstreperous little brat, she'd never wanted me to model her lovely clothes anyway and was only doing it as a favour to Mum. I didn't mind the insults at all, but I did object when she refused to pay me for the work I'd done already,' I said reminiscently.

'I hope you threw a tantrum until she was obliged to honour her agreement,' Hamish said surprisingly. 'So you've really been quite respectable. Shame, I thought at the very least you must have parked in the chairman's space or whipped his special chocolate biscuits,' he added in a regretful voice. 'But Gabrielle wasn't being spiteful about you, in fact she kept on saying how much she liked you.' Chalk another one up to the power of round blue eyes and a lisp on a thirty-year-old woman when it comes to completely occluding the normal powers of masculine judgement. Except that his expression was just a little bit too bland; he didn't believe she liked me either. He shrugged slightly. 'The only things which did come up were she said you had had rather a lot of jobs –' she said I didn't last for more than a couple of weeks in any of them – 'and yes, she did mention you had a bit of a temper when things get difficult.' (She said I threw things and generally made life hell for everyone when crossed. I know how Gabrielle's tongue works.)

Honestly, with his capacity for linguistic obfuscation, he could have made it big as a diplomat – or a politician, I thought sourly. I wasn't in a mood to admire it. He appeared to have believed her. 'Did she mention child-beating too?' I asked.

'Er, she did say something about how you were completely unfit to be allowed anywhere near a child, yes,' he agreed, smothering a smile.

'But all the same you still agreed to inflict a workshy, child-abusing virago on Stephen,' I said crossly.

I noted he didn't bother to deny my words. 'Stephen's a grown man, it wasn't up to me to make his decisions for him, so I did what Rose wanted.' Thanks a bunch for the vote of confidence! I thought bitterly. Then he smiled slightly, 'And I thought you might be just what he needed. Apparently, he used to make his last PA cry with frustration when he mucked up her arrangements, If only a quarter of what Gabrielle says is true you'll probably threaten to keelhaul him if he does it to you! It'll be interesting to see if it works. He needs shaking up a bit.' He rose to his feet, thanking me for the drink, and left me to wonder whether he'd been serious or not. I was beginning to think that Hamish Laing wasn't quite as stuffy as he'd first seemed.

CHAPTER 5

Well, if Hamish thought I was workshy he should have seen me this week, I thought, pushing back my chair and checking the property details I'd just been compiling from Stephen's scribbled notes. He was an extraordinary mixture of chaos and meticulousness. I knew quite well that all the measurements were perfect to the nearest centimetre, if not the millimetre, but the descriptions were both illegible and, when I could read them, often idiosyncratic, with comments that were supposed to be transcribed into decent English for the property details. Some were straightforward, like 'original Victorian wallpaper' and 'checked marble floor', some not so clear, such as 'ten minutes' jog to station'. How many minutes' walk did that make? Then there were comments not meant for the general public: 'claw-foot iron bath (off a builder's skip and looks it)' or 'immaculate flock wallpaper – typical curry-house style'. And the longest section, where I was supposed to decide in Stephen's absence what was supposed to go in and what wasn't. 'Off main road (on train line – literally).' 'Renowned village shop (wife ex-page-three model).' 'Delightful views of river (in river when it floods).' And the ambiguous 'many improvements installed by the owner'. Then the final part which included things like 'charming matured garden with ??? trees – check please, Susie.' How? I'd think crossly. Somehow Stephen managed never to be in the office when I got to those bits and he had an uncanny ability for knowing when *not* to answer his mobile. I felt completely wrung out. Normally when you start a new job (and believe me I've had far too much practice at that) everyone tiptoes around you, handing you the odd file to read so you can assimilate everything to do with the company, and saying they'll show you what to do when they have a minute. By halfway through the second day you're so bored you're pleading to be allowed to do the filing and rearrange the stationery cupboard. Not at Bailey-Stewart Estate Agents you weren't. I'd barely found out where the loo was, and hadn't yet located the coffee machine, when Stephen dumped a pile of files on my desk and asked me to see if I could sort through them while he was out. He then left at a run, saying he was already late for his appointment. That was my sum total of orientation into my job. Sometimes I wasn't surprised his previous assistant had thrown in the towel after two weeks. (It was rumoured that she had left in hysterics, saying she hadn't been taught to cope with such chaos at college.) Luckily, Amanda, one of the agents, took pity on my woeful ignorance and spent a morning showing me what was what or we might have had quite a few disgruntled clients wanting to know things like why their bijou cottage was being advertised in the *Dubai Times* and why the management charge for the rental properties had risen by 300 per cent overnight. I had to spend the best part of a day working out what the cryptic squiggles in Stephen's diary might possibly mean. It was quickly made apparent that one of the chief essentials for this job was a considerable degree of psychic ability, otherwise how on earth was I supposed to know that 'X B'd C' pencilled in for Friday afternoon meant 'Contracts due to be exchanged on Bowfield Cottage'? And Stephen always seemed so surprised if I couldn't instantly divine what he meant. He was, without doubt, one of the vaguest people I had ever met, though I couldn't help thinking if he hadn't possessed quite so much charm and ability to get people, usually female, to smile tolerantly and pick up after him he would have been quite capable of dealing with the boring bits himself.

Nearly two weeks into the job I was at last beginning to have some success in divining what it was he wanted, so I wasn't endlessly asking Amanda or Jenny the secretary for help. I was surprised at how much I was enjoying myself. My experiences at temping had led me to think I wasn't best suited to being someone's assistant, I've always been better at telling people what to do rather than being told, hence the reason I made it to the dizzy heights of school prefect (until I was sacked for going to a horror film in the local town with Rose). But given Stephen's general methods of working I had plenty of scope for working on my own initiative and, though I would never have thought to hear myself admitting this, I was finding estate agency in general infinitely more interesting than the money market.

Amanda came in, wearing the self-satisfied smile of someone who knows they've been extravagant and doesn't regret it one bit. She was carrying a glossy dark-blue bag I recognised as matching the frontage of a very smart little lingerie shop in the High Street. Frampton had some surprisingly expensive shops, there must be plenty of money around locally. And Amanda was adding to the general wealth by blowing a large part of the commission she'd just got for selling a des res on an executive estate ten miles away. At very little prompting, no prompting at all in fact, she undid several layers of parchment-coloured tissue paper and held up some extremely delectable silk wisps; calling them a bra-and-pants set was much too pedantic. I tried to quell my instinctive pang of envy by telling myself firmly I really had better things to do than handwash my underwear, and I'd bet that paper-fine silk needed ironing too. It didn't make me feel much better. I still coveted them desperately. My grandmother used to say the first thing a woman did when she had her eyes on a man was go out and buy new underwear. It made me wonder if she was talking from experience. She had very liberal views for someone of her generation, but all the same, it's hard to imagine your *grand-mother* doing that sort of thing, especially as by the time I knew her she was white-haired and settled into relatively sedate old age. I realised with a slight pang that all I'd bought in the lingerie area for the last two years were three-packs from Marks and Sparks, practical, but hardly the high spots of glamour. It said something about the way my relationship with Arnaud had drifted into the 'comfortable old shoe' mode that it hadn't even occurred to me to go and buy something as small and transparent as the items Amanda was holding up.

'I presume those are for Bill's benefit?' I asked.

Amanda grinned. 'You bet! He's been working really hard recently, so I thought I'd give him a bit of a treat. He might even stop thinking about that blessed computer of his for a bit!' She adored grumbling about her husband, forever grous-ing that if she'd known her married life was going to consist of tenderly cooking the most delectable morsels only to see them eaten with one hand while the other continued to roam over the keyboard she wouldn't have bothered with a trip up the aisle. However, judging by the smile of cat-like contentment that she wore most mornings, it didn't seem that Bill spent every waking moment examining the type of figure that appears on a screen.

'If he continues to prefer the computer to you when you're

in those it'll be grounds for divorce!' I commented, eyeing her purchases wistfully and thinking perhaps I should wander down and look in the lingerie shop window myself. But then I decided there was no point gazing at stuff I didn't need (although I can't say that has ever put me off before), more importantly, had no one to see me in – I had no idea when Arnaud was going to be able to fit a trip ninety miles up the M1 into his busy itinerary – and, what should be the primary consideration, which would certainly send my overdraft up to implosion point. I was sure when Mr Brown had so kindly offered me that increased overdraft by 'new clothes' for my new job he hadn't meant flimsies. Well, maybe he had, I didn't know him well enough to hazard a guess, but I still couldn't afford it. I stretched and said, 'Stephen wants me to take some brochures over to the other office and pick up a few things, so I might as well do it now.'

Amanda looked at me with exaggerated amazement, 'You're going to spend the whole of your lunch hour going over to Market Burrough and back?'

'Of course I'm not!' I retorted. 'I love nosing around new places so I'll grab a sandwich there and wander around.'

'Yeah, I was beginning to wonder about such conspicuous dedication,' said Amanda. 'No one who works for Stephen should take the job too seriously – that route leads to insanity. Though, of course,' she added thoughtfully, 'there are many, including Cheryl, who was here before you, who say working for Stephen is a route to insanity in itself!'

Sometimes I had distinct sympathy with that sentiment, but at least working for Stephen was fun, I thought as I made the pretty journey through back roads to the other branch office about fifteen miles away. It was almost solely staffed by Stephen's father's original negotiator, an old boy called Maurice

Young, who was long past his retirement date, but refused obstinately to retire on the grounds that he had nothing better to do. A more ruthless businessman than Stephen would have put Maurice out to grass long ago and merged the two offices, but as he said to me with a rueful smile, they didn't actually lose money on Maurice's office, and sometimes due to simply having been around for so long Maurice came up trumps in an entirely unexpected way. This brochure I was delivering publicising a small Georgian gem was a case in point. He'd sold it to its elderly owner forty-three years ago, and she'd been so charmed with the idea of dealing with the same man again that she'd refused all the blandishments of the bigger chains and given us sole agency.

I carried in the boxes of brochures and stopped for a few minutes to chat with Maurice, whom I'd only spoken to on the phone before. He was charming, telling me how nice it was going to be having a pretty young thing visiting him from time to time, and generally making the sort of remarks which if he'd been in America would have had a sexual-harassment suit slapped on him before he could say, 'Delighted to see you.' He was of the old school that believes firmly that it's a gentleman's duty to flirt with every female who crosses his path and I didn't mind at all. It was rather nice to be made to feel you were the sole cause of whatever spring there might be in the step of that particular sixty-seven-year-old. I collected the files Stephen needed – we had learnt from experience not to ask Maurice to fax anything unless strictly necessary (the repairman had had to come back three times on the last occasion) – and dumped them in the boot of my car before wandering off in search of my sandwich.

The choice appeared to be limited to two; a sandwich bar of the type where you get free salmonella with every bap and a badly over-renovated pub. At least the pub looked clean. I was contemplating whether it was one of those places a woman feels comfortable in on her own, or whether I should go and get a newspaper first so I could make it quite clear I wasn't looking for a pick-up, when out of the corner of my eye I saw a familiar man walking down the street towards me, talking to two others. I turned automatically and did a double-take. It wasn't possible!

'Hello Martin,' I said in a funny high voice, quickly running over in my mind what I was wearing, praying desperately that my skirt hadn't worked its way round so I had an unflattering and fattening seam running down the middle of one thigh and that I hadn't pressed my face up against a grubby window since I last looked in a mirror. At least I'd washed my hair last night and brushed it just before going in to see Maurice, so it wouldn't be doing a haystack impression. 'Are you here to see Maurice as well?'

Stephen's senior negotiator slowed down, looking at me without particular pleasure. He didn't seem to like me, and I couldn't work out why, unless he objected on principle to women who were taller than himself. I hadn't done anything to annoy him, at least I thought I hadn't. I hadn't made sarky comments about dictator complexes (I'd been tempted) and I'd done the last-minute work he'd thrown at me without (much) complaint, but he still continued to treat me as if I was terminally inefficient, not an attitude I appreciate. But needs must. I smiled at him broadly as I spoke. He nodded slightly in my direction, said, 'Susie,' and was carrying on, without breaking his stride, when I exclaimed loudly, 'Oh, hello! It's Luke, isn't it? How nice to see you again. What a coincidence!'

I'd half convinced myself my memories of Luke Dillon

were highly over coloured, no one could possibly be that good-looking. Well, maybe they were a bit exaggerated, but they weren't that far off, I thought incredulously as he smiled at me. So the sunlight wasn't quite as flattering as the rose-tinted light from the pink lining in the marquee, but the now visible lines around his mouth gave him, in my biased opinion, some added character. And like most women who grew up on a diet of Georgette Heyer I'm a complete sucker for a man who looks just a bit dissipated. God, he looked as if he'd been born to wear a beaten-up leather jacket and jeans, I thought, my hormones going into overdrive. It was almost too much. 'How are you?' he asked politely, with no signs of recognising who I was at all.

'Susie Gardener,' I prompted, and then, as he seemed to need further help, 'We met at Rose and Jeremy's wedding.'

'Of course,' he said, in a tone that made it clear he was none the wiser. While, unlike Martin, he was basically too good-mannered to even think of looking at his watch with an impatient sigh, it was apparent from his blank expression and the way his eyes shifted over my shoulder that he wasn't in any hurry to renew his acquaintance with me. He did, however, appear to be eager to go in the pub and get to know a pint. Well, I supposed men like him virtually had girls flinging themselves in front of them like Lady Walter Raleighs, but bang went my chances of something to eat. I could have risked Luke Dillon thinking that I was pursuing him, especially if it got a result (well, a girl can always hope), but no way was I prepared to have Martin Prescott going back to the office and informing them all in his snide way that I was such a sad, desperate act I had to resort to following men into pubs.

'I mustn't keep you,' I said, as Luke eyed the door to the

pub again in a longing manner, and I was chagrined to see that he looked distinctly relieved.

Then the third member of the party said, 'I'm not surprised that Luke doesn't recognise you out of that terrible bridesmaid's dress! The present outfit is an enormous improvement! I wouldn't be surprised if you refused to ever speak to Rose again.' He put his hand out as Luke at last began to look at me with some degree of recognition. 'I'm Nigel Flaxman, we haven't met, but I have heard of *you* before.'

I took his hand. He had the bluest eyes that I'd ever seen in my life, the colour even more intense against the tanned darkness of his skin. I'd have suspected coloured contacts except there was something about him that suggested he wouldn't be bothered with anything so frivolous as eye enhancers. I'd been far too busy gawping at his friend to do more than briefly glance at him at the wedding, but now I realised he was a good bit older than Luke. His greying hair was still thick and he had the trim figure of the naturally slight and small-boned, but there were quite heavily marked lines around his eyes and mouth which said he had to be in his forties. But still, most men would be delighted to be in such good shape at thirty-five, let alone forty-something. He twitched the lapel of an immaculately cut blue pin-striped suit into place and said, 'And what are you doing up here?'

'I've just started working for Stephen Bailey-Stewart.'

'Really? Why didn't you say Susie was working with you, Martin?' he asked reproachfully. Martin glowered at me, while Nigel said with a smile, 'We're just popping in here to grab a bite to eat, why don't you join us? It would be so nice to meet you properly.'

Martin shifted in a way that suggested an inarticulate protest. No doubt his idea of a fun lunch wasn't one with me.

Nigel turned to him and said, 'Susie and I have an old friend in common, the new Mrs Ashton.'

Martin looked at me as if he hadn't expected me to have such important connections and mumbled something like, 'Right, do join us, Susie.' He still didn't look particularly enthusiastic about the idea, but Nigel's tone had made it quite clear that it was he who was calling the shots here and if he wanted to natter about Rose to me over a pint then he would.

What could I do but accept? I mean, it would have been positively rude to refuse, wouldn't it? And it would give me an opportunity to do some scouting around, find out a bit of what lay between Luke and Rose. Find out if the way lay clear for me. I muttered with great insincerity that I couldn't possibly impose on their lunch, and allowed my protests to be over-ruled with only the minimum of protest. Within minutes Martin was despatched to fetch our drinks while I was being installed on a banquette, or I would have been if I'd obeyed orders and not nipped off to the ladies to do a surreptitious complete makeover. Sharing a table with a man who is much prettier than you are is not good for your confidence. A couple of minutes later I returned, feeling much happier with myself now I was properly remascaraed and lipsticked, though I had to regretfully acknowledge that my emerald-green dress was not the most fortuitous choice for the Royal Oak. The refurbishment, despite the traditionalism of the pub's name, was of a quite staggering tastelessness. Someone must have gone through the colour chart and chosen two at random, for that could be the only explanation for the combination of lime-green and brown. I wasn't surprised that the cheeky chappie behind the bar had elected to wear dark glasses and, judging from the empty expanse of biliously coloured carpet, the local pubgoers had voted with their feet and gone somewhere gentler on the eyes. At least it meant we got served quickly, though when I cast a professional eye over our plates of sandwiches I decided they were nothing like as good as mine. Luke downed his lager in a few long gulps, and began to look more alert. I realised belatedly we'd been dealing with a man in the throes of a full-blown hangover, so it wasn't really surprising that he hadn't recognised me. It had probably hurt to see. The colour scheme in here wouldn't have been doing him any favours either.

Nigel had been establishing how I'd come to be working for Stephen via a few crisp, short questions, all of which demanded a proper answer. This was uncommonly like the interrogation techniques used by lawyers in old Hollywood films; I hoped I was being classified as a friendly witness. He regarded a dry edge to his sandwich with critical displeasure and began to break it off, murmuring, 'So you've burnt your bridges and moved up here. How very courageous of you. I expect Rose is thrilled about it.'

'She doesn't even know yet. They're doing a grand honeymoon tour of the States visiting Jeremy's various American cousins, and should be back at the weekend,' I said as I virtuously sipped my mineral water. (I'd have killed for a glass of wine, but given Martin's still-sour mood because I'd joined them I thought it would be more politic not to give him an excuse to say any mistakes I made that afternoon were due to drinking in working hours.)

Nigel's mouth curved slightly as he said, 'I must confess, I wonder whether Rose arranged for you to have this job for her own benefit or for yours.'

'It's occurred to me too,' I admitted, 'but since I benefit either way it doesn't really worry me.'

'How very philosophical of you,' he said, looking at me with approval.

Martin raised his head from where he'd been staring sulkily into his pint, distinctly put out he was being excluded from the conversation. 'But Stephen was saying only the other day he was looking forward to meeting Jeremy Ashton's wife. If he's never met her, how come she gave your name to him?' he demanded suspiciously, as if I'd just made the faux pas that conclusively proved I was an imposter. I felt sure he would have been delighted.

'She didn't actually do it herself, but she'd heard he needed an assistant and got Hamish to make contact with him,' I explained.

'Hamish?' queried Nigel sharply. His fingers mauled the crust into crumbs. 'Is that Hamish Laing?' he asked slowly, eyes fixed on my face.

'Yes,' I said, a bit surprised at his tone.

'Well, well, well. Of course, he was best man at the wedding, wasn't he? And you were chief bridesmaid. How very fitting. Are you a particular friend of his?' There was a quite unmistakable emphasis on the 'particular'.

'Good heavens no!' I said quickly. Fortunately, it was no hardship to be so honest, even while a basic bolshiness in me resented intensely being asked a question like that by someone I hardly knew, but I wouldn't have dared say anything else. I certainly wasn't brave enough to stand up to the degrees of permafrost that had abruptly settled in Nigel's eyes as I mentioned Hamish's name. I felt a quite inordinate pang of relief as he smiled slowly at my words, and wondered what lay behind such blatant dislike. I didn't feel like asking.

'Are you sure?' Luke asked slyly, apparently almost entirely restored to life by a second lager. A little smile curved around his lips. 'I saw you in very deep conversation with him at the wedding.'

He'd been watching me? I thought, with a quite disproportionate shudder of delight, then realised with a little pang that what with Hamish's height and me in billowing pink silk we were hardly an unnoticeable couple. 'I hardly know him,' I said truthfully. 'I've only seen him once since the wedding, when Stephen asked him to help me move into the cottage.'

Luke picked up his glass and examined it as if he was checking there was really nothing but drops in the bottom of it. 'Oh, does he live around here now?' he asked idly. 'The last I heard of him he was working in London.'

'He's got a new job in Leicester,' I said.

Luke shrugged, putting his glass back on the table with a regretful look, and said, 'Rather him than me. I suppose someone has to work in provincial cities, but if I had to I'd insist that it was one with a bit more glamour, like . . . Edinburgh.'

'I don't think the Scots would appreciate hearing you describe their capital city as provincial,' Nigel said dryly. 'I particularly wouldn't try doing it on Burns Night.' He tore another piece off his sandwich, examined it and put it to one side. 'I presume as you were in pole position behind Rose you two are still best friends. Do you still discuss everything?'

I sipped my water slowly, wondering what he was getting at. 'Most things,' I replied evenly, and looked at him. 'She didn't tell me much about you though, I was abroad when she knew you,' I added, wondering if he was worried Rose had been massively indiscreet.

That must have been it, for he smiled and asked me when I thought I'd be seeing her. 'I was glad to be able to see her get married, it's a long time since we last met.'

'She seemed to be quite surprised to see you,' I said carefully.

'I'm amazed she even noticed us in that crush,' said Nigel.

Luke laughed. 'Come on, Nigel! She couldn't help it, you nearly mowed her down in the porch!' He glanced sideways at me, eyes glinting. 'I have to confess, we were just a little bit naughty about that, or I was. I knew Rose would have invited us if she'd known Nigel was back from the States and I was going to ring her, but I forgot . . . So we came anyway.' He smiled at me beguilingly, expecting instant forgiveness. He was absolutely right. I would forgive a man who looked at me like that a lot more than merely gatecrashing a friend's wedding.

'And he didn't tell me about it until after we'd got there,' said Nigel, with a touch of grimness in his voice.

'You'd have been even more angry if I'd told you before and you'd felt your scruples wouldn't allow you to go,' pointed out Luke with what seemed a fair degree of justice.

I'd been watching him closely while he was talking about Rose and, to my relief, whatever feelings she might be harbouring about him, he didn't appear to show any undue sensitivity about seeing her while she'd been busily getting married to another. Though, to be frank, close observation of my brothers has convinced me men aren't particularly hot on showing sensitivity about matters of the heart anyway. Their greatest sign of emotion is to down a pint rather quickly, and that certainly doesn't mean anything in itself.

'I'd have been more worried she'd insist that I was immediately thrown out!' Nigel said. 'Rose and I weren't very friendly for a while, that's why I didn't contact her myself.' Those amazing-coloured eyes were fixed on my face, seemingly awaiting my reaction. I nodded to show that I understood. 'So I was pleased to have the opportunity to mend a few fences.'

I couldn't help feeling a letter might have done just as well. The truth was probably he hadn't been able to resist going along to see who his former girl was hitching herself up to.

'Well, she was delighted to see you,' I said, a touch mendaciously, and turned to Luke. 'Didn't you say you've got a house up here? Do you know Jeremy too?'

He shook his head. 'I know *of* him of course, but,' he grimaced slightly – 'I don't really move in those circles. Hunting and shooting definitely isn't my style.' No, I couldn't imagine Luke on a horse or striding across a ploughed field potting pigeons myself. His skin was too perfect, he looked like he'd never been windblown in his life. He seemed to belong somewhere glamorously decadent, Happy Valley in Kenya or Cairo before the war perhaps, lounging around with the sort of women who kept cheetahs on jewelled leads and wore shoes with diamond heels.

'Have you lived here for long?' I asked curiously, wondering how such an exotic creative had landed up in this rural place.

'He shook his head. 'My grandparents lived here and I used to visit as a child, of course, but I only decided I should have a base up here about a year ago – that's how I met Martin. He showed me around several places.'

'And he didn't buy any of them!' Martin interrupted wryly.

Luke glanced at him. 'I promise I'll buy the next one through you!' he said. He turned his attention back to me, looking at me as if I was the only person in the world he wanted to speak to. I was sure it was a natural gift he'd been born with, but even so, it didn't dampen the warm pleasure inside me. 'I'm really only an extended weekender. I freelance, so I've got a bit of scope when it comes to arranging my time, and I like to come up here on a regular basis so I can keep an eye on my grandmother, who's getting very frail. You know, pop in and make sure that the gutters are kept clear, all the little things she doesn't notice any more.' He grinned ruefully. 'She doesn't thank me for it, she can't see why I won't come and live in the house. Frankly, there are limits!' He rolled his eyes. 'A ninety-year-old asking you what you've been up to is a definite cramp on your style.'

'Just be grateful you're male,' advised Nigel. 'Luke's grandmother is of the type who believe that men are free to sow prairie loads of wild oats, while their sisters should stay at home and embroider the odd firescreen.'

He looked up, his eyes meeting Luke's. I wondered if there was some story here, one undoubtedly supposed to be unsuitable for the tender ears of women. The cheeky chappie behind the bar stopped admiring his reflection in the polished metal of the fittings for long enough to mince over to us and ask if we'd like refills. 'Another water, Susie?' asked Nigel. 'Or will you be daring enough to have a lemonade shandy this time?'

I shook my head and got up. 'I'd better go, there's a lot to be done this afternoon,' I said with real regret. I would have liked longer to try making an impression on Luke. Get real! I told myself. Your only chance of making the sort of impression you want to on someone like Luke would be to tie him to a chair and hypnotise him. So you could have knocked me over with a feather (a very large feather in my case) when on my return from the ladies I stopped to say goodbye to everyone and Luke looked up with that incredible smile of his and said, 'It's been really nice seeing you again, Susie. Shall we meet for a drink sometime?'

'Yes, of course,' I said instantly, biting my lip just in time to stop myself blurting out, 'When? Where? Can we make it tonight?'

'How do I get hold of you? At the office? Or have you

managed to memorise your new number at your cottage yet?'

I scribbled it down, though I was so fizzy with pleasure that I had to make two attempts to get the numbers in the right order. I could still feel the imprint of Luke's goodbye kiss on my cheek five minutes later as I drove, somewhat distractedly, out of town. Like a teenage fan of a pop star, I played with the idea of never washing the place where his lips had touched me, until I remembered that one of my few good habits is always to take off my make-up at night. Funny, Nigel had kissed me too – and I'd felt nothing, I thought with a grin. How had he and Rose got together? I wondered. He wasn't the sort of man she usually went out with. She liked her men malleable, so she could run rings around them without being checked. I couldn't imagine anyone daring to do that with Nigel, he looked far too in control of himself, and of those around him. Maybe that was why they'd split up unamicably, because he wouldn't put up with her games. Despite an easy charm, he'd struck me as one of the coldest men I'd ever met in my life, and that wasn't just because I'd been comparing him to the smouldering appeal of his friend – which was another odd pairing, when you came to think of it. Nigel was so much older than Luke, and a lot tougher. If I hadn't been absolutely convinced down to the marrow of my bones that it wasn't so, I might almost have thought the pair of them were gay, they seemed to know each other so well, but even if I sometimes doubt the accuracy of my own antennae, I have absolute confidence in Rose's. If there had been any question of it she'd have told me directly, rather than dropping those infuriatingly elliptical hints about Luke. She took the pursuit of men much too seriously to allow me to waste my time in that way. And if she didn't like what I was pursuing, too bad. The only man she had any business to stop me going near was Jeremy, I decided, as I had to brake to avoid a couple of old women who were gossiping their way slowly across the road. And I'd better start concentrating on driving and not indulging in rose-tinted daydreams.

Naturally, I was bursting with my news and longing to settle down to have a good gossip with Amanda, who is a soul sister after my own heart. She fully understands the importance of imparting information and is still close enough to the heady days of her own bachelorgirlhood to be able to thoroughly enjoy the stories of someone else's. But when I went in, my arms laden with the files I'd got from Maurice, she had a young couple with her, laboriously going over every possible first marrieds' house that we had on the books. From the look of it, she'd be tied up for a couple of hours.

I had my head down and was typing out a couple of confirmations of offer for Stephen when Martin came back, mid-afternoon, strutting in with his hands in his pockets as if he owned the place. He reckoned that as Stephen's senior negotiator he was in charge when Stephen wasn't there and didn't fail to make his belief abundantly clear at every possible opportunity. He stood over Amanda for a few seconds, as if judging whether she was doing her job properly or, as I'd been told was his habit, assessing whether this couple was going to spend enough money to make it worth his while annexing them as his clients. Half a minute of hearing about two-bedroom cottages convinced him they weren't. 'Any messages, Susie?' he asked in a self-important voice, from the other side of the office.

I looked up. 'Yes, from the Ridleys. They went to see The Cedars in Gossington and want to put in an offer of—'

He forgot about being too grand to approach a mere assistant and strode over to my desk. 'Haven't I told you before that I don't want you interfering with my clients?' he snapped.

I stared at him, amazed. Yes, so he had said something along those lines, but all I was doing was taking a message. Had something gone wrong with Nigel and Luke after I left? And I was being held responsible? Probably. Or was he just generally teed off I'd joined them at all? But I was still in such a sunny mood about Luke that I didn't give into my immediate impulse, which was to tell him where to get off. Instead, I shrugged and said, 'Suit yourself. Next time I'll tell them to ring back.'

'You will not!' he snarled. 'You will take their number and tell them I will ring them back as soon as I get in. I will not have amateurs mucking up my work! Understood?'

'Perfectly, sah!' I said, saluting smartly.

Amanda went into a coughing fit which imperfectly disguised an acute attack of the giggles. She'd suffered from his 'I'm the one who's got qualifications and you're just some jumped-up typist' attitude many times in the past. Even Jenny, who was normally the soul of placid discretion, made a noise like a snort. Martin's face went red and I had a feeling that despite the young couple, who were still there making up their minds if they could manage to fit in viewing ten houses over the weekend (they were in a hurry to move, they said), I was about to get bawled out, when I was saved by the bell, literally. The telephone went. I gave Martin a non-apologetic look and picked it up, saying in my best receptionist's manner, 'Bailey-Stewart. HowmayIhelpyou?'

'Could I speak to—' Then there was dead silence and an incredulous squeak. '*Susie?* Susie, is that you? What are you doing answering the telephone?' gasped Rose.

'Working of course!' I retorted primly.

'Good Gad, girl, you're a quick mover!' she said in an astonished voice. 'I didn't know you had it in you! I was just ringing Stephen to ask him if he'd contacted you.'

I grinned. 'Actually, it's Stephen who's the quick mover, I had very little to do with it, I can assure you. Anyway, what on earth are you doing thinking about my employment prospects? Aren't you supposed to still be on your honeymoon? Weren't you coming back on Sunday?'

'We were supposed to be,' said Rose in a disgusted voice, 'only Jeremy didn't notice the return date was down as the thirteenth, not the eighteenth, and we couldn't get it changed without paying hundreds of pounds, because it was a special fare. He said it wasn't worth it for a few days.' Oh dear, I thought, this did not bode well for a harmonious start to the Ashton marriage. 'But,' she added, her voice brightening a little, 'he did let me go just a bit wild in Donna Karan as a consolation. The prices are so much lower in New York, it would have been mad not to. Jeremy quite agreed with me.' I'll bet he did! I thought with a smile. Anything for a peaceful life. 'And he even came with me and helped me choose. He's a very good judge, those clothes can be cruel if you've got the slightest bulge. He knows exactly what makes me look fat.' I daresay most of the stock, I thought, my estimation of Jeremy going up by the minute. 'Oh, I can't believe you're up here!' Rose went on in a delighted voice. 'This is incredible! What's he like, this Stephen? He must be quite something to get staid old you to kick over the traces like that! Is he gorgeous? Do you fancy him?'

'No! Of course I don't!' I said with emphasis, loudly enough to make the young marrieds look up at me in surprise. I wasn't staid. Was I? Perhaps compared to her, I was, but Rose wasn't exactly your normal benchmark as a measure of sedate behaviour. 'Look, Rose, I am supposed to be working,' I said repressively, afraid she was going to carry on with intimate questions about Stephen, who might walk in at any moment and hear me making blunt denials of finding him attractive. And if he didn't, then Martin, whom I could see out of the corner of my eye was writing a little note about my gossiping on the office phone and was listening to every word, would be bound to tell him. 'I can't spend all day nattering on the phone.'

'Tush! Working's never stopped you gossiping before,' Rose retorted with a certain degree of exaggeration. I drew in my breath audibly with irritation and she said quickly, 'OK, OK, I get the picture. You've turned over a new leaf.' I ground my teeth, but silently. Trust Rose to say something which I could neither agree with nor refute. It's that sort of thing which sometimes makes me wonder why I haven't brained her a long time ago. I can never come up with a reasonable answer. 'Anyway, we can catch up on all the news later. When are you coming round to see us? This evening?'

'This evening?' I repeated blankly, looking at the telephone in mild surprise. I know Rose's appetite for socialising is truly prodigious, but surely even if she wasn't suffering from jet-leg wouldn't she want to spend the second evening in her new home alone with her nearly as new husband? 'This evening? No, I can't. I'm having a drink with one of my neighbours in Little Dearsley.'

'Is that where you're living? It's practically next door to us! Well, only about ten minutes away. Oh, I can't believe this!' she burbled. 'Come tomorrow for supper then, about six—'

'So I can help cook it?' I interrupted.

'Of course,' she responded serenely. 'That's the only way you'll get an edible meal, you should know that! And stay for the night too. I know you could virtually walk home, but we've got far too much to catch up on for the miserable quantity you're allowed with the breathalyser. As you know, we aren't exactly short of spare bedrooms.'

'Won't Jeremy mind?' I asked tentatively.

'Considering I had to put up with his mother coming round last night with a covered tray, on account of the fact she was sure I wouldn't have found my way around the kitchen yet, and then staying to polish it off, if he does mind he can lump it! Besides, he won't. You're prettier than his mother, not difficult I must admit, and he says you make him laugh.'

'Do I?' I asked in surprise, not entirely sure whether I should be pleased at this completely unexpected compliment or worried that from now on every time I met Jeremy I was going to feel obliged to do a party trick known as Susie Amusing Jeremy. 'Of course I'll come, I'm longing to see you.'

'Good,' she said happily.

CHAPTER 6

Despite Rose's airy assurances I was a bit uncertain whether Jeremy would really be very keen on seeing me so soon after coming back from honeymoon, but when I trolled up the next evening to a front door of truly baronial proportions he seemed flatteringly pleased I'd arrived. Of course, it could have had something to do with the way his mother, despite being a good foot smaller, was standing in front of him in the unmistakable manner that tells you a lecture is in progress, or rather, judging by the finger being waved in front of his face, more of a full-blown harangue. However, you have to hand it to her, the moment she heard my wheels on the gravel she stopped in mid-sentence and turned in my direction with a social smile plastered on her face. I wondered if being gracious to strangers when you're in the middle of a row was the sort of thing they taught you at Lucie Clayton. A small hairy white dog that had been frisking around her feet dashed over to the car, scrabbling up against the door with long black claws.

'You must have been introduced to Susie, Susie Gardener, at the wedding, weren't you?' said Jeremy, who to my surprise didn't look nearly as incandescent as most men would when they'd been caught having a telling-off from their mother. Either he was even better natured than I thought he was or he was used to it. Though I noticed his voice perhaps held a bit more venom than was strictly necessary as he snarled, 'Down Mallory, you horrible little mutt!'

Mrs Ashton held out a limp hand towards me. 'Of course I was, how nice to see you here,' she said, though the way her eyes flickered up and down me suggested she was unsure exactly how nice it was. She was one of those small-boned, exquisitely made women that give off an aura of being much too fragile for the everyday events of ordinary life. They usually have several men in tow, only too happy to perform the necessary tasks for them. However, according to Rose, she was about as delicate and helpless as an anaconda. She pursed her lips thoughtfully. 'Gardener . . . I know some Gardeners. Are you from the Somerset Gardeners?'

I was tempted to say no, municipal Gardeners, but decided it wouldn't be polite, besides, it was a bad pun. 'No, we come from Sussex.'

'I don't know any Gardeners from Sussex,' she said. That meant, presumably, we weren't worth knowing. The dog jumped up at my leg, leaving a liberal deposit of mud on my fawn jeans in its wake. I pushed it down. His owner looked momentarily annoyed that I had dared do any such thing, then cooed at him indulgently, 'What a naughty boy you are, Mallory. You mustn't spoil Susie's nice trousers.' She smiled at me benignly. 'I'm sure it'll brush off. When you live in the country you have to get used to a little mud.'

What did she think Sussex was? A suburb of London? I thought indignantly, as I picked off a couple of large clods that Mallory had transferred to my trouser leg.

'It will be so nice for *dear* Rose to have you here,' she said in a gracious voice. 'I'm sure having one of her friends living around here is going to make settling in *much* easier for her.' She glanced at her watch. 'Goodness, I must go and start my

100

dinner. Do you like cooking, Susie? I'm sure you find good food needs plenty of careful preparation.' She smiled at her son. 'Jeremy, you'd better take Susie to find Rose. I expect you'll find her relaxing with a book in the morning room.'

I wondered how long it would be before Rose buried the hatchet with her mother-in-law – right in the centre of her skull if she went on making remarks like that. Jeremy flicked his mother a glance that clearly said he didn't particularly appreciate being ordered around in front of guests, but since getting away was obviously more to his taste than staying to argue the point he set off for the front door at a near gallop, merely saying a terse, 'Follow me, Susie,' over his shoulder as he left the starting blocks. We slowed down once we got inside and out of sight. The contrast between the sunny outside and the wood-panelled gloom of the hall, only relieved by dim light from high narrow stained-glass windows, was so extreme that if I'd been in a hurry I'd never have seen the suits of armour flanking either side of the door and would probably have gone into one of them. As it was I bashed an arm with an embarrassing clang. I jumped backwards with a startled exclamation.

'I really ought to get those moved,' said Jeremy, who was negotiating several large oak chairs dotted around the room with the skill born of long practice. 'People are always bumping into them, but Mother likes them there. She says they lend gravitas to the hall, but I think they'd look just as good over by the fireplace. What do you think?'

Actually, suits of armour aren't my first choice when it comes to decorating, but I thought they'd look just as good anywhere they weren't menacing the entrance for innocent visitors. I told Jeremy I agreed with him. My eyes were getting used to the gloom, which wasn't quite as deep as I'd thought,

101

merely very woody-coloured from acres of well-polished parquet flooring, carved panelling to the ceiling and a lot of heavy, dark oak furniture. I wondered how long it would be before Rose decided to brave maternal-in-law rage and did some redecorating in here. Replacing or removing the heavy red velvet curtains which were draped across the windows and obscured a lot of what light there was would be a good start, even if Flavia did claim they were some kind of family heirloom.

Contrary to what Flavia Ashton had said, Rose wasn't relaxing with a book at all, though the green velvet sofa in the morning room did bear signs of having been fairly recently occupied. A paperback lay on the floor beside it and an apple core sat on a plate next to a crushed soft-drink tin. We ran her to earth in a huge, deliberately old-fashioned kitchen, complete with Aga and wooden drying rack suspended on chains from the high ceilings. There was even a working fireplace down one end, with a sitting area around it and bunches of herbs hanging decoratively from a beam. I was prepared to bet that it hadn't been Rose who had put them there. The only Herb she's familiar with is an American boyfriend she had when she was seventeen. One wall was completely taken up by a long, built-in dresser painted white, which had a decorative arrangement of plates, arranged by colour and graduated size, on the shelves, and neat stacks of artfully arranged bowls lower down. It wouldn't stay like that for long, I could already see signs that Rose was making her mark. A lipstick nestled next to a Delft plate and a shocking-pink clock in the shape of a daisy had been put in front of a jug. Rose was staring in a puzzled way at a cook book propped up on a long pine table, scrubbed nearly white over the years, presumably by generations of diligent dailies, while around her the surface was covered in various untidy heaps of raggedly cut-up meat and a couple of half-chopped onions. A large black-and-white pointer with a turned-up nose sat a few feet away, staring solidly at the table top, willing the meat to levitate and tumble on the floor. A Siamese cat, stretched out decoratively on a cushioned ladder-back chair, watched both dog and meat through half-closed eyes and made it quite clear who was going to get the prize if the miracle did ever happen.

Rose dropped the book with a pleased shriek when I came in and raced over to give me a hug. 'Susie! I didn't expect you so early. Oh, this is great! I'm so glad to see you!'

'Me too!' I said, though I was well aware that at least part of her delight was due to an expectation I'd help her work out what she was supposed to do with the piles of raw food she had around her. Rose hadn't had many encounters with basic ingredients before. And few of them had had particularly happy results. I stepped back to have a look at her. She was looking fantastic, I noted enviously, wondering if the figure-hugging teal-blue top she was wearing under her 'Head Cook' apron was one of the things she'd persuaded Jeremy to buy for her in New York. The colour was superb against her newly tanned skin and sun-streaked hair. One of the great grouses of my life is that I don't tan. I've got the typical redhead's skin, which goes scarlet, peels and then goes white again. Except for my nose. That freckles. I'm a walking encyclopaedia on the most effective sun blocks and I have a huge collection of large hats. 'Don't you look well! Married life must suit you.'

'Oh, it does!' she said promptly. 'You ought to try it. Have I got lots to tell you!'

Jeremy cast her a look of alarm, whistled to the dog, and started backing out quickly, muttering about needing to go and see a man about a field. 'He's worried we're about to launch into "girl talk",' said Rose with a smile, 'discuss the latest hairstyles and what's in vogue.'

'He can't know you very well if he thinks your girl talk is on such innocuous subjects,' I said.

She opened her eyes wide. 'Surely he doesn't think I'm about to disclose honeymoon secrets?' she demanded with outraged innocence, then grinned broadly. 'Well, he might have, but he was probably more afraid I was going to hand him a bag of spuds and the peeler. By the way, Susie, what does "parboil" mean? Look at this recipe here . . .'

She pointed to 'daube de something or the other', written by a chef who evidently had never thought that your average home cook doesn't have the full range of a restaurant kitchen available when trying something out, nor the services of the two sous chefs who'd have been needed to complete this recipe. We decided it would take us until tomorrow evening to finish looking up all the words we didn't understand before we could even start on all the parboiling, sautéing and clarifying demanded and Jeremy was likely to be rather hungry by then. So I did my infallible man-satisfying recipe, which is basically pouring a bottle of wine and some herbs over the meat and shoving it in the Aga. If you're really taking a lot of trouble you can add some veg. (That is if the one wearing the apron with 'Head Cook' on it can be persuaded to chop up the rest of the onions. She claimed the tears were spoiling her make-up.)

The recipe is then completed by the cook and her assistant, who sit down and finish what's left of the cooking wine to help them recover from their labours. I'm by no means brilliant at cooking, it's just that anyone who likes food and lives with my mother either has to learn the basics or live with permanently shrivelled taste buds. She is a truly imaginatively bad cook, her ideas made even worse by her habit of chucking a handful of pulses or some tofu for their health-giving properties into whatever it is that she's making, even, as I discovered once, in a birthday cake. A sponge lentil cake is quite something, though to be fair even she agreed it wasn't a success and she bought my cakes from Marks and Spencer after that. I think my friends were a bit disappointed, they rather enjoyed the sense of adventure you got with a Gardener cake.

We got through a couple of glasses each while Rose rattled away about the honeymoon (clean subjects only, Jeremy would have been relieved to hear); two weeks in a beach-front hotel in St Lucia, where they could walk straight out of their room on to a private beach and into the sea, followed by ten days in New York, visiting friends and relations of Jeremy's and by all accounts doing a lot of shopping. Jeremy had gone shopping too, and not just to Donna Karan. He was either very long-suffering or deeply in love. Or perhaps he was merely worried for the safety of his credit card.

Rose pushed back her chair. 'Do you want to do the grand tour before it gets dark?' she asked. Of course I did, though it would have been more than my life was worth to have said no, even as a joke. Rose was obviously tremendously proud of her new home, though she nonchalantly declaimed in a very Roseish manner how ridiculous it was to call it Moor End Hall. Since the East Midlands aren't exactly overloaded with moors, the house was at least a hundred miles from any moors to be at the end of, and as far as anyone knew there had never been a Yorkshire Ashton who sentimentally called his new house after the views he missed so much (or was glad to be shot of). It was impressive in the sense that it was big, but pretty it wasn't. Two Victorian Ashtons in succession had fancied themselves as architects and had transformed what had originally been a relatively plain large Georgian box by adding wings, battlements, turrets, a tower, crenellations and several gables, all in different variations on the Dutch style. 'There was another wing to that side,' said Rose as we stood in the gardens, looking at the back of the house, 'but luckily it got dry rot in the sixties and was pulled down. I wish the same could happen to that one,' she added, pointing. I looked at her enquiringly. 'That's where Flavia lives,' she added meaningfully.

Flavia had ignored all Jeremy's suggestions that now he was getting married it was really time she moved out to the very nice house on the estate that had been prepared for her. Her eyes had brimmed over with tears and she'd asked Jeremy in a choking voice how he could be so cruel as to turn her out of the house she'd been brought to as a bride by his father, where she had so many happy memories (despite the many witnesses who'd heard her complaining about the damp and cold and draughts), if she really deserved to be put out on to the scrap heap like that and so on. Rose said sourly that what Flavia really objected to was changing address from Moor End *Hall* to Moor End *Farmhouse* and all her objections would have vanished like smoke if she'd been able to move into the Dower House, a William and Mary gem. Unfortunately, it had been sold to cover death duties after the war. The net result was that Jeremy folded under an assault that would have downed many stronger men (even Rose admitted that) and agreed his mother could stay on in the house, though he did manage to stipulate she had to move into the wing and leave the main part of the house to him and Rose. She had, weeping bitterly about being made to leave her home under duress, and had taken most of the best furniture and pictures to console herself for her cruel upheaval. Rose had no great expectations that this experiment in shared living would be harmonious. I also had a feeling she wasn't going to go out of her way to try and make it so either. 'The problem is Jeremy won't stand up to her,' she said in a disgusted voice.

'He was standing up to her all right when I arrived,' I said. 'I haven't got a clue what it was about, but every particle of her body language said she wasn't getting a simple walk-over.'

'Oh, that'll be about this idea for the new estate,' said Rose gloomily. 'She hasn't stopped banging on about it since we came back, even though it's really none of her business. It's our affair, not hers.'

I'd stopped to admire an urn full of scarlet and yellow tulips at the bottom of an elegant flight of stone steps. 'What's it all about?' I asked idly, rather amused at her proprietorial tone.

Rose shrugged. 'There's been a development proposed for a site near the back gates for ages. Something really luxy, forty-odd houses, private swimming pool for the residents, the lot. Probably even a gym by the sounds of it.' She raised her eyebrows. 'We're talking about aiming at *serious* money here. The developer virtually had it sewn up, planning permission and all, when out of the blue some naturalist discovered there was a colony of incredibly rare toads or something right where they were going to put the access road. You know they really do stop these things for toads,' she said in a voice of complete amazement. 'Or maybe it was frogs. I can't remember. Not that it matters. It was something that hopped. Personally, I'd have been tempted to put down toad poison and claim they'd all caught a rare toad plague.' She saw my expression and laughed. 'OK, I wouldn't, but I might have caught them all and taken them to a toad luxury development elsewhere. But this lot weren't quick enough off the mark, and the pond where the toads live was designated a SSSI or whatever they call it, and basically they were told they could only have their development if they moved the access road and some of the houses right away from Toad Hamlets. The only possible place for the new road is the farm track, which would be quite sensible, except they want to buy an extra five acres for the houses that would have gone near the toad pond, and it's a bit close to the house, and we'd have to make an entirely new farm road. Apparently, executive house-dwellers object to the mud that comes off tractor tyres. Flavia is dead against the whole thing. She says she'll leave the house rather than see it desecrated by crass commercialism. Actually,' Rose said pensively, 'that's the best reason I've heard so far for going with the developers. Problem is, I think that when push came to shove you'd find she'd decided that her duty lay here.' She smiled suddenly. 'Amazingly enough, for once I side with Flavia, but not just because I don't fancy having the hoi polloi so close to us. I don't think we need this sort of development, the houses in the village are already priced way too high for the people who were born here. We need houses they can afford to buy, not executive nests for rich townie yuppies.'

'I had no idea you had a social conscience!' I said teasingly and a bit unfairly. Rose's always enjoyed involving herself in causes, and being mistress of the Big House was going to give her loads of opportunities for finding them locally. At this rate she'd be standing for the Parish Council before too long, and heaven help them when she got on it. Underneath a rather flippant exterior, she's extremely bossy. She stuck her tongue out at me. 'What are you going to do?'

'Jeremy hasn't made up his mind. They only approached him a couple of weeks before the wedding, so he hasn't really had time to go over the ifs and buts.' She perched on the edge of a balustrade, ignoring the chill rising up from the stone. 'It sounds like a lot of money, but he says when you look into things like tax and the costs of making a new farm track it mightn't add up to so much, and of course he doesn't like the idea of selling his land. The nearest house would be just behind that little hill there,' she said, pointing down the valley.

I leant against a pillar alongside her, and followed her gesture over lawns that swept down to a lush field, the various greens of grass and hedge darkened by the gathering dusk. A few peacefully grazing sheep stood out as lumps of light grey and some bird, I couldn't identify what sort, was warbling in a rather desultory manner from a copse of trees. It was very quiet, barely possible to hear the cars from the main road. From somewhere in the direction of the village a dog barked questioningly then waited for a reply. It was difficult to imagine what it would be like with forty houses, their occupants, animals and probably two or three cars per household only a few hundred yards away. 'I can understand why Jeremy's reluctant to risk spoiling all this. Once it's gone you'll never get it back, will you?'

Rose nodded. 'And Jeremy thinks that the company behind the scheme might be dodgy too. It's one of those outfits where you can't find out who owns it, and since he wants to become a JP he's certainly got no intention of getting into business with some outfit that might turn out to be completely crooked. So he's taking his time and they're getting impatient for an answer.'

'If it's that important to them they'll just have to wait, won't they?' I asked.

'Well, it's not as if they can do anything else,' said Rose practically. 'Shall we get a move on? I'm freezing. We can get back to the kitchen this way,' she said, pointing down the wide terrace running along the whole side of the house which must be a veritable sun-trap on sunny days. Right now, it was feeling distinctly dank.

'What's that?' I asked, looking at a ruinous heap halfway up a hill at the end of the garden. 'Another Victorian improvement that didn't quite work?'

Rose laughed. 'No, it's the original house. The Mrs Ashton of the day wanted to go and live in London, and to help her husband make up his mind she burnt the house down.'

'A bit drastic, surely,' I said.

She nodded. 'It didn't work either. He decided the ruins would make a really superior folly and it would do his wife good to see them every day from the windows of the new house. He promised she could go to London once she'd presented him with a proper family. I believe she got to twenty-two before he finally relented! There's a portrait of her upstairs with about twelve of them all grouped around her, so it can't be too much of an exaggeration.'

I laughed, 'I trust that Jeremy isn't going to try and make the same sort of bargain.'

'I'd like to see him try!' retorted Rose grimly. She glanced down at her enviably flat stomach and shuddered. 'Can you imagine having morning sickness *twenty-two* times?' she asked in a voice of horror. 'Gabrielle felt so ill with Alexander she couldn't get out of bed until midday.'

'Gabrielle always suffers worse than anyone else,' I said. 'And you wouldn't exactly object to staying in bed till midday either!' Rose grinned at me. She's never been known as the queen of the early risers. 'And you might get lucky and not have it each time. Only maybe half the time, that's only eleven bouts of morning sickness.'

'Thanks a bunch!' she retorted. 'But if I have anything to do with it I won't have *any* bouts of morning sickness!'

I stopped, looking at her in surprise. 'Aren't you intending to have children at all?' I asked.

She shrugged defiantly. 'Not all of us have a maternal instinct!' she said defensively. 'I suppose I'll have to have at least one eventually, it'll be unfair on Jeremy if I don't. He loves children. But I'll delay it as long as I decently can –' she glanced sideways at me – 'if only so I can annoy Flavia!' I wasn't entirely sure from her expression if she was joking or not. 'The woman's already started dropping hints I should leap into brood-mare mode, and keeps pointing out that Jeremy was a honeymoon baby. And can you imagine what my life would be like with the grandmother from hell? She'd never stop interfering. As she won't move out, I'm going to have to wait until she's popped her clogs to be able to have a baby in peace, which since she's disgustingly healthy means I'll probably be the first woman to have a baby while operating a Zimmerframe!'

'Well, considering how short your engagement was, you'd probably be advised to wait for a bit anyway, unless you want a lot of counting up on fingers,' I said.

Rose beamed at me, bad mood forgotten. 'Clever Susie, I'll tell her that next time she tries to nag me!' We went into the welcomingly warm kitchen, which smelt strongly of casseroling alcohol. She bustled around, opening oven doors and peering inside, shoving baking potatoes in, and generally trying to give an impression of someone who was completely au fait with the workings of her kitchen. It wasn't absolutely successful. I was forced to point out she had in fact put the potatoes in the plate-warming oven.

'I thought it seemed a bit cool,' she said thoughtfully as she moved them over to a hotter one. She waved me to go and sit down on an elderly sofa opposite the fire, presumably the place where a complete pig would once have been roasted on a spit, judging by the size of the hearth. The two logs burning away looked rather dwarfed and can't have been throwing out much heat, since the cat had curled itself up comfortably on the edge of the hearth and was toasting his back. He only flicked his ears when one of the logs spat firework sparks up the chimney, but Rose hastily put the bottle and glasses she was carrying down on a low wicker table and picked him up, scolding him in a loving, silly voice for being a reckless cat who was about to be covered in scorch marks. He dangled limply from her arms, blue eyes glinting like jewels, used to this treatment. Once she sat down, he curled himself up comfortably in her lap and began to purr raucously. She stroked the shiny fur with one hand as she leant forward to fill the glasses, a movement which spoke of long practice at doing these different actions with both hands.

'How's Phuket settling in?' I asked. The cat had been named after a particularly memorable holiday Rose had had in Thailand.

'He's still a bit upset about that horrid cattery, aren't you, darling?' she cooed, rubbing his ears. 'But he's just about achieved an entente-not-at-all-cordiale with Dexter. They pretend neither exists. He's still got a bit of a way to go with Jeremy though,' she added reflectively.

'You mean he bites him whenever he gets the chance?' I asked.

She laughed. 'Something like that. He's just a teeny-weeny bit jealous, aren't you, my darling?' she crooned, stepping up the stroking. The cat leant back with a thoroughly self-satisfied expression on his face, looking completely sweet, adorable and strokable. I knew better. My hand still bears the marks from the last time Phuket took me in that way.

'This is lovely,' I said appreciatively, making sure I kept a safe distance away from Phuket's claws. He was only pretending to be half asleep. 'I've always wanted to live in a house where you can have a fire in the kitchen. It's the ultimate in cosy chic, isn't it?'

'It was just chic when Flavia was in charge,' said Rose, lighting a cigarette and leaning back with a satisfied sigh. 'The sofa in here was *white*, can you believe it? Luckily, she wanted it for her wing, because there would have been enormous offence taken if I'd said I wanted her precious sofa recovering.' She shook her head disbelievingly. 'That woman's not human! White in a kitchen! Jeremy found this one in a back room somewhere. It's much more me.' She grinned at me, 'If you make as much mess in a kitchen as I do it's better to have the sort of furnishings where an extra bit of flour doesn't make any difference.'

'Or a paw print or two,' I said, looking at the arm of the sofa.

'Dexter was never allowed in here when Flavia was in charge, because he used to try and eat Mallory, not that we blame him for that – we all sympathise with a desire to bite Mallory – but it hasn't sunk into Dexter yet that this sofa isn't for dogs. Still, I forgive him, he's very good at clearing up. I hardly ever have to wipe the floor!'

'As a matter of interest, what do you do with this flour that you spill on the floor and the sofa?' I asked. 'Does it come from whipping up a nice little sauce?'

'Don't be stupid!' Rose said robustly. 'I do peanuts and things like that. I don't want Jeremy to start taking my cooking skills for granted –' I nearly choked on my drink – 'he might start expecting me to whip up nice little somethings for him every evening. At the moment, he's still properly impressed I know how to take the foil off the top of a pack of chicken Kiev. I intend it to stay that way for some time!'

She stubbed out her cigarette and poured some more wine in both our glasses, sighing happily. 'This is great! I never expected to be able to entertain you quite so soon. Having you around makes me feel I haven't quite lost touch with when I was single and that I don't have to become a fully paid-up member of the ranks of sober and godly matrons, as they put it in the marriage service, quite yet.'

'Bit of a lost cause expecting you to become sober and godly, isn't it?' I asked lightly, though with a twinge of alarm. So I might look at marriage through highly tinted spectacles, but surely you weren't supposed to hanker after your single days *quite* so soon after getting married?

'It's the matron bit I really object to!' she said with a giggle as she took a swig from her glass, proving that for the time being at least she definitely had no intention of being sober. 'In fact, I don't think Jeremy'd like it very much if I joined the ranks, so I'd better stay the way I am,' she said, looking at me with a contented smile that suggested my alarm had been quite groundless. 'But I still can't believe that you threw everything in and moved up here at a moment's notice!' she said with mild amazement. 'Though when you decide to do something you always really throw yourself into it, don't you? Are you sure it has nothing to do with Stephen? Do you really not fancy him, not the teensiest little bit? Have you met anyone interesting since you made the great move?'

I glanced over at her cautiously. There she sat, drink in one hand, the picture of marital contentment, albeit not sober, godly or matronly marital contentment, so surely she wouldn't give a toss about my bumping into Luke. Yet – I couldn't forget the expression on her face as she'd told me to lay off him. I wasn't worried about her reaction to me, I wasn't *that* spineless, well, I didn't think I was, but surely if she didn't know he was living quite close it would be better all round to delay enlightenment until she was more settled in her marriage. Well, that was my rationalisation anyway. Besides, I wasn't lying when I said that the most interesting man I'd met here was the charming gay owner of the second-hand bookshop, who shared my taste for truly trashy literature to read in the bath. I hadn't actually met Luke here, had I? I didn't get the chance to add anything to this somewhat mendacious statement, as there was a tentative little tap on the door and Flavia popped her head around.

'Oh, there you are!' she said, in a voice of artificial surprise, as if just before dinner she'd have expected to find Rose anywhere but the kitchen. 'I just popped in to get my copy of *Mrs Beeton*, which I must have left here. I can't find it in my new little kitchen. You won't have any use for it, will you, Rose?' she asked kindly.

'Personally, I find it a bit old-fashioned,' Rose drawled through clenched teeth. 'I prefer something more modern – like Delia Smith.' I was extremely impressed Rose knew the names of any cook-book writers.

Flavia stood up from where she'd been examining the shelves of a near-empty bookcase. She didn't look particularly surprised not to find her book. 'Oh, you must mean the back-to-basics book? Yes, I hear it's very useful for those who need to start from scratch.'

By the look on her face, Rose might well have been in danger of committing mat-in-law-ricide if Jeremy hadn't come in at that moment with a whirling, bounding mass of black-and-white energy which promptly decided that I was in need of a good wash. While I was fighting Dexter off and persuading him I really preferred not to be licked, Jeremy despatched his mother with a speed and skill that spoke of long practice.

'Hamish'll be here soon,' he said over his shoulder, as he poured himself out a glass of whisky. 'He's got some papers for me and as he's coming from some conference in Peterborough he thought he might as well drop them in on the way home. It is a bit out of his way, so I'll have to offer him a drink at least.' He looked hopefully at his wife, judging her mood. Her face was still stormy.

'I suppose that means you want me to invite him to stay for dinner,' she said, looking extremely put-upon.

'Well, yes, if you could. That would be very kind of you. But are you sure that you've got enough?' asked Jeremy eagerly, apparently completely oblivious to her slightly martyred air.

Rose hesitated, then relented. 'There's enough for a complete regiment of guardsmen. Of course Hamish can stay if he wants to.'

He cast her a relieved glance. 'Great, and I'm sure he will. It smells delicious!' he added with slightly unflattering surprise. 'Have you been using that cook book that my mother gave you?'

'The one entitled *Cooking for Complete Wallies*?' Rose enquired in an acid voice.

'Was it really called that?' he asked innocently. 'No, it can't have been. You aren't *that* bad, darling.'

Rose looked distinctly unappeased by the endearment. I cut in before she could start making him suffer for his mother and make the sort of remarks that were obviously trembling on the edge of her tongue, along the lines of, 'If you think it's so easy, why don't you try doing it yourself, buster?' or 'If you wanted a cook you should have applied to the domestic employment agency.' She's a strong believer in all those feminist adages about women not being subjugated by domestic tasks. But since she doesn't believe in wasting a sense of humour on such unworthy subjects, it doesn't make for a relaxed atmosphere when she starts to get shirty about them.

'Er, Jeremy . . .' I began. He looked at me and having caught his attention I floundered around for something with which to follow it up. 'Er, what does Hamish do exactly? I can't remember what Rose told me.'

Rose's delicately arched eyebrows rose slightly. Trust her to put a completely unwarranted emphasis on my unexpected interest. 'Is *that* why you don't fancy Stephen?' she asked *sotto voce*.

'No, it is not!' I snapped, equally *sotto voce*, glaring at her meaningfully before turning my attention back to Jeremy, who didn't appear to assume anything untoward in my enquiring about his friend.

'He's a solicitor. He handles the estate business for me, which is why he's dropping around some bumf this evening.'

'Oh,' I said. Rose had been quite right. Soliciting wasn't a very interesting thing to do. 'Is that why he came to work around here, so he could do your business?'

Jeremy shook his head. 'But of course I handed it over to him as soon as I knew he was coming up here. He's a very clever bloke, much brighter than me, always has been,' he said completely matter-of-factly and not sounding as if he gave a toss about it. 'He used to work for one of the top London firms, specialising in company law.'

'If he's so clever, why has he given it all up to become a country solicitor?' I asked, as Dexter, recognising a soft touch, pushed himself against me adoringly and rested his chin on my hand for me to scratch.

'Er, I think he likes the country,' Jeremy said, patently

snatching the first thing he could think of out of the air. He might just as well have been holding a sign above his head with 'I'm trying to prevaricate about something' on it. I could see Rose was going to have a very easy married life in some respects, Jeremy was far too transparent to ever be able to have a mistress. He'd be rumbled before the first longing look.

'Really?' I asked sceptically. I saw Rose's antennae swivel my way again attentively. She was still wearing a slightly offended air about the cooking remarks, so I decided that a bit of teasing from her later would be worth it if I could get her thinking of other things. And there's no quicker way to distract her attention than a man. 'Even if Hamish suddenly developed a passion for the country, couldn't a big shot like that find a firm where he could continue specialising and make a name for himself?' I persisted. 'Or was it really just some excuse because he wasn't good enough and blew it?'

Jeremy looked confused and worried, searching for something to say. 'I expect he got bored with all that technical stuff.'

'Come off it!' I said disbelievingly.

'Actually, Susie's right. I blew it all right, but not, I believe, in the way you think,' said a voice from behind me. I twisted around in horror, sending what was left in my glass slopping over my knee, as Dexter gave joyous voice and leapt at Hamish, who was standing in the doorway, looking very respectable in a dark suit, holding a large envelope under one arm. I wanted to smother myself in the sofa cushions. I'd have crawled under the sofa if there had been room. There's nothing like being caught out being really rudely curious about someone for a major humiliation factor. Hamish pushed Dexter off and stepped forward to kiss Rose and hand the envelope over to Jeremy, who promptly offered him a glass of whisky. I felt I needed one too.

Hamish turned to me. 'Hello, Susie. Nice to see you again.'

Liar! I thought bitterly, feeling my cheeks burn. 'I'm sorry,' I muttered. 'That must have sounded very rude.'

Instead of instantly denying it, he considered for a moment. 'I should say more nosy than rude.'

Nettled, I began, 'No, I'm n—' and fortunately realised just in time it would land me even further in the soup if I was to grandly declare I wasn't interested enough in him to be nosy. Not true either, as I was now burning with a curiosity, that even I could see wasn't going to be satisfied, about exactly what had happened to his job in London.

'Sit down, Hamish, and have your drink,' said Jeremy expansively, gesturing at the place on the sofa next to me. He had taken one of the armchairs, Rose was perched on the edge of the other. For a humiliating moment it seemed as if Hamish was considering Jeremy's knee as the lesser of two evils and then he plumped himself down near me.

'You don't seem to have any wine left,' he said, his eyes flickering briefly but noticeably to the damp stain on my knee. I'd spilt my wine last time I saw him too, hadn't I? I remembered gloomily. No wonder he was so reluctant to sit next to me, not only might he have to listen to tactless remarks, he probably thought he was next in line for an alcoholic bath. I might have imagined that I saw him smile as I crossed my legs hastily, realising just too late I was giving my other trouser leg a nice rub-down of red wine too. Now I was going to have two stains to soak off my fawn trousers. He reached over for the bottle of wine and offered me a refill. I was tempted to refuse, but decided that would be just childish. Also, he must be interested to see if I was capable of keeping any liquid in a glass for longer than a couple of moments.

Rose looked at us both and decided a bit of social emollient

119

was needed. 'We haven't shown you the photographs of the wedding yet, have we?' she asked brightly, reaching towards a large package in the middle of the low table. Hamish made an involuntary movement towards his drink, as if he feared the worst. We might have to sit through the video next. Rose looked up and grinned. 'Don't worry, Hamish. This won't take more than an hour. We can look at all the honeymoon photos later.'

'Not *all* the honeymoon photographs, surely!' said Jeremy in an alarmed voice.

Her eyes opened wide in horror. 'Oh, Lord! I forgot! I gave them to your mother.'

He half rose from his chair. 'I'd better go along now and see if I can get them back. She might not have looked at them all yet,' he said in acute anxiety, then slumped back down again as Rose collapsed in giggles. 'You wretch! You nearly gave me a heart attack!' he said reproachfully, taking a restorative swig of his drink.

'You should have seen your face!' she crowed gleefully and riffling through the pile of photographs in front of her pulled one out. 'Look, Susie, I think this one of you is rather good, don't you?'

I hate nearly all photos of me, since despite what my fond mother claims, I don't think I'm in the least photogenic. I have a tendency to look like a scared rabbit notwithstanding the most valiant efforts of the photographer. Something to do with having round eyes, I think. I couldn't see that this one of me talking to Rose was much better than average, though at least it had been taken after I'd taken off the wretched topknot of flowers. Gosh, and I hadn't realised taking off that fichu thing from the neckline would make it quite so low cut, I thought, seeing for the first time quite how much of my

120

cleavage had been on display, especially in the candid shot where I'd been leaning down talking to Grace. (Or it might have been Clemmie, it was no easier to tell them apart in pictures than it had been in real life.) Still, Rose's Uncle Julius appeared to be enjoying the display, judging by the way his eyes were bulging.

Hamish had put the photographs between us on the table, so we could both look at them at the same time, and was leafing through them slowly, commenting on various people he knew, laughing at a couple of very candid ones, and saying all the proper things about the ones with the bride in them. Rose glowed. She did look fabulous actually, but then her small features always photograph beautifully and with a figure like hers (to say nothing of the basque) she need never worry about the supposed fattening effects of photographs.

'Extraordinary how you don't seem to get to meet even half the people who come to your own wedding,' said Jeremy. He gestured expansively at the pile of photographs, 'I don't even recognise lots of them, but then I suppose it's because most of them are old flames of Rose's. There were certainly enough of them there,' he added reflectively, with the slight complacency of the man who has beaten them all to the post.

'You invited all your old girlfriends, didn't you?' asked Rose. 'Including that dire female Clarissa, who went around telling everyone how you'd ruined her life and she'd never look at another man.' Jeremy began to look rather pleased with himself, until Rose pulled out a picture and said in a disgusted voice, 'If I'd known you could look like *this* I'd have told her she could have you, with my blessing!'

I was leaning forward, giggling at it, my knee brushing slightly against Hamish's when I felt his leg stiffen next to mine. His hand was resting on a contact sheet, his eyes fixed on the picture in the top left-hand corner in which you could just see Nigel talking to some unknown woman and the back of Luke's head half out of the frame. He bent and examined it closely. 'I'd begun to think I must have imagined seeing him. Evidently I didn't. Is Nigel Flaxman a friend of yours, Rose?' he said in a neutral voice.

'Nigel Flaxman?' asked Jeremy, glancing up quickly. He took the sheet, examining it with interest. 'Which one is he? Oh, I see. I certainly can't remember coming across *him* at the wedding. Another old boyfriend, darling?'

'I used to know him,' admitted Rose, with a degree of circumspection quite unusual for her, 'but I didn't even realise he was in the country. You must have asked him.'

'Not me,' said Jeremy firmly. 'Never set eyes on the blighter in my life before. You must have forgotten you invited him, Rose. You were in such a flap over all the arrangements, it wouldn't be surprising if you forgot a casual invite to someone you met in the street.'

'I'm not the sort of idiot who'd forget asking an . . .' began Rose in an irritated voice.

'Maybe he simply gatecrashed,' suggested Hamish in a mild voice, trying to cut off any argument.

'He did, but he didn't mean to,' I cut in without thinking. Three pairs of eyes swivelled around to look at me. I squirmed uncomfortably under this combined scrutiny. 'Actually, Luke was supposed to ring Rose's mother for an invitation, but forgot.'

'Luke?' asked Hamish. 'Luke Dillon?'

I nodded. 'But he didn't tell Nigel they hadn't actually been invited until they were at the reception.'

Rose surveyed me coolly, as if I were a dog caught doing something naughty on the carpet. 'And how do you know this,

Susie? Was this something Luke let slip while you were talking to him at the reception?'

I shrugged as casually as I could. 'No. I bumped into Luke and Nigel in Market Burrough a couple of days ago and we had a drink.'

'What were they doing there?' asked Hamish casually.

'Haven't got a clue,' I replied. 'I imagine that Nigel was visiting Luke or something.' I glanced up and saw Rose's intent face and sighed inwardly. Well, she'd have to know sometime, I supposed. 'Luke's got a weekend cottage quite near there, at Wickham,' I ended up unhappily, sensing rather than seeing Rose's sudden alert interest.

'Really?' she enquired frigidly, with a glare that promised I was going to be made to pay later for holding out on her. 'You seem to have garnered quite a lot of information over the course of this one drink.'

Fortunately, the acid annoyance in her voice was lost on Jeremy, for even he might have started to wonder what she was getting so cross about. He broke in with, 'Wickham? I didn't know that, but then I've never had much to do with Luke Dillon. He's not really our sort.'

This earned him a cold stare from his wife. 'Do you mean he's not grand enough for you?'

'Certainly not!' exclaimed Jeremy promptly. 'Nobody would *dare* say old Mrs Dillon isn't grand enough, or any of her descendants. She's the most terrifying old tartar, she can out-handbag Lady Bracknell any day, I promise you!' he said with feeling. 'She's loaded too. Luke's the favourite grandchild and is going to cop the lot, so I hear, but apparently away from his grandmother's censorious eye he mixes with a pretty wild crowd. I outgrew that sort of thing a long time ago, of course.'

I saw Rose begin to smile at this rather untypically middle-aged statement from her husband. 'Outgrew what? Loose women, fast cars and too much to drink? Come off it, Jeremy! The only one of those you've given up is the first!' she said. 'Or at least you'd better have!'

In Jeremy's loudly protesting denials the sticky moment was temporarily forgotten, though I knew that I wasn't off the hook yet. Sure enough, a few minutes later Rose, with a fine disregard for gender equality, motioned for me to get up and help her lay the table, while the men stayed in front of the fire to attend to the serious masculine business of discussing the one-day international against Australia. She dumped a pile of knives and forks in my hands and said with a tight smile, 'Well, you're a close one, aren't you?'

'I can't think what you mean,' I said blandly.

She cast me a fulminating look from under half-closed eyelids. 'Can't you?' she asked meaningfully, clattering the plates down with more force than was strictly necessary.

'No,' I said flatly, and untruthfully. And then showed myself up by adding, 'But perhaps you'd like to tell me exactly what this is about. Is there something going on between you and Luke?'

'Of course not!' she said, so promptly I reckoned she really was telling the truth. 'I've never so much as kissed him, if you must know!' she declared loftily. I had the feeling that she wasn't too pleased about this. She glanced at the two men, deep in conversation about batting averages, then turned to me with a serious face. 'But I meant what I said before, Susie. Don't get mixed up with Luke Dillon.'

'For what reason?' I asked, manfully swallowing the rider of, 'Other than you fancy him yourself.' There were certain cans of worms I thought it best not to open, even with my closest, just married, friend.

'Um, well . . .' She concentrated on arranging the water glasses just so, at forty-five degrees to the ends of the knives. Her mother would have been proud of her. 'As Jeremy said, Luke's rather wild.'

'But yesterday you said I was staid,' I said dulcetly. 'What better way to liven myself up a bit than to have a fling with someone like Luke.'

'You're not!' she squeaked, loud enough for the men to lift their heads and look at us curiously.

I giggled at her horrified face. 'Come on, how fast a mover do you think I am?' I demanded. 'Have I ever launched into a fling with someone on two very brief meetings?' I didn't wait for her answer, which would have been something along the lines of, of course not, but if I was going to tie myself up with a foreigner for years what could I expect? 'All I did was have a well-chaperoned glass of mineral water with him in a horrible pub, when he was so hungover he probably couldn't even focus on me. Hardly the start of a great romance. So you don't have to worry, he's still free for you!'

'Is he really?' she murmured, in a most disquieting manner, then screwed up her face comically. 'You forget that I've got an impediment in the shape of Jeremy.'

'Is that going to make any difference?' I demanded, only half joking.

'We-ell,' she began slowly, then grinned. 'When you're faced with temptation in the shape of someone like Luke Dillon, perhaps the best thing is to give into it,' she said, returning to her normal teasing manner.

The only problem was I had a horrid feeling it wasn't teasing.

CHAPTER 7

An untidy heap of papers landed without warning on the desk in front of me. 'I need this report for two. I'll pick it up when I come back from lunch,' said a voice disappearing around the corner.

I gazed in its direction with a baleful expression. I supposed that meant for the second time in a week I was going to miss my lunch. Of course, it wasn't going to do me any harm to skip a meal, I thought, with a rueful glance down at my lap and automatically sucking in my tummy, but I do like to be asked if I mind being put on an involuntary diet. Not that bloody Martin Prescott ever *asked* me to do anything, I thought bitterly, he barked orders with a slight sneer in his voice that said he reckoned I wasn't going to do anything properly. And I wasn't even supposed to be working for him, I only helped out when Jenny was snowed under, but Jenny, wise woman, wouldn't dream of working through her lunch hour and even Martin knew better than to suggest she should. She was in her mid-thirties, married with a couple of children, and completely unambitious. She worked for money, did her set hours conscientiously and left promptly each evening to go back and cook tea for her family. Amanda said it had taken some persuasion to convince Jenny that if the clock struck five while she was in the middle of typing a letter she ought to finish it rather than leave it half done until the next morning. For obvious reasons, she found it very difficult to cope with Stephen.

She looked up briefly from her computer screen, made a face at Martin's disappearing back, and said, 'Tell him you had an appointment to do your hair or something. Teach him a lesson and make him more considerate in future.'

It was a distinctly tempting idea, except I had a feeling the only way I'd ever be able to drum a lesson into Martin Prescott would be at the end of a sledgehammer. In the days since I'd bumped into him with Luke and Nigel he'd been even more odious and off-hand with me than before. He'd also made a couple of comments along the lines of 'people who make fools of themselves pushing in where they aren't wanted'. I'd have made some smart and inflammatory remark in reply if an uneasy little voice hadn't pointed out that in fact I had pushed myself in quite deliberately and maybe, despite Nigel and Luke's good manners, they hadn't particularly fancied an extra in a boys' drink out at the pub. Not that I always bother to listen to what my conscience tells me, but for once I attended to the wiser half that pointed out going head to head isn't always the most sensible way to behave. I should know that from past experience, but sometimes I have difficulty in remembering it. There was no point in blowing on the embers of Martin's hostility any more than I had done already. I'm not always so restrained. Besides, he was the senior negotiator and, when push came to shove, was rather more important to the success of this firm than I was. If Stephen had to choose between the two of us I was well aware of who it would have to be. I must be growing up, I thought, as I picked the report up and looked over Martin's crabbed writing, I never used to be this circumspect. I sighed. Maturity could be very boring.

'You're too soft, Susie, that's your problem,' said Jenny, returning to the complexities of the 3D maze she was currently negotiating on her computer screen. She adored playing games on the computer, not the sort where you shoot down aliens or find treasure in ancient Peruvian tombs, complete with sound effects and a lot of splashy blood, but mind puzzles that were so complicated just reading the instructions made my eyes cross. According to Amanda, Jenny was reputed to be quite startlingly bright, but these puzzles, and apparently a certain ability at computer hacking, were the only signs that she had a stratospheric-level IQ concealed behind her placid unambition.

It's nice to be able to report that just sometimes virtue has its own reward. Or I suppose the reward would have come anyway, even if I'd been thoroughly badly behaved and had sloped off to buy the book I wanted, but it would have come a bit later. The phone went and I picked it up with one hand while I suppressed a naughty word as I saw the report was just a bit too long for three pages and I was going to have to respace all the paragraphs. One of Martin's obsessions was presentation, even in draft discussion documents. Although I had a sneaky suspicion he was rather more adamant about perfect presentation with me than he was with Jenny, who would simply say calmly she'd do it like he wanted if she had time. Which she usually didn't. Whatever, it meant another two minutes juggling lines and I didn't want to spend even another two seconds on Martin Prescott's business.

I'd just about given up hope that Luke would ever contact me about that promised drink. Actually, I'd begun to spiral into gloom when he didn't ring me that very same afternoon, telling myself it hadn't ever been much more than a casual suggestion and I'd probably read much too much into it, yet still jumping as if I'd been stuck with a pin every time the telephone went. If he ever did ring, I certainly wasn't going to fall over myself accepting his invitation, I decided, he must be bored to tears with that sort of reaction from girls. No, *I* was going to be icily cool and sophisticated, indicate that perhaps I could find a gap in my busy social schedule in about a week or so. Cool? Like hell I was! When I heard his voice I almost dropped the phone, leant obliviously on the keyboard so Martin's precious report had four pages of h's in the middle of it, and agreed to meet him that evening almost before he'd managed to get the words out. I have to confess I would have preferred to meet him somewhere a little more picturesque than my local pub, but he explained apologetically that he was in Brum doing something for Nigel and had to leave for London later that evening, Unless we made it strictly local he didn't think he'd have a chance to see me at all. Put like that, in honeyed tones audible even through the come and go of a car phone, how could I say anything other than the pub sounded just perfect?

For once, I was just like Jenny and beetled off on the dot of five, though I was absolutely sure she never did it so she could spend two hours washing and blow-drying her hair so it was sophisticatedly straight rather than curly and countrified, bathing, making up and trying on every single garment in her wardrobe, only to reject nearly all of the same. All so I could look like I'd just had the time to dash into the cottage, fling off my office clothes and reappear a minute later in casually understated glowing natural beauty. Some hope. The best you could say is I didn't look as if I'd just spent two hours dolling myself up. And I have to admit Luke didn't immediately cover his eyes when he saw me, muttering, 'Get thee away from me.' In fact, he grinned and said I looked super, so even allowing for polite exaggeration I suppose the effect wasn't too bad.

Naturally, he was as stomach-churningly fantastic as ever. He was wearing a pair of black jeans that fitted him so well he might have pre-shrunk them to size in the bath that afternoon, and a tight black tee-shirt, his golden hair swept back untidily from his forehead, the fallen-angel air accentuated by the slight bags under his eyes. He said he'd had a bit of a rough evening the night before. I felt an acute pang of jealousy grip me, until I realised that men don't have that sort of evening with girlfriends whom they want to be a bit more than just friends with, if you get my gist. And he hadn't said anything about spending it with a girl either. Even better.

The Dearsley Arms doesn't have what you might call the most romantic ambience in the world, even if compared to the Bull and Bush its floral carpet and bentwood chairs are positively drenched in hearts and roses. Though for me, going to the pub with a desirable man is like trying to conduct a romance in front of the computer, it smacks a bit too much of work and I can't help automatically assessing how quick the service is and which are the most popular brands of beer. But at least on a mid-week evening it was quiet in the saloon bar and we were able to find ourselves a corner table where Luke installed me on a banquette while he sat down opposite. For a moment I was disappointed, my mind had been lightly running along the lines of our thighs gently brushing each other under the table etc., and then I realised that not only was this being just a bit forward and presumptuous, but this way I could lean my chin on my hand and feast my eyes on his face. (Without making it too obvious, of course.) Honestly, a man who looked like that didn't need to have any other social attributes, I thought dreamily, as he went to fetch us a white wine and a half of bitter respectively, and then brought myself abruptly back down to earth as various other essentials in a man besides looks occurred to me, such as non-hairy hands and decent table manners. Well, Luke definitely passed in both those areas. And I insist on regular sock-changing too. As far as I could tell without getting too close, he scored a perfect ten there as well.

'Evening, Susie,' said my next-door neighbour as he slowly made his way to the darts board, carrying his half of Best and breaking into what was becoming my increasingly pernickety list of requirements in a man. 'Haven't seen you in here before. Here with your young man?'

'Just a friend, Mr Tanner,' I said.

His wife, who was almost as aged and bent as he was, chuckled, saying, 'I remember saying that to my mam about our Bert here in nineteen thirty-three! But nice girls didn't go in public houses then, we had to make do with walking up the chestnut path to Nisby. Those were the days, 'specially when the chestnuts was in flower! That scent! It proper heats your blood, don't it, Bert?' She dug him in the ribs, making his half wobble around dangerously, and chuckled again. 'Not that I'm not saying the pub's warmer in winter and more convenient like, but if he's being a bit slow get him to take you for a walk under the chestnuts.' She tapped the side of her nose. 'Never fails!' She glanced towards the bar, where Luke was handing his money over and waiting for his change. 'If I was you, I'd get that one up under the chestnuts sharpish! Lovely boy that! Now if I were fifty year younger . . .'

'I'll remember that, Mrs Tanner,' I said quickly, praying that she'd leave and take her embarrassing remarks with her before Luke got back and was subjected to some heavy geriatric flirting. Mr Hodges from across the green, who enjoyed a (reasonably) friendly rivalry with Mr Tanner over who grew the finest radishes and cucumbers, came in from the snug and, waving his stick, called triumphantly that he'd just had a special delivery from the horticultural society which was going to sweep the board at the flower and produce show this year. The two Tanners immediately hobbled over to begin a lively discussion about seed varieties as Luke came back with the drinks.

Over our drinks we did a bit of exchanging of life stories. He was engagingly self-deprecating about his previous career as an accountant. I was quite sure he couldn't have been as incompetent as he made out, even though it was difficult to imagine anyone as exotic as Luke doing something quite so mundane as number-crunching. He was also impressively open about how he accepted an allowance off his grandmother so he was free to keep a watchful eye on her and manage her affairs, though Grandma did have a permanent live-in carer. Most men would have been far too proud to admit it. It was nice of Luke to care so much about his grandmother, most men thought taking care of relatives was a job for the females. What a find he was; good-looking and good-hearted, I thought dreamily. In fact, just about the only shortcoming I could find in him was that he was a friend of Martin's, and I supposed that was more of an error of judgement than a character fault. It did mean I had to keep a grip on my tongue when talking about work though.

'And what's the freelancing?' I asked. 'Not accounting, I take it?'

'God no!' he said with a grimace. 'I sort things out for Nigel on an ad hoc basis, sort of troubleshooter I suppose.'

That sounded impressive. 'What is Nigel's business?' I asked curiously. 'I got the idea that most of it was in America.'

Luke drained his glass. 'Only some of it. He's in property

management basically, you know, rentals and the like, in places like Nottingham and Birmingham, though he's got one or two little projects going in the States too. He doesn't do badly out of it,' he said casually and gestured towards my glass. 'Another?'

Naturally, I accepted and he went off to the bar. 'Have you seen Rose yet?' he asked as he came back and sat down with the glasses. 'How is she?'

I was used to my friend being the centre of attention when we were together, she simply assumes that she's going to be the focus and like a magnet she is, but frankly I could really have done without her making an invisible third while I was trying to wow Luke Dillon. Was he just using me as a method of trying to get to her? I thought with sudden despondency. So he wasn't looking at me as if I was the most attractive thing he'd ever seen (but then men don't usually behave like that in pubs, which is why your average woman prefers dimly lit restaurants), but that certain light definitely didn't go on in his eyes when he mentioned Rose's name either. He was probably just making conversation. After all, she was a friend we had in common. 'I went over and had supper with them the other night. She was on great form, though I could have done without her telling Jeremy and Hamish some of the stories about what we got up to at school,' I added darkly. 'She made them all sound as if it was my fault, when in fact she was always the prime mover!'

Luke leant back in his chair and looked at me from under half-closed eyelids. 'Hamish?' he queried softly. 'His name seems to crop up a lot in your conversation. Do I take that to mean you were telling Nigel a tactful little porkie when you said you weren't particular friends with him?'

I shook my head vehemently. 'I was telling the absolute

truth! Hamish just happened to drop in with some papers for the estate and stayed on.'

'Oh, come on!' he said sceptically. 'He can't work for Jeremy!'

'In a way,' I assured him. 'Hamish does his legal stuff apparently, and was delivering something. Though frankly, with the way Nigel looked when Hamish's name was mentioned, I would happily have sworn on my grandmother's grave I didn't know him, even if we'd been having an affair to rival the steamiest pages of the *Kama Sutra*!'

As Luke laughed I was emboldened enough by a glass and a half of Portuguese white to lean forward and ask, 'Do tell me. What is it between those two?'

'What do you mean?' he asked guardedly.

'Come on! It's obvious Nigel can't stand him, and I gather Hamish isn't ready to fall on Nigel's neck and swear undying friendship either.'

Luke looked at me with dancing eyes. 'Have you ever heard about what happened to the cat, Miss Gardener?'

'Oh, I suppose it's something confidential,' I said with resignation.

He shrugged. 'Nigel doesn't like people gossiping about him. You must understand I have to respect that.' My face must have shown I found this a very disappointing attitude for him to take, for he grimaced slightly and said, 'All I can say is Hamish was acting for one of Nigel's companies, and well – to be honest, it was a complete cock-up. Nigel lost a lot of money.'

Was that what Hamish had screwed up about? I thought. Yet, Jeremy, who despite his good humour was no fool, had deliberately moved his business to Hamish. Surely he wouldn't do that with someone who was incompetent, even a good friend. There had to be more to it. I eyed Luke speculatively, intending to get him to expand on this interesting subject, drop in a few clues, surely he couldn't be so unnaturally close-mouthed as to refuse to say anything at all about what was obviously a very heated subject, but he distracted me most effectively by murmuring that he was glad I wasn't tied up with Hamish. The unspoken meaning behind his words was so unmistakable that I immediately went shooting off into daydream city, half my mind hanging on every word he was saying, the other half speculating in the most delicious way about the future.

'I got an invitation to some charity do at Moor End Hall next month, in aid of that specialist learning centre for mentally handicapped adults,' he said idly as we were draining our second glasses. 'I know I should support a good cause like that, but I'm not sure if I could stand a whole evening. I'll send a donation – if I remember,' he added with a rueful smile. 'The last one of these things I was inveigled to going to was full of the dullest and worthiest people in the county – the ones I try hard to avoid – and we had to watch a very amateur fashion show, modelled by women who should have known better than to display themselves on a catwalk. *Then* we were served with a fork supper provided by the ladies of the committee, comprising gluey rice salad and coronation chicken which was long on the coronation and short on the chicken!'

I laughed at his expression of disgust. 'Actually,' I said, 'this one is going to be a wine-tasting, so your visual sensibilities needn't be too offended, and the wine is coming via Jeremy's cousin, who's a wine merchant, so it should be quite drinkable. He'll have to answer to his Aunt Flavia if it isn't! Although I'm afraid at the moment we're still in for the ladies' committee's offerings for the fork supper, but Rose is being pretty tough about it. She put her foot down very firmly about Mrs Richardson doing something interesting with the cut-price ham she can get from the Cash and Carry.'

Luke looked like he didn't even want to contemplate what you could do with cut-price ham. 'Rose's really becoming the county lady if she's already getting involved in charity affairs. Next thing we'll know she'll be running the local pony club.'

'I doubt it; she gave up riding when she decided it was making her bottom spread. But this isn't by her choice. Flavia promised the chairlady of the committee they could hold the event at the house without consulting Jeremy and Rose, and then promptly announced that as Rose is now the mistress of the house she has to do all the liaison with the charity, which basically means most of the organisation for the party! Rose was not happy to come back from honeymoon to be greeted with the news that in under a month she has two hundred people turning up for the evening,' I said with great under-statement, remembering the way she had sounded off during supper. 'Especially as the chairlady keeps on saying how very kind it is of Flavia to allow them to hold it there.'

'So, are you going to be there?' asked Luke. This was accompanied by such a meaningful look I'd have promised to be at the South Pole on New Year's Day if that was what would please him.

'Rose informs me my life won't be worth living if I'm not! She's put me down to sell raffle tickets already,' I said.

'I'll buy raffle tickets off you any day,' said Luke, with another of those stomach-clenching, toe-curling, spine-quiver-ing looks. I was quivering so much I was going to start resembling a jelly if I wasn't careful. 'In fact, you can put me down for several books.'

'Thank you,' I said, smiling at him. 'So you're going to

come?' I asked, finding that an event which I'd been looking forward to with a certain degree of gloomy anticipation suddenly seemed as if it might be fun after all. 'I'm sure you'll find it more enjoyable than you thought it was going to be.'

'If you're going to be there, I'm sure I will,' he said simply, in a manner that was very bad for my fantasy levels. My daydreams were skyrocketing upwards. 'And I've always wanted to have a look at the house, I've heard it's rather impressive.'

'Big, certainly,' I said. 'And the setting's lovely too.'

'Yes, it's a very pretty part of the world.' He frowned slightly. 'Didn't I hear a rumour about a new village or something being built in the estate grounds. Three hundred houses and a shopping centre? That's going to spoil it a bit, isn't it?'

'It's a bit of an exaggeration,' I said. 'There's talk of a new estate nearby but I don't know if it's going to go ahead.'

He offered me the last peanut in the bowl, which I refused, and asked, 'Why not? Are there problems with planning permission?'

'I don't think so, Jeremy isn't sure that he wants it.'

Luke raised his eyebrows disbelievingly. 'Not *want* it! Come on, every landowner *dreams* of winning the equivalent of the lottery by discovering he can get planning permission. Or he does if he's in his right mind! I'd have thought Jeremy would grab a large cash injection with both hands and go singing all the way to the bank!'

'Well, it's quite close to the house, for one thing, and Rose isn't very keen either. She wants some low-cost housing, something which would be better for the community.'

Luke snorted with laughter. 'Since when has Rose been an environmentalist? Or a bleeding-heart liberal?' he asked incredulously. 'Still, in the end it's Jeremy's land, isn't it? He might have promised to share all his worldly goods, but I bet when it comes down to it he'll decide anything to do with the estate is his and make up his own mind.'

'Probably,' I agreed, 'though I think he listens to Rose as well. If she stays adamantly against the scheme it's going to be very difficult for him to go ahead.'

He nodded vaguely, losing interest in theoretical building developments, and asked me something about how I was getting on at work.

To my acute disappointment, my evening with Luke lasted for rather less time than it had taken to doll myself up. I'd rather hoped that our drink would extend itself into a quick dinner at least, but he explained apologetically he had promised to drop in and see his grandmother before leaving for London. Not even in my wildest dreams could I seriously expect he'd start taking me to meet the family on the first date (if you could give a drink in the local pub such an exalted title as a date), so I didn't have any valid reasons for feeling let down, I told myself firmly. It worked a bit. But any gloomy suspicions that he might have just been undertaking a tiresome social duty he wanted to get over as quickly as possible were quashed when he said he'd ring me as soon as he got back later in the week and perhaps we could go out then. I didn't play it cool about accepting that invitation either, though this time I did let him finish the sentence first.

I let myself into the cottage, humming gently to myself, knowing that I was going to be reliving many times the moment when he kissed me goodbye under the light of a pale half-moon, still low in the sky. OK, so it wasn't a passionate triple-violin job, more of a peck with attitude, but we had to start somewhere. It was definitely a move onwards from when he'd kissed my cheek in Market Burrough last week and the way he'd looked into my eyes and murmured he wished he could stay a little longer made up for any amount of actual physical contact. I have a very good imagination.

The telephone rang as I was off to bed to indulge in some exotic fantasies. I picked it up gloomily, afraid that it was my mother. Even a merely mildly horny daydream is killed stone dead with the first reproachful, 'Hello, darling, I haven't heard from you for *ages*.' It seems to come with the maternal territory, along with Ovaltine and good winter coats. But to my surprised pleasure it was Arnaud, who was just the tiniest bit indignant I hadn't been there to answer the phone when he rang earlier that evening, and even less pleased when he heard that I'd been out for a drink with a man, though he did manage to fit in some Gallic aspersions on the cold-blooded-ness of English males who left women on doorsteps. Oh, and he'd been missing me. He had? I thought, stunned. He was going to try to arrange his next trip over to London with meetings on both Friday and Monday, so he could spend the weekend with me. Would I like that? I blinked slightly, astonished he'd even thought to ask. Normally, Arnaud made a (quite justified) assumption I'd simply fall in with whatever he wanted. Even if it wasn't very convenient for me. Well, I'd been doing exactly that for the last four years. Except I'd had to turn him down last time he wanted to see me, hadn't I? And I hadn't been in earlier this evening for his call. Rose had been telling me for ages that if I wasn't going to chuck him at least I could stop running every time he crooked his finger, and it seemed she was right. It did bring results, I thought, as I assured him that indeed I'd like it if we spent the weekend together.

I went to bed with that pleasant feeling you have when you feel yourself in demand from several quarters (not something that happens often enough to me, especially on the same evening) and I had some very nice dreams indeed. Disconcertingly, the male person who was doing such very interesting things didn't turn out to be either Luke or Arnaud, but in the way of dreams I didn't feel in the least guilty about it, just rather pleased with myself.

CHAPTER 8

I'm not very good at letting sleeping dogs lie. Which is probably one of the reasons I don't seem to do very well in the sort of jobs where women are basically supposed to be decorative and not muddy the waters by asking questions. So yesterday I'd rung Rose and arranged to meet for lunch in Frampton's answer to the brasserie phenomenon so that we could have a serious talk. As far as I was concerned, she could either fess up about all those mysterious hints about Luke, or shut up. But that had been before I'd had that call from Luke. Now, as I shot down the High Street towards Chez Bruno, late because Stephen had decided to rewrite something at the last minute, I couldn't help wondering if I was about to be given the third degree. I know very well how quickly the bush telegraph works in the country, so it was quite possible someone had already been on the blower to Rose to tell her I'd been closeted in the corner at the Dearsley Arms virtually having it off on the table last night with Luke. It wouldn't put her in a particularly propitious mood for our discussion.

She'd continued to be in a funny mood all during what was otherwise a very relaxed dinner the other night, throwing in the odd remark about my various menfriends, commenting especially on Arnaud, and generally making it sound as if I was the next best thing to Mata Hari in the man-trapping stakes.

143

I saw Hamish looking at me in slight bewilderment more than once, as if he was trying to square this honey-pot vision being created by Rose with the mundane reality sitting next to him in the wine-splattered trousers. It didn't take a genius to work out she was in a thorough snitch about Luke, though I wished I knew what the hell she was so antsy about. Maybe she knew something dreadful about him, like his being a drug dealer or something. I then thought of his incredible face and decided if your average dealer looked like that there'd be a far greater drug problem amongst the female population, so it was unlikely.

She was already seated at a table in the window, staring with a certain disbelief at the menu, which tends to be long on glasses of indifferent wine and short on inspirationally good French cooking. Or even brasserie staples like *steak, frites*, and croque-monsieur (their version had shavings of Parma ham and Parmesan. Parma ham isn't improved by grilling, in my opinion). But the wine bar on the other side of the street, which did have a reasonable cook, usually had most of the office in it and the chances of a private gossip were practically nil. For one thing, the tables were placed so close together that you weren't only able to eavesdrop on the next-door table's conversation with ease, but the one on the other side of that as well. And I'd decided after the depressing session I'd had yesterday evening, trying to ease a pair of trousers over my hips and discovering they were no longer slim-fitting but positively constricting, it would be a good thing to lunch where I wasn't tempted to eat a lot.

I eyed Rose warily as I approached the table, fearing a storm. But she looked up with a smile that seemed perfectly genuine. 'Am I glad to see you!' she exclaimed. 'Do I need to talk to someone! Honestly, Susie, I knew it was going to be no picnic sharing a roof with that woman, but I had no *idea* how impossible it was going to be. Do you know she was around *again* last night, poking around the kitchen? She *said* she'd left her best saucepan behind and was looking for it.' She snorted indignantly. 'As if that was likely! She cleared out everything, even half-full packets of salt! And then she said Jeremy shouldn't be eating . . .'

I hadn't even had a chance to sit down yet. 'Hello, Rose,' I said across her diatribe and pulled out my chair, as unabashed she continued outlining the iniquities of Flavia who, according to Rose, was being thoroughly tiresome about the arrangements for this charity do and despite saying it was now nothing to do with her was insisting on interfering with everything. Rose had, as she called it, 'stuck to her guns' about whether the local bank's dance band should be invited to play for the evening (a.k.a. being thoroughly bloody-minded and refusing to concede a single point), while Flavia had said pityingly that she knew dear Rose was doing her best, but she wasn't used to living in the country yet and didn't really understand how country people thought. Apparently, you couldn't call Hertfordshire real country any longer, Rose added, fuming, so many people commuted to London from there it really counted as a mere garden suburb. Poor Jeremy, who had bravely stepped into the middle of this battle royal and tried to keep the peace between his womenfolk, had ended up being blamed by both sides for being too weak to properly support the correct point of view.

'But why are you letting her get under your skin so much?' I asked, as she ground to a halt while two rather limp 'Provencal Country' salads were being placed in front of us. They must think the inhabitants of Provence live mainly on semi-grilled goat's cheese and sun-dried tomatoes, I thought, wondering belatedly if something else, anything else, would have been a better bet. 'Before you got engaged you were going out with Jeremy for how long, six months? OK, so you weren't actually living with him, but you must have got some idea of what Flavia was like. You used to laugh at her.'

Rose forked about her salad in a dispirited fashion, picking out a bit of bacon and examining it closely before she put it in her mouth. 'That was before, wasn't it?' she asked gloomily. 'Now I'm stuck with her for good, or as long as I'm married, in any case.'

I stared at her in alarm. 'Rose! You aren't suggesting . . .!' I exclaimed.

'No, of course not!' she said, promptly enough to quell my worst fears. 'But I wish we lived in France,' she said in a longing voice. 'Then I could kill her and claim it as a *crime passionnel*! I lay awake for hours last night, planning ways I could murder her. You wouldn't believe how much better it made me feel! Would you like to hear some of my sure-fire methods?'

'No thank you!' I said firmly.

'Chicken!' she retorted.

'I'm trying to eat my lunch,' I pointed out, knowing from experience how gory Rose's imagination can be.

'Can't think why you're bothering, those tomatoes are truly sun-dried. I now understand all about the damage too much sunbathing is supposed to do to your skin. World of Leather, here we come!' She pushed the plate away, signalling to the waiter to bring her an ashtray. She watched him thoughtfully as he reached up to fetch one from the clean stack on a shelf above the bar, lean and lithe in white shirt and black trousers. He was well worth looking at, with the oval face, olive skin and dark curls more usually associated with some figure out of

146

an Italian Renaissance painting. Amanda had already informed me he was actually a farm labourer's son from a smallholding near Peterborough and was only waitering while he hung around to see if he'd succeeded in his bid to become a policeman. 'Mm, nice figure. Very nice figure indeed,' murmured Rose, eyeing him up as he shimmied back around the bar and placed the ashtray carefully on our table.

'Which is why, despite the quality of the food, the place is packed. And why the clientele is almost entirely female,' I said. 'Except for Jack over there –' the owner of the second-hand bookshop looked up and waved at me – 'and he comes for the scenery just like the rest of us.'

'It looks like life in the sticks has its compensations after all. I'll be coming here again,' Rose said, eyes still on the waiter as he bent over another table. 'Still, he's not as good-looking as Luke, is he?'

I looked at her warily, wondering what was coming next. She started tracing idle circles on the tabletop with one long fingernail, as if she was choosing her words carefully. My apprehension increased. It wasn't like Rose to be this hesitant.

She sighed shudderingly and said abruptly, 'I'm sure you need another glass of wine, Susie. I know I do,' and signalled the waiter to bring over another two glasses of red.

I waited with impatience while they came without haste, the waiter favoured a measured tread, and she then slowly lit a cigarette, watching the end glow red as if she was a Girl Guide trying to get her firestarter's badge. 'I think I've been a bit stupid,' she said finally, to my utter amazement. This was even more unlike Rose. 'There isn't any reason why you shouldn't go out with Luke, it's just that . . .'

'Just what?' I asked eventually, after it became apparent she was more interested in watching her cigarette slowly burn

147

down than in saying anything. I'd crown her out of sheer frustration if she didn't get on with it soon. 'That you've got the hots for him yourself?'

Her head shot up. 'Of course not!' she said indignantly, too indignantly, in my opinion. Then she smiled faintly. 'I used to, of course, but I expect you've already guessed that.'

'I did have some glimmering,' I admitted.

She sighed wistfully, idly playing with a lock of hair that had escaped from its ponytail. 'Only it was a bit more than the hots. I was bonkers about him,' she said flatly. And then added in a rush, 'In fact, he was the love of my life.'

I gaped at her. I couldn't have heard right. *The love of her life?* Me, her best friend, whom she told everything to, knew absolutely nothing about this at all? Had never even heard her mention Luke's name? Impossible. It had to be some sort of belated April Fools' joke. But she didn't look like she was joking, in fact, she looked deadly serious.

She glanced up with an air of defiance. 'It's true, I promise,' she said sadly. 'I was so infatuated with him I used to walk up and down outside his flat just to look in the windows and imagine what he was doing. I stole one of his shirts and used to cuddle it at night, pretending it was him. I stopped wearing Diorissimo and switched to CKhomme because that was what he used. I let the second and third holes in my ears close up because he didn't like them. I was even prepared to give away Phuket if he turned out to be allergic to cats . . .' She smiled wanly at me. 'Do I need to go on?'

I shook my head mutely, too awed by this long list to say anything. Gosh, I'd thought I was well lost for love when I first met Arnaud, but it was never anything like this. I used to go into chemists' and spray myself with Egoiste so I could smell like him, but I never resorted to nicking his clothing.

How typical of Rose to fall in love with such superb excess, I thought ruefully, not quite sure if I was envious of such passion or relieved I'd never had my life disrupted to quite that extent. And she'd kept it all from me. Miss Motormouth herself had never, ever breathed a single word. If she hadn't been so obviously, desperately sincere, I still wouldn't have believed it was possible. 'Why didn't you tell me?' I asked at last.

'You were so busy rabbiting on about the Frog I couldn't get a word in edgeways.' I looked at her in slight shock, wondering if it was really true, and she sighed, saying, 'That's a bit unfair, I suppose. But you were in Montpellier, having the time of your life, and there was I hopelessly addicted to an unobtainable object. I didn't want to admit to being absolutely miserable while you were canoodling with this supposedly gorgeous man –' a trace of the normal Rose resurfaced as she lifted a sceptical eyebrow – 'and then when you came back and we were both apparently in the same boat I'd locked it all away inside me and didn't want to talk about it. It was too strong, too personal.'

Now I came to think of it, she had been very quiet during that time, but I'd been too wrapped up in my own miseries to even contemplate that anyone else could be unhappy. But that she hadn't said a word . . . I shook my head disbelievingly. 'So why didn't anything happen? Why didn't you ride off into the proverbial sunset with Luke for the affair of the century? He isn't gay, is he?' I asked in sudden suspicion.

'No, of course not! What do you think I am, a fag hag?' she asked indignantly, then added, 'Though he's not a rampant skirt-chaser, if you know what I mean.' She looked at her cigarette in surprise to see it had burnt away without her noticing and lit another, taking a long draw. 'To answer your question,' she said, blowing out smoke, 'firstly, I never had any indication that Luke fancied me.'

I raised a sceptical eyebrow and she laughed a bit sheepishly. Rose knew and I knew, she had never ever failed to land an object of desire and heaven knows there had been enough different personalities, ages and nationalities to be able to say with confidence that her skills went right across the board. If she didn't know whether Luke fancied her or not it could only mean she'd never put it to the test.

'Well, of course I couldn't come on to him because of Nigel,' she explained earnestly. 'I met him through Nigel, but not until a couple of months after we'd started going out together. Luke had been away doing something for one of Nigel's companies, Nigel uses him as a roving troubleshooter . . .'

'Really,' I said non-committally, reckoning it was more tactful not to mention I'd already heard this from the horse's mouth.

She nodded. 'Nigel once said Luke mightn't have the greatest business brain in the world, but that charm of his is worth ten MBAs – whatever they are,' she added dubiously, 'but apparently they're a good thing for high flyers to have. He's brilliant at smoothing ruffled feathers, getting people to see his point of view and believe it was actually theirs in the first place. Nigel said he was worth his weight in gold. Anyway, Luke had done even better than usual and Nigel arranged a celebration dinner at Le Gavroche.' She stopped for a moment, her eyes fixed unseeingly on the distance, and sighed heavily. 'He was late, as usual,' she said in an indulgent voice. 'Nigel and I were already halfway down our aperitifs when I looked up and there was this gorgeous man coming across the room. It was as if he had a spotlight centred on him; everyone was looking at him as if he were some kind of star. I'd never seen anything like it. I was in love before he even sat down and said a word to me.' She shook her head wryly. 'Sad or what? There was I, properly in love for the first time in my life and not able to do a bloody thing about it because I was already involved with his friend and employer.'

I could see this would have presented a distinct problem. 'But you could have broken it off with Nigel and then gone after Luke after a decent interval,' I suggested, thinking this was what she would have done normally.

Rose shivered and reached for her wine glass. 'Not with Nigel,' she said firmly and took a large swig. 'He's very possessive. He doesn't allow people to muck around with his possessions, and as far as he's concerned his women are his possessions. And you stay his possession even after you've broken up. There was no question of starting something with Luke, I didn't even need Nigel to say anything, he's got a way of looking at you that sends shivers down your spine and promises if you step out of line he'll have his revenge, no matter how long it takes him. And having an affair with Luke would have been stepping out of line with a capital S.'

I felt a shiver of my own go down my spine as I remembered the effect Nigel had had on me, who hardly knew him, when he was cross-questioning me about Hamish. Poor Rose. Talk about being stuck between the devil and the deep blue sea. 'So what did you do?' I asked at last.

She looped her finger in the thin gold chain around her neck and began twisting it around her finger. 'I got over it, as one does,' she said flatly. 'I don't have it in me to nurture an undying, unrequited love for the rest of my life.' There was an uncomfortably hard edge to her voice as she said this. 'You've got to have something to feed an infatuation like that. You have to see the loved one from time to time, so just as you

151

think you're getting over it you meet him again, and whoosh! Back you are in a quivering heap of palpitating, mindless, uncritical love and desire.' She looked up, meeting my eyes. 'Bit like you and Arnaud, actually.' There was a silence. 'For six months or so after I broke up with Nigel I couldn't stop torturing myself with the odd glimpse of Luke, having a word at a party, even going out to the cinema with him in a group . . . Then I finally got the sense to get right away so I never saw him, didn't even hear his name. I dropped everyone in that crowd, got that job in Dublin for a few months, made sure for the first time in my life I was so busy I couldn't think . . . Eventually, all that hot passion just withered away and died from lack of nurture.' The chain had been twisted around so many times it was now almost garrotting her. She began to unwind in the opposite direction.

Had it really all died? I thought uneasily, but didn't dare ask. 'What about Luke's shirt?' I demanded eventually, seizing on a minor point. 'Did you have a ceremonial burning of it?'

She lowered her lashes demurely. 'Well, I kept it for a bit,' she admitted sheepishly. 'I'm not that strong-minded! Then I met Richard. You remember, wild Irish Richard with the black hair who was so brilliant in bed?'

'I just took your word on the last bit,' I reminded her.

She grinned. 'I'd have had something to say if you'd tried him out! Well, he was. He was fantastic, what that man did to you could make you forget any amount of heartbreak! You wouldn't *believe* the size of his . . .' She appeared to realise that two middle-aged women just passing our table had stopped with pleasurably shocked expressions on their faces. 'Hands,' she said firmly, to their disappointment. 'He had *very* big hands. Someone like that's an excellent cure for yearnings after the wrong bloke. In fact –' she regarded me thoughtfully –

'maybe I should have passed him on to you after all. He'd have made you forget the Frog in no time!'

I decided to let that one go without comment. 'I still can't conceive of how you found the strength to cut Luke off like that,' I said sincerely, absolutely sure I wouldn't have been able to do it myself.

She made a face. 'It's lot easier when you've got Nigel breathing down your neck!' she retorted.

'Did he know you'd fallen in love with Luke?' I asked.

'I'm not sure,' she said slowly. 'He's such a strong, confident man I don't think it would occur to him that his woman might have the temerity to look elsewhere, certainly not if she knew what was good for her anyway! But we didn't split up over Luke, we did it because I found out Nigel was married, though needless to say he didn't think a mere wife tucked away in a house in the country was a good enough excuse for me to chuck him. He was livid, he likes to be the one to do the dumping when he's good and ready.' She thought for a moment. 'Actually, he might have suspected something, for he said quite clearly I'd better not be leaving him for anyone else.'

She smiled slightly. 'It was enough to make me contemplate going into a nunnery! Even Nigel would balk at going after God! And believe it or not, I wasn't just thinking of myself. If by some chance Luke and I had got together Nigel would have gone after Luke first, not me. He's such a deep-dyed in the wool misogynist that he thinks women should be treated like children and not held responsible for their actions – it doesn't stop him using them when it's necessary though. And since Luke's his right-hand man and mascot he'd have been even angrier, because the betrayal, as he saw it, would have been that much greater.'

'Gone after him how?' I asked open-mouthed.

'Nothing like quick-drying cement and motorway bridges, if that's what you're imagining!' she said. 'Nigel doesn't do violence, says it's counter-productive. But there are plenty of other ways to bring someone down. For instance, Luke does a bit of recreational coke. How easy to tip the cops off as he's making a purchase. Can you imagine Luke in prison?' she demanded.

I shook my head.

'Exactly, and even if he'd got off for a first offence, someone would have made sure his grandmother knew and he'd probably have been disinherited – and so one could go on. Nigel used to say everyone has skeletons in their cupboards, it's just a question of finding out what they are and using them.'

'So that's why you were so worried about seeing him when he turned up at the wedding,' I said.

Rose started. 'No, not at all. It wasn't that. Well, maybe I did wonder if he was going to be unpleasant. But –' the chain had come back out to its full length, and she began to twist again – 'I hadn't seen Luke for nearly four years and just for a bit, I thought . . .' She sighed and said in a rush, 'I was feeling a bit claustrophobic about the whole wedding thing, if you must know. Call it post-wedding nerves. It had suddenly occurred to me what I'd done, that I'd committed myself to one person, and –' she smiled ruefully –'I've not been terribly good at fidelity in the past, have I? I like variety. I was quite prepared to give all that up for Jeremy, really I was, but when I saw Luke again it struck me that even Nigel might have allowed me to have a crack at him after all this time and it was too late. That's why I got so shirty when you said you fancied him yourself. You were free to go after him and I wasn't. And I couldn't take that. Not then. Oh, blast it!' The chain had

154

finally given up under all the twisting and broken in two and the little frog pendant on it fell under the table. Rose reached down to retrieve it and put it next to her ashtray.

She shrugged apologetically. 'In other words, I was as jealous as hell! That's why I told you to lay off him. But don't worry, Susie, I've seen sense now. Just after the wedding all that commitment seemed terrifying, it is a big step you know, especially after you've just made it, but now it's wonderful, exactly what I want. I've got the most super husband, whom I love dearly, even if he does hog the remote control,' she added darkly, 'and I'm not going to risk all of that by mooning around after someone who really doesn't mean anything to me any longer. Luke Dillon's nothing more than a fond memory to me, so you're quite free to go ahead and do what you want with him. And do it with my blessing.'

It was nice to know she wouldn't be kicking up a fuss about me and Luke, but I still eyed her cautiously, deeply uneasy inside. I didn't want to believe this was a case of the lady doth protest too much, but I couldn't help a few niggling suspicions. For someone who'd felt so strongly, she was giving him up a damn sight too easily. Still I was going to take what she said at face value. It was going to make life easier all round if I saw Luke again, as I hoped I would. Oh yes! I thought, as pleasurable quivers began to vibrate through the pit of my stomach. I sternly commanded my imagination to behave itself. I was due back in the office in a few minutes and this type of thought was not conducive to concentrating on in-agency conveyancing, which was on the agenda this afternoon.

'Thanks for the benediction,' I murmured.

'Any time!' Rose said irrepressibly, impervious to sarcasm.

CHAPTER 9

The weekend had started off pretty promisingly. Claire, from the old flat, had broken her journey to her cousin's twenty-first on Friday night with me (though I would have thought even someone who hadn't done Geography at school should know there are more direct routes to Norwich from London than going via Leicester) and we'd had the usual very late-night girly gossip session, catching up on everything. She was flatteringly impressed with the cottage and my new life, though when I started to describe Luke I saw a distinctly sceptical eyebrow go up until I fished out a photo of him taken at Rose's wedding which had arrived that morning with a scribbled note saying, 'Look and enjoy!' on it.

She gaped in the most satisfactory fashion, more so after I nonchalantly said it wasn't even very flattering. 'Wow!' she breathed. 'And you got him after you read those books Trish and I gave you?' She took no notice of my denials I had read them, pointing out that the spines were broken on a couple (well, all right, I did have a look), and announced that if they got that sort of result she'd better buy a set for herself. I saw her off before lunch on Saturday, looking somewhat fragile and short of sleep, and wondered what time she would arrive in Norwich. She appeared to be heading towards Nottingham, so it might be quite late.

After that, things went downhill somewhat. I was restless and distrait, looking for something to do so I wouldn't have to admit that I'd reverted right back to being the sort of person who hangs around eyeing the telephone and waiting for it to ring. It didn't. In an effort to distract myself, I cleaned the whole cottage from top to bottom, even going so far as waxing the brick floors in the kitchen and sitting room, which gives a good idea of my desperation. Serious domestic effort is not my favourite way of spending the weekend. But the cottage was so small the whole thing only took a couple of hours (perhaps I'm not that particular about doing *all* the corners), so I settled down to watch a Marilyn Monroe season on the box, half an ear cocked for the preliminary 'breep' of the telephone. It was completely silent.

Later that evening I discovered Mr Bell from the end cottage had decided in an excess of spring fever to clear up his garden and in particular to lop some of the overhanging branches off the ash tree by his back fence. It must have been shortly after I'd resolved to stop picking up the phone every five minutes to check if it was working that he neatly lopped a branch on to the telephone line that serves our four cottages. He's a nice old boy (who at his age definitely shouldn't be doing stupid things like going up ladders to cut down branches) so even without the jar of his wife's best homemade plum jam by way of an apology I wouldn't have been able to give vent to my roar of frustration about being incommunicado until Monday at the earliest.

In the meantime, I watched Marilyn, trying to tell myself in a thoroughly Pollyanna-ish way I appreciated the chance to see *Some Like It Hot* and *Gentlemen Prefer Blondes* again and *The Seven Year Itch* for the first time, without having the telephone interrupting me in the good bits, but it didn't make

158

me feel much better. Not surprising really. I thought I might as well occupy my time by genning up on the general arts of trapping a man, so after drawing the curtains, just in case anyone should be passing and see what I was reading, I settled down to work my way through my extensive library of self-help books and read them properly instead of merely telling myself I was just glancing through. According to *The Rules* and the other how-to-catch-a-man books, being unavailable just heightens a man's interest. Even so, nothing could make me think Luke being unable to contact me was A Good Thing. In my experience, if a woman is unavailable to a man like Luke he doesn't hang around pining, but moves on to the next one on his list.

So, all in all, I'd had a lot too much time to hang around and think, my general preoccupation interspersed with worrying whether Luke was ever going to ring me, about Rose and her incredible revelations and whether she really meant it when she claimed she wasn't holding a giant-sized candle for Luke any longer.

Still, I thought, when halfway through a Monday morning that was promising to be as much a lift for the spirits as the weekend had been, there was nothing I could do about Rose – or Luke, for that matter – so just stop worrying. Easier said than done, of course, but what really did the trick was Stephen bowling in a few minutes later in one of the foulest moods that I have ever seen on man or beast. After that, I had no time to think about anything except what was going on within the four walls of Bailey-Stewart. It was as if my mild-mannered boss had taken a quick trip to Dr Jekyll's lab for a bit of that nice potion. Within half an hour I'd been hauled over the coals for using the telephone for personal calls (a call to the garage to book my car in for a service) and informed that if the agency went to the wall it would be entirely my fault for misspelling a village name in some property details, thus leaving us liable to be prosecuted under the trades descriptions act, with all the consequent penalties. Five minutes later I was threatened with the sack for misfiling a letter, something which Annette never did, apparently. When I protested I was still learning the job and wasn't a trained secretary either, I was given my second warning.

A shell-shocked Amanda and I slipped out to the wine bar for a much-needed restorative glass of wine at lunchtime, before we could be informed by the ogre in the big office that drinking within working hours was now a capital offence. To our surprise, a few minutes later we were joined by Jenny, who virtually never came in here but announced meaningfully she'd decided to escape the flak. Stephen had taken to muttering about her playing her computer games on company equipment. Amanda took a large swig, followed immediately afterwards by an extra-strong mint. It's her patent way of neutralising alcohol fumes before they even start to swill around on the breath, much more effective, she claims, than eating the whole packet of mints at the end of a drinking session. She's tried to get me to do it too, but I'm not fond of the combination of Sancerre and mint.

'Wow!' she said, leaning back in her chair.

'Does he get like this often?' I asked.

Jenny sipped at her spritzer. 'Sometimes, but I've not seen him as bad as this before.'

'I have,' said Amanda. 'Don't you remember last summer, when Martin was ill and Stephen had to take on all his work and that tiresome woman was threatening to sue us for misrepresentation because we'd described a house as Victorian when in fact it was Edwardian? And Liddy kept nagging him to go to that seminar in Worcester with her.'

'Yes, I do!' exclaimed Jenny with round eyes. 'I nearly gave in my notice.'

'I didn't,' said Amanda wryly. 'He might have accepted it. It was me who thought Victoria died in nineteen hundred and three.' She cupped her chin in her hand thoughtfully. 'I wonder if Liddy's been giving him a hard time about something again.'

'Surely not enough to put him in this sort of mood!' I exclaimed.

'You haven't heard her when she gets the bit between her teeth. I have,' said Amanda darkly.

Stephen's girlfriend, Lydia, was a byword, and not a particularly favourable one, in the office. She was a dark, intense brunette given to taking herself very seriously and had firm feminist principles. These did not preclude her wearing tight wrap-around dresses and tops that served to display her slim waist and large bust (suspiciously large, according to Amanda, who had known her when she was two cup-sizes smaller), but they did mean she'd taken on board all the hoary old shibboleths about the basic beastliness of men and their wish to grind every woman into the dust under their feet. Every time Stephen hesitantly mentioned that perhaps they should think of making it permanent and even consider starting a family she would round on him and accuse him of wanting her to waste her brain on menial tasks and become nothing more than a domestic appendage. In vain, Stephen offered to employ a nanny or look after the children himself. She would declare grandiloquently that he wasn't the one who was going to have to give birth, was he? He had to admit defeat there.

But the biggest bone of contention was when Liddy started accusing Stephen of holding her back in her career. She was a management consultant in Leicester and doing very nicely indeed apparently, but according to her she should be shining in a larger centre, such as London, Edinburgh or Manchester. It was only her loyalty to Stephen that kept her here in the sticks, away from all the big career opportunities, but when he suggested that if it meant so much perhaps she could take a job somewhere else and come back at the weekends he was attacked for wanting to get rid of her. It didn't seem that there was any way in which the poor man could win. But since he was basically too nice to work off his temper after one of these extended nagging sessions by throttling his girlfriend (many people thought it was richly deserved), he'd come into the office and take it out on his staff, as Amanda and Jenny informed me.

'It looks like this one was a real humdinger,' said Amanda in a depressed tone. 'He'll be in a filthy temper all week. And I was about to ask him if I can have a week off next month to go to Ibiza.'

'Better not,' said Jenny. 'He'll give you a flat no.'

'Too right. But we're supposed to give the travel agent a decision by Wednesday. It's one of these specials. The agent owes me one, I sold his last house at a very good price for him, so I'll see if I can get him to hold on until next week. Even Stephen can't make a mood last that long.' She didn't sound completely convinced. 'I can't think why he doesn't get rid of the cow,' she said loudly.

'He loves her,' Jenny said mildly, finishing her spritzer. 'I must say, I'm glad I'm not in the front line.'

'Me too,' agreed Amanda.

They both turned around to look at me in an ominous fashion. 'I don't envy you, Susie,' Jenny said finally. 'Perhaps you should go on sick leave for a week.' She pursed her lips.

'Nah. He'd be round there with his own doctor to give you a full medical to check if you're skiving. All I can say is, if he sacks you don't take any notice. Not the first time anyway.'

'And practise ducking,' said Amanda.

I glared at both of them. 'Thanks a bunch, girls.'

Even without their warnings, I had a sense it would be a good idea to make myself scarce for a bit, so the first thing I did when I got back to the office was concoct an excuse to go and see Maurice at the other branch. I spent a blessedly peaceful half hour drinking tea and being told that he wished he was fifty years younger. Getting in the swing of things, I retorted I was glad he wasn't, since seven was much too young for me, which pleased him no end.

Stephen's general mood was no better when I finally made my dilatory way back to the office, though I was glad to discover that contrary to what Amanda had said his temper was restrained to words and didn't extend to throwing things. He was still being perfectly impossible, but I did manage by dint of double-checking everything I did and holding my tongue to avoid being given my third warning in a few hours. By the end of the day I felt rather like a rag that has been through the wringer. I was in the mood to accept almost anything if it was going to get me out of there, even a projected grappling session with Edward Fairley, he of the hairy hands. Actually, maybe that was going a bit too far. But when Luke rang to say he'd tried to get hold of me over the weekend and would I like to come out for something to eat at a rather well-known local restaurant I almost fell on his neck with gratitude, if such a thing were possible down telephone lines. 'Do you want me to meet you there?' I asked.

'Certainly not! I'll pick you up,' he said, with a flattering promptness that made my heart sing. I'd already looked up

163

exactly where he lived in Wickham in my *AA Road Atlas* and had worked out it was a good thirty-mile round trip. And the restaurant was much closer to him than me. It was going to make him awfully late getting back home tonight. Or maybe he wasn't intending to go home . . .

I was going to have to do some serious thinking about Arnaud. Not that I believed he ever considered the merits of fidelity in relation to me when he had a blonde with long legs and green eyes in his sights, and I know that what's sauce for the gander should be sauce for the goose etc., but I just find it difficult to think that way. Actually, it came as a bit of a shock to realise that despite my protestations to Rose about keeping all my options open the only fling I'd had since Montpellier was with a seriously fey graphics design artist – and that was during a six-month break-up from Arnaud. It had already withered away by the time Arnaud was transferred to London and we picked up the reins all over again. I might have declared airily that of course I was looking around, but in truth I'd put my sex drive into cold storage, sublimating it to the desire to make it big in the money markets, and only taken it out when Arnaud made one of his flying visits. It was a bit of an unnerving glimpse into my morality too. I'd secretly always been a bit smug about being so choosy and so rigorously faithful, but it's quite easy when you don't fancy anyone else, isn't it?

I had my chin resting on my hand and was gazing rather blankly at the tumbling houses that someone had chosen as the screen-saver (they must have been very pleased with themselves) when I heard a throat clear ominously from behind me. I turned around and looked up into the cross face of my boss. 'Private calls again, Susie?' he asked with heavy sarcasm.

Behind his shoulder I could see Martin's rat-like face give a distinct smirk. I bet I knew whom I had to thank for Stephen being 'accidentally' informed that his PA was chatting in office time yet again.

'Just the one,' I said blithely, pushing my chair back and standing up. 'Considering all the unpaid overtime I put in you can't really complain about that, can you?' I smiled at him sweetly.

He looked as if he jolly well could complain and was about to. I slipped out while he was still formulating the words and raced off for another extended session of deciding what to wear. They seemed to be becoming a habit.

It was the thrum of a powerful car being parked on the other side of the green that made me look out of my bedroom window and realise I had precisely a minute and a half to clothe myself or I'd be opening the door in my underwear. It was a bit early, both in the evening and in our relationship, to start doing things like that. I also had to brush my hair, put on my earrings, apply lipstick and stuff all my discarded clothes back into the wardrobe just in case other eyes were to see my room tonight. Blind panic like that is a wonderful aid to concentration. In a flash I'd put on a green jacket that unbuttoned nicely to just the right place, a black skirt with a discreet slit up one side, and had got as far as finding my other shoe by the time I heard the front gate being opened. I tore down the stairs, flipped open a book and laid it face-down on the arm of the sofa, so it looked as if I'd been indulging in a bit of mental activity rather than rushing around in a flat tizz discovering I had nothing to wear. As the bell went I had to rush back to check said book wasn't one of the how to get a man variety. Dorothy L. Sayers, nothing wrong in that. Some people even call her a classic. I headed for the door a second time, wondering nervously if I was going to be overdressed.

Luke was uncharacteristically smart in a dark jacket and yellow shirt with a button-down collar, so it seemed I had got it right on the apparel front for once. I noted approvingly he was just as eye-catching as he was when he was less formal. He hugged me and kissed me on the lips. This was more like it! My heart flipped. It was like being kissed by a matinee idol, I thought dreamily, or by James Dean, which had been an early adolescent fantasy of mine. (I conveniently ignored the fact he had been dead for many years by now and the kiss might not have been quite so pleasant as I fondly imagined.)

To my regret, he didn't come back for a second go, but apologetically announced that he was running late (he was too) and we'd better get a move on. The Flying Duck had a nasty habit of giving away tables if the punters were more than ten minutes late. There was always later, I thought philosophically as I locked the door.

On the face of it, the Flying Duck was nothing much. It was in a small house just off the main road, with some rather naff fairy lights twinkling over the porch – or maybe the manager had been too busy to take down the Christmas decorations – and a lot of rather dated eighties-style country-house pastels and chintz decoration inside. But it was also remarkably crowded for a Monday evening, so it must have had a good reputation. The clientele were a mixed bunch, some of the local worthies, a few younger couples like ourselves, and a group of businessmen entertaining some bemused visiting Japanese who had probably thought they were being taken out to an example of ye olde English cooking and instead got an eclectic mixture of Italian crossed with Indian with a bit of Caribbean thrown in for good measure.

With a certain amount of regret, I passed on the most

delicious-looking mussel risotto which I sniffed at appreciatively as a portion was carried past me to the next table. It would also have been just the ticket for keeping vampires at bay and though I was sure Luke wasn't the type to object to just a faint whiff, there are limits. Making the inside of his car smell like a garlic growers' convention was probably one of them.

I needn't have mourned the risotto, in true novelistic style I was far too busy talking and listening to really taste what I ate, other than register dimly that it was considerably better than what my mother might produce – admittedly not a difficult task for the chef. I almost had to pinch myself several times so I could be really sure such a bloody awful day was ending in such a delightful way, with good food and an even more delicious object on the other side of the green-covered table. He was as lively and amusing as he'd been the other night, telling me a couple of stories of when he'd known Rose while she was going out with Nigel. I scanned his face closely, watching for signs that he might have returned her hopeless passion, but unless he was considerably cleverer at concealment than I thought he was he only thought of her as a friend's ex-bird. Poor Rose. How dreadful to have wasted all that passion.

We got on to talking about the cinema for some reason, and I was a little disappointed, but not entirely surprised, to discover he had a penchant for the sort of crime caper that has me cowering under my seat, hiding my eyes so I don't have to watch body parts flying around all over the screen. Men have appalling taste sometimes. 'Well you certainly won't find me coming to the cinema with you then!' I said firmly, realising just a bit too late that the subject hadn't come up as yet. To cover up my faux pas, I added quickly, 'Rose and I are going to go and see the new Meg Ryan comedy together. Jeremy says he thinks it sounds "soppy" and only for the girls. The next-door cinema in the multiplex is playing *Blown Away 23* or something, maybe you should go with him.'

'I'd rather go and see Meg Ryan,' Luke said promptly. 'Better company and I fancy Meg Ryan rotten.' His eyes glinted at me wickedly. 'Perhaps you two could count me in as an honorary girl and let me tag along when you go and see it.'

I almost spluttered into my wine glass. Luke an honorary girl? It would be about as credible as having Cruella De Vil as head of the Dalmatian Rescue Association. Despite the curling eyelashes and guinea-gold hair, he was indisputably male. 'Of course you can come with us,' I said finally, 'but think it would be best if you came in your own masculine guise.'

'Good,' he said with relief. 'I hate drag. I can't get the hang of pulling up tights without laddering them! When are you planning to see it?'

'Possibly later on in the week or next week,' I said. 'As usual everything depends on how Rose can sort out her busy social diary. I'll give you a ring when I know.'

It was getting late, all the other tables had been vacated and the waiters were beginning to stand around in that hopeful way that indicates they'd like you to push off so they can go home, thank you very much. Since the Flying Duck was a classy establishment, they didn't resort to putting the chairs on the tables or noisily clattering cutlery as they prepared the tables for the lunchtime crowd, just hovered meaningfully. Luke looked at me ruefully and said, 'I think it's time for us to go. What a shame.'

I agreed with him entirely. I would have been quite happy to stay for another hour or two just talking and sipping wine, though I realised there was a certain degree of funk in this feeling. My frankly lascivious thoughts of earlier in the evening about the man whose knee was just brushing mine under the table were beginning to be tinged with an element of panic now that the hour when erotic thoughts might be put into action was approaching rapidly. Wasn't all this moving a bit quickly? And there was Arnaud too. Yet again I'd wimped out of making any proper (or improper) decision. Well, I supposed that if things got a bit much I could claim a sudden tummy upset (though it was a bit unfair when I'd just been taken out for a superb meal). But you needed something off-putting enough in those circumstances. When I was seventeen I'd claimed a migraine as a means of getting rid of a bad case of wandering hands, which rebounded completely. He solicitously suggested I should go and lie down and he'd massage me better.

It began to rain as we stepped outside. As we ran for the car Luke nobly held his jacket above my head to stop my hair getting wet and going into infuriatingly wild curls. 'Your shoulders are soaked,' I said in a remorseful voice once we were safely inside.

He shrugged. 'Doesn't matter. The heater's pretty powerful, I'll dry off in no time.' He grinned at me. 'But I think when I'm seeing you across the green I might let you have the umbrella in the boot rather than my jacket!'

So he was intending to come in, I thought, as I stretched my damp feet out and wriggled my toes under a welcome blast of warm air. Maybe I should just let things run their course and not worry about them until they happened. The charm of that philosophy was it sort of implied that I wasn't really responsible for whatever was going to occur. As a victim of circumstances, I couldn't really be held to blame if I ended up in bed with Luke, could I? And my moral principles would

169

still be intact. (Maybe a bit dented though, even I couldn't rationalise that away entirely.)

Happy and content I'd come to this sort of vague decision, I surrendered to the fuggy warmth in the car – as Luke had promised, the heater was very effective – and leant back, closing my eyes. I'd already discovered he didn't enjoy talking much while he was driving, so I was free to listen to Dusty Springfield belting out from the CD player and indulge in some very pleasant daydreams.

I heard him curse as he realised he'd taken a wrong turning and the car abruptly did a U-turn. I opened my eyes to see if I recognised where we were but all I could see were some still-bare trees, hedges and ditches and a light shining outside the front door of some unknown house set back slightly from the road. We roared up to a T-junction and he hesitated, reading an old-fashioned wooden signpost, before he put his foot on the accelerator and swung the car to the right, heading towards Barkby 4 and Great Harton 7. He looked around at me with a slightly tight smile as I sat up. 'Sorry, I always find this way difficult in the dark. But the main road is always crawling with cops and the chances are you'll get breathalysed.'

He seemed to think that I was exuding disapproval or something for, keeping his head turned towards me, he said apologetically, 'With a car like this you're always getting stopped and frankly I'm bored with the hassle, whether or not I actually think that I might fail the bloody thing—'

'Luke!' I shrieked and grabbed his arm incredulously as I saw a large dappled shape planted right in the middle of the road in front of us. 'Look out!'

He whipped his eyes back to the road and went, 'Shit!' and swung the wheel to the right as he braked violently. The car began to slide on the wet road and he wrenched the wheel back to the left, overcorrected, and the car mounted the verge, seemed to wobble for a moment and started to slip sideways. We were still only yards from the junction and Luke's acceleration surge hadn't reached full blast, so instead of hurtling into the drainage ditch we more sort of inexorably slid down it. He was still saying in an unbelieving voice, 'Who's the bloody idiot who let that *fucking* sheep out on the road?' when we hit the bottom with a thump. Or rather *I* hit the bottom, as the car was sliding down on my side and despite what were presumably state-of-the-art seat belts I was thrown against the passenger door with a bone-shuddering impact. Half a second later, Luke thumped into me as well, managing to knock my head against the door pillar. Swearing dreadfully, he reached up and grabbed the strap above the window and levered himself off me, his seat belt bearing most of the weight of his body.

The engine was making an odd coughing sound. I had some very unpleasant images of scenes from films where what seemed like the smallest roll down a hill would instantly make the toughest car burst into spectacular flames. 'Hadn't you better switch it off?' I asked nervously, half fearing it was already too late.

Luke nodded and did so. For a few seconds we sat, too stunned to speak, even to think, the only sound rapid breathing and Dusty, still belting it out into the night air. He stretched out a shaky hand and turned the CD player off. 'Are you all right, Susie?' he asked, his voice strained.

'I think so,' I said. Actually, I was still too dazed from the knock on my head to know if anything hurt or not. I moved my legs cautiously. Apart from listing distinctly to the left because of the angle of the car, they seemed to be OK. Ahead of us, the headlights of the car cut into the darkness, illuminating the ditch with blinding clarity and half the road. An

171

extremely stupid face with a long muzzle and a magnificent pair of curly horns thrust itself into the light.

'I wasn't imagining it! I was beginning to think that you'd put something in my drink! It *is* a sheep. But what kind? It looks like some kind of rare breed to me.' I squinted at it as it ambled towards us curiously, horns shaking from side to side menacingly as it made up its mind whether we were dangerous or not. From what I could see of Luke's face, the sheep was going to find he was very dangerous indeed unless it got the hell out of there before he managed to scramble out of the car.

'It's going to be very rare, extinct in fact, if I get my hands on it!' Luke muttered, making an ineffectual effort to get out and do just that. The sheep baa'd at us and when it got no response turned around and began to meander back down the road, stopping every so often to snatch a mouthful of much greener grass from the verge. 'What sort of bloody fool allows his sheep to run around loose on the sodding road! And in the dark too,' Luke growled as the sheep's very woolly bottom began to disappear into the darkness. 'It's a complete danger to the public. A ram too. Everyone knows they attack people. I'll kill him! He should be sued, locked up . . .' After venting a lot of steam in this manner he obviously felt a lot better, though I was developing a headache, and he began to try to get himself out of the car.

It took him five minutes of panting, groaning effort. He would doubtless have been much quicker if he hadn't been trying to make sure he didn't kick me as he heaved his way out, but eventually, after a lot more bad language, he was standing on the verge looking down at me.

'Come on,' he said, bending into the car and holding out his hand, 'let's get you out and then we can go to that house down the road for some help.'

It was drizzling and I was wearing a pair of strappy slingbacks which were definitely not the right footwear for a tramp in the dark of a mile or so. I didn't want to ruin them either. But I might have been prepared to ignore these trifling matters, and show I was made of the same stern stuff as Victorian lady-explorers, if a rare burst of common sense hadn't pointed out Luke would go much quicker on his own, and be dryer too, since he could use the umbrella himself instead of chivalrously holding it over my head. And there was another not so minor point; I was beginning to feel decidedly odd and wasn't at all sure if I'd be able to walk that far.

He was still arguing whether it was safe to leave me alone in the car with only a curly-horned ram around to protect me against any passing predator, when we heard the welcome sound of a car engine in the distance.

He dashed out into the middle of the road, waving his arms about and shouting, 'Hey!' as a mud-splattered Range Rover rounded the corner and came to a halt. From my vantage point I could see a large pair of wellingtons come down the road and then stop opposite the car door. 'You've met my ram then,' a country voice said in a tone of deep resignation.

'It's *your* bloody ram?' exclaimed Luke incredulously. 'What the hell do you think you're doing, you stupid idiot, allowing your livestock to roam free around the roads? We could have been killed! You know what you can do with your sodding ram, don't you?'

'Don't think I haven't thought of having old Houdini with a bit of redcurrant jelly many a time. He's a devil for getting out. Though maybe now at his age he'd be better in a Lancashire hotpot, I'd have to ask the wife. But my son won his first prize at the County Show with our Houdini and won't hear of it,' said the voice with a tinge of regret. 'Two hours and

173

more I've been out looking for the old bugger tonight. I'm right sorry for all the trouble he caused you. We've never had an accident before, usually people go so slow around here they have time to stop when they see that dratted beast. But I've already made up me mind, this is the last time. Young Miles might like to see Houdini in the field, doing what he does with the ladies,' he chortled richly, 'and he does that well, I can tell you! But this one stays locked up in the stable from now on. I can't be doing with all this chasing around . . .'

'Yes, yes,' interrupted Luke rudely. 'But I'm not interested in your sodding animal! My car's in the ditch and my friend is inside it.'

'Your friend?' exclaimed the farmer sharply. He bent down and a round, red face peered in through the window. 'Evening, miss, I'm sorry to meet you under these circumstances. Tom Cartwright's the name,' he said, with excruciating politeness. 'Er, um, I didn't mean no offence.' I assured him that I was brought up in the country and knew quite well what rams did with the ladies. He smiled in relief and looked doubtfully down at me. 'Now what are we going to do about you? Do you think if I give you a hand you can climb out?'

'No,' I said firmly, having already discovered by dint of experimentation it hurt like hell to move my left arm. Even with help, there was no way I could put any weight on it while I got myself upright.

'Right you are,' Mr Cartwright said cheerfully when I explained. 'We'll have to tow you out. It's lucky that I got the rope in the Range Rover then, isn't it?'

I'm sure that he tried to drag the car out of the ditch as smoothly as he could, but it wasn't possible without a certain amount of jerking and bumping, which of course thumped me back against the door each time. I was feeling sick and more than a bit dizzy by the time the car was at long last level on the road and Luke rushed around to lever the door open.

'Don't – touch – my – arm,' I warned him through gritted teeth as he put out a helping hand. He jumped back, looking shocked.

'Oh God, Susie, have you broken it?'

I leant back against the car for a bit of support. My legs were so wobbly I think I'd have fallen over otherwise. 'I've never broken anything, so I don't know what it feels like. But –' I did a little experiment – 'I can move my fingers, isn't that supposed to be a good sign?'

'I wasn't suggesting that you were paralysed!' said Luke, frowning.

'The lass had better get to hospital, she's going to need one of them X-rays,' said Mr Cartwright. He bent down and gloomily inspected the front wing of the car, which seemed to have taken the brunt of the impact. 'Well, you won't be driving this again until the panel beater's got that off the wheel, but it seems you were lucky, there ain't much else in the way of damage.'

'With no thanks to your ram,' muttered Luke, a bit churlishly, I thought, but perhaps in the circumstances forgivable.

'True enough,' Mr Cartwright said imperturbably, 'and I'm right sorry about that. Don't worry, I'm fully insured.' He chuckled. 'Took a five-year plan out as soon as I saw what that ram was like. Never seen another bugger like him for getting out, begging your pardon, miss. Paid the premium up front too. That insurance chappie thought he were so clever in getting all my money at once, now there ain't a thing he can do to try and cancel it!' He rumbled with laughter again. 'Course, I didn't tell him the ram's name was Houdini. Even that daft

175

so-and-so might have realised something was up then.'

He reached into the car, got my handbag out of the footwell and closed the passenger door. 'Right you are, I'll take ye both to the hospital. Lucky the casualty aint too far away and they aint closed it yet, though they keep talking about it.' As Luke seemed to be about to protest he said firmly, 'The car'll be safe enough where it is if you lock it and I'll get the garage to tow it in the morning. They might want to see you in the hospital too.' He looked pointedly at Luke. 'You can inform the police about the accident afterwards. That should give you enough time.'

'I can assure you I didn't put the car into the ditch because I was drunk!' Luke said frostily. 'I was talking to Susie.'

'Well, I'm with you there, a fine lass like that is enough to distract anyone,' said Mr Cartwright, with considerable generosity, I felt. Just as I'm not the sort to escape a red nose and swollen eyes when I cry, I was also absolutely certain I wasn't one of those rare individuals who could come out of a minor car accident without looking like a wreck.

'I've got a few things I don't want to leave in the car,' said Luke, opening the boot and putting a couple of small packages and a paperback into his pocket. He went around the car, carefully checking each door was locked, and then pronounced he was ready to go.

'But what about your ram, Mr Cartwright?' I asked weakly, mind fixing on trivialities.

'He'll be up the road there. We'll go by slowly and I'll put him in a field and collect him on the way back.' He scratched his chin thoughtfully. 'That is if he hasn't gone too far up towards Jackson's oil-seed rape. In that case, he'll have to go in the back of the car.' I sincerely hoped he hadn't gone as far as Jackson's oil-seed rape. I was sure Houdini was a delightful

176

character once you got to know him, but I didn't really want to have to travel with him. 'Now, lass, do yer need a bit of help to get into the car?'

I could have done without having to climb up into a vehicle the height of a Range Rover. What I would have liked was a sort of motorised stretcher on to which I could simply topple over sideways and lie supine while I was transported to a place where I sincerely trusted I was going to be given several very large pills to take away the feeling that somebody had just tried to cut off my arm with a blunt saw. I'll draw a blank over what I said when Luke accidentally took hold of my elbow while helping me up. Suffice to say that Mr Cartwright chuckled and said that young girls knew some right funny words these days.

I had rather hoped that my first ever visit to casualty would be rewarded by George Clooney bending over me solicitously, wielding a stethoscope and murmuring soothingly that he'd get this sorted out in just a minute and I wasn't going to feel a thing. Instead, I got Bob Geldof, whose red-rimmed eyes suggested that all that stubble wasn't a sartorial statement but the result of not going to bed for the last week and missing out on the early-morning wash-and-shave routine. I'd read all those scare stories about overworked doctors who cut off the wrong leg because they were so tired they couldn't read their notes, and I'd taken them all with a pinch of salt – until now. I couldn't sink back into that nice feeling of mindless trust that you're supposed to have in hospital. Especially after he started examining my nose for damage, when I'd quite clearly pointed out I'd knocked my head on the side. He said he was looking in my eyes for dilated pupils.

Several hours later, I was pronounced unbroken in every area, not even concussed, though severely bruised all down my left side. I hadn't needed six hours in hospital to tell me that. My shoulder had already turned interesting shades of purple and pink. Neither did I need Bob Geldof to inform me it was going to hurt like hell. I knew that too. It already did. But he was decent enough to give me a large bottle of pink pills, with instructions to take a satisfyingly liberal dose up to four times a day. 'And take this week off work too,' he said firmly.

I brightened slightly. So there really was a silver lining behind every cloud. Stephen might have recovered his temper by next week. And even in his current mood he could hardly accuse someone who had one arm supported in the largest sling I'd ever seen of skiving.

'And what sort of car have you got?' Bob Geldof asked.

'A manual,' I said, surprised.

'Well, I doubt you'll be driving for at least a week,' he said definitely. 'You aren't going to enjoy changing gear with that arm.'

I hadn't thought of that. But I could see he probably had a point. 'But I'm supposed to be driving to Sussex for the weekend,' I said.

He laughed hollowly to indicate that I'd made a very unfunny joke. 'Take the train,' he said succinctly. 'But travel light, because you aren't going to want to carry anything. Or see if you can get someone to give you a lift,' he suggested, already losing interest in me and yawning. He was no doubt thinking about moving on to the 515th patient he was about to see since he had got out of bed a few days ago. 'Call your GP if you have any problems,' he said in clear dismissal and, taking the hint, I got up and left.

Luke was half asleep outside, slumped sideways on one of those moulded-plastic orange chairs that seem to breed in doctors' and hospital waiting rooms. He'd escaped with only a slight bruise along one cheekbone, the result of banging it as he climbed out of the car. Unfairly, along with the dark shadows under his eyes, it only served to increase his good looks, giving him an air of romantic fragility. Whereas I looked more as if I'd just stopped off on my way to the morgue. Dr Bob's nurse said rather stiffly I should be grateful I'd escaped from a car accident so lightly (though, frankly, when I tried to move my arm 'lightly' seemed a distinctly relative word) and not be worrying about my pallid face, scruffy hair and the mascara track leaking from one eye. At my insistence, she announced frostily she'd give me five minutes' wash-and-brush-up time in the ladies and no more. Unfortunately, the contents of my bag, designed only to give a quick lick and polish during the course of one evening, were completely unable to rise to the task of turning me into an interesting replica of La Dame aux Camélias so I had to settle for merely clean and brushed, which was a considerable improvement in itself.

Not enough, evidently. As I approached, Luke jerked upright into wakefulness. 'God, you look awful!' he said immediately. 'Aren't they going to keep you in for observation?'

As downers go that one took quite a lot of beating. 'Nope. The doctor says I can go home. I'm not seriously damaged enough to stay here,' I said.

He gave me another searching look. I had a nasty feeling that *my* bruise on my cheekbone was rapidly spreading upwards to my eye and was generally a lot less fetching than his. 'Can't think why not!' he retorted. But the damage to my ego was partially massaged by the immediate look of contrition on his face. 'I'm so sorry, Susie, it's all my fault.'

'You couldn't have been expected to anticipate a sheep in the middle of the road at midnight,' I pointed out.

He looked down. 'But if I'd been concentrating . . . It shouldn't have happened.'

'Well, as I doubt I'll be suing you for damages, it doesn't really matter how culpable you are.' I could see from the surprise on his face it had come out a bit more sharply than I'd intended. But I was tired, everywhere that wasn't already agony was beginning to ache and I just wanted to get home, to bed, to sleep. I could ease Luke's guilty conscience when I felt more like the full quid, but until then he'd have to live with it. I yawned, swaying slightly. Luke sprang up, hand outstretched to catch me, then recoiled at my look. No doubt he was remembering the last time he'd touched my left arm. And the grey-haired nurse with the ferocious perm behind the reception desk looked far too respectable to hear that kind of language.

'Could you call a taxi?' I asked wearily.

'Of course, of course,' he said quickly, hovering protectively as I sank down on to a chair. 'Can I get you anything? Tea, coffee, something from the machine?'

I shook my head, suddenly too exhausted even to speak, and sank into a sort of restless and uncomfortable doze as he went off to find the phones and some change.

I woke with a stiff neck to add to all my other minor and major aches, and to the sound of a familiar voice. I blinked, still too dopey to work out what or who it was in front of me, until it said, 'Susie! Wake up! Are you sure she's not concussed, Luke? She looks completely do-lally to me. Do you think we'd better call the doctor? I don't like her colour . . .'

I lifted my head a bit, unglued my eyes, and managed to focus. 'I was asleep, that's all. I'm fine, they say. What are you doing here, Rose?'

'I've come to take you home,' she retorted cheerfully. 'Luke had the sense to ring me and I came straight over.' For once this seemed to be no exaggeration. She had no make-up on, her hair was untidily bundled back into a ponytail, and she looked as if she'd got dressed in the first things that came to hand, including several garments that must have belonged to Jeremy. Rose never wore jeans that baggy.

'But I could have taken a taxi back to the cottage,' I said stupidly. 'There was no need to drag you out of bed at this hour just so you can ferry me there. You aren't ever up this early.'

She smiled at me in a very determined manner. 'You aren't going back to the cottage. You're coming back to Moor End with me and staying until you're back on your feet again.' As I opened my mouth to protest she cut in firmly with, 'Don't be stupid, Susie! It was Luke's idea and he's quite right!' Behind her shoulder I saw Luke give a pleased smirk. 'He didn't think you should go back to the cottage on your own. You need looking after. For one thing, what would you do about things to eat?'

Probably better than relying on her cooking, but that would have been a cheap shot so I stayed silent. Besides, there was no point in arguing, I knew Rose when she had an expression like that on her face and she didn't take no for an answer. So though I felt everyone was making much too much fuss (the pills were kicking in with some very pleasantly euphoric effects) I said, 'That's really kind of you, Rose. Thank you. I really appreciate it.' I yawned hugely. 'But could we go, please? I'm so tired.'

CHAPTER 10

Jeremy, poor man, had the task of half carrying, half dragging me up the wide oak stairs to a pretty blue-and-white room with a heavily curtained four-poster bed and a view over the garden and the ruins of the old house, not that I was in any fit state to appreciate scenery just at that moment. Rose went and raided her own possessions for such necessities as nightdresses and a spare toothbrush to tide me over until she could go over to the cottage and get some of my own things. She bossily shooed Jeremy out, saying I had to get undressed, though I would have quite happily crawled under the bedclothes fully dressed and, worst sin of all, without taking off what remained of my make-up. But Rose had stronger moral fibre than me, especially when it came to inflicting it on other people, and insisted I followed all the right procedures. I muttered resentfully as my make-up was being creamed off that I was surprised she wasn't making me floss my teeth as well. She hesitated for a moment then said she thought it would be a bit difficult one-handed and it wasn't really something she could help me with. I could see I was in for bed-baths next if I wasn't careful.

Actually, she made a much better care assistant than I would have expected, gently easing my jacket over my arm as if she were playing one of those games you find at church fêtes, where you have to pass a loop of wire along a twisted shape. A bell rings if you accidentally jog it. Like me. But she did pretty well, all told, I only nearly hit the ceiling squealing about three times. They had suggested in the hospital that as they couldn't just drape the jacket over my shoulders, since I only had a semi-transparent bra on underneath, they cut the arm off to make undressing again easier. I'd indignantly refused, something I was rather regretting just now. Rose had even found a nightie that did up with ties on the shoulders so I could step into it and didn't have to manoeuvre any armholes, which would doubtless have prompted another burst of bad language. But then she's used to it. Her vocabulary is much bigger than mine too.

I found it quite extraordinarily frustrating to be able to use only one hand. The toothbrush kept going all over the place and finally, with an eldritch wail of rage, I had to ask Rose to put the toothpaste on for me. 'I think those pink pills must have affected my coordination,' I grumbled as, finally clean enough for her liking, she led me to bed and instructed me to get in and stop talking. 'I'd have been in here ages ago if it hadn't been for you,' I pointed out.

She majestically ignored me. The bed might be quaint and very pretty, but it was a damn sight too high for anyone shaky on their pins, I thought, as I sat on it and tried to swing my legs up. I wriggled into the bed at last and leant back against the pillows, trying to place my shoulder so it was resting against a bit of support.

'Here, let me do that,' she said, leaning over and tweaking one of the pillows out so my arm fell down on the mattress. 'Oops. Sorry. I didn't hurt you, did I?'

When I could speak again I said through gritted teeth, 'Just a bit. Never mind, it's good practice for when I become a secret agent and have to get used to being tortured on a regular basis.'

'I didn't mean to do it!' she protested, then asked doubtfully, 'Would you like me to leave you alone?'

I nodded, closing my eyes. 'Yes please.' I think I was probably asleep before she'd even got as far as the door.

I spent nearly the whole of the day drifting in and out of sleep, so dopey that I barely noticed the discomfort from my aching shoulder. I was vaguely aware of Rose coming in and out. Once when I opened my eyes a large vase of lilac had appeared on the mantelpiece, the next time there was a jug of water and a glass resting on the bedside table. She popped her head around the door later that evening and, seeing I was awake, came in with an armful of books and magazines. 'Here's something for you to read,' she said, dumping them on the bed beside me. The thoughtfulness of her gesture was only slightly marred by the magazines that landed on my knee, which though damaged in a strictly small-fry way still didn't appreciate having three months' worth of *Tatler* dumped on it. She stood over me, hands on hips, while she examined me carefully. I'd have been more impressed by the level of scrutiny if I'd thought she had any idea of what she was supposed to be looking for. 'Well, you look better, at least,' she said at last. 'This morning you looked as if you were about to pop your clogs at any moment. Do you want something to eat?'

'I'm not really hungry,' I said, 'but thanks.'

She frowned in a quite terrifying imitation of my mother. 'I'm sure you should eat. How are you going to get better if you starve yourself?' she asked in a worried voice. There goes Mum again, I thought, but thought better of saying it. Fond as she is of my mother, I didn't think that Rose would appreciate being compared to an ageing ex-hippie who conceals

185

her spreading waistline under brightly coloured gypsy caftans. 'What about Heinz Cream of Tomato soup and Jacob's crackers?' she asked coaxingly. 'I'm sure you could manage that.'

I had to laugh. An unwise move, as my shoulder didn't appreciate the vibration. Though it was one of the few things that we'd never compared notes on as far as I knew, it seemed that Rose and I had shared identical nursery comfort food. 'That would be super,' I said knowing well that if I refused the next things on offer would be boiled eggs, soldiers and hot Ribena.

Actually, it was just the ticket and made me realise that it was nearly twenty-four hours since I'd had my last meal at the Flying Duck. It takes a lot to make me lose my appetite and it never happens for long, hence the reason I'm a 'fine figure of a woman', as Maurice had told me last time I saw him. So much for all my worries about the manner in which the evening was going to end, I thought, as I crumbled a cracker into the soup so that it made a lovely gooey mess. Luke put paid to that. I hoped the rather drastic manner in which he'd done it hadn't been intentional. No, I was sure it wasn't. He couldn't have been that desperate to get out of giving me a goodnight kiss, not even I could denigrate myself to the extent that I'd believe he'd rather go to hospital than get fresh with me. Besides, what man deliberately damages his own car? It'd be like damaging a certain part of his anatomy and I doubted Luke was that different from other men.

'What's happened to Luke?' I asked, swallowing a mouthful of tepid soup. Rose had taken the instructions to heat it over a gentle flame to extremes. 'Did he get back home all right?'

'He got a taxi from the hospital,' she said, sitting on the end of the bed and performing two tasks at once; entertaining the bedridden and painting her nails a new shade of browny red. 'He was going straight off to see about the car, and then to bed, I should think, but he said that he'd probably call in here to see how you are tomorrow.' She grinned at me. 'Don't worry. I'll help you wash your hair and titivate yourself up into looking like the thoroughly glamorous modern invalid.'

'I reckon I'll need all the help I can get,' I said gloomily. 'I'm mirror-cracking material at the moment.'

She examined me closely, head cocked to one side. 'Not precisely,' she said carefully, 'though you do look a bit *battered*.'

'What, like a chicken? Thanks a lot!' I retorted.

'You know that isn't what I meant,' she said, unruffled, as she held out her hand to admire the effect. 'Mm, it is a good colour, isn't it? Sets off what's left of my tan perfectly,' she commented, putting her hand back on her knee so she could apply the second coat. 'Did I hear Luke right? Did you really go into a sheep?'

'It was a ram called Houdini and, Houdini-like, it escaped,' I confirmed.

She giggled. 'Oh dear, it's not the coolest cause of an accident, is it? And Luke's fond of his image too,' she said indulgently. 'Do you think he'll ever live it down?'

'At least he didn't go into a pig,' I said. 'There'd be something about telling people your car was wrecked by a Gloucester Old Spot that would make even the most miserable git giggle!'

'If I were you I wouldn't offer that as comfort. He didn't seem to me to be in the mood for flippant comments,' she said with unwonted severity. 'He's going to have enough of a problem explaining everything to the insurance company. But when they've stopped laughing they'll have to pay up, won't they? Or the farmer's insurance will. It's not as if it's Luke's fault or anything, is it? But he's awfully worried you're going to blame him for the accident,' she added casually, examining her index finger carefully and rubbing off the tiniest smudge with a cotton bud.

I shrugged, which was a mistake. They seemed to have had time for a pretty extended chat. 'If he hadn't been in a filthy mood about missing the turning, driving too fast and apologising to me all at the same time it wouldn't have happened.' She looked up at me reproachfully. 'OK, OK, if Houdini had been properly in his field it wouldn't have happened either. It's just one of those things. I'm not badly hurt and let's look on the bright side,' I added, as she still seemed to be worried on Luke's behalf, 'with luck, by the time I get back Stephen'll be so glad to see me he'll have forgotten he tried to sack me twice yesterday!'

'Twice? What did you do *this* time, Susie?' she asked in a tone of deep resignation.

'Nothing!' I said, hurt by the implication. 'His girlfriend's giving him a hard time, that's all.'

She looked at me through narrowed eyes. 'I'm sure you're telling the truth, but it's funny how you're the one who always seems to get it in the neck and yet it's never your fault!' I felt like telling her not to bully invalids. 'I can't think what you've done to put his back up,' she said severely. 'He sounded so *nice* on the phone. He was really worried about you when I rang to say what had happened. He wanted to know if there was anything you needed and if he should come round.'

'Probably needs to know where something is,' I said, and earned myself a shocked look for my cynicism. I yawned, hoping Rose would take the hint. She didn't.

Five minutes later she looked at her large brightly coloured Swatch. 'I suppose I should be going down to get something ready for Jeremy's supper,' she said without urgency.

My eyelids were growing heavy. Heinz Cream of Tomato beats Mogadon as a soporific any day in my opinion. 'Well, don't let me keep you,' I said hopefully.

'It won't do him any harm to wait for a bit!' she retorted. 'I bet he's round in Flavia's wing anyway. She summoned him to discuss this property thing, we had another letter this morning . . .'

I yawned again, this time a real stretcher with loads of sound effects and in-drawing of breath and little groans in the back of the throat. Even Rose couldn't ignore that. 'You look sleepy,' she announced as if she was making a discovery, 'I'd better leave you to get some rest,' and got up, sending a pile of magazines hurtling to the floor. 'I'll look in later and see if you're awake,' she promised.

I grunted and slid further down into my pillows.

It was daylight before I was woken again by the noise of something at my bedroom door. I turned my head slowly to see a large Crimplene-covered behind backing slowly in, using a weighty hip to barge the door open. The figure revealed itself to be a grey-haired woman in her late fifties, wearing a brightly coloured floral pinny and carrying a loaded tray. She looked over my way. 'Oh, good, you're awake, miss. I'm Mrs Miskin.'

'Good morning,' I said. I'd heard all about her from Rose. Mrs Miskin first came to work here for Jeremy's grandmother when she was fifteen and reckoned she knew far more about how the establishment should be run than any of the supposed ladies of the house. She and Rose had already had one battle royal over the handwashing of Rose's silk shirts, with the inevitable result that Mrs Miskin had now gone firmly over to Flavia's side, and Rose suspected she was actively engaged in spying activities and was reporting what she discovered back to the other wing.

She acknowledged my greeting with a remarkably regal incline of her head. 'Mrs Jeremy said she thought you oughter have some breakfast, so I've brought it up for you.'

She staggered over with a tray which looked as if it held enough food to feed all the inhabitants of the house. I wondered who had been in charge of portion control. Surely, Rose couldn't believe that I needed feeding up, or was it Mrs Miskin's idea of a light repast? It would certainly explain the width of the hips.

I was feeling much better. Not get up and run a marathon sort of better, let's not exaggerate here, or even a brisk stroll around the grounds sort of better, but no longer feeling as if I'd been put through the hot wash on the extended spin-cycle. I pushed myself up, a sharp twinge from my shoulder reminding me I might feel better, but not that good, and quickly took a couple of my pills.

I was delighted to see Rose come in mid-morning with a bag of my things which she'd fetched from the cottage. My own nightie was going to be a great relief. Hers, though absolutely gorgeous and trimmed with lace that had probably been made by a whole convent of nuns, was the sort of thing to be seen in and perhaps even have taken off you if you're lucky, but not so hot for actually sleeping in. For one thing, all that lace was rather scratchy and it was floor-length and quite narrow, which made climbing up into that high bed about as easy as if I'd been wearing hobbles. I went off to my enormous en-suite bathroom, firmly ignoring all Rose's suggestions that she should hang around in case I got into difficulties getting out of the bath. 'I'm not eighty, you know!' I said. 'And if I get into trouble I promise I'll let you know by letting the water out in three short bursts at a time – all you have to do is watch the drainpipe.'

'But I wouldn't know what drainpipe to watch,' she began. 'Maybe I should leave my mobile with you . . .'

'Don't be stupid!' I interrupted. 'I'll only drop it in the bath and probably electrocute myself! Go on, I'll be fine!' I said, shooing her out and wondering when her enthusiasm for playing Florence Nightingale was going to come to an end. I was finding it quite exhausting, but at least since even Rose wouldn't smoke in a sickroom I got a respite from all that care every so often while she rushed out for a nicotine fix.

I'd been thinking vaguely about getting dressed after my bath, but instead I decided the bed looked more inviting and climbed back into it for another kip. I'd be going for the world sleep record at this rate, I thought drowsily as I nodded off. I woke to a familiar sound that I couldn't place for a moment. A car backfiring? A pop gun? Then I realised it had been a champagne cork coming out of the bottle. There was the clink of glasses and then I heard Rose's distinctive low throaty laugh, followed by the murmur of another voice. Curious, then as Rose laughed again, suspicious, I climbed out of bed and went over to the sash window, and looked down at the terrace below.

'The cow!' I breathed furiously as I saw Rose, dressed in jeans and a shirt tied at the waist, sitting on the terrace wall, half-empty champagne glass in one hand, laughing as she made some remark to Luke, who was lounging back comfortably in a white iron chair. Why hadn't she told me he was coming over? She'd promised to help me wash my hair. I needed make-up, a complete makeover, you name it, before he could be allowed to see me, I thought in a panic. I dashed into the bathroom, where I'd brushed my teeth and washed my face earlier in near-darkness, with the light over the basin mirror turned off. I'd had to see my left side while I was having my bath and that had been bad enough. It was now a spectacular yellow and purple most of the way down and I hadn't dared check to see if it matched my face. And I'd thought pink was a bad colour to go with my shade of hair.

Now, taking a deep breath, I stood in front of the mirror, flipped the light switch and braced myself for the worst. It wasn't quite as bad as I'd feared. I won't say I looked great, but I didn't think that any passing dog in the street would start barking at me. At least the bruise on my cheekbone hadn't exploded into a rainbow of colours, even if it did look disconcertingly as if I'd skimped on several weeks of the cleanse, tone and moisturise routine in that area. Feverishly I got to work, concealing, highlighting, lining, shading, mascaraing, brushing, combing, until I looked a reasonable semblance of my normal self. I contemplated the merits of glamour over comfort in the matter of nightwear. Glamour won hands down. I dived feverishly into the laundry basket to retrieve Rose's nightie, only to find it empty. Mrs Miskin must have been in while I was asleep, I thought in annoyance, so Luke would have to feast his eyes on me clad in my present from Granny last Christmas. Unfortunately, a present from respectable Granny, not wicked Granny, so it was very high-necked, voluminous and definitely from the serviceable rather than the enticing end of the nightie range.

I knew Rose well enough to be sure she'd come up after the bottle was finished and not before. I wandered over to the window to judge where the tide mark was and guess when I should expect them. A bottle and two abandoned glasses lay on the table. They must be on their way up, I thought and then hearing a distant sound craned my head to look along the length of the terrace. They were walking off across the gardens towards the ha-ha and the old folly, Rose's hand tucked companionably in Luke's arm as they chatted. They'd gone off for a walk around the grounds without even bothering to come up and see me first!

It was a good hour and a half before Rose's flushed, slightly contrite face peeped around the door. 'Oh, you're awake!' she said. 'We looked in before but you were asleep . . .'

'We?' I asked frostily.

'Mm.' She nodded. 'Me and Luke. He didn't want to risk disturbing you, so he sent you his love and said he was delighted you seemed to be so much better.' She giggled. 'I told him you were getting bossy again so it must be a good sign!' Belatedly she took in my made-up, primped and scented appearance and her hand flew up to her mouth. 'Oh God, Susie, I'm sorry! I didn't realise you'd woken up!'

'It didn't occur to you that all that carousing on the terrace might have woken me?' I asked, unmollified.

'You call *that* carousing? We only had one bottle!' retorted Rose indignantly, coming in and perching on the side of the bed. 'And *between* us too.' She smiled at me contritely. 'Really, he turned up unexpectedly. I thought he was coming this evening and I did think you were asleep.' I eyed her severely for signs of insincerity. She looked back at me with wide, clear, untroubled blue eyes. It almost certainly meant that she hadn't been too particular in checking to see if I was really asleep, probably stood at the other end of the corridor and hissed, 'Susie, are you awake?', not surprisingly getting the non-reply she wanted. She could then go off with only a slightly spotted conscience and indulge in a pleasant hour or so of wistful remembrance of what might have been.

'We spent a bit longer than we intended on our walk, so when we got back here he said he had to go. He was running really late, as usual. He's borrowing his grandmother's car while his is being sorted out and he had to have it back by three so

193

the carer could take Grandma to the clinic, otherwise he'd have come up to see you, I promise.'

'So where did you and Luke go?' I asked, leaning back against the pillows, hoping that my casual tone wasn't revealing the sudden spasm of sickening jealousy that had made my hands curl for a moment into little claws. *Why* had they spent longer than they intended? Had what I'd presumed was simply going to be a bit of mild flirtation on Rose's part – par for the course really, as she can't resist flirting with most males out of nappies – developed into something altogether more steamy and passionate? Had she been unable to resist the temptation to see what she'd missed out on five years ago? How dare she! She was married, for heaven's sake, and she had no right to move in on my territory, I thought venomously, ignoring the horridly common-sensical and disgustingly honest voice pointing out that in fact Luke *wasn't* my territory. Not yet. I scanned her quickly for tell-tale leaves and grass stains on her white shirt, but all I could see were damp lines around the bottom of her jeans, a legacy from walking in long grass.

'Just around,' she said vaguely, which did absolutely nothing to reduce my general suspicion level. Then perhaps even she felt a little amplification was necessary, for she went on, 'There are one or two nice walks through the woods, you'll have to come with us one day. Dexter's a hoot, he spends his whole time trying to climb the trees and get at the squirrels. We went along the back drive and skirted the farm, and ended up having a look at the infamous toad pond. We didn't see any though, so I can't think what all the fuss was about, but Luke was interested in seeing it because he says he was quite a naturist in his younger days.'

'He *was*?' I asked, my mind filling with some very interesting visions. What exactly did Luke mean by his younger days?

I thought happily, as I dwelt on the pictures being flashed up by my ever-fertile imagination. I hoped he meant at least sixteen and not six, that would be too disappointing.

'Yes,' said Rose, puzzled, then caught on and began to laugh. 'I think I probably mean a naturalist, don't I? Oh dear, what a shame! And here was I hoping we could persuade Luke to demonstrate his latest toad-watching techniques!'

The last remnants of my jealous fit were washed away in a prolonged session of giggling as she made a few unrepeatable suggestions about what naturists might have to wear by means of protective gear when out wearing their naturalist hats.

'You know, I'd never been down there before,' she said thoughtfully after a few minutes. 'I mean I'd passed by, I knew it, of course, but I hadn't actually walked around it. I'm beginning to wonder if a development there would be such a bad thing after all. It's not *so* close to the house and it'd be completely screened by a belt of trees. We'd hardly know it was there. And I bet lots of the locals would find jobs on the building site too. That's another thing I hadn't thought of.'

'What about it being the wrong sort of development, with the wrong sort of houses?' I asked.

'Maybe I was too prejudiced,' she said. 'It's reverse snobbery, isn't it, refusing to allow townies the benefits of the countryside? It's not as if they could overwhelm the village, there's seven hundred already living there, so it can easily cope with another seventy or so. And people like that do bring wealth into the area, they've got lots of money to buy things and they offer employment too.' She sat thoughtfully gazing out into space, tapping one fingernail against her tooth. 'There'd be more children to go to the village school too, that's always a good thing.'

'Wouldn't they be sending their children to the private

school in Frampton?' I asked. 'The one where all the children walk in crocodiles and wear hats?'

She thought for a moment. 'Some of them mightn't,' she said hopefully. 'It's one of the things they like about the country, it allows them to indulge their socialistic leanings by sending their children to a state school, but without making their education suffer like it would in some run-down inner-city suburb.'

She got up off the bed, stretched, and said, 'Oh well, I'd better stop gassing and get a move on to clear up the terrace before Mrs Miskin comes back after her lunch. Otherwise she'll be straight round to Flavia to report I've been *drinking* in the middle of the day, and the next thing you know Flavia will be having little consultations with Jeremy, telling him how worried she is about the amount "Dear Rose" –' her voice dripped poisoned honey in an excellent imitation of her mother-in-law – 'is drinking each evening and now she's afraid it's started at lunchtime too. I swear she's bribing Mrs Miskin to tell her exactly how many empties go in the bin; though the old witch has been working for the head cauldron-stirrer for so long she probably doesn't need bribing.'

'You could always ask your mates to save all their empty gin bottles for you, and then stack them up in the wardrobe one day and wait to see what happens,' I suggested.

Rose hooted with laughter. 'I might just do that! It would serve her right too! I wish I could sack her!' she added vehemently, then seeing my slightly puzzled expression said with a strained smile, 'I'm talking about Mrs Miskin! She may be poisonous, but you can't get rid of people who've worked in the place for as long as she has. I wouldn't mind getting rid of Flavia too, though I expect you've gathered that! But since the only way I can think of getting rid of *her* involves a large quantity of arsenic and I don't want to spend the next few years in prison I suppose I'll just have to learn to put up with her. I'll see you later.' When she reached the door she turned and gave me the critical once-over. 'I must say you've done a pretty good job, you'd never guess what you looked like yesterday morning. Shame it was all wasted!' she added callously. There are some times when I don't feel I like Rose very much. This was one of them.

'I'll tell you what though, you needn't let all that effort go for nothing,' she said kindly. 'I'll let Jeremy come up and see how you are, you can try vamping him.'

'You shouldn't be encouraging me to vamp your husband,' I said severely.

'Probably not,' she agreed serenely. 'But then I'm quite safe. He's tramping the bounds or something. All I know is that it involves a lot of walking around and Jeremy and the farm manager knowing better than each other. After a long day like that the only thing likely to get a response out of Jeremy is a glass of whisky.' The pleased smile that accompanied this statement showed that she wasn't speaking the truth.

I was spared the effort of trying to vamp Jeremy from within the voluminous confines of Granny's Christmas present as Rose was forced to admit after a certain amount of argument on my part that I was well enough to get dressed and join the grown-ups downstairs. I'd had enough of lying around in bed and I was determined that if by any chance Luke did pop round again I would be reclining, pale but interesting, downstairs, so there was no chance of Rose getting away with going off for another little walk with him. In the event I did have visitors, but not Luke. The first was Stephen, carrying a bunch of tulips and looking distinctly shamefaced. I got the feeling his mind had been running along tabloid headlines of,

'My last words to tragic road-accident victim were so cruel . . . if only I'd known what was going to happen later that evening I'd have never . . .'

He was almost falling over himself to be nice, telling me to take as much time off as I thought I needed, and not to worry about a thing at the office, in such a comical contrast to his mood on Monday that I began to wonder if it might not be worth getting injured on a regular basis. 'But you don't happen to know what happened to those notes I made on the house at Colby?' he asked casually.

I shot Rose a triumphant glance. 'The last I saw of them you were about to throw them at me. I didn't hang around to see what you did with them, but I imagine they're somewhere on your desk.'

'I didn't think of that,' he said, looking a bit self-conscious. 'Perhaps I should clear away all the mess.'

'Please don't!' I said quickly. 'I'll never find anything again, you know that!'

I had to force him to swear absolutely he wasn't going to file so much as one bit of paper away. I'd already experienced Stephen's somewhat eccentric attitude to filing, which for reasons best known to himself didn't always follow the same rules, so correspondence relating to the same house could be found under house name, owner's name, village or part of the county. The infuriating thing was he always knew where he'd put them and couldn't understand why I didn't.

He didn't stay for long, asking us to convey his regrets about missing him to Jeremy and saying that he had to get home as Liddy was expecting him.

'Next time you come here you'll have to stay longer,' said Rose, who had taken one of her shines to him and kept on sending me 'Are you mad to be letting this slip through your fingers?' looks. 'You are coming to the charity wine-tasting I'm having here, aren't you?'

'Er, I don't know,' he said vaguely, with a 'I'm dumping the responsibility for this on someone else' look that I recognised. 'Liddy handles all the things like that.'

'You must,' she said firmly, beaming at him. 'I'm in charge, so it's going to be good fun. Susie can give you another invitation as a reminder when she comes back to work.'

I watched with amusement as Stephen at last met his match in a purveyor of the same sort of juggernaut charm as he had himself. Rose held his eye firmly until he gave way and said, 'Yes, of course we'll come.'

'I'll put both of you down on the list as definites,' she said, with a look that suggested she'd have been quite happy if there had only been one to mark down. He blinked, looking bewildered but also rather pleased.

'Isn't he a poppet?' she asked, coming back from seeing him out and throwing herself down on the sofa.

'You wouldn't think so if you'd seen him a couple of days ago!' I retorted.

'Tush! You don't know how to handle him, that's all!' she said infuriatingly. I eyed her sourly, but said nothing. Rose doesn't believe that anyone, especially me, is as good as she is at manipulating men. I have a nasty feeling she might be right, but I still thought she'd have met a pretty insuperable challenge in Stephen last Monday. 'Honestly, I can't see why you aren't going in there with all your guns blazing and wrenching him away from this Liddy. Forget female solidarity, he's gorgeous and she sounds like a complete pain in the neck!'

'She is,' I agreed, smiling. 'Yes, he is nice-looking but . . .'

'He's not your type!' she said with a disgusted sniff. 'Honestly, Susie, you write off ninety-nine per cent of the male population because they aren't smaller than you and don't have a foreign accent!'

'Actually, I was about to say I'd got my hands quite full enough at the moment, thank you very much,' I said with offended dignity.

She looked up with a quick smile. 'Yes, I'd forgotten that you've been branching out a little . . .'

'What's Susie branching out with?' asked Jeremy, coming in, looking tired, well exercised and rather pleased with himself, with an equally tired and happy-looking Dexter at his heels. 'This sounds interesting! Glad to see you up, Susie. Hamish'll be pleased too. He's parking his car and'll be here in a minute.' He bent down to give Rose a kiss with an enthusiasm that belied her claim that he was only interested in a glass of whisky after a day on the farm. I studied the view out of the window for a minute or two. It had been a gorgeous warm, sunny day, the sort which gives you a bit of faith that there might actually be an English summer this year, and the honeysuckle climbing rampantly around the wall-length window made a very attractive frame for the lawns and a rather nice weeping cherry tree in the mid-distance. Even so, I'd drunk quite enough of my fill of the view by the time movements alongside me told me it was safe to allow my eyes to wander back to the interior again. Rose was tucking a piece of hair behind one ear with a silly expression on her face, while Jeremy politely turned his attention to me. 'I must say you're a considerable improvement on yesterday,' he said on a note of surprise.

'I get the impression that the average corpse was an improvement on me yesterday,' I said.

He thought for a moment, then shook his head. 'No. Corpses either smell or they come alive and leap up and bite you on the neck. Both are pretty nasty. I preferred you, even if you did look a bit ragged around the edges.' I didn't feel I was being measured against a very high standard. There was movement behind him. Dexter had realised I was there and, remembering I'm a dab hand at scratches under the chin, was bounding forward to give me one of his enthusiastic greetings. I held out my hand defensively, my arm might have been better, but it still didn't need fifty pounds of high-speed dog landing on it. Jeremy snapped his fingers and said sternly, 'Here!' To my surprise, Dexter halted in mid-bound, and was back at his master's feet almost before the words had stopped ringing on the air.

'I wish you could train your mother's bloody dog like that!' said Rose, clearly impressed.

'I suggest you train Dexter to eat him!' said Hamish, pushing the door open and looking decidedly irritated. 'The little sod has just been firmly attached to my ankle. I thought I was never going to get him off.'

'Don't tell me,' said Rose in a weary voice, giving a very fair imitation of Flavia, 'you enticed him to do it in some way.'

'I hope not!' he said, sounding startled.

'Come on, darling,' said Jeremy. 'Hamish's love life might be a bit piano at the moment, but I'm sure he hasn't got so desperate he encourages the dog to roger his leg. He'd at least choose a bitch!'

As she laughed, Hamish turned to me with a smile. 'Sorry to hear about your accident, Susie, though apart from that rather impressive sling you're sporting I wouldn't have known that anything had happened.' I could have flung my good arm around his neck and kissed him, it felt so good not to be told that I looked as if I'd just been resurrected. 'I came to see how you were, but I can see that the answer is, recovering quickly.'

I smiled at him with a certain degree of cynicism. He had a

black leather briefcase under one arm. 'Don't you mean you came over to give something to Jeremy, heard about the accident, and decided to earn a few brownie points by a bit of sick visiting at the same time?'

'Not true at all,' he said promptly, sitting down on the sofa alongside me. 'I could quite easily have faxed these over, in fact I was going to, but then I heard all about the dramatic events of the other night from Stephen, who is suffering from a bad case of acute conscience and seems to imagine he provoked you into hurling yourself in front of a goat. I couldn't resist coming to see how you were for myself.'

'It's very nice of you, thank you,' I murmured, feeling absurdly pleased with myself for some reason.

'Stephen's already been round to see Susie,' said Rose.

'Only because he couldn't find a file,' I said.

'You're so cynical!' she complained. 'He was worried about you and you put the worst interpretation on it. And he brought you those flowers too. Honestly, I'm not surprised he threatened to sack you if you have that attitude around him!'

Hamish looked at me with deep interest. 'He didn't mention that! Was that why you tried to top yourself by goat? What exactly did you do to merit the sack so soon after starting a job?'

I thought for a moment. 'I was there,' I said finally. 'And before you ask, I did absolutely nothing to warrant having a file thrown at me, apart from ask him to decipher a word I couldn't read! Anyway, he didn't actually sack me, he didn't get as far as the third warning – though that was probably because I bolted out of the door before he could issue it!'

Hamish chuckled. 'No wonder you felt like taking it out on a goat. What state is it in, or shouldn't one ask?'

'It's a sheep,' I corrected. 'Houdini by name and Casanova

by nature, so I hear. Unless Mr Cartwright's carried out his threat to turn him into Lancashire hotpot, he's fine. He was peacefully munching grass in a field when we left him. It was Luke swerving to avoid him that caused the accident, and his car wasn't in such a fine state.'

He was stretching out his hand to accept a glass of red wine from Rose, but at this he turned his head sharply. 'You have got to know Luke Dillon well, haven't you?'

'No,' I said evenly, wondering what was up with these three men. They seemed to bristle like territorial dogs when each other's names were mentioned. And I didn't get the impression I was the bit of disputed territory. 'I was simply having dinner with him.'

My look challenged him to say anything more about it. He murmured, 'Not enough of it if it was necessary to pick up a bit of extra mutton on the way home,' and then to my relief asked me what I'd done to myself, a nice innocuous subject with no nasty undertones.

'Just bruising, but I had no idea that something minor like a bruise could hurt so much,' I said with a grimace. It reminded me it was time for my evening pill, so I fished the bottle out of my pocket and washed one down with my orange juice.

'I had these a couple of years ago when I broke my collarbone,' he said, picking the bottle up and examining the label. 'They're very good, but strong.'

I nodded. 'I know, they're fantastic! I can already take fewer than the doctor said I could have and they seem to work perfectly well enough on a lower dose.'

'What's the point of lying there suffering if you don't have to?' asked Rose. 'I like my painkillers a bucket at a time, I don't want to feel anything at all. In fact, let me lie there in a blissful dreamy state, not knowing what the hell is going on, like they used to in the olden days.'

Hamish laughed. 'I think that was because they were taking opium on the basis that if you stayed high for long enough you would either have got better or died before you came back down to earth again.'

'Oh,' she said, then grinned. 'It's not a bad way of being ill, is it? Do you think that people were constantly calling the doctor in and saying, Doctor, I've got a bad finger and it's sooo painful, could I have a little of your wonderful medicine?'

'Probably not, in case he suggested amputating it.'

'Maybe aspirin's not such a bad idea after all then,' Rose said thoughtfully.

CHAPTER 11

I insisted on going back to the cottage the next day, saying I felt much better, which I did. My whole left side still ached like hell, but it was quite supportable and I could get around easily, even if I was heartily glad I was right-handed. A relaxed and very congenial supper the night before had done more for my wellbeing than any amount of medication, even if Rose, backed infuriatingly by Hamish (who was even more sure he knew best than she was), had insisted I was sent to bed at ten o'clock. Also, I didn't want to outstay my welcome, which I could see becoming imminent. Rose had loads of other things to do, like attending committee meetings about this charity do, which was now only ten days away. To give her credit, she tried to make me stay on for another couple of days and Jeremy nobly seconded her invitation. I was sure the last thing he wanted hanging around in the evenings with him and his new wife was a redheaded gooseberry. Besides, I was gloomily aware there were boring domestic matters to attend to at the cottage. If I didn't get the milk out of the fridge soon it would be battering on the door and claiming it was owed parole.

Rose dropped me off on her way to her meeting, and lingered with anxious enquiries as to whether I was going to be all right, making me absolutely swear to ring her if I needed anything. In the end, I had to threaten to have hysterics in the middle of the green where everyone could see if she didn't get in her car and go *now*. It was bliss to be back in the cottage again, even if it did feel more shoebox-sized than ever after the grandeur of Moor End Hall. I paced it out, and discovered that, as I'd suspected, the total downstairs area of 3, Green Cottages was the same as that of the bedroom I'd just been sleeping in. Though it was a big bedroom even by Moor End standards. Somehow, in less than a month this place had become home in a way that the flat in London, which I'd lived in for years, never had. I'd supplemented Preston's minimalist tastes with my own clutter, adding ornaments and knick-knacks that I'd collected over the years, slinging the bright tapestry cushions my mother makes as a hobby all over the sofa to offset his passion for neutral colours. There was one covering the wine stain on the arm too. There was room on the deep bookshelves for a row at the front of colourful, and frankly, scruffy (bath-read) paperbacks that all but obliterated the serried ranks of theatrical biographies Preston favoured. I hadn't dared to ask how the weight of this useful arrangement might affect the stability of the screws holding the shelves.

I poddled around, tidying up, releasing the milk and something else that looked like I should have remembered to send it to the great dustbin in the sky some time ago, then headed out to the shop to stock up again. I hadn't even unlatched the gate before Mrs Tanner was ever so casually out of her door, supposedly on the same errand, but in actual fact on a mission to find out what I'd been doing not coming back to the cottage for three nights. She was a one woman Neighbourhood Watch and there were many more like her here. I wasn't surprised Little Dearsley had one of the lowest crime rates in the area. The burglars wouldn't even be able to get as far as casing the joint before they were asked what they were doing. Mrs Tanner was horrified to see my arm in its sling (very useful for stowing my purse so I didn't have to bother with a handbag) and, after I'd disabused her of her fantasies about a near-escape from death, confessed that she'd been hoping I'd been doing a bit of 'you-know-what' with that young feller of mine. 'Not, of course, that I 'xactly approve,' she said, sucking air in through a gap in her teeth, 'but when yer with a looker like that one you want to grab him any way you can! Don't let him slip through your fingers, young Susie!'

With a furiously blushing face I assured her I was trying to make sure he didn't, while praying desperately that no one was sitting behind half-open windows, listening to every word. And probably laughing their heads off, I thought grimly, as Mrs Tanner launched into more of the same. Thank heaven, at last even she ran out of steam, and interest. Mysteriously, she decided she didn't need to go to the shop after all and the last I saw of her she was hobbling off as fast as her walking stick would take her towards the village hall and the over-sixties' club.

I was almost as much of a sensation in the shop, which was full of mothers enjoying a brief period of peace while their offspring were at the playgroup. I knew several of them by sight, though being at work all day I hadn't really penetrated the young-marrieds crowd in Little Dearsley. They tended to look at me a bit askance, with the same sort of suspicion that is reserved for newly divorced women, as if, single, and presumably desperate, I must be after their husbands. It's difficult to know what to do to allay that sort of suspicion. If you assure them you wouldn't dream of touching their husbands in a thousand years, not even to save you from a fate worse than death, you risk causing even more offence by maligning their taste. But since all the village men had been safely accounted for during my absence, they felt free to metaphorically fall on my neck, saying how worried they'd been about me and, without giving me a chance to say what had happened, launching into what other people had imagined. Mercifully, all these speculations about my disappearance had been confined to the dead in a ditch sort, rather than the rolling around in the biggest pile of hay you've ever seen type, so I didn't have to suffer any more embarrassing commiserations on failing to land my man. I was beginning to rethink my sentimental thoughts of a couple of hours ago about how much I felt at home here and was wistfully remembering London where I didn't even know the name of the man who lived in the flat above and had such a noisy sex life, when Bob, who keeps the shop, leant forward across the counter and said, 'Ladies, it's ten past. The kiddies'll be out in five minutes.' Within seconds the shop had emptied as they streamed down the road towards the playgroup. Bob winked at me and said blandly, 'I just discovered my watch is ten minutes fast. Now, what can I do for you, Susie?'

He refused to allow me to carry anything back home, whistling his son, an enormous adolescent who was on a study day, out from the back and telling him to act sharpish and get my two carrier bags over to the cottage at once. Mr Patel at the corner shop round from the flat had been incredibly helpful, but even he drew the line at getting his family to deliver shopping. My faith in village life was completely restored.

I turned over in bed around five-thirty the next morning and woke myself up swearing as my weight hit my shoulder and I discovered it wasn't as well healed as I'd thought. I'd spent so much time in bed during the last few days I was completely over-rested and knew there was no way I was going to be able to go back to sleep again. I had a bath, got dressed and mooched down to the kitchen, where I made some coffee and read my book for a bit. But I'd done a lot of reading in the last couple of days too, and it wasn't even a very good book. So after I'd polished the coffee machine, washed my one mug and wiped the sink, I looked around for things to do. I'd done too much cleaning last weekend, so there was absolutely nothing, apart from heavy work like cleaning the windows, and I wasn't bored or well enough to do that. By nine o'clock I was virtually going up the walls. I was marching around, frustrated and resentful that my bad arm prevented me from getting on with weeding the garden, though it has to be admitted I hadn't actually wanted to until I realised I couldn't. The day seemed to stretch out very long in front of me, as did the whole bloody weekend, now that my trip to Sussex had been cancelled.

I was going to go mad if I had to hang around here any longer, and decided that I might as well go into work for half the day at least. It was only about seven miles into Frampton and I was sure that whatever Dr Bob said I could manage the driving, providing I didn't do too many racing-driver-style gear changes as I screamed around corners. I could get another book and get my hair washed in the hairdressers in the High Street, I thought happily, the notion of getting out of here seeming more attractive by the minute. (I'd already investigated 'Mary Anne, Hairdresser' in the village about getting my hair washed, as it was one thing I couldn't do one-handed. Mary Anne, who'd set up just after the war and was still giving her contemporaries perms and blue rinses, hadn't been happy about the idea of letting me out of there without a nice set, held in place by plenty of lacquer, at the very least. I'd decided I'd rather have dirty hair.)

If I'd hoped everyone would be delighted to see me and impressed by my noble effort in coming in, I was sadly mistaken. 'What the hell are you doing here?' asked Amanda bluntly as I came in. 'You're on sick leave. This is showing far too much dedication to the great God Work for my liking. You're queering the pitch for all of us! Go away before Stephen begins to think all of us should come in when we've got a sick note!'

Jenny nodded wisely. 'You've got to give yourself time to recover, otherwise you'll have a relapse.'

Martin looked up from flicking through a copy of *Estates Times*. 'I don't know who you're trying to impress. You're no bloody use to anyone only able to use one arm, or is that thing just for show?' he sneered, looking at the sling which I'd prudently put on just before I went in, to make it absolutely obvious he couldn't land me with any of his ruddy typing at lunchtime.

I bared my teeth at him. 'You're such a sweetie, Martin, I do love you. You say such *nice* things.' Amanda and Jenny sniggered as his mouth clamped into a straight line of annoyance.

Stephen poked his head around his door to see what the noise was about, and blinked when he saw me. 'You're supposed to be off until next week, aren't you?' he asked doubtfully. 'Hadn't you better go home? I'm sure we can manage without you, Susie.' So much for any notions of thinking myself indispensable, I thought wryly. 'I don't want to be responsible for any damage you might do to yourself by coming back too soon,' he added.

'Is this concern for my wellbeing or concern that you might find yourself being sued?' I asked.

He stared at me blankly, glasses slipping down his nose.

'For yourself, of course!' he began indignantly and then laughed.

'I can assure you the only damage done today will be to my head as I beat it against the walls if I go home,' I said firmly. 'I had to come into Frampton anyway, so I thought I'd just do a half-day or something.'

'Oh,' he said, 'I suppose that'd be all right.' He pushed his glasses back into place and beamed at me. 'As you're here . . . You don't know where the copy for the ads for next month's *Country Life* has gone, do you?'

I found it on top of Stephen's bookcase, jammed between a pension proposal and an Ordnance Survey map of East Leicester in the nineteen fifties, and took the opportunity to remove various important things and take them back to my own desk where I could sort them out at leisure. Amanda was on her feet, about to show someone around a house, and shrugging herself into a gorgeous red jacket that I would have given my eye teeth to be able to wear (not with my colouring though). 'Don't go before I come back, will you?' she asked, patting her pockets for her car keys. 'I want to hear all about it, especially –' she rolled her eyes – 'exactly what you were doing in the back lanes with the scrumptious Luke Dillon! When I met him it was lust at first sight! If Bill hadn't been with me I can't say what might have happened, ripped-off clothing and swinging chandeliers, I expect!'

'Don't be crude, Amanda,' said Martin, without raising his eyes from the pages of his magazine, *Estates Gazette* this time. 'It gives a very bad impression to any clients who might come in.'

'Dear me, Martin, what a sheltered life you must lead if you think that was crude,' she said mildly. He glowered ferociously at his magazine and pretended not to have heard.

211

Within a couple of hours I began to realise Dr Bob might have had a point when he'd told me to take the whole week off and not do any driving. It wouldn't have occurred to me before how much more tiring it was doing simple, mindless tasks, like working out what Stephen had done with the bill for his mobile, than lying on a sofa, reading a racy novel. Naturally, the five-thirty get-up this morning hadn't helped either and my shoulder was aching dully from the drive in, though if I hadn't been in a fairly martyrish mood through being in the office when I was officially on sick leave I would probably barely have noticed it.

I was on the verge of throwing in the towel and going off to get my hair washed and buy my book when Jenny bit into a toffee and left the crown off her front tooth poking out of it. There was a general panic while the normally unflappable Jenny burst into tears. Her husband was having a big office do that evening, she'd bought a new dress and shoes, and now she wasn't going to be able to go. Her dentist's receptionist said in a sniffy voice that they couldn't possibly fit in even an emergency appointment until tomorrow afternoon at the very earliest. And frankly, in her opinion, a missing crown wasn't an emergency. Jenny opened her mouth to show a large and visible gap. 'I can't go out like this! Alan's going to be so cross!' she wailed. 'And he's going to say it's all my fault, and it is! I've been told not to eat toffees, but I do love them so. I've ruined his evening!'

Surprisingly, it was Stephen who took charge. He rang his own dentist and, through a mixture of cajolery and threatening to take his teeth elsewhere, persuaded her to fit Jenny in later that afternoon to do a temporary gluing job. He told Jenny the good news and then said, 'Martin, can you cancel your appointment for this afternoon? Amanda and I have to go to

Lincoln and won't be back before Jenny has to leave.'

'No, I can't,' said Martin abruptly. 'The Woodrows are coming up from London to see The Grange, they're probably already on their way.'

There was a silence. Stephen turned and looked at me, his eyes saying he wouldn't dream of imposing on me when I wasn't even supposed to be here, but . . .

'I'll stay,' I said with heavy resignation, feeling rather annoyed that for once I couldn't accuse Martin of being obstructive and unhelpful. That's not to say he probably wouldn't have given the same response even if his had been an easily cancellable appointment, but still . . . 'We can't have poor Jenny spending the evening with her hand in front of her face.'

It was almost as boring being in the office alone without much to do as it had been at home. I whiled away a few minutes playing minesweeper on the computer, in the full knowledge I could never hope to match Jenny's times for completing it at every level, and then started idly flicking my way through back files on completed sales. A surprising number of them were password protected, which I presumed meant they must be Martin's, what with his passion for keeping his clients to himself. I hoped it wouldn't be logged somewhere that I'd tried to get into his files or I'd be in for another earbashing. But what happened if he was out or on holiday and something needed to be checked urgently on one of his files? I wondered vaguely. Probably someone in the office had a master list of passwords, I decided, and forgot about it as I came across a house that we seemed to have sold about four times in the last ten years. I was tracing the files back, wondering if it was haunted or something to have changed hands so often, when the phone went for the first time since I'd been left in charge.

It was Rose, ringing to check Stephen really was coming to her charity do. She wasn't best pleased to discover who was acting as telephonist and said so at length.

'I was fed up and needed something to do,' I said plaintively when she had finished at last. My ear was aching. Rose on her high horse is quite something.

'But aren't you supposed to be going off to your parents' this evening?'

I sighed, 'It just wasn't possible. I couldn't ask anyone to come and collect me, could I? It's a three-and-a-half-hour drive, and the taxi fare to Leicester station is more than a return airfare to Paris, so that pretty well stymied that option. I'm going in a couple of weeks instead, but it won't be the same. Rob and Kitty are there this weekend, and I haven't seen them for ages, not since Christmas.'

'I'd be delighted if I could go from one Christmas to the next without seeing *my* sister-in-law. Unfortunately, I'm not so lucky,' said Rose dryly. 'Though I admit the brother isn't too bad, even if he does have a questionable taste in wives.'

I couldn't disagree with her there. 'Hey! I've got an idea!' she went on. 'You're at a loose end and need cheering up, and so am I. Well, I don't need cheering up, but I am at a loose end because Jeremy's had his arm twisted into going to one of these NFU things this evening and I'm all alone. Why don't we go to see that Meg Ryan film we were talking about?'

'Well, I don't know,' I began. I was getting to the stage where flopping in front of the telly in my dressing-gown was the most attractive option for the evening and one of the three books I'd bought in my dash out at lunchtime was sending out a particularly loud siren call of 'read me'.

'Oh, come on,' she wheedled. 'I'll come and collect you too, so you'll have chauffeur service. You can't complain about that! It'll do you good to have a really good laugh and you were saying how much you wanted to see it.' As I hesitated she went on, 'Oh, do come, Susie, you know I'll never get to see it otherwise. Jeremy won't go and I don't think he'd be very pleased if I started buzzing off and leaving him alone at home already!'

'Well, maybe you should start getting him trained now,' I said. 'I thought you had no intention of being the sort of woman who stayed at home attending to her husband's every whim.'

She laughed. 'Believe me, I'm not! But I do try to make the odd concession. And there's a cocktail bar next door to the cinema. We can pop in afterwards and pretend we're really sophisticated.'

'I'm not allowed to have cocktails,' I said primly, seizing on the one concrete objection I could see. 'No alcohol with these pills I'm taking.'

'There are non-alcoholic cocktails too!' she said loftily, probably sensing she was winning. 'Instead of a Long Slow Screw Up Against The Wall, I'm sure they can do you a Quick Peck On The Cheek In The Front Porch.'

'Have they really got one called that?' I asked, fascinated.

'I don't know,' she replied blithely, 'but there's bound to be something for good little non-boozers like you. I'll ring and book the tickets. Which performance do you want? Seven-thirty or nine-thirty?'

'Seven-thirty,' I said, realising too late that once again I'd been manoeuvred into agreeing to do something I didn't really want to by Rose, even if she really did think it would do me good to go out and have a bit of fun. Naturally, she wasn't averse to a bit of fun herself. I yawned, glancing at my watch. Maybe she was right. If I went home and straight to bed as I longed to all that would happen would be another five-thirty wake-up. And this was hardly going to be a late night either, more a respectably middling one, since Rose wanted to be home for Jeremy when he came back from scintillating the NFU. Probably even Dr Bob would admit that this mild entertainment could do me no harm.

I got home, sat down for a couple of minutes, and promptly fell asleep on the sofa. I woke up about five minutes before Rose was due to pick me up and one panic-struck look in the mirror convinced me that I'd better forget all about the sandwich I'd been planning to make and do something about my face. Crease marks down the cheeks as a result of sleeping on an embroidered cushion are hardly de rigueur even on the quietest night out with the girls. The sacrifice of stomach in the interests of face turned out to be well worth it when Rose, hair pinned up in an artfully messy bun and wearing a new pair of shocking-pink trousers that made her legs look as if they ended in her armpits, casually told me she'd remembered about Luke wanting to see the film and he was meeting us at the cinema. She was sorry she hadn't rung to tell me, but she'd been too busy to get to the phone.

Judging from her immaculate make-up, she'd been too busy titivating herself, I thought sourly, then more pressing matters occurred to me. 'I can't wear this!' I shrieked in horror, looking down at the skirt and shirt I'd worn to work and which had seemed just about passable a couple of minutes ago. 'I must change!' I called, heading for the stairs.

'You look fine,' Rose assured me, following me at the gallop. She knows my dressing habits well, and I expect she wanted to see the first half of the film. 'Though –' she looked doubtfully at my crumpled, slept-in shirt, weighing up delay against the potential shame of appearing in public with such a scruff bucket – 'perhaps . . . What about this?' She picked up a dark-orange silk jersey top.

'I'm not sure about the colour,' I began.

'It suits you, really,' she said, then, seeing me waver, said with an irresistible firmness, '*Put it on.*'

I did. But I made her wait while I chose the right pair of shoes.

I'd been hoping to buy myself a hot dog or something from the foyer of the cinema as Stephen had swept most of my lunchtime sandwich on to the floor with the edge of his briefcase on his way out. As it landed bread-side down and didn't explode its contents all over the carpet, I would have picked it up, dusted it off and finished it if he hadn't turned round to remind me about a call he was expecting and trodden on it. Unfortunately, when I suggested going off to the hot-dog stand Rose, with unnerving practicality, pointed out that Luke hadn't arrived yet and there were few less glamorous things than to be seen by the object of your desire eating a hot dog, whether or not it had extra onions and mustard. 'And it doesn't do great shakes for your breath,' she said kindly.

It was with great regret that I had to admit she was right; he probably wouldn't appreciate chocolate stains around my mouth either, I decided sadly, going for some popcorn, which might be more elegant, but didn't do a great deal for satisfying the appetite. In the event, I could have had two hot dogs, followed by a Polo chaser for the sake of the breath, as he was so late he only slipped into the seat between us five minutes after the film had begun. We were in the middle of the row too. The couple in the seats behind us were not pleased, even less so when Luke began whispering apologies, claiming problems with traffic and parking. A ham-like hand was placed on his shoulder with a muttered imprecation that he'd have a

217

good few more bleeding problems if he didn't shut his gob now. Luke stopped talking.

I'm sure that the film was very good, I could hear Rose chuckling in several places and sniffing in others, an even greater compliment, though Luke seemed fairly unmoved. Perhaps he'd discovered he didn't fancy Meg Ryan as much as he'd thought he did. The cinema was overheated and stuffy and I had a disconcerting desire to go to sleep. I'd have given in and taken the opportunity to have a quick cuddle by using Luke's shoulder as a pillow if he hadn't been on my left side – I didn't want to lean on my bad arm. It was already aching dully in a way that was making me feel a bit queasy and I was longing to fish around on the floor for my handbag and get my pills out, but given the irascible temperament of the man behind us I didn't dare in case I rattled the bottle and drew down a rain of curses on my head. It wasn't until the music was playing over the credits at the end that I was at last able to grab a couple of my lovely pink pills, but by then it was too late. I hadn't been able to concentrate on the film and, worse, for I could always see the film on video eventually, because I'd stupidly bogged up the seating arrangements I hadn't been able to concentrate on the pleasure of having Luke so close to me for an hour and forty minutes in the dark either.

'Oh, wasn't that super?' said Rose with shining eyes as she stood up. 'That last scene, I thought they were never going to find each other. I felt my heart was going to stop with tension when he got caught in the traffic jam, didn't you, Luke?'

'Er, yes, it was very good,' he said.

She didn't notice the lack of total enthusiasm. 'I could watch it all over again, just to see that last bit. I really could.'

I looked at her in slight alarm, afraid that she might really suggest we see it through again. Luke must have had the same thought, for he said hastily, 'It's Friday night, there won't be any tickets left.'

'You're right,' she said equably. 'Let's go around the corner and have a drink. You're on for one, aren't you, Luke?' She looked at me and winked in a ludicrously suggestive fashion. 'I know Susie is.'

Susie wasn't, as a matter of fact. She was far too bloody tired and not even the thought of seeing Luke for the next hour or so could stop me from thinking I'd far rather be in bed, and given the way I was feeling, be alone too. But there are certain rules between friends, and not being a complete party pooper is one of them, so I smiled, hoping she'd notice it was a bit wanly, and said a drink would be lovely. I also hoped she'd notice the emphasis on the singular.

I could see why Rose liked the cocktail bar. It exuded chic, money and the latest style consultant, who had evidently thought long and hard before deciding on a designer fantasy of a Tokyo bar. Sliding paper screens hid the customers from the hoi polloi passing by in the street outside, tatami mats covered the floors, and low cream-covered squares cunningly imitating futons were grouped around almost floor-level black-lacquer tables. Anybody with rheumatism was going to have the devil of a job standing up again, except that presumably if you were old enough to have rheumatism you were too old to go to a joint like this. Even the staff were dressed in black kung-fu outfits. I was quite surprised to see that they hadn't carried the Japanese theme to the limit by insisting everyone take off their shoes and put on slippers. Needless to say, the place was packed and there were a few hopeful people hanging around the edges waiting for the opportunity to sit down. 'Look! Those women in the corner are just picking up their handbags. They must be getting ready to go,' exclaimed

Rose, who has an excellent eye for these things. 'Quick, Luke! Do a dirty dash and get that table, before those men over there!'

Luke displayed impressive speed and technique, reaching the table just in front of four hooray Henries, who stopped, looking non-plussed and bolshy. One of them began to protest and Luke said something, indicating my arm. The man turned around, looked at me sceptically – unfortunately I'd left the sling at home – then sighed heavily, evidently giving the table up for lost, and stumped off grumpily with his friends to perch on stools by the bar. 'Luke's always been good at whipping tables away from people who think they have a right to them,' said Rose in a pleased voice as we began to weave around the tables towards him. 'Hey!' she whispered excitedly, stopping and nudging me hard. 'Look! Over there. It's Hamish! With a woman. Who do you think she is? A colleague from work or his girlfriend?'

I shushed her, afraid that her carrying voice would carry even over the buzz of conversation, and glanced over to where she was pointing. Hamish, long legs slanted sideways to fit them in the limited space, was sitting next to a dark-haired woman wearing what looked to me very like a Chanel suit. It had that something about it that said it was no high-street copy. He was leaning towards her, saying something in her ear, leaning his weight on a hand that was virtually on her knee. She'd bent her head to listen, so all we could see was a fall of impeccably cut hair, so glossy it looked as if it had been French polished.

'I must find out who she is!' whispered Rose. 'So much for Jeremy saying Hamish's love life was on the flat side at the moment. Not with that one around it isn't!' And before I could stop her she had bounded across saying loudly, 'Hello,

Hamish! Fancy seeing you here. Have you been to the cinema as well?'

He raised his head, his smile taking just a bit too long to replace the faint frown of displeasure between his eyebrows. 'Rose, Susie,' he said evenly. 'How nice to see you both.' His eyes said he didn't mean a word of it. 'You must be feeling a lot better, Susie, if you're up to braving Leicester on a Friday night.'

'I am, thank you,' I said. There was a little silence and I was all for turning around and shooting off to our corner as quickly as possible but Rose was standing her ground, staring at him meaningfully.

When he didn't respond she smiled brilliantly at the woman. 'Hello, I'm Rose Ashton, my husband is a great friend of Hamish's, and this is Susie Gardener.'

A faint shadow of resignation passed over Hamish's face. 'This is Merial Carstairs,' he said, indicating his companion and, displaying what I was beginning to recognise as a particularly annoying trait of his, not giving any clue as to who she actually was. Well, it was easy enough to guess. I'm certainly not sexist enough to say that solicitors can't look like Merial, but that suit was altogether too stylish and in the mode for a member of the legal profession. I expect her skirt length would be a severe danger to the blood-pressure levels of the judiciary as well. And the way Hamish had been eyeing her certainly didn't indicate she was some sort of impersonal colleague. And who could blame him? I thought dully, finding that I suddenly felt scruffy and unattractive in comparison. The only way to describe her was drop-dead gorgeous. I felt an overpowering need to find she had even one fault, but it didn't seem as if she'd got any, except that perhaps her mouth was too big. And that's dead sexy. She had huge, liquid brown eyes, a flawless complexion, and the sort of beautifully cut blunt bob that will always fall back into place, no matter how much of a gale blows it about. Natural justice would say that somebody with so perfect a face, and loads of money, judging by the suit and hair, should have a size-ten top and a size-fourteen bottom – after all she was one of the few people who could pay for the expert dressing to conceal it – but I just knew somehow that both halves matched perfectly.

'Nice to meet you both,' she said, flashing us a smile (perfect teeth too, life really isn't fair) and glancing quickly at Hamish with a rueful expression. Oh God, they thought they were going to have to invite us to join them, I thought in dismay, and tugging Rose's arm said vaguely we must get to our table before Luke began to think we'd gone home without him.

Hamish looked at me quizzically. 'You're trusting yourself to Luke's driving so soon? That shows admirable faith.'

I could feel myself blushing stupidly. 'Rose drove me,' I said quickly. 'She thought a night out would do me good.'

'I hope it will,' he said politely. Even Rose, who was being more than usually thick-skinned in her determination to discover what Hamish was doing with Merial, had to take the hint after that and allowed me to take her away quite meekly. The subject occupied her for some time afterwards, rather to the irritation of Luke, I thought, who not unreasonably didn't have very much interest in whether Hamish had found himself a new woman, no matter how good-looking. Rose shut up for long enough to order our drinks from a very supercilious waiter and then launched into one of those interminable arguments where neither party is prepared to concede a single point. This one was about the future of the countryside; Luke accusing Rose of wanting to keep rural areas like some gigantic theme park, Rose claiming he was the type who let big business do what it wanted in the interests of short-term profit and hang the long-term consequences. I'd have found all of this a lot more interesting if I hadn't heard Rose on this particular hobby-horse not long ago, on the way into Leicester in fact, so I sat back in my corner and tuned out, idly watching Hamish and Merial over on the other side of the room, who seemed to be getting on very well, and sipping abstractedly at some fruit confection Rose had selected for me. I hadn't realised Hamish had such an attractive smile once he dropped the slightly guarded reserve he wore like a coat, I thought, as he laughed at something Merial had said. In fact, looking at him dispassionately, he was all-round rather attractive. Merial certainly seemed to think so, judging from her body language. She leant towards him and touched his knee to emphasise a point. I swung my eyes away abruptly, taking a long swig from my tall glass. It was very nice. Too nice, actually.

'What's this got in it?' I asked suspiciously, looking up at Rose and breaking into an impassioned declaration about the effects of agribusiness or something or other. 'It doesn't taste teetotal to me.'

She looked at me under lowered lashes, ready to brazen it out, then something in my face must have made her change her mind. She shrugged guiltily. 'I didn't think one drink would do you any harm.'

'But I told you that the doctor said –' I began.

'You know how overcautious those doctors are,' she interrupted. 'If they had their way you wouldn't be allowed to have a drink for a month after you'd taken an aspirin because of possible side-effects. It's not as if you're going to be driving or operating heavy machinery, is it? So what do you have to worry about?' She paused for a moment and, seeing that I still looked annoyed, added placatingly, 'You said your arm was

223

hurting and alcohol's a great painkiller.'

Luke leant forward, 'She's right. My mother used to put brandy on a piece of cotton wool when we had toothache as children and it was brilliant. Worked every time.'

'Things have moved on a bit since then. I find that the pills I've just taken are rather more effective,' I muttered through gritted teeth. Rose looked hurt, as if she was afraid I was about to accuse her of ruining my evening. Perhaps I was being a bit too much of a goody-goody. A little bit of alcohol wouldn't harm me. It wasn't as if I was downing half a bottle, merely a measure diluted with a goodly quantity of fruit juice, which meant lots of vitamin C and that had to be good for me. And the ache in my arm was lessening and I was beginning to feel pleasantly relaxed. I smiled. 'Well, don't do it again, understood?'

She nodded meekly and turned back to Luke, apparently picking up in mid-sentence from where I'd interrupted her in the middle of a spirited denunciation of out-of-town superstores. I felt rather narked about the way she was monopolising Luke, but since changing the subject, or even talking at all, would use up far more energy than I had, I couldn't be bothered to get cross. Instead, I relaxed in my comfortable seat, deciding philosophically that even if I did have precious little chance of holding Rose to her promise to leave after one drink, at least watching Hamish and his girlfriend was a damn sight more interesting than watching the walls at home. It was this mood of unusual resignation that led me to weakly agree that perhaps a second of those cocktails wouldn't do me any harm, or perhaps that had been why Dr Bob warned me not to drink with the little pink pills. It had nothing to do with the possibility that I might be trying my hand at driving an HGV and everything to do with the combination of booze and pills putting your common sense through the shredder.

I paid for it, of course I did. I woke up the next morning with a fuzzy mouth and that feeling that tells you it might be unwise to move your head too quickly. I lay there with my eyes shut, wondering if I was going to be greeted with a blast of pain if I opened them or if it was just troubled conscience operating. How could I have been so stupid? Wasn't I already in enough pain from my bashed arm and shoulder to satisfy the average martyr without adding a hangover to it as well? How much had I drunk? I only had the vaguest memories of travelling home, some of them seemed to have a distinctly dream-like quality about them, and I certainly couldn't remember coming in the front door. I was still half dressed too. You've got to have been seriously plastered not to have had the coordination to take your bra off. At least I'd made it into bed. I shifted slightly, experimenting to see how much it hurt, and was relieved to note that apparently I didn't have a headache after all. I contemplated going back to sleep and wriggled to a cool spot on the pillow, my cheek brushing an embroidered trim around the edge of the pillowcase. All desire to sleep fled like the wind. My pillowcases have a frilled edge, not a trim.

Not daring to open my eyes, I patted the edge of the case to make sure. There was a thin line of braid under my fingertips. I wasn't in my own bed. My heart seemed to miss several beats, then started up again. Of course, Rose must have decided I needed more TLC and had taken me back to Moor End last night, she'd been banging on about how I shouldn't be on my own. That was it. I moved to get more comfortable, burying my nose in the pillow, and my heart did another unpleasant lurch. This didn't *smell* like the bed I'd slept in at Moor End. That had a vague smell of lavender pot-pourri and linen sheets

225

about it. This pillow had another scent, intangible, not unpleasant at all, rather nice actually, but definitely not feminine. Masculine, in fact. Oh God.

I opened my eyes very, very slowly. I closed them again rapidly, my heart plummeting down to my toes. I'd been right. It wasn't my pillow. It wasn't my bed either. I don't have striped sheets. But neither was it any room at Moor End Hall I'd ever seen.

Where the hell was I?

CHAPTER 12

I was paralysed with horror. I've done various things in my life which I don't like to think about too closely, which by any standards must rank as being staggeringly stupid, but never, *ever* before had I not known where I was when I woke up. Or not known exactly what I'd been doing to get there either. Well, that's pretty obvious, I told myself in dismay, you went home with Luke. It had to be him. Well, I hoped it was. My whole body shuddered at the thought I might have gone to bed with someone, anyone, while I was too drunk to know what I was doing, but at least I *knew* Luke.

At least, I was still in my underwear, I thought in relief, patting myself to make sure that I hadn't imagined both bra and pants were still safely in place. That was something, unless in some excess of modesty I'd put them back on again afterwards. Oh, bloody hell, why couldn't I *remember*? I thought in desperation. I froze at a noise, Oh God, was he still here in the bed with me? Very slowly, I turned on my back and with my eyes tightly shut inched my hand over the sheet, anticipating with a thumping heart the moment the tips of my fingers brushed against bare, warm flesh.

My stomach churned with relief as my searching hand fell over the edge of the bed into space without meeting anything. I dared open my eyes and looked around cautiously. Enough light came in through a gap in the curtains at the window for me to see that I was in a large bed with a basketwork headboard in a square, sparsely furnished bedroom. But whose bed? Whose bedroom? I sat up slightly, looking around for clues. A pair of formal black shoes had been kicked off in a corner, a pale-blue shirt with a button-down collar was draped casually over the back of a chair and, most telling of all, a shaver was being recharged from a power point by the door. Good deduction, Susie, I told myself, heart beating with unpleasant anticipation, so it's a man's bedroom, and one which he appears to sleep in, so you can't fool yourself that you're respectably encased in a spare room which you've dossed down in for some reason. But *which* man does it belong to? Unfortunately, he hadn't been considerate enough to leave his cheque book or a handy letter by the bed so I could check his name.

I eased myself out of bed, feeling as stiff as if I were a hundred and ten, but I definitely wasn't suffering from the mother and father of all hangovers. Surely I should be if I'd drunk so much last night I had virtually no recollection of anything past the second cocktail arriving? I shook my head from side to side to test for ill effects and the only thing that happened was I felt a bit fuzzy. Even my arm and shoulder felt infinitely better than they had last night. How very curious, I thought. My skirt and top from last night were lying on a chair. I eyed them askance, my heart doing that nasty little skip again. I'd never have put them away that neatly. Well, at least I could get dressed, I'd worry about how they came to get off me later. I felt very vulnerable in bra and pants and I was hardly in the traditional position of most girls who overnight like this and can swipe their host's dressing-gown. You ought to know who it is that you've slept with before you start borrowing his things.

I nipped into my clothes at the speed of lightning, he might hear me moving about and come upstairs, though it was a bit late to worry about the mystery man seeing me in my underwear. It wasn't even my best bra either, though at least it wasn't the one with the tear in the lace in a rather provocative place. If I was brave, the sort of person who faced up unflinchingly to the consequences of her actions, I'd go straight out of that door and discover whom it was I'd gone home with last night. I mean there couldn't be any doubt any longer that I'd gone off with someone, could there? But, being an absolute coward who procrastinates whenever possible, I decided it would be helpful to gather some information about him by casing the joint a bit first. Besides, there was no way I was going to meet Mr Mysterious with panda eyes from sleeping in my mascara, unbrushed hair fanning out like the proverbial burning bush, and a mouth full of night breath. Presumably it was for Luke I was trying to repair the ravages of a night spent in make-up, I thought tiredly as I scrubbed away at mascara streaks with only the aid of a wad of loo paper and some water in the little bathroom that led off the bedroom. Except that the aftershave sitting on top of the bathroom cabinet didn't smell like the musky one Luke used. This one was nice, I thought, taking another sniff, and seemed familiar, but I couldn't place it. Mr Mysterious didn't run to much in the way of male cosmetics and didn't appear to have a girlfriend who left useful things like make-up remover and moisturiser in his cabinet either, but I helped myself liberally to his deodorant and cleaned my teeth with his toothpaste and my finger. It was more effective than I thought it would be.

I'd spent as long as I could with the limited materials at my disposal, and all things told hadn't done too bad a job at all, I thought, examining my reflection critically. This situation was bad enough without feeling I looked like the interior of the cat's basket. I emerged to explore the bedroom, which wasn't going to take very long as it didn't have much furniture in it – a couple of chairs, an oak chest of drawers and the bed. It was a very big bed too, I thought, eyeing it and wondering nervously what had gone on in it last night. I shuddered as I realised I'd no doubt find out for sure quite soon.

I padded over to the window and pulled back the curtains to let in some more light, and looked out on to a short drive and a quiet road fringed by tall clumps of cow parsley. In other circumstances I would have thought how pretty it was, now it just seemed worryingly isolated. I must have absorbed more of estate agency than I'd realised, for instead of instantly riffling through his drawers I stood admiring the moulding around the ceiling and the panelling in the door, thinking that it might be a bit down at heel, but it was going to be lovely if Mr Mysterious ever got round to doing it up. That reminded me, I looked around for clues, but the room was disappointingly bare of personal possessions, no photographs, no bits and pieces, not even a bookcase, though there was an untidy heap of books stacked on the floor by the bed. As I balked at actually going through his sock drawer, I was walking around to examine the books to see what he read, when I saw a picture hanging above the marble fireplace. It was of a hilly landscape, painted with a wonderful use of colour and a freedom of line that made it look slightly unreal, yet instantly recognisable, as if it came from a half-remembered but familiar dream. There was another picture by the same artist hanging on the opposite wall, this time of a lake in winter, with graceful trees around it bowing down under the weight of ice and snow. Whoever Mr M. was, he had good taste in his pictures, I thought, trying to find consolation in the fact I had been picked up by an art lover. I didn't.

The noise of a door closing downstairs made me jump and realise sickeningly that even I couldn't procrastinate any further.

I tiptoed over to the door and eased it open, half afraid of what I was going to see. It was a reassuringly normal scene. Sunlight slanted in through a sash window on to a small landing which judging from the experimental blocks of paint on the wall opposite, was next in line for repainting; a broad staircase with nicely carved banisters curved away to the lower floor from where I could hear the distant sounds of a radio drifting up. And smell coffee. My stomach lurched with need for a caffeine shot.

Heart thumping horribly, I reluctantly shuffled down the stairs, one at a time, to a small hall with a black-and-white chequered floor and, following my nose and ears, went quietly down to the door at the end. I stood with my hand on the knob for a few seconds, almost too afraid of what I might find to push it open, then, taking a deep breath, turned it and stepped in.

It was a long kitchen, crossing the width of the house, which though, at a guess, had last been modernised some forty years ago was still immensely attractive, with windows on two sides looking out on a slightly scruffy garden, and a wide pair of French windows opening on to a little paved terrace. A large battered table took up the middle of the room and someone was sitting on the other side of it, face completely hidden by a large newspaper, a pair of bare feet stretched out comfortably to one side. The door slipped from my fingers and crashed to. He jumped, swore, and dropped the paper on the table.

'Morning, Susie. Sorry, I didn't hear you come in,' he said, looking up and smiling. 'I didn't realise that you'd woken up. I expect you'd like a cup of coffee? Or you can have tea if you'd rather.'

It was so normal that for a moment I couldn't take it all in. Scattered all over the table was the paraphernalia of a leisurely weekend breakfast – mug, crumb-covered plate, marmalade, a couple of sections of the paper, already read and folded none too tidily, shoved to one side – the sort of sight familiar in my own kitchen. Except that I didn't normally have Hamish, unshaven and wearing an elderly San Francisco 49ers tee shirt and faded black jeans, stretching his legs out behind my table. Suddenly, feeling distinctly wobbly in the knee area, I pulled out a chair and almost fell into it. My first reaction had been a blazing sense of relief that it wasn't Luke behind the newspaper, the second, following instantly on its heels – What the hell had I done? Had I really just spent the night with *Hamish*? Surely, judging from the way he'd been talking to Merial, if he'd been making any arrangements of that sort they wouldn't have included me, I thought in bewilderment.

He looked at me questioningly. I realised that he expected an answer. 'Coffee'd be lovely, thank you,' I said faintly, mind buzzing with questions and not knowing how to frame a single one. I stared at his back as he got up to fetch a mug from the draining rack, noticing how tall he was. Surely, no matter how drunk I'd been, I should have remembered *something* about going to bed with someone that big? I thought miserably. I swallowed hard. 'Hamish.'

'Yes?' he asked, sitting down and pushing the full mug over to me.

Hell, didn't he *know* what I wanted to ask him? I thought resentfully, my annoyance giving me the courage to frame the question. I cupped my hands around the mug, as if the warmth could give me a bit of extra much-needed bottle. 'Er, what went on last night? I mean, what was I *doing* in your bed?' I asked in a rush. 'It *is* yours, isn't it?' I added nervously.

His eyes flew open. 'Of course!' Then he stared at me in amazement. 'Don't you remember anything about last night at all?'

I eyed him suspiciously. I didn't appreciate the note of sympathy in his voice. What on earth had I *done*? 'Well . . .' I thought hard for a moment, then admitted, 'Rose and Luke were comparing ski resorts. I don't ski, so I sort of tuned out.'

'Don't blame you for that,' he said with a faint smile.

'The next thing I knew for certain was waking up here,' I said, trying to keep my voice even and not let him see how worried I was. I thought I did have one or two memories of last night, or they could be dreams. I hoped to God they were dreams.

He reached out and patted my hand. 'Poor Susie. And you've been imagining rape, pillage and worse. Don't worry, it didn't happen,' he said reassuringly. Except that drunken advances were neither rape nor pillage, and, being a man, he probably wouldn't count them as 'worse' either, I thought in despair. 'It's quite simple, you went to sleep.'

'You mean I passed out,' I said. God, what must he think of me? One and a half cocktails and she's anybody's. Cheap or what?

'I suppose you could call it that,' he admitted. 'Those painkillers of yours don't react well with booze. In fact, in conjunction with alcohol they're complete knock-out drops. That's why the bottle has that large label saying, "Do not drink alcohol while taking this medication" in big red letters on it.'

'I didn't think one drink would do any harm,' I said in a small voice, resolving to obey the doctor's every last instruction in future. And the dentist's too, I vowed in sudden remorse. I'd even go for a check-up every six months.

'It does with those,' he said. 'I should know.' I stared at him in surprise and he smiled ruefully. 'Me too,' he confirmed, 'though I was in my own flat. I woke up halfway through the next afternoon, so really you haven't done too badly. You're up by –' he looked at a severely plain watch on his wrist – 'ten-thirty. Positively crack of dawn, considering.'

I wasn't in a mood to be comforted. 'But I should have had the sense not to drink on an empty stomach anyway, let alone when I'd only just had a couple of those pills,' I said gloomily, determined on self-flagellation. I stared miserably into my coffee, feeling an utter, total, bloody fool. 'God, how stupid of me!'

'You're a loyal friend, aren't you?' he said after a moment. I lifted my head to look at him, puzzled. 'Rose was so petrified when she couldn't wake you up properly she admitted she didn't tell you the drink was alcoholic when she ordered it for you. She thought she'd poisoned you or something. She's the one who needs her head examined!' he said savagely.

'But I finished it,' I said, surprised at the venom in his tone.

'You wouldn't have *started* it if it hadn't been for her,' he said coldly. 'Though I will give her she was quite up-front about what she'd done. You were half awake, obviously not in a coma, and you hadn't drunk very much, so we thought you could go home to sleep it off.'

'So what happened?' I demanded.

Hamish shrugged. 'Rose didn't think she could manage to get you home on her own –' his eyes slid towards me – 'Luke said he had to be at his house for an important telephone call.'

His voice made it quite clear that he didn't think this was much of an excuse. Neither did I. Hadn't Luke got an answerphone? 'I offered to follow her and help, but she was running late and had promised Jeremy she'd be back by midnight at the latest, so we decided that I'd be the one to take you back. Except once in the car you fell absolutely sound asleep. I had to stop to get you off my shoulder, you were stopping me from changing gear, and I knew the chances were I was going to end up having to carry you across the green from the car.' He smiled at me. 'Without being rude, Susie, I didn't fancy it much. It's one hell of a long way.'

'And I weigh a ton,' I interrupted, thinking he probably would have been quite happy to carry the diminutive Merial the whole distance. What had happened to her, by the way?

'Do you?' he asked, looking at me with interest, as if I was one of those 'Guess the weight of the piglet' competitions. 'You must have heavy bones for you don't look it.' I barely had time for this to sink in before he said, 'But even if I'd been able to wake you up enough to get you to walk, it wouldn't have done your reputation any good to be seen staggering across the green at midnight in the arms of a man. There's no way that I could have got you in last night without that old bag in the end cottage finding out. She's on permanent net-curtain alert, and it'd have been all round the village by now that you're a loose drunk who has to be rolled home by her fancy man.'

'I don't think she'd have put it in quite those terms, she likes me,' I said doubtfully.

'I doubt she likes you more than the opportunity to tell a good story!' he said dryly. 'On the other hand, it's only five feet from car to front door here and one of the unfairnesses of the double standard is that even if one of the neighbours did see me taking an attractive redhead home at midnight it'd only add to *my* reputation, so it didn't seem as if there was any contest. You woke up as I was getting you out of the car and seemed quite happy to spend the night in the spare room. Don't you remember?'

I shook my head. 'But I didn't spend the night in the spare room,' I pointed out.

He shrugged as if it was of no importance. 'I got you upstairs and remembered the spare-room bed was covered with rubbish, so rather than leave you propped up against the wall I laid you down on my bed. And then it seemed too much effort to wake you up again, so I left you there.' He smiled reassuringly at me. 'So there you are. End of story. Nothing to it.'

I wasn't as comforted as I might have been. It wasn't the end of the story. How come my clothes had ended up on the chair? And where had he spent the night himself? 'Um, er . . .' To my fury I could feel a blush heating up my cheeks. I stared down at the red Formica tabletop desperately. 'Did we *do* anything?' I blurted out.

'Of course not,' he said promptly, with a note of faint hauteur in his voice. 'I can promise you I don't jump on comatose women.'

I looked up, seeing that he really seemed quite annoyed. On reflection, it was rather insulting to imply he was so desperate for a leg-over he had to fumble someone who was fast asleep. 'I'm sorry, I didn't mean to suggest you did, but I was more worried about myself . . .' There were those dreams. The ones about having my arms around someone's neck. And the ones that went a lot further than necks. And if I'd been harbouring any illusions about my bad arm being some sort of guarantor of chastity a surreptitious waggle of it knocked that one right on the head. It might not be in perfect condition, but it was perfectly fit for a bit of rolling around in bed . . . That wretched blush was intensifying. 'I thought perhaps I'd woken up slightly and come on to you . . .' My voice trailed away in hideous embarrassment. The worst part about it was the realisation that with Merial hanging on his sleeve he would have been completely uninterested in any lures I might hold out, drunk or sober.

To my relief, his frowning displeasure had been replaced by amusement. 'Susie, you were so out of it last night that anyone attracted to you would have to have been seriously into necrophilia. I can assure you that's never been one of my vices! You didn't make any improper advances to me either, you were far too fast asleep.' Oh, thank God! I felt breathless with relief. 'More's the pity!' he added regretfully. I glanced up to see his eyes gleaming with mockery. Well, of course he hadn't meant it. 'You'd even managed to struggle out of your top and skirt on your own so I didn't even get the usual hero's perks of being able to remove the lady's clothing,' he went on in the same light tone.

I glanced at him suspiciously, not entirely sure if he was telling the unvarnished truth, then decided that even if he had had to help me he wouldn't have laid more than the most reluctant finger on me if he'd accidentally touched me while easing my top off.

'Thank you for all you did,' I said in a small voice. 'I'm sorry to have been such a nuisance.'

He shrugged. 'What are friends for?' Oh well, it was nice to know that despite my stupidity I'd been raised to the ranks of his friends. I hadn't thought he liked me enough to regard me as a friend, I thought, with a surprising degree of pleasure. He rubbed the back of his neck ruefully. 'And one good thing's come out of it. I now understand why my parents were so willing to let me have the bed in the spare room. I'm going to have to get a new one before anyone can stay.'

'You slept in the spare room?' I said before I could help myself.

'Of course. It would have given you the fright of your life if you'd woken up and seen my head on the pillow next to you,' he said with complete accuracy. 'Besides, there wasn't room for me. You were lying across the mattress, taking up about three-quarters of it. Do you always hog the bed like that?' he asked in a tone of mild interest.

He was about to ask me if I usually snored as well, I thought, sending him a meaningful glare and daring him to do just that. At least indignation had banished embarrassment. He laughed and, standing up, asked me if I'd like any breakfast, thereby restoring himself to my good books. My stomach was just getting to the point where it was going to start rumbling embarrassingly. He started rustling around the kitchen in an impressively competent manner, doing the sorts of things that my brothers never remember to do, like putting the plates to heat up and actually knowing where the kitchen scissors were when he wanted to snip the bacon rind off. It was even more impressive that he didn't appear to expect me to make any contribution, telling me to sit down and take a look at the paper if I wanted, while he set to work at the stove, producing a vast quantity of eggs and bacon. 'I couldn't possibly eat that much,' I protested, wondering if he saw me as the sort of person who went in for pie-eating contests.

He looked over his shoulder and smiled. 'Don't think you're going to get it all! I'm having some too.' Even so, the plate that was put in front of me would have satisfied the appetite of the average navvy. Hamish's was even more heavily loaded, and he added several pieces of toast to it as well.

'Do you eat a breakfast of this size every morning?' I asked, once I'd satisfied the first, most pressing hunger pangs. Surely even someone with his rangy frame couldn't manage a constant diet like this without getting fat.

He shook his head. 'Like you, I didn't get any dinner last night. We were working late and Merial had already eaten at the hospital, so I didn't bother.'

'She's a doctor?'

'A consultant at the General,' he said, as he speared his last piece of bacon.

And someone who must do a lot of private work if she could afford clothes like that, I thought, finding suddenly I didn't approve of doctors who worked outside the NHS. Especially when they're that beautiful. 'Is Merial working with you on something?' I asked casually, eyes fixed on a piece of bread I was using to mop up some egg yolk.

'She's helping with a possible medical-negligence case, which isn't really my area. I can't even pronounce half the names, let alone understand what the condition is supposed to be,' he said. So she was just a colleague, I thought, then realised that you don't normally sit thigh to thigh in cocktail bars with colleagues. My first impressions had been the right ones.

'Have you been living here long?' I asked.

He looked slightly surprised at the abrupt change of subject. 'Only a couple of months, I haven't even unpacked most of my stuff yet. As you can see, it's got what Stephen would call a lot of potential. Bags of it in fact, enough to keep you busy at B & Q for years. But since I'm not your natural DIY type the work is going slowly, very slowly,' he said, with a wry twist to his mouth. 'But it's got a good garden and at least the doorways are high enough for me to get through them without banging my head, which is more than I can say for a lot of the places around here!'

I could see Hamish would have problems living somewhere like my cottage. The church swear-box would be making an absolute packet. 'It's going to be fantastic,' I said, looking down the long kitchen, thinking that I wouldn't mind having a kitchen big enough for me to get round the table without brushing against the units. Though perhaps the answer to my situation was a diet. Then it occurred to me I'd delivered a somewhat backhanded compliment, so I added hastily, 'It's lovely already, it's got such good proportions.'

Hamish smiled at me somewhat cynically. 'You don't have to fall over yourself to be polite. You should hear what my mother says about it! It's one stage above a dump, the best you can say is that it's thoroughly tatty because no one's touched it for fifty years.' Mercifully, he didn't look in the least bit offended and offered me another piece of toast.

I contemplated it then, remembering the circuit around the kitchen table in the cottage, declined. I leant forward, saying honestly, 'I think the house is super, really, but what I really covet are those two paintings in your bedroom. They're absolutely fantastic. In fact, if you ever find them gone you know where they'll be.'

'Keep your sticky fingers off them!' he warned, smiling. 'I like them too. But Gina'll be pleased to hear she's got a fan. Being a typically neurotic artist, she's always needing her ego massaged.'

I stared at him. 'You know her?'

He nodded. 'She's my sister, and before you ask, no I don't have any of her talent. She's a complete one-off, the rest of the family are hard put to draw a recognisable gibbet when playing hangman, let alone do the hanged man himself. It's the sort of

240

completely unexpected gift that leads people to count backwards on their fingers to when the mother last went to the Summer Exhibition. Luckily for Ma's reputation, Gina looks remarkably like my father.'

'I'm going to put one of her pictures right at the top of my list of must-haves for when I win the lottery,' I said dreamily, leaning my chin on my hand. 'I'd like to have one hanging opposite my bed so I could see it when I went to sleep every night.'

'They're very restful,' he agreed. 'But I doubt you'll have to wait until you win the lottery. I don't know exactly how much Gina charges these days, but I don't think she's that expensive.'

I had a feeling that there was probably a wide gap between what Hamish and I classified as 'expensive', therefore what he probably meant was her prices hadn't yet reached stratospheric levels. 'You could always ask her and see,' he suggested.

There wasn't much point; given the current state of my bank account, unless she was giving them away, I still wouldn't be able to afford one of her pictures. However, it's embarrassing to go into details like that, so I nodded and said, 'I will if you give me her telephone number.'

'Better than that, I'll take you to see her. She doesn't live much more than an hour's drive away and then you can have a look at her studio too. She loves showing it to an appreciative audience.'

'Oh, thank you,' I said vaguely, thinking it was one of those meaningless things people say and never intend to carry out. 'I'd like that.'

'Good,' he said, holding up the coffee pot, and when I shook my head emptied it into his mug. 'Rose said your plans for the weekend had been cancelled because of your accident. If you aren't doing anything else, shall we go today?'

'Today?' I squeaked. 'But I don't want to put you out . . .'

'You wouldn't be,' he said bluntly. 'I ought to go and see her anyway, I owe her a birthday present which has been sitting on the hall table for three weeks now. And she's not going to expect you to buy anything, so you don't have to make excuses about running out of cheques.'

That was an uncomfortably accurate observation. I hesitated, thinking I'd really like to go, but since I'd just seemed, amazingly enough, to have established some form of friendship with Hamish, I didn't want to bog it up right at the start by outstaying my welcome.

I stammered, 'You've already done so much for me . . .'

'I've offered a bed for the night and breakfast to loads of people before, so don't make a big deal of it.'

'Except that I'm sure you haven't offered house room to loads of drunks before!' I said tartly.

'You'd be surprised!' he retorted, grinning at me. 'Law students behave just as badly as medical students, I'll have you know.' Having gone out with a medical student for a while during my first year at university, I found it difficult to believe. 'Besides, you weren't drunk,' he said firmly, 'so do stop going on about it. Now, are you going to come with me to see Gina and Tony? You'd be doing me a favour, honestly. Artists are supposed to be selfish, sacrificing everyone and everything for the sake of their art, but not our Gina. Unfortunately. She likes to paint with one hand and sort out the problems of the world with the other.' He made a face. 'And at the moment she reckons her biggest problem is me. She's one of those mother hens who doesn't believe men can live on their own without either suffering from malnutrition due to a diet of baked beans and beer or being suffocated in a mountain of unwashed socks.'

242

'Sounds just like my younger brother's flat,' I said, thinking of the last time I'd dared to visit.

'She should know better with me. I don't even like baked beans very much. And I'm her *older* brother too,' he said with emphasis. 'But if you come with me she won't feel able to grill me about the contents of the laundry basket and whether I'm airing the sheets properly. And she'll enjoy meeting you, she knows Stephen too and she's very hospitable, loves visitors, especially the ones who have the taste to like her paintings. So please.'

He smiled pleadingly at me, eyes crinkling up at the corners, the unshaven, tousle-headed creature leaning back lazily in his chair a very different animal to the formally attired solicitor I was most familiar with. For a moment, I forgot he was inveigling me into protecting him from an over-motherly sister and imagined he was smiling at me just because he liked what he saw on the other side of the table. My stomach did an involuntary lurch and I dropped my eyes quickly, before I could betray that at that moment I was definitely enjoying what was on the other side of the table.

God, what's happening to me? I thought. Didn't I have enough to occupy myself, fancying both Luke and Arnaud at the same time, without adding a third to the list? I was becoming positively *rampant*. It must be because I'd slept in Hamish's bed last night, I must have absorbed some of his pheromones or something which made me more attuned to him. It'd wear off. It would have worn off by now, I decided firmly, daring to look up. He was still looking disturbingly unstuffy, but I couldn't fool myself his smile was anything more than a polite enquiry as to whether I was going to fall in with his plans or not. I suppressed a pang of disappointment.

'Put like that, how could I refuse?' I asked lightly. At least

243

he looked genuinely pleased I was coming. 'But could I go back to the cottage to change first?'

'Of course,' he said, and stretched. 'I'll go and ring Gina, tell her we're coming, and then we can leave.'

I stared at his bristly chin. 'Excuse me for pointing this out, but won't going unshaven count as Not Looking After Yourself?'

He rubbed it thoughtfully. 'Whatever happened to designer stubble?' he asked sighing. 'OK, make that we leave after a call and a shave.'

I only just had time to do my bit of stacking the dirty plates in the dishwasher and wiping the crumbs off the table before he returned, obviously someone who didn't believe in spending a lot of time on his appearance, but I already knew that from the paucity of male accoutrements in his bathroom. (Arnaud had shelves of bottles and potions in his bathroom. In fact, they overflowed on to the table in his bedroom and it always took him at least half an hour to go anywhere. I never minded, providing he let me have a bit of the mirror.) Hamish had achieved a lot in his five minutes; besides a speed-shave, he'd brushed his hair into something approaching order and had found some shoes and socks too. I wouldn't say he looked like someone who would bring joy into the heart of the average father – he was still way too far from his weekday respectability – but he probably wouldn't be refused entry to Harrods on account of breaking their dress code any longer.

I did my best to emulate his speed-changing, but with less success, even though I'd been given firm instructions that jeans were de rigueur in Gina's household due to the quantity of mud and animals. I was still given free choice about what to put on top and duly spent the requisite amount of time dithering. Hamish was deep in the second chapter of the Michael Dibdin I'd just bought by the time I came downstairs, feeling rather pleased with myself because I hadn't had the usual struggle to do up my jeans and my green shirt had slipped really easily into the waistband. 'You look nice,' he said, looking up with approval. 'That green suits your colouring.'

I felt quite ridiculously pleased at the compliment. I tucked a piece of hair behind my ear and said gruffly, 'Do you want to borrow that?'

'Thanks, I'll return it, I promise,' he said, standing up and immediately seeming to take up a large amount of the space in the room. Well, he did, his head nearly brushed the large centre beam. He tucked the book into the back pocket of his jeans. My jeans are never loose enough to put things in the pockets. 'You've brightened this place up a lot, it looks good. I can't say I go for all these greys and whites, even if they are the latest fashion,' he said, looking around. He picked up a photograph frame from the table. 'Who are these? Your parents? And this?'

'That's Arnaud,' I said.

He looked more closely at the picture. I'd taken it on my last visit to Paris, when we'd been having a drink at a pavement café. Arnaud was holding a glass in one hand, head lifted towards me. I'd called to him to look up just as he'd picked up his wine and he hadn't thought a mere photograph warranted delaying the first pre-lunch drink of the day, even if it was only by thirty seconds. It showed in his expression. I didn't like the photograph very much, but the only other recent picture I'd got of him was one taken for some office journal, in which he looked impossibly stuffed-shirtish and not at all the enthusiastic bon viveur I'd fallen for. 'Oh, the French boyfriend, the one Rose claims to dislike so much!' Hamish said thoughtfully. 'Mm, I can see why they might not get on. Not enough room centre stage for both of them.'

245

I looked at him, startled, and laughed reluctantly.

'What does he think of this place?'

'He hasn't seen it yet. I doubt he'll be impressed, country cottages aren't Arnaud's style.' I suppressed a rather disloyal thought that at least he'd be able to walk through the doors here without ducking, unlike Hamish. Rose's heightism must be catching. 'He's probably coming here next weekend though, so I'll find out.'

'Good God, you aren't intending to take someone like that to Rose's charity do, are you?' Hamish asked in surprise.

I too had balked slightly at the vision of the combination of Arnaud's Parisian chic and a fork supper when he'd rung to say he'd got appointments in London on Monday week so what about coming to see me on the Saturday before. 'I can't not. Rose has threatened me with disembowelling if I'm not there to sell raffle tickets.' I hadn't dared tell Arnaud about it yet, reckoning that, like injections, it would hurt less if he didn't know it was coming, especially as he'd informed me he'd checked his Michelin guide and though there weren't any starred restaurants locally he'd discovered one with a good reputation. 'He'll love going to the house though, and it'll give him a real insight into English country events, something to talk about when he goes back to Paris,' I said, hoping without expectation that this would be enough to make up for missing out on the subtle delicacies of Rushton Hall's dining room. 'Are you going as well?' I asked.

'I've been press-ganged into helping with the bar,' said Hamish, putting the photo frame back down again. 'I doubt there's anyone Rose knows locally who's being allowed to simply come to this thing in peace and enjoy themselves. I trust your Arnaud isn't going to be too sniffy about the wine.'

'Of course he will be,' I said, 'he is French, after all.'

CHAPTER 13

Hamish's sister was as pleased to see us and as unfazed to have two extra arriving for lunch as he had promised. She lived with her husband, an executive in a local firm, on the other side of Lincoln, in a redundant farmhouse that had once belonged to a small farm now swallowed up with about seven others in a three-thousand-acre grain prairie. It was a low red-brick building, built for serviceability rather than beauty, with an old brick barn to one side which had been converted into Gina's studio. She rushed out as soon as we drew up in the car, with a flaxen-haired toddler clinging limpet-like to one hip, and hugged Hamish enthusiastically, saying reproachfully it was far too long since she'd seen him and he'd lost weight, if he wasn't careful he'd get too thin. She then turned to me with a broad smile, surveying what her brother had brought to her house with frank interest and making me wonder uneasily if she'd got the wrong end of the stick about why I was here. She bore a distinct resemblance to him, being tall with the same rich-brown hair and heavily lidded eyes, though luckily for her she didn't have his craggy nose or his big bones. But she still didn't fit into the romantic ethereal ideal of what an artist should look like at all.

'How nice to meet you, Susie, I've heard all about you,' she said warmly. You have? I thought, shooting a quick look at

Hamish. His resigned expression said this was a mere fishing expedition. 'But look, we mustn't stand out here, it might be nearly summer but this wind is perishing,' she said, ushering us into a mercifully warm hallway. I had it on good authority that the wind which had been whistling around us outside came straight from the Russian Steppes. After a couple of minutes of standing in it I could well believe it.

She led the way into a large, messy kitchen, warm and welcoming with the heat from a brick-red Aga and a very good smell coming from a large saucepan. It looked as if it was the nerve centre of the household; a huge pinboard covered in notices took centre stage on one wall, fairly orderly heaps of papers were stacked alongside a telephone on the dresser, two miniature chairs and a table were pushed against one wall, and children's art was proudly displayed on every available vertical surface.

There was also a large black-and-white cat sitting in the middle of a big pine table, licking his paw thoughtfully. Gina raced forward with a scream of dismay. 'What have you been into now, you bloody animal! If you've been in the milk again you can start thinking tennis rackets,' she said in an exasperated voice, as she looked around for drips on the table or paw prints in the butter, and scooped it up unceremoniously with her free hand and dropped it on a chair. 'He's called Art, short for the Artful Dodger, named for obvious reasons,' she informed me darkly. 'One of these days he'll take one thing too many and he'll find himself being made into a fur hat!' She cast an indulgent smile in the direction of the cat that indicated she didn't mean a word of it and turned back to Hamish. 'How's the house? Have you had the central heating fixed yet?'

'It is nearly June, Gina, getting the heating fixed isn't really an urgent priority at the moment, I'm hardly going to die of cold,' he said, throwing a glare in my direction as I smothered a giggle. So he hadn't been exaggerating about the mother-hen tendencies. His sister looked as if she was about to say more on the subject, but he adroitly diverted her by holding out the beribboned, elaborately wrapped present he'd brought with him. 'Happy late birthday,' he said.

'I thought you'd forgotten all about it!' she exclaimed, putting the toddler down and reverting to being aged about six as she turned the package over and over, feeling it and shaking it slightly to see if it rattled, then carefully undid each bow on the ribbons and lifted the Sellotape up without tearing the gold embossed paper. 'Oh, Hamish, it's gorgeous!' she cried, as she held up an enormously long silk scarf in shimmering shades of green, iridescent blue and indigo. She wrapped it twice around her neck, leaving the ends to dangle and make a fine contrast with her elderly sweatshirt and Levi's with a paint smudge on the knee. The brilliant colours of the scarf looked stunning against the warm shades of her olive skin and brown hair. She kissed Hamish delightedly and dashed over to a mirror to see what she looked like.

She was still preening in front of the glass when the back door slid open and a balding, pleasant-faced man in his late thirties tried to sneak in unnoticed. Half hidden behind him was an object covered in so much mud it was barely recognisable as a child. Gina spun round with an outraged shriek. 'That,' she said to me, 'is Tony, my husband, and I presume *that* –' she pointed in open-mouthed disbelief – 'is my eldest child.'

'He fell in the ditch,' Tony explained laconically. 'And then, as he was already dirty, he decided to do a bit of rolling about. We hoped we could get him cleaned up before you noticed.'

Gina rolled her eyes to the ceiling. 'Did you?' she asked grimly.

'The mud's all squishy,' the child offered, an unrepentant grin showing startlingly white teeth against his mud-coloured face.

Hamish leant towards him confidentially, though I noticed he prudently kept out of touching range. 'You should have taken your shoes off, Benjy. It feels even better when the mud squelches through your toes.'

'Hamish!' exclaimed his outraged sister, galvanised into action, whipping off her precious scarf and folding it carefully before pointing dramatically at the door to the hall. 'It's bad enough Tony allowing him to fall in the ditches, without you going all out to corrupt him! Right, young man, into the shower with you. No, *not* upstairs, unless you feel like scraping mud off the stair carpet yourself. The shower in the laundry room.'

'Wouldn't the washing machine on the hot cycle be a better idea?' asked Hamish.

His sister cast him a dirty look while leading her errant child out of the room, gingerly making sure no part of her came in actual contact with his wet and messy exterior. Shortly afterwards, we could hear protesting yells and some pretty bad-tempered motherly comments drifting down the passage towards us. Tony shuffled his feet in a shifty manner and said, 'I'm thinking perhaps I'd better get on with chopping a bit of wood. Never too soon to get next winter's supplies ready.'

'Exactly,' agreed Hamish solemnly. 'You might not have time to do it later.'

There was the sound of a door being flung open and Gina saying, 'I do not want to have to change your clothes again today. Understood?'

'Maybe we should go to the woodshed now,' Tony said hastily, opening the fridge and getting out two cans of beer. 'You get very thirsty chopping wood,' he informed me with a wide-eyed innocent expression as he sidled out of the door. Footsteps came up the passage and Hamish followed him in short order.

'Have they left you on your own?' asked Gina with a disapproving frown as she came in with a clean, though not noticeably subdued, child who calmly went over to a painted toybox and began sorting out bits of Lego as if he hadn't been yelling his head off two minutes ago.

'They've gone to chop some wood,' I explained.

She laughed. 'Tony needn't think he can escape the wifely wrath that easily! He's on extra washing-up duties for at least a week for this! Two weeks if when I go to the shed all I find is beer cans and no newly cut wood,' she added with the voice of experience. She was looking around like someone who wants to get on and do things, so I asked if there was anything I could do to help. 'If you wouldn't mind laying the table,' she said. 'We'll eat in here, it's less smart, but it's much easier to clean up the floor. Josh –' she looked fondly at the toddler who was intently galloping a model horse along a chair seat over and over again – 'hasn't quite mastered the art of getting food straight from plate to mouth yet. I daresay he'll get the knack eventually. About the time he's twenty, I expect!'

She whizzed around the kitchen, making a salad, putting a huge pan of water on to boil for spaghetti, whisking up egg whites for a Queen of Puddings in a way that made me feel positively lazy, and chatting to me as she worked. I'd been afraid she might ask me some awkward questions about Hamish, like how come I'd just happened to be there when he made up his mind to come and visit her, but to my intense

251

relief she was far more interested in talking about Stephen, who had been her first love. 'He was the most gorgeous thing I'd ever seen, completely knocked Champion the Wonder Horse off his podium from the moment I saw him,' she declared, whisk momentarily stopped as she relived all the intensity of a nine-year-old's passion. 'One holidays, when he was fifteen, he taught me how to serve overarm at tennis. Oh, I was smitten! This girl, at least, was quite prepared to make passes at guys who wore glasses, not that I was absolutely sure what a pass involved. I used to pray each night I'd grow a bosom and quickly, because Alastair, our oldest brother, was always teasing Stephen about how much he fancied Lucy White, who was the local femme fatale and *very* well endowed indeed. And when they didn't sprout overnight I stuffed a couple of apples in my vest and hoped Stephen wouldn't realise they weren't real. He didn't even notice them. Hamish did though!' she added in a darkling voice.

I laughed, guessing what had happened. I know brothers. 'So what happened?'

She smiled wryly. 'I saw him kissing Lucy behind the potting shed and I thought it looked quite yukky. Even worse than when we did mouth-to-mouth resuscitation in life-saving classes. So I gave up on love for several years and went back to regarding boys as an inferior species to be put down on every possible occasion.'

'And you didn't fall in love with Stephen all over again once you realised it would actually be rather nice to go behind the potting shed with him?' I asked.

She laughed. 'Wouldn't it just! No, that particular flame had been firmly blown out, not that Stephen ever showed any signs of wanting to do any such things with me, worse luck!' Her eyes danced. 'I wouldn't need to be in love to go behind a potting shed with Stephen. There's something about men like him that arouses all your protective instincts – and a lot more – don't you find?'

'Well, actually, I'd rather find a man who feels protective about me,' I confessed, 'but they're in rather short supply, on account of the fact most men can't feel protective about a woman who's taller than they are!'

'You aren't that tall, there must be lots of men bigger than you,' she protested, smiling. To my horror, I could almost see a thought bubble appear above her head. 'Like Hamish,' she said, eyeing me speculatively.

I fought to keep my face expressionless as I remembered all he'd done for me last night. By any standards it was protective. Looked after me, given me his own bed – and protected his own back when he decided not to risk carrying me across the green, I thought with a smothered bubble of laughter, which eased away the knot of embarrassed self-consciousness in the pit of my stomach.

'Stephen likes his women good and bossy like Liddy – good thing too,' Gina continued, as if the conversation hadn't momentarily veered sideways. Was she being extraordinarily tactful or was my overactive imagination putting in some unnecessary overtime? 'Can you imagine what he'd be like if he was shacked up with someone as disorganised as he is? He'd never get out of the door in the mornings!'

'It hadn't occurred to me there was anything good to say about Liddy,' I said thoughtfully, 'but I can see you've definitely got a point.'

'Oh, she isn't too bad once you get to know her,' Gina protested. 'And she may be a pain sometimes, but have you ever thought of what absolute hell Stephen must be to live with? I suspect half the time his vagueness is covering up that he simply doesn't want to do something.'

I nodded in agreement. That had occurred to me too.

'Sometimes I wonder if what makes Liddy hesitate about committing herself isn't that she'll be held back in her career,' said Gina, as she spooned the pudding into a bowl, 'but the fear she'll have a lifetime of being married to a man who'll continually "forget" to get up for the baby in the night or go to the supermarket when he's promised to!' I laughed, thinking I must tell Amanda this insight into Liddy's character. 'How did you come to meet Stephen anyway?' Gina asked, her eyebrows going up somewhat when I confessed it had been Hamish who had done the introductions, albeit at a distance and at Rose's prompting. 'So how long have you known Hamish?' she asked casually.

'Since the wedding, or the rehearsal, to be precise.'

'Not long then,' she said meaningfully. 'What do you think of his house?' she added casually. I could visualise the points being ticked off in her mind as I made some vaguely polite reply – he got her the job, she's been to his house, he's brought her to lunch – and they all added up to one seemingly logical conclusion. Hamish and I were an item and this was the first stage of doing the rounds and meeting the family. Didn't she know about Merial? I mean it was fairly evident there was something going on between those two. God knows I'd studied their body language for long enough while Rose and Luke had been deep in their own conversations, I should know. How could I have been so naive as to presume that any sister is going to believe that the female whom her brother springs on her for a surprise lunch is merely an art lover? I certainly wouldn't fall for that one if my brother turned up with an even half-decent female, and if she was positively indecent it'd be even more likely they had something going, I thought wryly. Had Hamish deliberately presented me as a sort of smoke screen, so he could get on with his real love affair away from the searchlight gaze of his female relations? Quite possibly. It was exactly the sort of thing my own unmarried brother would do. I was about to work up a fine head of annoyed steam about being used when I recalled uncomfortably that I wouldn't have been in a position to be used at all if Hamish hadn't looked after me last night. He was well justified in thinking I owed him one. My indignant guns well and truly spiked, and by myself too, I could hardly inform Gina that she was barking up entirely the wrong tree if she thought I'd bring myself to lay a single finger on her Machiavellian brother (which would have been rude as well as not necessarily true, I realised uneasily). Instead, I looked around wildly for a safer, more innocuous topic and found it in a small drawing hanging next to the fridge.

It was a pencil sketch of Tony relaxing back in a chair, with a very small baby balanced on one arm and a larger child leaning up against the other. They all appeared to be watching something out of the sketch intently. 'Is this one of yours?' I asked.

'Yes, that's Tony introducing the children to the joys of "boys' things" – spending an hour and a half watching Arsenal get trounced! Josh was all of three weeks old. His favourite tape now is a compilation of football chants. I ask you! Whatever happened to nursery rhymes?'

'At least they haven't been watching the rugby internationals,' I said.

She looked at me in awe. 'Gosh, I hadn't thought of rugby songs! I don't think I'll ever complain about "Herewego, Herewego" sung in a loud monotone ever again!'

I managed to lead her into a nice safe discussion about her

paintings, interested to see how she lapped up my unfeigned praise. I would have thought with a talent like hers she would have got quite used to compliments, even a bit blasé about them, but it didn't appear so at all. 'I'll take you around the studio after lunch if you like,' she said, looking delighted when I assured her I would like very much. 'Which of my paintings have you seen?'

'The ones Hamish has got. They're wonderful.'

'Mm, I liked those ones too. They were a house-warming present.'

Too late, I remembered where the pictures were hanging. Did he have any others? I thought hopefully. Like in his sitting room? Except that he'd said on the drive here his sitting room was empty of everything except a few packing cases, as he was in the middle of stripping the wallpaper. Did she know? Talk about putting your foot in it and giving *entirely* the wrong impression, Susie! I thought in irritation. I hoped that it was blissful oblivion and not tactfulness that made Gina go blithely on, 'Heaven knows he needed something for the house. He brought virtually nothing from his flat in London. Well, there wasn't much to bring really, apart from that enormous bed of his,' she continued, while I turned my head to study the cover of the current *Farmer's Weekly* with acute assumed interest until my self-conscious expression righted itself. 'He always claimed his flat was a shrine to minimalism, but I reckon he couldn't be bothered to go out and buy any furnishings!'

Gina looked up as the door opened and her husband put his head around it cautiously, testing the atmosphere, his face creasing with relief as she smiled at him and he saw he'd been forgiven. He extracted a couple more beers from the fridge for himself and Hamish, announcing with a certain amount of pride that he'd split the whole pile of logs and, if she didn't believe him, she could go and look for herself. Gina declined the invitation, claiming the need to watch over the huge vat of spaghetti on the boil. 'Has Gina told you she's got an exhibition coming up near you?' Tony asked Hamish. 'In Frampton, in a place run by a friend of hers, the Stable Gallery.'

'I know it,' I said. 'It's the other end of the High Street to the office. It does all sorts of craftsman-made things, doesn't it? I've never dared to go in, it looks like the sort of place where they charge you for entry.'

'People who live around Frampton have a lot of money to spend. Sally's always amazed at what she can shift,' Gina said, with a cynically satisfied smile. 'I'm hoping we might do quite well. You'll both come to the opening thrash, won't you? Lots of booze and eats, and a special offer for the first evening – you'll be allowed to leave without buying anything!'

After a protracted and informal lunch we wandered over to look at the studio, which had been made out of the old stables and still had the original wooden stall partitions down one end and iron hay-mangers halfway up the wall. 'Very useful for stacking the smaller canvases,' said Gina. I wandered along, leafing through canvases stacked up against one wall, mostly landscapes of local scenes and some of near where Gina had been brought up, though there were a few figurative scenes as well. 'Those aren't very good,' she said, making a face. 'I only keep them so I can reuse the canvas someday.' I thought they were lovely, I would have given my eye teeth for most of them, but then as she took me over to show me the much smaller pile she was actually proud of even I, with my limited ability for art appreciation, could see these were a completely different kettle of fish. I would have sold my grandmother for one of those, both grandmothers actually, as I had a feeling that one granny probably wasn't worth enough.

After a few minutes Josh, who was being held safely aloft in Tony's arms, well away from the tactile delights of those nice squeezy tubes of paint, began to wriggle restlessly and demand to be put down. 'Don't you dare,' Gina said, without looking up from a folio of drawings she was trying to undo. The ribbons holding it closed at the top had got hopelessly tangled into a tight knot. 'The last time he got loose in here he scribbled over a whole pad of art paper and it was a week before I could get into town to buy a new one.'

Josh opened his mouth to roar his protest at not being allowed to wreak havoc. 'Why don't we go and see the pony?' suggested Hamish quickly.

'Good idea,' said Tony, rushing Josh out before he could decide whether he approved of this plan or not.

'No wonder Hamish was so scornful of my prowess at controlling the pages at Rose's wedding,' I said. 'If I'd been able to think of diversions as quickly as that we'd never have had the Penknife Incident.'

'It's easy to control children if you're an uncle who doesn't have to see them every day,' said Gina, with a certain degree of cynicism. 'Even Hamish would have problems persuading the average eight-year-old that a pony is a suitable diversion from causing mayhem with a penknife. You don't tend to find ponies in churches either. They eat the flower arrangements. Not to mention making messes that do nothing for the bride's train.' She finally managed to get the knot untied, cursing slightly. 'It's not surprising I can never manage to keep my nails,' she grumbled, as she opened up the folio. 'These are what I do for myself, pleasure work, you might say, all the non-commercial stuff and odd sketches of what interests me.'

I began to leaf through them. They were of a varied bunch of subjects, from a lovingly detailed study of the spire of

Lincoln Cathedral, to a frog half submerged in a pond, to Gina's mother industriously weeding a herbaceous border and wearing one of the most disreputable gardening hats I'd ever seen, and they are by nature a disreputable species. I turned a drawing over, and Gina reached over and whipped the one underneath away before I could get more than a glimpse at it. 'Oops! I forgot that one was in there, that's a bit *too* interesting.'

I giggled. 'Tony's got a very nice figure, I must say.'

'It wasn't his *figure* I was worried about you seeing!' she retorted.

The next picture was also of Tony, but he was safely attired and leaning on a gate, rather than against a pile of pillows on their bed. The one after was of Hamish, a quick study of his head as he smiled at something in the distance. 'When did you do this?' I asked curiously, thinking how relaxed he looked.

Gina looked at it thoughtfully, screwing up her face. 'The summer before last maybe. No, three years ago.' Three years ago? I thought in disbelief, picking up the picture and examining it. Unless she was the artistic equivalent of those society photographers who airbrush out all the lines and several double chins from their subjects, Hamish had aged about ten years since this was drawn.

'He's changed,' I said carefully.

'Well, it was drawn before he got tangled up with Bettina,' Gina said flatly. She looked towards me and smiled. 'At least he seems to be getting over all that at last. I can't tell you how relieved I was to see you weren't a tiny little brunette!'

Over what? I thought blankly. Some romance, evidently. 'Bettina?' I asked.

'You don't know about her?' Gina asked in surprise. 'God, Hamish likes to keep things close to his chest!' she muttered. She looked at me, obviously weighing up how much the bounds of discretion allowed her to tell me, now that she'd let a small part of the cat out of the bag. To my disappointment, it turned out not to be very much. 'She was a married woman he got involved with, but she decided to go back to her husband. Hamish was very cut up about it.'

You'd need to be more than very cut up about something to change that much, I thought, looking at the drawing. 'Is she why he left London?' I asked, my thoughts running vaguely along the lines that he might have found it too awkward to stay where he was if she was a neighbour or something, but primarily hoping I might be able to nudge Gina into disclosing a bit more.

Her eyes flickered my way. She hesitated and sighed. 'Yes. Her husband was one of the firm's clients. He complained to the Law Society, and Hamish ended up nearly being struck off. Solicitors are a bit like doctors, can't lay a finger on their own clients. Obviously he couldn't stay with the same firm, so he moved to where he is now.'

So that's what he'd meant when he'd said he'd blown it, but not in the way I'd imagined, I thought in amazement. That was certainly true enough. I would never have believed that controlled Hamish could endanger everything for passion, but I was wrong, wasn't I? And at one time I'd believed he was cold . . . What was this Bettina like then? Tiny and dark, evidently, and stunning too, presumably. Well, a mousy little woman might have made him forget all his professional rules about relationships with clients, but it seemed unlikely somehow.

And there must be more to the story than this. For instance, why hadn't he simply moved to another firm in London? I mean it wasn't as if he'd been embezzling his clients' trust funds, and it would be reasonable to assume he'd learnt his lesson about affairs in unwise places. I was about to try more probing, but Gina signalled the topic was closed by pointing to a sketch of the village cricket team. 'While I was doing that their star batsman scored a six – right through the pub landlord's bedroom window!' I smiled dutifully, accepting this forced change of subject.

We had almost finished looking at everything when a call from outside took us to the window. Hamish was leading a small, shaggy piebald Shetland pony with a very bolshy expression around the stable yard while Benjy, perched on its back on a felt saddle, waved at us frantically. Josh sat behind him, short legs almost horizontal over the pony's stout girth. Tony hovered protectively alongside, stopping him from falling off backwards. 'Hold on!' called Gina anxiously, as Benjy wobbled precariously and Hamish shot out a hand to balance him. 'He's overconfident,' she said gloomily, 'I'm expecting any day he'll be brought in minus his front teeth, and he hasn't gone out of a walk yet! Though I suppose if he has to knock them out he might as well do it now with his milk teeth,' she added in resignation. 'All Tony's family start riding before they're out of nappies and Benjy's a real chip off the old block. Horse mad, or pony mad in this case! He even wants to sleep with Biscuit, can't understand ponies don't like curling up in baskets like the dog. He may look sweet, but he's an absolute little sod, I can tell you!' she said with feeling. For a moment, I wasn't sure if she was talking about son or pony, then true to her character assessment the pony gave us a stroppy look, aimed a bite in the general direction of Tony, who smartly lifted his charge off its back and stepped away, as the pony headed off out through the archway towards its field.

'They're supposed to be the strongest and most self-willed of the British ponies, now you see why they have that reputation,' said Gina, leaning against the window frame and watching Hamish, almost large enough to have stepped straight over the pony's back, being towed willy-nilly away.

I laughed in agreement and turned from the window, knocking my elbow against a tall easel folded up against the wall. 'Blast it!' I said, rubbing it gingerly. 'The one thing I don't need to do is muck up my other arm as well.'

'What did you do to your arm?' Gina asked idly as she packed away her drawings and tied them up safely. 'Didn't Hamish say something about a car accident? I hope he wasn't driving.'

To my surprise, I hadn't even got to Houdini and his appearance in the middle of the road when she let the portfolio fall back on its side as she turned around to stare at me in blank astonishment. 'Luke? You mean it was Luke Dillon whom you were with?' she asked. I nodded. 'You're going out with him *and* Hamish at the same time? You like leading a dangerous life, don't you, Susie?' she exclaimed, shaking her head in disbelief.

I looked at her, trying to frame the words to tell her that, whatever she might think, I wasn't going out with Hamish. Or with Luke, for that matter. 'Does he know?' she asked, with a lot less friendliness in her voice than had been there previously.

'Who?' I asked stupidly. 'Oh, Hamish, about Luke. Yes, of course he does. And I was only having dinner with him,' I added defensively; realising with a district sense of déjà vu it wasn't the first time I'd made this excuse to a member of the Laing family. 'Anyway, what's wrong with Luke, apart from him not having a regular job?'

Gina looked at me thoughtfully, as if she were a barrister and I an unfriendly witness, then sighed and turned away, picking up her portfolio. 'Well, he's a bit of a cokehead, isn't he?' she said at last. 'It's not surprising he put you in the ditch.'

That hadn't been what she was going to say, I was sure of it. Or maybe I was imagining it, I thought uneasily. She was probably just getting on her high horse about her brother's supposed new girlfriend playing fast and loose with another man. Whatever, she continued to treat me with a degree of reserve for the rest of the time we were there.

Inevitably, Hamish noticed the lack of any warm invitations from his sister to me to return at some later date, though Tony obliviously told me repeatedly how nice it had been to meet me and I was welcome at any time. 'Did you say something rude to Gina about one of her paintings?' he asked curiously as we were driving home.

'Of course not!' I said indignantly. 'But she thinks I'm two-timing you with Luke.'

He glanced over quickly with raised eyebrows, then returned his eyes to the road. 'Whatever gave her that impression?' he asked mildly.

'Not me!' I said promptly, and probably not very flatteringly.

He chuckled. 'It's a good thing she doesn't know about your Frenchman then. Gina's surprisingly conventional. I don't think she could cope with the idea of me being *three*-timed!'

CHAPTER 14

The next Saturday afternoon I was doing the last-minute clearing and tidying up before I had to leave to collect Arnaud from the station. Actually, I was just polishing the same bits again and again for something to do and work off my nervous energy. It didn't take long even for the most meticulous and houseproud person to totally spring clean a space as small as this and Arnaud may have had his faults but running his finger along the picture frames to check for dust had never been one of them. Not getting out of bed early in the morning was certainly one of them, I thought grimly. He'd said firmly he couldn't possibly get a flight before midday at the earliest, he worked hard during the week and needed a lie-in on Saturdays. I'd noted before that he appeared to be perfectly able to get up early when it involved doing something like going out on a friend's boat. So he wasn't going to be here before about six o'clock. Oh well, at least it meant I could spring our evening supporting charity on him at the last moment and not give him much of a chance to complain about it. I was sure he still would.

I checked my watch. Time to go. Arnaud had intended to hire a car and drive, but I, who have endured many white-knuckle rides with him, told him at imaginative length how terrible the M25 was, *especially* on a Saturday afternoon, *much* worse than the Peripherique, and as for the M1, well, you moved along quicker in your average NCP. Really, though naturally InterCity services couldn't match up to the TGV, the trains to Leicester were fast, punctual and very frequent I assured him. I thought it more tactful not to say that at least in a train I could be sure he was keeping on the right side of the tracks.

I was strangely nervous about seeing him. Maybe because it was such a long time since we'd been together, nearly six months, I realised in some surprise; it didn't seem that long and yet in some ways it seemed much longer. Normally we picked up exactly where we'd left off before, which was a major reason why our affair had gone on for such a long time – we were good friends as well as lovers. But now, as I drove towards the station, I found myself wondering what I was going to talk to him about. Our paths had diverged so much in the last few months; I was absolutely certain that he wasn't going to find the minutiae of life in the country very thrilling, especially since there was so much I couldn't very well rabbit on about. My social life, for one thing. He cordially disliked Rose and wouldn't want to hear about what I got up to with her, and though Arnaud reckoned he was perfectly entitled to play away from home and paid lip-service to my right to do the same, if there was any actual hint I might be taking advantage of it he got a bit stuffy. So, no talking about Luke then. Not that there was any playing at home or away going on with Luke just now. He'd been completely hectic with something or other, so apart from when he'd dropped round on Sunday with a huge bunch of flowers and fulsome apologies about not taking me home himself I hadn't seen him this last week, though we'd chatted a couple of times on the phone. Frankly, I'd been rather relieved. My life had become

unnervingly complicated enough without adding the possibility of things with a new boyfriend going a stage further just
before the current model arrived for the weekend, I thought
wryly, as for the third time I tried and failed to overtake a
caravan that was ambling along at sightseer's pace.

And I'd have to keep quiet about Hamish too, not that
there had been any playing going on there either, but there
was no way Arnaud was going to believe a man would take a
woman along to visit his sister's studio without an ulterior
motive. Especially after she'd spent the night in his bed, but
Arnaud *certainly* wasn't going to know about that. Neither was
anyone else. Rose had been most curious about what had
happened, she'd rung several times last Saturday to check I'd
got home safely and had only got the answerphone. I'd
muttered some excuse about switching the bell on the phone
off so I could sleep and then going out to lunch with people in
the village, and she'd been so wracked with guilt over the
equivalent of slipping me a Mickey Finn that she'd failed
entirely to see the holes in my story. Good thing too. If she'd
had any hint that the last time I saw Hamish hadn't been at
my door on Friday evening, but late afternoon on Saturday, I'd
never have heard the end of it.

Thanks to the caravan and the driver's dozy habit of
wandering into the middle of the road whenever a good
overtaking opportunity came up, I was late. Only a minute
and a half late and the train was only just beginning to draw
out, but all the same Arnaud was standing on the platform
looking around with all the forlorn reproach of a child who's
afraid he's not going to be picked up at the end of term. For a
moment I felt as if I was looking at a stranger; this neat man
with the short brown hair and the sharp features, in his
impeccably cut beige linen jacket and navy trousers, didn't

seem to have anything to do with me at all. A passing woman turned and gave him a second look and I still felt so distant that it didn't arouse anything in me, not vicarious pride he was here for *me*, nor a pang of jealousy that he'd returned the look with interest. Then he put his hand up to smooth down some imagined ruffled lock of hair in such an incredibly familiar gesture – I must have seen it literally thousands of times before – that my heart skipped involuntarily with remembered pleasure and I ran towards him, full of apologies.

'You have lost weight,' he told me, giving me an immediate and automatic once-over. 'I think I laike it –' all my efforts to get him to pronounce his i's in the English way had failed – 'but do not lose any more. That –' his eyes rested appreciatively on my bosom – 'is one of your better features.'

'I'd have to lose one hell of a lot of weight before I became flat-chested,' I pointed out reasonably and hugged him, that awkward feeling of not really knowing him finally being pushed away under an enthusiastic and expert kiss.

We chatted in a fairly desultory manner as we drove back to the cottage; about his flight, the inadequacies of the Tube as compared to the Metro (naturally) and the surprising fact that he'd been quite impressed with the train. I got the impression he was on his best behaviour. He praised the scenery we passed, saying how pretty it was (it was an attractive route to Little Dearsley, admittedly, but nothing stunning in my opinion), admired the lushness of the grass and hedges (Arnaud had never been a nature freak before, to my knowledge), and even forbore to comment on the cruel way I'd left him standing for ages on the platform at Leicester station. He was very polite about the cottage too, saying he could see that it suited me perfectly and it looked like I was living in a very nice village. After he greeted with something approaching equanimity the news that instead of having dinner in a Michelin-recommended restaurant we were going to be tasting Chilean wine and eating rice salad amongst a whole lot of local worthies, I began to wonder uneasily if he'd got religion. (Though his benign mood might have had something to do with my forethought in settling him down with a large glass of good wine before I broke the news.) He was even decent enough to say he'd enjoy the chance to have a look at a proper English country house. I warned him Moor End Hall wasn't exactly in the top echelons of architectural grandeur, but he didn't appear to mind, saying that it was *le style Anglais* that he wanted to see, all chintz and gundogs. This wasn't the normal cheerful selfishness that I'd come to expect from the man I knew and loved, I thought, taking a sneaky feel of his forehead to see if he had a temperature under the pretence of brushing his hair back. That wasn't to say I wouldn't take as much advantage of this unusual magnanimity as I could.

'We should be thinking of changing, I promised Rose we'd be there early in case she had anything she needed help with,' I said. Arnaud put his still-half-full glass down on the side table and began to get up, so I added quickly, 'Why don't you stay down here and finish that while I get ready? The bedroom's so small we'll just get in each other's way if we're there at the same time.'

He nodded equably, probably thinking that if I took my usual amount of time he'd have a chance to have another glass as well. I went upstairs, realising guiltily that lack of space wasn't the reason why I felt strangely awkward about the idea of getting undressed in front of him. It must be something to do with the length of time since I'd taken off my clothes while he was in the same room, I thought uneasily, as I stripped off my tee shirt and skirt and reached for my dressing-gown. It had to be a female thing, for I was sure that he'd have no objection to my seeing him in his skimpy Homs, in fact, he'd rather enjoy it. He was proud of his figure. With reason too.

As usual, the weather had done exactly what Rose wanted. This morning when it clouded over briefly she had rung me wailing she'd planned to have the tasting on the terrace so everyone could wander around and look at the gardens and now everything was threatened with being rained out at any moment. I looked out of my window, saw a single cloud in an expanse of blue, and said that in the event of an unexpected deluge they had plenty of room indoors. With eminent practicality she said if the guests had something to do, rather than just stand around, they'd drink less and there'd be more profit for the charity. I could see she was going to make a formidable fundraiser, though I think her real worry had been that she was going to suffer a barrage of 'I told you so's' from Flavia, who had said from the moment the plan was mentioned that it was quite ridiculous to even *think* of holding something out of doors in this country. But the cloud that had occluded the sun at eleven o'clock had drifted away, the day had been gloriously hot and was turning into a warm and balmy evening, absolutely perfect for tasting wine on a terrace. It meant I could wear the new dress I'd bought on a strictly window-shopping expedition with Amanda earlier in the week. She'd demanded I try it on and, over my nervous objections that I wasn't used to wearing things that . . . um . . . skimpy, had insisted that I bought it. It was the sort of garment that would make my father snort in a old-codgerish way and ask with laboured humour if it had been handmade by twenty skilled seamstresses, since he couldn't believe much of the purchase price had been accounted for by the cost of such a small amount of fabric. It certainly did seem to show rather a lot of me, I thought, looking doubtfully at my back view in the mirror, and the strapless bra made essential by the narrow little shoulder straps seemed to have had the unnerving effect of making my bust even larger than usual. Though, judging by Arnaud's look when I came back downstairs again, the only person who objected to that was me. I sent him up before he could demonstrate his interest in the subject – we didn't want to be late – and went off to put my make-up on in front of a mirror balanced on the kitchen table. I doubted strongly he was a reformed enough soul not to fight me for a place at the mirror in the bedroom.

Despite my best efforts the drive at Moor End Hall was already half full of cars when we arrived. I'd have like it to have blamed Arnaud and the length of time it took him to put on an outfit that would have been perfect for a yacht at Cannes – navy-blue silk jacket, white slub trousers, yellow shirt of cotton so fine it could have gone through a wedding ring – but in fact it was me getting cold feet over whether my barmaid's figure was really too much of a good thing in this dress. In the end the reflection that I didn't have anything else clean and ironed, not to say the thought of Rose's reaction when we turned up hours late, propelled me out of the door, to Arnaud's loudly expressed relief.

The matronly woman dressed in an alarming shade of puce who was taking the entrance money had a very pleasing pile of five- and ten-pound notes stacked up in her cash box. She obviously knew me, though I couldn't remember ever seeing her (surely I would have noticed the matching hair?), for she said with a slightly reproachful look that I'd been expected quite half an hour ago and it was so important to get on with the money-making activities *early* at events like this. She handed over sheets with prices and tasting notes for each of the twelve wines and spaces for the really earnest to write down their own comments, saying firmly, we did realise our entrance ticket only allowed us to have a single tasting of each wine, didn't we? She looked at me in a meaningful way while saying this. For a guilty moment I wondered if she'd been having cocktails in a certain bar in Leicester on Friday last week and was speculating how long it was going to be before the raffle-ticket seller was laid out peacefully snoring it off under one of the tasting tables.

Arnaud was studying his card with raised eyebrows and a dubious expression. My heart sank, for I knew from experience there are few things worse than a wine buff who reckons there is nothing fit for him to drink, then to my relief he pointed to one and said, 'That one might be reasonable. They have a properly trained winemaker. He is French.'

The woman beamed, her indignation at our tardiness forgotten. 'You're French! Oh, I do love a French accent, it takes me right back to when I was a teenager and I used to swoon over Louis Jourdan!' She gazed up at Arnaud in admiration. 'You remind me of him too!'

She must have been very short-sighted. Arnaud looked *nothing* like Louis Jourdan, he didn't have black hair, for one thing. But he accepted the compliment as his due and took her hand, kissing it in the most outrageously ostentatious fashion. '*Merci, madame*, you are too kind,' he said. She was still fluttering with pleasure as we walked away.

'Arnaud, that was the hammiest thing I ever saw!' I said severely.

'Hammiest? Like *jambon*?' he began, and when I fixed him with a reproving look, for though his pronunciation can be dodgy his knowledge of colloquial English is excellent, grinned and asked, 'But when in England should I not be what you

272

English think a Frenchman should be?'

'Not if you don't want to be lynched by half the men present!' I retorted. 'Englishmen aren't keen on their wives palpitating over a foreign accent, and as for hand-kissing . . .'

Despite the puce lady's reproaches, I delayed getting down to my work for another few minutes by taking the long way round to where the action was, so Arnaud could have a chance to look at the house and gardens before they filled up too much with guests. Whatever he might have been anticipating with his visions of *le style Anglais*, it certainly wasn't a house where about ten different architectural styles had been flung together in what was usually – but not always – a happy accident. It wasn't what he was used to, French châteaux don't tend to have bits added on at random, and he didn't altogether approve of it. (I warned him not to express his opinions to Jeremy – or Rose.) But he admired the gardens and the view thoroughly, saying that the English truly knew how to landscape a park, even when they didn't have the estimable Monsieur Capability Brown working for them.

We sat on a curved stone bench, enjoying the peace for a moment. A small herd of Jersey cows had positioned themselves centre stage in a field below the ha-ha with the instincts of a set designer looking for that final perfect touch, their coats almost gold under the rays of a slowly sinking sun, and a brilliant contrast to the long lush grass and cow parsley. Music drifted down from the house like some muted film score. Rose had lost the battle over the local bank's dance-band which had been installed at the bottom of the terrace steps, far enough away not to deafen the guests. The lead sax held considerable sway over the overdrafts of several committee members and it was generally felt it wouldn't be a good idea to hurt his feelings by not accepting his offer to play. Since Rose was moving her account to the same branch, she came round to their point of view.

There were a few other people wandering around, looking at the flowers and commenting on the quality of the weeding, though most of the early birds had headed for the booze and were huddled around the tasting tables that had been laid in a line down the far end of the terrace. They were studying their tasting sheets with frowning concentration and fantasising about being Jancis Robinson or Hugh Johnson as they swirled their wines around in their glasses and lifted them up to examine the colour. Arnaud's lip curled in an ominously familiar way and I threatened to kick him if he even started to make a rude remark. He lifted his eyebrows haughtily. 'Me, rude? I am honest, but if you do not want honesty...'

'Not here, I don't!' I said through gritted teeth, wondering not for the first time why it is that all wine buffs seem to think it's obligatory for them to be absolutely honest about what they've been given to drink, even if they're guests in someone else's house. After all, if your hostess says, 'What do you think of my new recipe for the lamb?' you don't reply, 'Well, actually, it's completely overcooked, you used too much seasoning and the coriander was a complete mistake ...' Well, not if you want to keep your friend. But the keen wine-fancier has no such scruples.

I hastily got Arnaud a glass of the wine he'd said was made by someone French and gave him mine as well for good measure. That might keep him quiet for a bit. I could see Hamish's dark head bobbing around further along the terrace as he served white wine, and was going to go and say hello to him. But I felt strangely shy about approaching him and decided he was probably too busy for socialising. Besides, I

274

was going to be in mega trouble with Rose if I didn't present myself for duty soon, so I looked around to see if there was anyone who would keep Arnaud happily occupied for a bit. The nearest possibility was Flavia, which turned out to be a stroke of genius. Like the puce lady, Flavia was a sucker for French accents, and even more so for a French accent which belonged to someone who had *de* in his surname. And Arnaud was equally happy to be talking to someone he could recognise as a genuine English Lady, even if she didn't actually have a title. Especially an English Lady who, unusually for the species, was dressed with enormous elegance and style and was looking a good ten years younger than her true age. I left them discussing lineage, they'd no doubt find out they were related in some way, since both were tracing their ancestry back centuries and eventually they were bound to get back to Adam.

Rose must have already had a couple of tasting glasses under her belt, for she was in a remarkably good mood and instead of receiving a rocket for my lateness I was greeted with a big smile and, 'Wow! Like the dress!' followed by a suggestive smile and, 'No *wonder* you're so late!'

'It was nothing like that at all,' I said stiffly and then spoilt my dignified air by adding, 'I see *you* must have been in a bit of a hurry getting ready. At least I remembered to put my dress on over my petticoat.'

Rose stuck her tongue out at me. 'Bitch!' she said equably. Score one all. She was stunning in a navy-blue slip dress, her legs looking even longer than usual in her one and only pair of Manolo Blahnik's, very high-heeled Roman sandals that laced right up to the knee. 'Now come on you, there's work to do! And no hanging around chatting up the talent while you're supposed to be selling!' she said severely.

I looked at the several middle-aged and rotund stomachs

that surrounded us. 'I don't think I'll feel inclined to.'

'No,' she agreed gloomily. 'Pretty poor showing so far. Still, there's time for more to arrive. Stephen, Luke . . .'

'Married women aren't meant to cruise parties looking for talent!' I told her.

'Why not?' she protested, wide-eyed. 'I don't see why I can't have some fun as well. Where's your particular bit of talent, by the way?'

For a moment I couldn't think what she was talking about, then I gestured down the terrace. 'There, talking to Flavia. They're getting on like a house on fire.'

She looked at them, open-mouthed. 'What a splendid combination!' she breathed. 'They could be made for each other! Why did I never think before that what Flavia really needs is a toy boy? I'm sure there must be something against it, but what could it be?'

'That Arnaud's going out with me?' I suggested.

She looked at me. 'I can't see that's an objection,' she returned serenely.

Two-one to Rose, I thought resignedly as I picked up a huge wad of raffle tickets and my money bag and began to go around persuading people that what they really wanted was to spend five pounds on the chance of winning a near-life-sized toy lion, a white handbag that looked suspiciously as if it was made of plastic, a vast jardinière in blue and green and a ten-pound voucher for Maison Valerie (specialising in special-occasion outfits for the fuller figure). It was much easier than I'd expected, everybody appeared to have come expecting to spend loads of money and bought one or two books of tickets at a time. The tombola stall was doing a roaring trade as well, though I couldn't help noticing that my bottle of Algerian red (a generous contribution on my part, I felt) had been won and returned twice so far and we hadn't even had supper yet.

I'd been keeping a sneaky eye out for Luke, just slightly worried that he might try to lay claim to me in front of Arnaud, that firm believer in the double standard, but in the event I needn't have worried. When Luke finally did breeze in, an hour late, but a sight for sore eyes as ever in tight black trousers and a snowy-white shirt, just like a Spanish waiter (a look that no one but he could have got away with), he barely stopped to kiss my cheek, saying he'd catch up with me later and he must go and say hello to his hostess. I eyed his admirable back-view as he threaded his way through the crowd towards Rose, not sure if I was annoyed or not at his cavalier attitude. So he might just be being tactful in not making a fuss of me in front of Arnaud, but it was still a bit of a downer to the ego to have him showing all the enthusiasm towards me that he would for his maiden aunt – and the one without the money too. Though I reckoned Arnaud would barely have noticed if Luke had enfolded me in the sort of embrace best confined to the bedroom. He was having far too much fun teasing his rival for Flavia's attentions, a portly man in his fifties with a close-cropped moustache, who had 'retired colonel' stamped all over him, to even look my way. The colonel, an upstanding example of the stiff-upper-lip type, didn't stand much of a chance against someone who had begun to perfect his flirting techniques while still at *maternelle*, and was driven to resorting to glaring at Arnaud with a 'who's this young whipper-snapper?' sort of expression while Flavia simpered and preened under blandishments that were getting more French by the minute. When Arnaud took her hand, tenderly turned it over and made as if he was reading her future, the colonel's face went so red I thought he was about to explode. But I knew that if I went over at least two of the party would find me about as welcome as an accurate mirror in a changing room, so I decided to leave them all to it.

So much for worrying about whether I'd be able to divide my time between my two men without annoying either of them, I thought sourly, feeling distinctly unloved. My money bag was getting heavy with the proceeds of my efforts, I'd dump it with the treasurer and go and find myself a drink. I reckoned I deserved a break.

CHAPTER 15

I had a frustrating time with the treasurer, who alarmingly confessed she'd never passed a maths exam in her life and had really just wanted to take notes at the meetings. She made me re-count the one hundred and forty-three pounds and twenty-nine pence I'd collected so far three times. The problem was the twenty-nine pence – the tickets cost a pound each and neither of us could work out how I'd come by the extra pennies. Eventually I bared my teeth in a smile and said through a clenched jaw that I remembered now, someone had given me his loose change as a donation. I hoped a thunderbolt wasn't going to come down and smite me immediately for lying, but it was in a good cause. The Susie not being kept here until midnight good cause. The treasurer nodded happily, bureaucratic soul satisfied, and wrote down painstakingly in her account book under 'Miscellaneous', Donation to raffle – 29p. I made good my escape and headed off towards that now really needed drink.

'Skiving off already?' said a disapproving voice behind me.

'And just how much money have you personally raised this evening?' I asked, turning around to a grinning Rose, noting slightly resentfully that judging from her sparkling eyes and slightly flushed cheeks she hadn't been too busy to get herself a single drink in the last hour and a half. Unlike me.

She raised her eyes piously upwards. 'I don't sully myself with actually touching the money. Someone has to be the fat cat who sits back and tells everybody else what to do, don't they?' She laughed at my expression and speedily changed the subject. 'I haven't seen Arnaud recently. Where is he?'

'Still charming the pants off your mother-in-law, I expect,' I said.

She opened her eyes very wide. 'Not literally?' she breathed.

'God, I hope not!' I said. 'On the other hand . . . you'd love Arnaud as your *beau père*, wouldn't you?' I laughed at her horrified expression and added, 'But he's got competition from a man with a toothbrush moustache who doesn't approve of him one little bit.'

'Oh goody, is there going to be a fight over Flavia? That should really make this a memorable do!' she exclaimed. 'That'll be Colonel Wilding. He's known Flavia for ages, but he won't make up his mind if he's really interested or not. Typical man! Oh, I do hope Arnaud's making him jealous enough to whisk Flavia off to his place in Yorkshire. He's a widower too. Just think how perfect it would be!' she exclaimed, eyes gleaming. 'Flavia a hundred miles away.'

'They might decide to set up their love nest in Flavia's wing here,' I pointed out.

Rose's mouth dropped open in dismay, then she shook her head firmly. 'Jeremy wouldn't allow it,' she said, though her voice held a note of doubt. She looked around at the crowd stretching down the terrace, chattering away noisily. 'It's going well, don't you think? Luke was saying how well he thinks I've organised everything.' Her face looked all pink and pleased at the compliment. 'In fact he suggested perhaps I ought to think of doing party organising. He says I've got a talent for it. What do you think?'

'That you do a good party or you should make a career of it?' I asked. Luke was absolutely right. She was very good at doing parties, and it was the sort of thing that suited her restless energy perfectly, as she never spent long enough on any one thing to get bored. But he couldn't possibly *know* how good she was at it, especially after half an hour. I hoped the nasty little sensation in my stomach wasn't jealousy that he was choosing to flatter her and not me. It probably was. 'It's not a bad idea,' I said, making a big effort to be fair. 'You should look into it, see if there's enough demand for that sort of thing up here. You have done this brilliantly.'

'I have to admit Luke gave me some good ideas,' she confessed.

'*Luke* did? When did he come around doing party planning?' I demanded, keeping my voice casual with a determined effort.

'He didn't come *here*,' she said quickly. 'Jeremy doesn't like him very much, though I can't think why as he hardly knows him.' If Jeremy had noticed his wife's expression each time Luke's name was mentioned I could think why very easily indeed. 'But I told him the other day I had some problems with little details so he's been ringing with suggestions. He's been really helpful.' She giggled. 'He said if he had to spend an evening supporting charity he wanted to make sure it wasn't too painful!'

She looked up with a broad smile as Luke threaded his way through the crowd with two glasses in his hands, dodging the first takers for supper, who were wandering around with dangerously loaded plates in their hands, looking for a table to sit down at. Two teenage girls, dressed up to the nines in black skimpy dresses, heavy eyeliner and Doc Martens, who had probably been dragged along on the grounds that their parents

281

didn't trust them alone in the house for the evening, were eyeing him with frankly lascivious expressions. One nudged the other as he came to a halt in front of us, and they began to sidle purposefully our way.

'I'm so sorry, Susie, I'd have bought you a drink too if I'd known you were here,' Luke said and held up his glass. 'You can have mine if you don't mind my germs, I've already had a swig.'

'I'm sure you don't have any germs,' I said waving it away, 'but I wouldn't dream of depriving you.' I have to admit he looked distinctly relieved, especially when I assured him that he didn't have to go and fetch me a drink either, because I was on my way to do it myself.

He put his arm around my waist, hugged me, and kissed my cheek. 'What a star amongst women you are, Susie,' he said lightly. 'Beautiful, intelligent – and independent!'

I laughed up at him, feeling a pleased flattered tingle go all the way through me at the compliment, even though I'd come to realise that flattery dropped as easily from Luke's lips as curses do from a navvy's. Still, that was part of his charm, wasn't it? I thought indulgently, as he murmured a couple more ego-boosting things in my ear. It didn't necessarily mean that he was insincere – just that he liked women. The two teenagers had got to within about five feet and were staring at me with a venomous expression that was making me feel distinctly uncomfortable. I had a nasty feeling that they reckoned someone as old as myself had had her chances and blown them, so should make way for the younger generation. I left them to battle it out with Rose and, saying I'd talk to her later, made my way down the terrace.

I headed towards the table where I could see Hamish busy at work, collar open and sleeves rolled up, looking remarkably unrumpled and fresh despite the fact that, judging from the continual press of people around, he must have been opening and pouring almost solidly for the last two hours. He was answering a question from a middle-aged man and put his bottle down, glancing up in my direction. I smiled at him. His eyes slid over me as if I wasn't there. Someone bumped into me and trod painfully on my heel as I slowed to a halt, staring at him while he turned around to get a new bottle. Was he just too busy to notice me or had I annoyed him somehow? I thought in dismay. I'd had the impression we'd parted really good friends last week, certainly I hadn't enjoyed myself so much in ages. Apparently I was mistaken. Now my brief period of usefulness as a smokescreen was over, maybe he'd decided he didn't want to be bothered with me any more, I thought nervously, feeling an acute funk attack coming on. I was about to forget all about getting a drink when I saw Stephen, perched on the end of the table in a manner that must have been considerably detrimental to its stability, holding a glass up to the light. Well, that gave me the means to go up there without it looking as if I was thrusting myself forward for Hamish's attention.

Stephen was taking little sips from a glass of white wine and studying his tasting notes with frowning concentration. 'Can't say I can taste any pineapply, bananary or blackcurranty notes in this,' he grumbled to no one in particular. 'No strawberries either. And if I'd wanted them I'd have had a plate of bloody fruit salad! Who wrote this rubbish anyway? And why can't they make this muck taste of grapes, that's what I'd like to know,' he demanded rhetorically.

Liddy, hovering by his side, frantically tried to shush him, probably fearing the supplier of the wine was within earshot. 'Oh look, here's Susie,' she said, with an enthusiasm for my company that I'd never noticed in her before. For such an ardent feminist she didn't appear to be very fond of her own sex.

He looked up and exclaimed, 'Susie! Where have you been? I've been looking for you.'

'I've been selling these.' I held up a bundle of tickets. Always loath to let a sales opportunity slip, I said firmly, 'Once you've finished that glass of wine I daresay you'd like to buy some as well, wouldn't you? Even if you wouldn't *like*,' I added meaningfully, 'I'm sure you'll still buy some, won't you?'

He nodded in the resigned fashion I'd come to expect from everyone who saw me advancing and knew they were being given the opportunity to become the proprietor of a life-sized plush lion. 'Good party this, isn't it?' he asked, recovering and waving his glass. The motion made the table wobble ominously. 'I'm glad I let Rose persuade me to come. I was really doubtful about it, I can tell you, but I'm happy I came. You are too, aren't you, darling?' he asked turning towards Liddy.

She gave the tight-lipped smile of the one who lost the toss for who was going to drive home and sipped at a mineral water. 'Of course I am,' she said expressionlessly, giving the impression she'd be having more fun at a macramé class.

Stephen looked at me owlishly, blinking behind his glasses. 'Don't you look great,' he said reflectively. 'Your dresses aren't usually that . . .'

'Tight?' I suggested, as he seemed lost for a tactful adjective.

'Figure-hugging, I was about to say,' he replied, rising nobly to the occasion. 'Why don't you wear things like that to the office? It'd brighten the place up no end.' Liddy shot him a poisonous look. She didn't look like she was in a mood to listen to her man complimenting another woman, especially as she'd misjudged how dressy this evening was going to be, for the women at least, and was wearing an unusually sober knee-length dress that would have been perfect for a parent–teacher meeting. 'Don't you agree, Hamish?' Stephen asked.

Hamish stopped stacking empty bottles in a case behind the table and straightened up, looking at me with a slightly strange expression. 'That Susie looks super?' he asked. 'I'm sure she doesn't need me to tell her, enough people must have done that already this evening.'

Well, actually *not* enough people, I could do with another, I thought in slight irritation. And some compliments meant more than others because of who they came from.

'Or that she should wear it to the office? Not unless you want to switch from estate to escort agency,' he continued.

I heard Liddy snigger as I gave him a filthy glare. He looked at me blandly. 'Only the very best, most *respectable* class of escorts, of course!'

The ruddy man could run rings around me, I decided in exasperation, it wasn't worth trying to retaliate. 'Can I have a glass of the Sauvignon?' I asked abruptly.

'Arm completely better?' he asked, and smiled as I coloured. 'The Sauvignon is filthy, it needs to be icy cold to be tolerable and we're nearly out of ice. Try the Chardonnay instead.'

'Thanks,' I said, wondering if this was a peace offering. He handed over a full glass and I drank half of it in almost indecent haste.

'You aren't supposed to treat a fine wine like that,' he said with faint disapproval.

I obediently took a minute sip and did all the things you're supposed to do when tasting a wine, like making exaggerated facial gestures to show you're moving it around your mouth so it reaches all the taste buds, though I drew the line at the gurgling sound-effects that go with them or spitting it out on the ground. 'It isn't a fine wine,' I retorted when I'd finished.

He inclined his head slightly. 'True, but you still shouldn't gulp it as if it was Coke.'

'I *never* gulp Coke. I don't like it,' I informed him loftily and then added more quietly, 'And you needn't worry, Hamish. Even if I do get absolutely paralytic, you won't get landed with taking me home tonight!'

'No,' he said, equally softly, but with a distinctly hard edge to his voice. 'But have you sorted out who will yet?'

My eyes flew up to meet his for a startled moment. His face was completely expressionless and I was just deciding that, not for the first time, I was reading altogether too much into a situation when Stephen broke in unheedingly. 'It may not be a fine wine, but it's not at all bad. I might just try a bit more to see if I want to buy some. I'll have Liddy's glass as she isn't drinking. It's in a good cause, after all,' he said defensively, as Liddy gave him the pitying look reserved by the teetotal for those whose lips have touched the demon drink.

She took a deep breath. 'Maybe after we've had a walk around the gardens,' she said in a don't-you-even-think-of-disagreeing-with-me tight-lipped sort of voice. 'Shall we go before it gets dark?' Recognising the implacable note of command, Stephen didn't protest, though he called over his shoulder, 'See you later, Susie!'

'Bother, I didn't get him to buy those raffle tickets,' I muttered, 'still, I can catch him later. Now, Hamish . . .' I turned around, determined to exact my revenge.

But he was talking to a middle-aged couple who appeared to know his parents and was obviously going to be occupied for some time so, feeling distinctly and unreasonably deflated, I decided I'd better get back to work. Dusk was beginning to fall and various helpers were lighting hundreds of candles housed in every conceivable sort of container, from grand hurricane-lamp affairs to humble jam jars and mustard pots, and placing them along the wall and on the tables outside. The woman in puce called me over to help as it was taking much longer than they thought it would, principally because the matches didn't reach far enough down half the jars and the holder ended up singeing her fingers. This resulted in a few genteel 'Ouches' and 'Oh dears' from the puce woman or a lot of muffled swearing if it happened to be my fingers on fire. Fortunately, my contributions were drowned out by Arthur Crown and the Tellers, who were still playing their hearts out in their last set before they stopped for supper.

I'd been keeping a vague eye on Arnaud, pleased to see he'd seemed quite happy colonel-baiting each time I glanced his way. Now, however, though he was as attentive as ever, I could tell he'd had enough of being charming to Flavia and her circle, and as for the colonel, he was starting to look positively apoplectic, his eye almost bulging from its socket as he glared at Arnaud through his monocle. It looked like a duel by shooting sticks was imminent. It was time I broke this up. I went over and, tucking my hand into Arnaud's elbow said, 'I'm ravenous. Shall we go and get ourselves something to eat?'

'Good idea!' barked the colonel and before we could get any funny ideas about making a cosy foursome grabbed Flavia's elbow and forcibly bore her off towards the dining room, so fast she nearly came off her perilously high heels.

'I suggest you don't offer to join them at their table,' I murmured to Arnaud, 'not unless you want arsenic in your salad dressing.'

'I do not think I will need extra poison,' he muttered morosely as he took his first look at the huge spread laid out on the long oak table in the dining room. He was being a bit unfair, for though there were certain elements of the curate's egg about it, the salmon was overcooked and just the sight of the rice salad made the food snob next to me snort in disbelief, all in all the ladies of the committee had done themselves proud. They'd sensibly limited themselves to only offering a few choices for each course (Rose had told me the rows and negotiations over which ladies were going to be allowed to impose their favourite dishes on the others were something else), though not surprisingly there were great variations between the five separate dishes of coleslaw made in five different kitchens, and due to an oversight only one lady had been commissioned to do potato salad, with the result that it ran out after ten minutes. Even so, Arnaud declared that his ham had been properly cured and his stuffed courgettes were 'tolerable', and by the time we got to the puddings unbent enough to declare that actually his lemon meringue pie was 'very good'. I hoped that Amanda and Bill who were sharing our table realised what an enormous compliment this was.

Actually, most of the compliments were going Amanda's way. Having sharpened up his act for the evening on Flavia, Arnaud was really getting into his stride with Amanda, who was the sort of vivacious woman he adored. (She also had a C cup, which he liked almost as much.) He was having great fun playing the clichéd flirtatious, licentious Frenchman to the hilt and Amanda was lapping it up with enormous pleasure and flirting back with equal gusto. I cast a slightly worried look at Bill, a great big bear of a man, wondering dubiously how he felt about his wife doing virtually everything involved in making love in public apart from actually taking her clothes off and frightening the horses. He smiled tolerantly. 'She doesn't mean anything by it,' he murmured.

On the other hand, Arnaud might well mean something by

it, but I thought it wiser not to say so, since I wanted Bill and Amanda to look after him while I dutifully flogged the last of my raffle tickets. I passed the tombola, likewise now virtually denuded of all prizes, except one. My bottle of Algerian red was still sitting firmly in the middle of the table.

'Want a raffle ticket, Mary?' I asked.

'If you buy one of mine,' she replied.

'No fear!' I said quickly, and added in explanation of my churlishness, 'I might get that back!' I pointed at my bottle.

'Is it really that bad?' she asked, eyeing the bottle speculatively. 'Roger's ex-wife has invited herself to stay and I don't want to encourage her to linger . . . She's a bit of a wine snob too.' She giggled. 'I'll have five tickets. Look, what a surprise. See what I've won! Won't Alicia be pleased when she sees this in the middle of the table! I wonder if she'll make it to the end of dinner . . .'

It was nice to know that my bottle had at last found a home where it was really wanted, I thought with a smile, as I handed over my ticket stubs to the puce woman, glad that she'd commandeered two others for the tedious task of folding all the tickets for the draw. The wine tasting had finished with supper, though the bar was still doing a roaring trade, and I ended up helping Jeremy and a couple of others fold up a few of the trestle tables for collection the next morning while others busily moved the crates of empties around to the back. Then we wandered back to the dining room where the tables had all been pushed to the side and under the influence of several bottles of tasting wine Arthur Crown and the Tellers had bowed to popular demand and unpacked their instruments again. Right now they were giving a spirited rendition of Glenn Miller and Arnaud was beguining the beguine with Amanda with a touch more enthusiasm than might have been deemed strictly necessary by Bill. Jeremy looked morosely around the crowded room. 'Oh God! Now they'll be here all bloody night!' he muttered. 'And some of us have to get up at six tomorrow morning.'

'If you've got an early start, you could always slope off to bed,' I suggested.

'Not bloody likely! God knows what Rose would get up to!' he exclaimed bitterly, then shot me a guilty glance. 'Um, our room's above here anyway, I'd never get any sleep with all this noise. I bet this was her idea,' he added with feeling.

'Probably was,' I agreed, 'she adores dancing. Look, there she is, coming in from the terrace. Why don't you bag her for yourself before a queue forms?'

'Good idea,' he muttered, cheering up distinctly. 'If you'll excuse me, Susie.' He headed off purposefully towards Rose.

I breathed a sigh of relief as out of the corner of my eye I saw Luke being waylaid by one of the black-clad teenagers who stood meaningfully in his path until with a resigned smile he led her off to dance. Whereas it would have been nice if he'd been about to ask me to dance, for I'm keen on a bop myself and he looked like he knew how to move, I had a feeling he'd been heading for Rose. And the last thing we all needed right now was Jeremy and Luke in a neck and neck to get to Rose first. I felt certain that Jeremy would have been much more sanguine about the dancing if he hadn't been afraid his wife was going to spend too many numbers locked in Luke's arms. She'd been busy, dashing around doing one thing and another, but it had been noticeable, to me at least, that each time she chose to relax she did it in Luke's company. I had a chill feeling of disquiet. Was she playing with the idea of laying an old ghost to rest once and for all before she finally settled down? I shivered, hoping that she knew what the hell she was doing – and what she was risking. Jeremy didn't strike me as the sort of man who'd forgive his wife a fall by the wayside or two.

Then Bill came to claim me for a dance, presumably on the sauce for goose and gander basis, and since Rose was locked tightly in Jeremy's arms with every sign of enjoying it enormously I decided that perhaps I was worrying too much. After all, at a function like this in their own house you could hardly expect Jeremy and Rose to be together all the time, and though politeness would say she should have gone around talking to as many people as possible Rose had never suffered bores gladly. It didn't mean a thing that she'd spoken to Luke a few times, I thought, as I endeavoured to keep my toes out of the way of Bill's very large feet.

With admirable single-mindedness the two teenagers annexed Luke completely for the next hour or so. They stuck to his side like glue so he wasn't given a chance to talk to any one else, let alone dance with Rose. They followed him to the bar and outside for a breath of fresh air and since they apparently had no shame in the pursuit of what they wanted I wouldn't have put it past them to have hovered casually outside the gents when he went inside there. They were more effective than a whole posse of chaperones. Luke accepted it with remarkably good grace, merely rolling his eyes at me expressively while showing the more gothic of the two girls some advanced rock-and-roll steps. Arthur Crown's music was getting steadily more modern as the older generation went home. By the time the teenagers' parents insisted that this time they really were going to drag their reluctant offspring away we'd moved up to the early sixties. They departed with longing glances over their shoulders and looking very pleased with themselves. I expected their form common-room would be alive with some very colourful stories on Monday morning.

When Luke finally got his freedom I was dancing with Arnaud, so it would hardly have been politic to say I felt like a drink or something and then promptly abandon him while I made a beeline for another man. I had enough of a guilty conscience about Arnaud as it was. I'd neglected him shamefully this evening. Even with the blasted raffle tickets to sell I could have spent more time with him than I had, I realised, not caring to examine my motives too closely. Looking over his shoulder, I saw Luke wave a casual goodbye to the teenagers, then head straight for Rose on the other side of the room. Within seconds they were making a tight little couple in the middle of the dance floor. Jeremy stood in the doorway, watching them, looking displeased. With a sinking heart I thought I'd have to risk seriously offending Arnaud and go and do a Ladies' Excuse Me when with immaculate timing Arthur Crown announced he was playing a couple of fast ones to get everyone's blood moving then he must stop for fifteen minutes or so as he was parched. I could have flung my arms around his rather portly figure and kissed him as they broke into 'Twist and Shout'. I'd defy anyone to have a clinch while doing the Twist.

As soon as the music stopped there was a mass exodus towards the bar, the band leading the charge. I grabbed Arnaud's hand and made my way casually towards Luke and Rose, who were standing at the back of the crowd waiting for the worst of the queue to subside. Rose shot me a heavily significant look and raised her eyebrows while I introduced the two men. 'You enjoy taking risks, don't you?' she murmured under her breath as the two men were sizing each other up. Judging by the quality of the vibes that hung thick upon the air, I doubted they would ever be bosom buddies.

'What do you mean?' I asked blankly.

She gave me a feline and inscrutable look. 'Not even I have ever deliberately brought *both* my men together at the same time!'

Luke decided the queue had subsided enough to go and get the drinks and commandeered Arnaud to help him. I waited until they were out of earshot and then looked at Rose and said clearly, 'Luke isn't my man, but from the way you've been going on I wouldn't be surprised if half the party thought he was yours!'

She smiled in a particularly annoyingly knowing way. 'Do I detect a little bit of the old green-eyed monster here?' she asked teasingly. 'Honestly, Susie, there I am, keeping your seat warm for you and stopping anyone else getting their hands on him, and you're getting all narky about it!'

She fished in her ridiculously tiny bag for her cigarettes. 'You must have it bad!' she said with a grin. 'I've never known you get jealous before.'

'But I'm not,' I protested, and realised to my surprise that it was absolutely true. I really couldn't give a damn whom Luke spoke to or whom he danced with. Rather in the way that you probe a sore tooth when it stops hurting, just to make sure it's still there, I looked over to where his fair head caught the light as he spoke to the barman and tried to whip up a bit of feeling. Not a single heart-string twanged. Neither did anything less exalted heat up. He was just a good-looking, OK, *very* good-looking, bloke I liked. But didn't desire. It felt rather odd after all that fevered thinking about him. And disappointing. I'd been enjoying my visions of being Susie the man-trap. Still, at least it solved the problem of what to do about him and Arnaud, I thought with resignation.

Rose blew a smoke ring in the air, looking superior and

sceptical. This wasn't the moment to go into explanations, the men were coming back with the glasses, so I just shrugged and said, 'Seriously, Rose, if you really want to have Flavia banging on for the next few weeks about making an exhibition of yourself in public go on wrapping yourself around Luke by all means, otherwise I'd cool it if I was you.'

'Oh,' said Rose thoughtfully. I held my breath as I saw a knee-jerk give-two-fingers-to-Flavia reaction battle with a bit of common sense, and let it out in relief as she nodded in acceptance. 'No one else dances as well as him, that's the problem,' she grumbled, 'but I get what you're saying.' Then she grinned at me and whispered, 'Do you want me to take Arnaud off your hands for a couple of dances so you can have a go at Luke for yourself?'

She did just that, holding out her hands to Arnaud the moment the music started up again so that he couldn't refuse. I smothered a smile, neither of them looked too happy about it, and turned back to talk to Luke, who was still finishing his drink, when Stephen appeared at my side and grabbed my hand, saying, 'Come on, Susie, you're on for a bop, aren't you?' I was pulled willy-nilly into the still-substantial crowd, wondering what Liddy was going to say about this. Nothing good, I'd bet. Stephen had been drinking steadily all evening, and though he wasn't obviously drunk there was a careful enunciation in his speech and a glitter in his eyes that gave the game away. I'd been within earshot when Liddy'd demanded they go home and he'd refused flatly with an inebriated obstinacy. She was now sitting at a table at the side of the room, bristling with put-upon indignation and refusing to dance, foot tapping impatiently and watching us with an eagle eye. It didn't do anything for my coordination. I'd have been out first heat if this had been the modern-dancing section of

294

Come Dancing. Then my feet got even more tangled up with each other as Hamish sat down next to her and she leant towards him, saying something with a frown that was visible even at this distance. Stephen had one arm firmly around my waist as he moved arrhythmically to the music, the other resting heavily on my shoulder. I had a feeling it was for support more than the pleasure of being near my body, in fact I was being held so close I *knew* it was only for support, but I could just imagine what it looked like. I wondered whether he would fall over if I stepped backwards out of his grip, and decided even avoiding the excruciating embarrassment of apparently making a play for my boss in front of Hamish wasn't worth the risk of Stephen toppling like a felled oak and braining himself on the parquet floor. While I was contemplating whether I could persuade him to sit down, though judging from his closed eyes and dreamy expression I was going to have great difficulty making any contact at all, Rose and Luke shimmied into view. She hadn't danced with Arnaud for long, I thought crossly, as Stephen was tapped on the shoulder by Hamish, who said in a no-nonsense sort of voice, 'Hey, you've monopolised Susie for long enough. It's my turn now.'

For a moment I thought Stephen was going to argue, so I said in a bright voice, 'We've been dancing for ages and it's not fair on Liddy to leave her alone for too long, is it?'

'If Liddy'd dance she wouldn't be alone, would she?' he said with, I felt, a certain amount of justice, but somewhat reluctantly he slowly let me go and made his way over to her with admirable steadiness, considering, while I pulled down my dress which had become alarmingly rucked up at the back. I looked up at Hamish's unsmiling face and for some unaccountable reason felt like bursting into tears. Why couldn't he want to dance with me for its own sake, rather than because he was doing Liddy a favour? I thought dispiritedly, deciding I must be very tired to mind so much. To offset any danger of weepiness, I scowled at him crossly and said, 'It is normal to *ask* a girl if she wants to dance, you know.'

His eyes glinted as he said, 'I wasn't aware I'd said anything about dancing, merely that Stephen was taking up too much of your time.'

I stared at him open-mouthed. Oh, well done, Susie! Talk about hoisting yourself with your own bloody petard! I thought grimly. In a minute I was going to howl.

'But we can have a dance if you'd like,' he added kindly.

Any lachrymose feelings were wiped by an almost over-powering urge to kick him on the shin. I had to remember I wasn't nine any longer. I smiled at him sweetly. 'Well since you're so insistent we can have just one.'

He nodded. 'Just one. I'm on my way home. I only stopped to say goodbye.'

I was tempted again to do violence, then reluctantly I giggled. 'You are the most ungallant, ungentlemanly, con-descending, graceless, off-hand, uncivil, ungracious, unmannerly . . .'

Hamish held up his hands in a gesture of surrender. 'Do you go to bed with the thesaurus each night?' he asked, shaking his head.

It was a good thing he'd stopped me. I'd run out of adjectives. 'No, it's just you inspire me to depths I didn't know I had,' I said.

He smiled at me slowly. Something very odd happened to my heartbeat. 'I'm glad I inspire you to something, even if it's only to insults,' he said. 'Come on, let's have our dance.'

I nodded, not feeling capable of saying anything else. He

put his arm around my waist and led me to the centre of the floor. I felt a bit like Stephen, I needed to cling on to something desperately for support, only I didn't dare do anything other than rest my hands very lightly on Hamish's forearms. Otherwise I might give into the temptation to cast my arms around his neck and hang on like a limpet, and hadn't I already made enough of a fool of myself in front of Hamish in one way and another without adding flinging myself at him in the most blatant manner to the list? I kept myself rigid, concentrating on the view over his shoulder, resolutely ignoring the heady scent under my nose, a mixture of warm skin, aftershave and fabric conditioner, and the prickles that shot down my spine as his breath tickled the back of my neck. I sternly reminded myself of Merial every five seconds or so, otherwise I'd have found myself getting closer, closer . . . With her around I didn't have a chance, so I'd better remember that or it was rejection city here we come, I reflected bitterly. How could I have fallen out of lust with one man and into lust with another all in the space of one evening? What sort of trollop did that make me? One with much too vivid an imagination, I realised ruefully, as I visualised all too clearly that normally trollops do a lot more than dance with a man, and my knees began to shake all over again.

What was happening to me? I had an urge to stroke the back of his neck where the short hairs grew. I wasn't like this. I don't have urges to fondle any man who crosses my path. Except that Hamish wasn't any man . . . And I didn't have any desire to fondle any other man at all.

I went cold. Oh God. I was about to go home with another man, wasn't I? Another man who had every right to presume we were going to pick right up from where we'd left off before, like the familiar lovers we were, like we'd always done in the past. But everything had changed. What sort of mess had I got myself into now? I couldn't pretend to Arnaud that everything was as normal. Even if I could have brought myself to do it, he wasn't stupid. I closed my eyes in despair. He was going to be *furious* about this.

CHAPTER 16

Arnaud was. And I couldn't blame him either. Well, I wouldn't have been too happy if I'd gone over to see him in Paris only to be told once I'd got there it was all over. But it didn't make me change my mind. What he couldn't understand wasn't that I might have another boyfriend (and he was convinced I must for there could be no other explanation for me jettisoning a perfectly good relationship), but that I couldn't adopt his cheerful amorality – for this one night. 'He is going to think we are sleeping together tonight anyway, so what is the point of making me sleep in the spare room?' he asked with maddening reasonableness (from his point of view at least). 'We can have one last night to remember,' he added, flashing me one of his most beguiling smiles.

I was tempted. As he'd said, anyone who cared to think about it would probably presume we'd be at it all night, making up for lost time, so what harm would there be? Especially if it meant we could part on better terms. And despite everything I was still very fond of him. Completely platonically. That part of me which had thrilled to his touch had switched off, permanently. But since I hadn't wanted to really wound him by spelling out that it wasn't only scruples keeping me from falling into bed with him, I'd sort of skirted around the subject. Maybe I could use memories to whip up a bit of desire . . . I thought. But cheerfully selfish as he was in many ways, Arnaud wasn't selfish in bed, he'd know I was faking. That'd be even more humiliating for him in the long run.

I shook my head. 'I'm sorry . . .'

Once it really sank in I meant it and wasn't going to change my mind he didn't take it graciously. I suspected he'd had the idea that if our liaison ever came to an end for any reason other than inertia it wouldn't be him on the receiving end of the boot; probably hurt pride shared the responsibility with frustration for the major attack of bad temper that followed. I let him rant at me for a bit – after all, it was the least I could do after the way I'd treated him – and prayed desperately that Mrs Tanner didn't have a glass pressed against the wall and was listening to every word. If she repeated any of what he was saying my reputation in the village would be in shreds within hours. As he began to wind down I handed him a glass of wine and took a large one for myself. After the character assassination he'd just dealt out I needed fortification. It's even worse when you feel you've deserved it. I sat in a chair opposite him and took a gulp, the glass shaking slightly in my hand.

There was silence for a minute or two, then he said, 'I do not mean all of that.'

I smiled wanly at him. 'Thank you. I was beginning to wonder why you'd bothered with me for so long if that was what you'd really been thinking of me all this time.'

'You know why, we are good together,' he said matter-of-factly. 'And I think you are stupid. This small-minded English morality, I thought I had taught you to forget it, but no! I do not see why we should not enjoy each other, even if you have the other boyfriend. This is what makes me cross.'

Hopping mad would be more accurate, I thought wryly. It was a good thing he didn't know there wasn't another boyfriend;

he'd be even more furious if he realised I'd turned off him because of a passion destined to remain unrequited. He drained his glass and stood up. 'I think,' he said with dignity, 'it would be best if you take me to the station to catch the first train. Since you are being so *moral* –' he loaded the word with all the contempt only the French can give it and then looked at me hopefully. I stared back wide-eyed, showing I hadn't changed my mind – 'there is no point being hung for the lamb when it could have been a ship.'

It took me a few seconds to get my brain around this convoluted and mispronounced sentence. 'Oh Arnaud, you don't have to worry about what people think of me,' I began, once I'd worked out what he meant, heart warming at his consideration.

'I do not,' he said tersely. 'Fanny does not know that I am seeing you. I told the hotel to say I was asleep if she rings. But this way I will return in time to answer the telephone myself.'

'Fanny?' I repeated. '*Fanny?* The Fanny who's the daughter of your parents' friends?' I remember noting the name, since for obvious reasons it's not one you hear much in England any longer. 'The one at the Sorbonne, whose parents asked you to keep an eye on her?'

He shrugged and looked at me defiantly. 'So?'

If she was ringing him at his hotel she must be a fairly serious item. Arnaud didn't allow himself to be bothered unnecessarily by his women. Especially students he was merely 'looking after'. Just how stupid had I been to fall for *that* one? As far as I could recall, Fanny was an only child and her parents had a pretty little château near the banks of the Loire. I wouldn't have called Arnaud mercenary, well not precisely, but there's no doubt he believed in the old adage of not loving for money but making sure you love where money is. No wonder he'd been so nice to me when he arrived, he'd probably been gearing himself up to give me a Dear Jeanne, after we'd had an extensive session of 'enjoying' each other, of course. Though actually, knowing Arnaud, maybe not. It was more likely he'd been intending to wheedle me into agreeing to a very discreet liaison indeed, one that involved no telephone calls to his *appartement* or birthday cards, just me hanging around in a diaphanous nightie, waiting for him to call. And he'd had the nerve to take umbrage and tear me to shreds! I thought indignantly. Then the ridiculousness of the whole situation struck me, a half-decent playwright could turn this into a Whitehall farce in no time at all. I smothered a smile, thinking that even if I didn't have the upper hand, at least I wasn't still in the position of grovelling on the floor. 'I hope you'll both be very happy,' I said.

He looked rather startled. 'There is no question of that yet,' he said quickly, eyeing me warily. It must have occurred to him that it was my turn to make a scene, especially considering the number of times he'd made it kindly, but firmly, clear there was absolutely no question of our getting married, because he wasn't the marrying kind, and the agony and tears it had caused me. Well, it seemed he *was* the marrying kind, just not to me! I thought crossly, tempted to throw something at him. But maybe it was a good thing. The notion of being married to a man who would be faithful only if you handcuffed him to the bedposts had begun to lose its charm some time ago. I grinned at the thought. He'd probably have found a way around that, and enjoyed himself enormously in the process too.

'Is she pretty?' I asked.

'Yes,' he said promptly. 'Very.'

And rich. And I was prepared to bet that she had ingrained

chic, always remembered to use scent, hung up her clothes at night and would learn how to give those terrifyingly smart Parisian dinner parties. I smiled. 'Lucky you. I expect she'll suit you perfectly.'

Did I detect a touch of chagrin mixed with the relief that I was taking this so well? 'I don't think either of us are really in a position to throw stones at each other, do you?' I asked, as I fetched the bottle of wine and refilled his glass. 'So shall we cut out the recriminations?'

He considered this. I could see that he still reckoned that right was on his side, after all he'd been generously prepared to continue letting me have a small part of his time, but I think that, like me, he wasn't keen to let five years end on too bitter a note, so he nodded without much warmth. I made us both coffee and we talked about jobs, flats, the cottage, anything rather than our respective love lives. When I glanced at my watch, wondering how long it was before we had to leave for the station, I saw to my surprise it was nearly time to go. The dawn chorus was already starting up in the most infuriatingly cheerful way, and the sky was tinged with gold as the sun rose over the fields at the back of the cottage.

We were both silent on the journey, we'd said enough already. As I drew up in the deserted station, the only car in the quick put-down and pick-up section, Arnaud turned to me and, leaning over, kissed me on the lips. 'Keep safe, Susie, and good luck.' He drew back, holding my face in his hands. 'I still think you are foolish. It is possible to have your gâteau and eat it, you know.'

'For you maybe,' I retorted with a faint smile. 'Think how nice it's going to be to talk to Fanny later this morning with a clear conscience.'

He raised his eyebrows. 'But what would I have a conscience

about?' he asked with perfect seriousness, and got out of the car.

I watched five years of my emotional life walk away, a huge lump in my throat, feeling so bereft that for a moment I was tempted to call him back. But it was no good, that chapter of my life was closed. I didn't know if he'd even come if I did call. I blinked a couple of tears away from my eyes, put the car into reverse and drove off, unable to stop wondering if I'd just made an enormous mistake.

'Gosh, look who's had a *very* active weekend!' said Amanda suggestively as I arrived at work on Monday morning. She winked broadly. 'Did he let you have any sleep at all?'

I sighed wearily as I headed for the coffee machine. I knew exactly what one night without any sleep at all and another spent tossing and turning, deciding I was completely mad on several counts, had done to the bag quotient under my eyes. I was so tired that I could hardly put one foot in front of the other. It was a toss-up between falling asleep over the computer or waking myself up by giving my nerves a caffeine overload so large that Martin would be in a severe danger of having my letter-opener stuck in him if he even so much as made one unpleasant remark. I decided to let Martin take the risk and poured out a huge mug of the heavily stewed viscous brown liquid that masquerades as coffee in the office.

'So?' Amanda asked expectantly. 'Blast it!' she muttered, as a truly early bird came in to ask if she could take her to have another look at an empty house nearby. With a big smile for the client and a silent session of eye rolling at me, Amanda hissed, 'We'll have lunch. OK?' and grabbed her bag and the house keys.

I'd been hoping for a nice peaceful day during which I

could doze over my screen, but as always things didn't turn out that way. Jenny had gone down with a flu bug that was going around so I had to take on all her work, several people came in wanting to go over house details, which I had to deal with as Martin was out as well, and the telephone never seemed to stop ringing with requests for a brochure detailing a former rectory 'in need of some updating' that we'd advertised in the *Sunday Times* the day before.

'We've had thirty calls about the rectory already,' I said to Stephen as I took his post in during a brief respite. 'I know loads of them are just curious, but it's still not bad, is it?'

'Everyone likes the idea of being able to modernise something, they think they've got the chance of a bargain,' he said, taking off his glasses and rubbing them with a red silk handkerchief. 'Er, did you enjoy that party on Saturday?' he asked, fiddling with the pens in the large pot on his desk. He seemed curiously ill at ease, looking down at his blotter and refusing to meet my eyes.

'I'll certainly remember it,' I said with feeling.

The pen pot toppled over, sending pens flying everywhere. One rolled under the bookcase, another two fell in the wastepaper basket. I brushed against Stephen as I fished them out for him and handed them back. He jumped like a scalded cat. I looked at him curiously and he dropped his eyes quickly.

'Er, I hope they made plenty of money,' he said, appearing to snatch a subject out of the air at random.

'Getting on for at least two thousand pounds, I should think,' I said.

'Good,' he said vaguely. 'Look I've got something to work on this morning, make sure I'm not disturbed, will you?'

'Of course,' I said, about to leave, then I was gripped by a nasty little sense that I knew exactly what was wrong with him. I could hazard a fair guess that at best he had only a hazy memory of the latter part of Saturday night. But if he could vaguely recall being wrapped in a rather tight clinch with his assistant, whom he knew perfectly well he didn't fancy, he'd probably jumped to a seemingly logical conclusion as to why it had happened. God, he was probably terrified I was about to leap on to his knee, whip off his specs and breathe huskily, 'My word, but you're handsome without your glasses, Mr Bailey-Stewart.' No wonder he looked as if he wanted to keep a safe, unlungeable distance between us. It would be funny if it wasn't also desperately serious. I couldn't afford to brush this under the carpet. I took a deep breath. 'Stephen, what's the matter?' I asked directly. 'Is it something to do with Saturday night?'

His head shot up, and he looked at me with something that seemed very much like alarm. 'I was hoping you wouldn't remember,' he said to my surprise. 'I'm so sorry, Susie. I don't know what came over me . . '

'What are you talking about?' I asked in astonishment.

'Liddy says I . . . I . . .' he mumbled. 'That I made a complete fool of myself and I'll be lucky to escape a sexual harassment suit.'

'Rubbish!' I exclaimed, almost weak-kneed with relief that Liddy hadn't been saying it was *me* who'd been harassing him. 'You were leaning on me like a farmer with a gate, but that's all, I promise you! You didn't even tread on my toes.'

He didn't smile. 'Are you sure?' he asked doubtfully. 'Because Liddy said . . .'

'As I'm the one you were resting on *I* should know, however it appeared to Liddy!' I retorted. 'Look Stephen, I've had experience of being jumped by an employer and I can promise you that if you'd even *thought* about laying a finger on me

306

you'd have been picking up your own pens just now. I'd have stayed down this end of the room, out of reach.' As he still looked doubtful, I put my hands on my hips and glared at him. 'Believe me, I don't lie about things like this,' I said forcefully.

'Really?' he asked. I nodded. His face cleared. 'Thank you, Susie.' He hesitated. 'So can we forget it?'

'Consider it done,' I said, then just in case he was still harbouring any lingering doubts I added teasingly, 'Until I want a raise, that is.'

He'd recovered enough of himself to say, 'I think I pay you quite enough. And I enjoyed our dance very much.'

'Even though you had to take your second choice because Liddy didn't want to dance?' I asked teasingly from the door.

He was gallant enough to avoid agreeing this was true, but only just, I saw with a spurt of amusement.

I was telling Amanda all this over a glass of wine in the wine bar while we were waiting for Rose, who'd rung demanding to meet us for lunch. She nodded thoughtfully. 'I think Liddy got a real fright on Saturday. She's been giving Stephen hell these last two weeks and when they go out there you are looking stunning – in a dress I chose of course,' she added with satisfaction, 'and she begins to think maybe this time she's gone too far, she's pushed him into looking elsewhere.' She smiled wryly. 'And, of course, being Liddy, she over-reacts completely!'

'I just hope she doesn't over-react to the degree she badgers Stephen until he agrees to get another assistant,' I said gloomily.

Amanda raised her eyebrows. 'She wouldn't be so stupid! She knows how long it took Stephen to find someone who suited him last time. I don't think she'll want to go through that again!'

Well, that was some comfort, at least, I thought as I waved at Rose who was peering through the window to see if we'd arrived. She came rushing in, waving at the waiter and exclaiming she needed a drink, *now*. 'What a weekend! Am I glad to get away from the house and to see you two!' she said, sinking down in her chair and managing to get her cigarettes out all in one movement. She lit one, drew in a long puff with a blissful expression of satisfaction then, letting the smoke out, turned to me with a critical look. 'You look completely knackered,' she said, 'so I presume you had the sort of rapturous reunion with Arnaud that we all fantasise about.' She grinned. 'You lucky cow! I tried to ring you yesterday, get you both to come over and have some lunch, the atmosphere certainly needed lightening, but I couldn't get any answer.' She leered suggestively, 'I suppose you were both too busy to worry about things like the phone.'

'I was riding around Rutland Water,' I said. I'd had this idea that loads of physical effort exorcises restless, gloomy thoughts. All I can say is it doesn't work. Not for me anyway. All that happened was that after twenty-six miles on a rented bike I was exhausted, still had restless, gloomy thoughts, in bucket-fuls, and had to cope with a very sore behind as well.

'*Arnaud*? Was *bicycling* around Rutland Water?' exclaimed Rose incredulously, as well she might.

'No, Arnaud was back in London,' I said in a resigned voice as she sat up expectantly. I was going to have to spill the beans sometime, so I might as well get it over and done with. The explanations were complicated by the fact there was no way I was going to tell either of these massively indiscreet gossips I'd realised I didn't love Arnaud any more at the same time as I was fighting all the base instincts I'd never known I had that were telling me to launch myself at Hamish. Naturally, they were rather puzzled about what had caused this massive sea-change and my explanations were patchy to say the least, but fortunately they were soon running ahead with their own conclusions, which they didn't want muddled up by any accuracies from me. I would have expected Rose to be dancing on the tables, singing Hallelujah! at the news – heaven knows she'd told me enough times to get rid of Arnaud – but she seemed rather shocked and subdued by it, even saying in a low voice, 'Are you sure you know what you're doing?'

I nodded, a bit sadly. 'Absolutely.'

'What a shame,' said Amanda regretfully. 'I had a lovely time with him, but I suppose it's a bit much expecting you to keep hold of your boyfriend just so I can have a nice chaste clinch with him from time to time.'

'*Chaste?*' I exclaimed. 'Arnaud's never chaste!'

'Chaste enough,' she said primly. She winked at me. 'I suppose you wanted to have your hands free so you could get them on that lovely Luke, did you?'

'Not precisely,' I muttered.

Rose laughed, somewhat shrilly. 'Jeremy'll be delighted, for one. He made the most terrible scene because he thought I spent too much time with Luke on Saturday, even though I told him that I was just looking after him for you.' She glowered savagely at her glass. 'He doesn't have any *right* to talk to me like that!' There was an awkward silence for a moment, while Amanda and I tried to think of something that would deflect Rose from the memory of what must have been a humdinger of a row. In retrospect, riding around Rutland Water getting saddle sores seemed definitely the soft option compared to refereeing what must have been a thoroughly uncomfortable lunch yesterday.

Rose giggled suddenly. 'Jeremy's really cross with you, Susie!

He says you've got to learn to keep your boyfriends under control! One of them was all over his wife and the other was making up to his mother, and he's *not* going to have it!' She looked up, all her ill humour gone in one of her mercurial changes of mood as we all laughed. 'And guess what? This is a real hoot! The colonel's decided he's not having it either. Not any longer! He's damned if he's going to be outclassed by a young whipper-snapper, and a Frenchie to boot. He's invited Flavia to go and stay with him next week in Yorkshire. She's started packing already!' She rolled her eyes expressively. 'And you'll be pleased to hear I've decided to make my peace with her, and my first step in that direction is offering to go shopping with her in London to get some new clothes so she can wow the long johns off the colonel.'

'You'll both enjoy that,' I said, wondering if at last Rose and Flavia had found their common ground. Rose was an enthusiastic shopper.

She made a face. 'If Jeremy doesn't wreck it by making a fuss about all the money I might be spending. He found the credit-card slip for that dress I wore the other night and hit the roof. Honestly, you should have heard him! It wasn't *that* expensive and he'd be the first one to complain if I didn't look decent—'

'Decent is one thing you didn't look in that dress,' I interrupted.

She flapped an exasperated hand in my direction. 'I mean, if we need the readies that badly all he has to do is agree to this housing thing.'

'Oh, isn't it going ahead?' asked Amanda, with a certain degree of professional interest. She was particularly good at selling modern houses.

Rose shrugged, looking around for the waiter to call him

over for another glass of wine. 'Who knows? I'm quite keen on it now, but Jeremy's still deciding. As it's his property, I suppose I'll have to let him have the final decision,' she said with large-minded generosity, attention on getting the waiter to look our way. 'Ah! Three white wines, please. Now, Susie, explain, was it before or after you made your decision to chuck him that you found out about Arnaud's Fanny?'

The waiter delivered his wine to a table full of women nearly weeping with laughter.

CHAPTER 17

The phone was going the next evening as I walked in. It was Lauren, just ringing for a chat, so she said (on the Bull and Bush's phone, naturally), but actually to find out if I'd got anywhere with Stephen. I informed her truthfully that I hadn't, and it certainly wasn't because he was a poof, and less truthfully gave her the impression I had hunky country folk just falling out my ears. I couldn't resist feeding the impressed awe in her voice. 'You lucky thing,' she said enviously, and went on to grumble about Saul for quite fifteen minutes – it appeared his initial was about to join the line on the wall above Lauren's bed. He was getting possessive and unreasonable apparently, and on Lauren's nights off wanted her to stay in with him rather than go out with a bunch of girlfriends to watch a group of male strippers. (Was this a regular occurrence? I wondered.) I made all the right noises, but thought when she finally rang off (the customers were getting unreasonably stroppy about the barmaid nattering and not pulling pints) that actually I wouldn't mind having someone around who objected to my going out and leaving him. I had a thoroughly good wallow in self-pity for a few minutes until I was interrupted by a knock at the door and Mr Tanner offering me a bunch of radishes from his garden and another extensive chat. Twenty minutes later I got around to going upstairs to

313

change out of my office clothes, which were beginning to feel like limp dishcloths that had been used once too often. It was loweringly hot, the air still and heavy with the promise of a storm to come, though the sky was a cloudless metallic blue. I threw my dress on a chair, even short sleeves were too warm in this weather, and put on a pair of shorts and a sleeveless tee-shirt, twisting my hair up so its weight was off my neck and fixing it with a butterfly clip.

I was planning a glass of wine, a book and a chair in the garden when the bell went once more. Probably Mr Tanner again; he'd said something about having more lettuces than he knew what to do with, adding rather pityingly he'd seen over the fence that I'd planted some shop-bought seedlings and I should know they never did as well as ones you grew yourself. The slugs liked them just as much, though, I thought wryly as I went to the door again. But instead of a demonstration of superior home-growing it was a slightly battered paperback that met my eye.

'I'm sorry,' said Hamish apologetically. 'It got a glass of water knocked over it. I think I dried it properly so the pages don't stick together.'

'Don't worry, I read in the bath, so it was bound to get wet sometime,' I said, amazed my voice was coming out normally. 'But you needn't have bothered to make a special journey to bring it back.' My brain was screaming out dismayed protests. Why, oh why, couldn't he have dropped round just after I'd had an extensive session of making-up and hairdressing, instead of when I was wearing a pair of shorts so short they were nearly indecent and my make-up was virtually non-existent? I glanced down quickly to check that my tee shirt wasn't the one with the embarrassing stain down the side. It wasn't, which was a mercy, but neither was it my new one with the flattering scooped neckline. That was languishing uselessly in my cupboard. And I was prepared to bet that my face was positively glowing too, but not with the sort of shine that takes a beautician about an hour to apply. As for my hair . . . Hadn't that magazine article I was reading only last week said the only time you should wear a butterfly clip was in the bath? I wanted to put my head between my hands and howl with frustration – in every sense of the word.

Oh well, I thought gloomily, he'd shown on Saturday he was quite impervious to me even when I was looking my best, so what did it matter that I was looking like the 'before' in one of those magazine makeover articles? Needless to say, I found this philosophical reflection small comfort, but I managed to forget my mirror-cracking appearance for long enough to invite him in for a drink. The speed with which he accepted was some balm to my troubled spirit but, on the other hand, he might just have been thirsty.

And hot. I set the bottle down on the table in the garden and began to open it while Hamish threw off his suit jacket, ripped off his tie and stuffed it in his pocket, then rolled his sleeves up to his elbows. I watched his transformation from the formal solicitor with every button done up correctly who'd arrived at my door into something quite different with frank interest and not a little alarm. I could cope with a solicitor, not make a fool of myself, just be cool and act like he was any of my friends. After all it wasn't the solicitor who got my hormones racing (though, actually, he didn't do a bad job on them either) and it was the solicitor whom I'd invited inside. But a half dressed, even three-quarters dressed, solicitor was another affair altogether!

'I frequently wonder why I ever took up the law. If I'd been a video cameraman I'd never have had to wear a suit again,' he remarked idly as he undid a couple of buttons at his neck.

'Is that what you wanted to do?' I asked in rather a strangled voice, trying not to watch, and failing completely.

'Not really, I was always interested in doing this. Boring, isn't it?' he remarked, looking anything but as he ran his hand through his hair.

He looked around and saw me watching him. I could feel myself colour vividly. 'You must have air-conditioning in your car,' I said wildly. 'I'd have melted in about five minutes in this heat with that suit on.'

'I do. It comes into its own on about four days a year, and for those four days it's worth every penny it costs, especially when you've just been visiting an eighty-year-old who's very hot indeed on the appalling informality of the younger generation,' he said wryly. 'I didn't dare do so much as loosen my tie!' He took a glass from me and sat down on one of Preston's wrought-iron chairs with a sigh of pleasure. I flopped down on the grass in the shade of the tree, not just so that I could look up at him winsomely and make my eyes seem larger, but because it's not flattering to milky-white thighs, even ones a lot slimmer than mine, to be spread out over an only slightly whiter seat. And this way I could arrange my legs so the flabby bits fell in the most flattering positions.

Not that he seemed to be paying any attention to my legs at all, I noted resentfully as we chatted about the other night. Though unfortunately pale unless I've had time to apply fake tan, my legs are generally acknowledged to be quite a decent shape. Particularly my ankles. I drew my legs up so I could draw attention to my crossed ankles, but he didn't even give them a second look, just one brief glance, before carrying on with a story about a self-proclaimed wine buff who'd insisted that the Chardonnay at the party had been bottled under the wrong label and it was actually Sauvignon.

At least he didn't seem in any hurry to leave, I thought as I got up to pour the second glass of wine. Merial must be on duty tonight. 'What did you do with Arnaud on Sunday?' he asked as I sat down again. 'Did you do the grand tour around the area?'

My hand shook. Bugger it! I was going to do my traditional trick of pouring my drink all over myself in front of Hamish if I wasn't careful, I thought crossly. I put the glass down carefully on the grass beside me. 'No.' This seemed a bit short, so I added neutrally, 'He had to go back to London.'

'That's a shame for you. When's he coming to see you again?'

I dropped my eyes and began to study the varnish on my toenails with close attention. 'He won't be,' I said tersely.

There was a long silence. 'Poor bloke,' he said at last. 'You could have seen it coming, I suppose. It was pretty obvious the other night that your attention wasn't on him. I won't offer you my commiserations, because you don't look as if you need any.'

I looked up, stung by the acid note in his voice. 'Neither does he, actually! He insisted on leaving at the crack of dawn, not because of a broken heart, but so when his girlfriend from Paris rang him at his hotel he wouldn't have to make any awkward excuses about why he wasn't there at breakfast time.'

'You're joking!' he exclaimed, putting his glass down on the little iron table with a clink. He shook his head in disbelief, then added thoughtfully, 'Surely the answer was for him to tell her to ring him on his mobile, then she wouldn't know where he was.'

'Even Arnaud would draw the line at arranging to be called

317

by one woman when he's anticipating being in bed with another!' I protested.

'It doesn't appear he draws the line at anything much!' Hamish said, then looked at me curiously. 'You sound as if you were used to it. Didn't you *mind* about his other girlfriends?'

'Of course I did!' I replied. 'I hated it, used to pretend to myself it was only flirting and wouldn't lead to anything.' As Hamish raised his eyebrows sceptically I added, 'It didn't – most of the time. If Arnaud went to bed with all the women he flirts with he'd never have the energy to get up! We split up a couple of times over the more blatant cases, but he'd promise to behave himself and I'd believe him. Until the next time of course.'

'I see,' he said stiffly. 'So you'll be having a grand reconciliation in a few weeks?'

I shook my head. 'This was different. I didn't even know about her until afterwards.' I smiled wryly. 'It's the first time I've ever been *pleased* about one of his girlfriends. Knowing he's going to have some ample consolation helps me feel a bit less of a heel for dumping him like that.'

'It doesn't sound as if he needs an enormous amount of sympathy,' Hamish said dryly as he picked up his glass again, twirling it around in his fingers. 'And when will you be riding off into the sunset with Luke Dillon?' he asked, in a voice that was disappointingly free of jealousy.

'I won't!' I said promptly. I scuffed my toe around in the grass a bit and, since I was hardly going to tell him the *real* reason I'd lost all interest in Luke, said vaguely, 'I'm not going to have any more part-time boyfriends. I'm fed up of not seeing them from one week to the next. If he doesn't live within reasonable distance, all week long, I'm not interested!'

I hugged my legs tightly. 'In fact, he's got to work the same sort of hours as me too, no one who often works nights or weekends either.' I stared fixedly at a pair of daisies in the grass. 'You must find that very difficult with Merial, don't you?' I asked in an ever-so-casual voice, as if it was just any old afterthought.

'Merial?' he asked. 'What was she got to do with it?'

'Well,' I said, beginning to curse myself for starting this, 'her hours and things, being a doctor and all that. It must make it difficult to know when you're going to see her.' I rested my face on my knees, hoping to hide the crimson tide of self-consciousness I could feel creeping up my face in the most hideously embarrassing way.

'What on earth gave you the idea I had anything going on with Merial?' he said. Well, she was virtually sitting in your lap for one thing, and you weren't in any hurry to push her off either. 'She's just someone I consult from time to time. Of course she's very pretty.' You aren't kidding! 'And she's a bit of a flirt.' A *bit* of a flirt? I thought incredulously. She'd have been undoing his shirt buttons with her teeth given half the chance. 'But she doesn't mean anything by it.' Doesn't she? Was he being wilfully obtuse? 'We're just friends.' How very, very disappointing for her. 'Though I suppose,' he said, looking into the bottom of his glass thoughtfully, 'something could have happened, except I'm interested elsewhere.'

His words seemed to hang on the air. I didn't dare look at him in case I was fantasising, again. I glanced around uneasily and saw the brilliant blue of the sky was being covered by purplish-black clouds, which were advancing across the sky at a remarkable speed, especially considering that so far not a breath of wind had disturbed the heavy, still air where we were sitting. 'It seems the weather's breaking at last,' I gabbled, snatching with relief at the traditional English solution when faced with a potentially sticky subject. With immaculate timing, there was a low rumble of thunder in the distance to emphasise what I was saying. A minute later a fat drop of rain fell on my knee. 'We'd better go in before we get soaked,' I said hastily, as another drop landed on the end of my nose. I began to scramble up, but I'd been gripping my legs so tightly they'd gone to sleep. Hamish put out a hand to help me up, and I shot upwards a lot faster than I'd expected, stumbling over one foot. I'd have landed back on the grass, flat on my face, if he hadn't grabbed me around the waist so I cannoned into him instead.

'Thanks,' I gasped, cursing myself for my clumsiness. God, I really went out of my way to show myself in a good light in front of Hamish, didn't I? I thought bitterly. Spilling things, passing out, falling over. Now I could probably add winding him to the list as well, since my elbow had caught him squarely in the midriff.

'Are you all right?' he asked, somewhere in the region of my hair, arms still holding me steady.

'I'm fine,' I mumbled, eyes fixed on the two top buttons of his shirt, not daring to look up in case he read my every desire in my face. I had goose pimples everywhere despite the heat radiating from his hands on my waist, and I was burning hot at the same time. There was another rumble of thunder, much closer this time.

'Are you frightened of thunder?'

Before I could stop myself I heard my voice say, 'Not really.' Oh, brilliant! Another own goal, Susie! I thought crossly. There are times when you can be just too bloody honest.

He sighed deeply. 'Come on, give me a break, Susie!' he muttered in my ear.

320

'Oh!' I muttered stupidly. I looked up to see his eyes only inches from mine. My brain seemed to have turned to candyfloss, and for a moment I didn't have a clue what he might mean. Then I smiled at him slightly nervously. 'Actually, I've remembered I'm *terrified* of thunder.'

'That's better!' he said, drawing me closer.

What seemed like hours, yet was no time at all, later I had to come up for some air. I leant against his chest, feeling my heart thumping so rapidly I wasn't sure how it could fit the beats in. His breathing sounded none too steady either. 'Was that the sort of break you meant?' I asked against his collarbone.

'It'll do,' he murmured a bit unevenly, 'for a start.'

'We're getting wet,' I remarked as a breeze ruffled the leaves above us and dumped a small, warm shower on our heads. As ever, take refuge in the weather when actually you're feeling so knocked back that all you really want to say is, 'More! More!'

'So we are,' he said in an uninterested voice, arms tightening around me.

'We're also providing a display for the Tanners and the Hislops,' I said in a slightly strangled fashion just before he began to kiss me again. 'Hamish! *Stop it!* Not where they can see!'

He drew back reluctantly, looking at me with a slow smile that turned my legs to jelly. 'Well, let's go where they can't see then,' he said. We did.

'I had the most extraordinarily vivid dreams about doing this,' I said some time later. We were on the floor in the sitting room – a two-seater sofa had proved itself definitely not large enough for all the interesting things Hamish was demonstrating you could do while keeping your clothes on. Though my shorts were so short and my tee shirt so brief there was

321

plenty he could get at anyway. He wasn't a man who believed in rushing his pleasures I discovered to my mingled delight and frustration, while a spectacular thunderstorm with loads of sheet lightning provided a magnificent backdrop outside. The earth might not be moving, but the air was certainly trembling. My dreams were beginning to seem a bit too accurate for comfort, I thought uneasily as he nibbled my neck. As far as I know, I'm not psychic. 'Are you sure the other night . . . that I didn't . . .' I asked suspiciously.

He stopped what he was doing and lifted his head, the sides of his mouth quirking slightly. 'Well, you did try to kiss me . . .'

'What?' I squeaked in dismay.

'Only goodnight,' he said regretfully, 'and then went back to sleep. I kept hoping you'd wake up and continue where you'd left off, but sadly you didn't.'

I eyed him suspiciously. 'I thought you said you didn't molest comatose women.'

'For a few minutes you were *very* enticingly awake and I may be noble, but I'm not bloody inhuman!' he retorted. 'There is only so much temptation that a normal man can put up with, especially when he's been actively lusting from a distance.'

'Had you?' I asked in surprise.

'Mm,' he confirmed, annoyingly not telling me for how long. 'As it was, I spent most of that night cursing myself for not taking advantage when I had the chance!'

I snuggled closer to him. 'Well get on with it and make up for lost time then!'

I must be a lot less transparent than I thought I was, for no one seemed to notice I was walking around on air or the silly smile that kept on breaking out on my face. Stephen was completely wrapped up in his plans for going off to Paris for a long weekend with Liddy, Martin didn't appear to see anything strange in the fact I actually smiled at him, and Jenny was completely immersed in the complexities of a new computer game that had arrived the day before. Even the sharp-witted Amanda failed to suss out why I spent my lunch hour in the lingerie shop spending a good part of next month's salary on some stunning silky manpleasers. She just assumed that I was cheering myself up, which suited me fine. I wanted to hug my incredible happiness to myself for a bit, savour my secret in peace before it became public knowledge and I might be asked to give some embarrassing explanations as to why I had been apparently bowled over by one man, while I was being actually knocked for six by his opposite. Not to mention only just having got shot of the long-term boyfriend . . . It was a plot worthy of a soap opera, I thought, thoroughly enjoying having a properly dramatic leading role for once. That was why my heart sank when I heard it was Rose on the phone for me. Her talent for sussing out developments in her friends' personal lives borders on the uncanny and I braced myself for an extensive question-and-answer session, with most of the replies greeted with withering scepticism by the interrogator. But she couldn't have been less interested in me, she was rambling on in a most un-Roseish way about Flavia's new wardrobe and how after the success of the party she'd been asked to join a fundraising committee for a new hospice, then added in an ultra-casual fashion, 'Oh, by the way, if you happen to see Jeremy, I spent yesterday evening at your place.'

No you didn't! I thought smugly, then said sharply, 'What do you mean? What are you up to, Rose?'

'Nothing!' she said overcasually. Then she must have felt the vibes coming down the telephone wires for she said sulkily,

'OK, if you must know, he's being absolutely impossible. He's been in a filthy mood ever since the party because he thinks I flirted with Luke. And it's not true either!' she added indignantly. I was glad she hadn't asked me to agree with her. 'Last night I just couldn't take another evening of the silent treatment. So I decided to go and see that Meg Ryan film again, thought it would get me out of the house for a bit. Only I knew that in his present mood Jeremy would assume I was up to something if I said I was going to a film by myself, and one I'd seen before too, so I said I was going to see you. Just back me up if the subject comes up.'

'All right,' I said doubtfully. 'But listen, Rose, I'm not doing this again. Understand?'

'Gosh, you can be pompous at times!' she grumbled. 'But I hear you.'

I didn't like the sound of this at all. Of course, it could be nothing but the truth. Rose was no fonder of being in the wrong than the rest of us and it was quite possible that rather than face a reproachful husband she'd done a temporary bunk. I hoped so anyway. I didn't like to think of Jeremy's reaction if he found out she was deceiving him on a regular basis.

But I shoved Rose and her antics to the back of my mind, I had more important things to think about. Like if I had time to wash my hair before going to Hamish's house tonight, his reaction when he saw my new underwear, what I was going to buy for our dinner, whether he was going to have to work late like he'd warned me he might.

He didn't, to my relief, and his reaction to the new underpinnings was everything that I could have hoped for. As a result, we were rather late in getting around to making the dinner, so it was a good thing I'd opted for the strictly simple and speedy. I left him to do the masculine bit, grilling

324

the steaks and opening the wine, while I made the salad and the dressing and found some candles so that we wouldn't have to eat under the brilliant striplight above the kitchen table. Then, while he finished the steaks off, I picked a few sprigs of honeysuckle from the profusion around the kitchen door and stuck them in a jam jar in the middle of the table.

'That looks nice,' he said approvingly as he put the plates on the table. 'It's what men need women for, their civilising influence. It's not the only thing we need them for, of course,' he added with a sideways look at me.

I was brought up not to waste food, so I ignored the suggestion in his voice. 'If you think women are civilised, you should have seen where I lived in London,' I said. 'The only time it ever got cleared up was when one of us had a man coming round. At one time we all went through a bit of a dry patch on the man front and I don't think the carpet saw the Hoover for about six months! Though I don't think Katie ever worked out how to use it,' I added reflectively. 'She doesn't get on with electrical appliances, so she used to crawl around on her hands and knees, picking up fluff.'

He grinned and said, 'And was Rose handy with the Hoover? I find it difficult to imagine.'

'Oh, we've never shared a flat. But we've been on holidays together, and were still speaking to each other at the end of them, which was quite something. On a couple of occasions we weren't on speaking terms in the middle, though,' I added. 'But I can promise you that if Rose had been in our flat it would've been cleaned top to bottom every few days. She was *never* without a boyfriend, usually had two or three of them at the same time. She was very generous with them too, always trying to pass the spare ones on to her girlfriends, like me.

She's a reformed character now, of course,' I said hastily. 'She only sleeps with married men.'

Hamish laughed. Then he said with a slight edge to his voice, 'So that's what she was trying to do, pass Luke Dillon on to you.'

'Oh no,' I said instantly. 'She couldn't. She never went out with him.'

'But I thought that was why he turned up at the wedding . . .' His fork stopped halfway to his mouth, and he stared at me incredulously, eyes narrowed into slits. 'Are you saying it was *Nigel Flaxman* she went out with?'

I nodded. 'Not for long though. She found out he was married . . .' My voice died away and I stared at him, brain whirling frantically. Then I made one of those lightning deductions I make very occasionally and which led my teachers to believe I was very much brighter than I actually am. 'My God! It was *his* wife you had the affair with, wasn't it?'

A quick look at his face showed that I was right. 'No wonder you two detest each other so much!' I breathed. 'I knew it had to be more than what Luke said.'

'What did he say, as a matter of interest?' Hamish asked mildly.

'That you lost Nigel a lot of money over an error.'

'What a miserable little crawling skunk he is,' he said levelly. I glanced upwards. Though his voice had been even, his eyes glittered with anger. 'He's tied himself so thoroughly to Nigel's coat tails he'd go around telling everyone his own sister turned tricks in King's Cross if that was what suited Nigel. Still, I daresay it's one of the things he's paid for – to do Nigel's muck-spreading for him.' He put his fork down with a slight clatter. 'Nigel did not lose one *penny* through me,' he said emphatic-ally, as if it was me who had made the accusation. 'He couldn't

326

even claim that I alienated his wife's affections, as they used to put it. He had a string of girlfriends, including Rose, so it seems.' He shook his head in amazement. 'And Bettina was indifferent to everything except the weight of his wallet by then. I wasn't even her first lover either.'

'So was it just spite that made him report you to the Law Society?' I asked.

'Gina *has* been busy,' he said mildly. 'Partially, he disliked me even before he knew I was sleeping with his wife. What did he call me when I'd just joined the firm? A "pompous young prig", I think, probably quite justified too.' He smiled wryly. 'I was very earnest in those days. I ventured to point out that his methods of rent collection didn't bear too close a scrutiny, and neither did some of the pay-back clauses in his leases. He's a mean-minded, vengeful sod by any standards, but where I was concerned I reckon he couldn't resist the chance to bring down someone who was too cocky by half, and of course I'd been idiot enough to lay myself wide open. I knew perfectly well what the rules were too.' He sighed ruefully, 'But it seemed worth the risk at the time.'

'What was she like?' I asked, avidly curious to know what sort of woman could have made Hamish chance so much.

'Bettina?' He reached over and refilled both our glasses, thinking for a moment. 'Very, very glamorous –' I loathed her already – 'even though she was a good bit older than me –' that was better – 'one of those tiny little women who look like they could fit in your pocket –' I hated her even more – 'who make you think that they need looking after –' I was definitely going to tear her into pieces if I ever met her. 'She was a director of a couple of Nigel's companies. I first met her when she came in to sign some papers. I thought she was the most stunning thing I'd ever seen.' I'd already gathered that. 'Of course she sensed it, women like that do, and she was looking for amusement. And I was available,' he said flatly. My fingers curled into vindictive little claws. 'I didn't realise how stupid she was until later,' he went on thoughtfully, 'or how vain. She had a mirror on the ceiling above her bed, not for erotic reasons, but so she could lie and admire her reflection. There were mirrors all around the bath too, but she complained they used to steam up.'

I smothered a snort of disbelief. He looked up and smiled. 'True, I promise you! It would probably have petered out eventually, except Bettina was writing down when she was meeting me in her diary – I said she was stupid – and Nigel happened to leaf through it on one of his rare visits to the family home and worked out immediately that this HL she was meeting all over the place wasn't her hairdresser as she'd claimed. For one thing, she'd gone to the Lake District with him. It took him two seconds to get the truth out of her, then he snapped his fingers and she came rushing back to heel, ready to do anything he told her to. No matter how dissatisfied she was with him she wasn't prepared to live without the lifestyle his money brought her, so there was no question of standing by a shortly to be disgraced solicitor.' He took a long swig from his glass, then gazing into the distance said, 'I knew he'd go all out to get me once he found out, but I really didn't expect he'd try and put me in prison.'

'Prison?' I gasped. 'Why?'

'Revenge, of course,' he said matter-of-factly, as if it was a quite normal reaction. There were some times when I thought I would never understand men. 'He was furious I only got hauled over the coals by the Law Society.' His mouth twisted. 'That wasn't exactly a bundle of laughs, I can tell you, and being told by the firm they'd like to shake my dust off their feet as quickly as possible wasn't particularly fun either, but it wasn't enough for him. He'd wanted me to be disbarred. By chance, he discovered his financial director had been skimming money off each time they sold a lease on one of Nigel's properties and he informed the Old Bill that I'd been colluding in it as well.' His fingers tightened so hard around his wine glass that I was afraid the thin stem would snap. 'Have you got any idea what it's like being asked to account for *every* minor financial transaction over the last three years? What you did with the two hundred pounds you took out of the cash point a year ago or why there was a cheque for seventy-five pounds twenty paid into your account? It took six months of delving into everything before they realised I'd virtually never even spoken to the bloke and certainly hadn't accepted any money off him, but by then the whispers had gone around that I was being investigated. And, believe me, mud sticks. That sort of mud, in particular. Nobody likes a shady lawyer. If I didn't have a few good friends and colleagues I might still be jobbing around, looking for some proper work.' He bared his teeth in an unamused smile. 'That's why I'm not very fond of Nigel Flaxman.'

He looked as if he wouldn't be in any hurry to fetch the lifebelt if Nigel was drowning in front of him. I wouldn't bother to get it at all, I thought vindictively. 'No wonder he spent most of Rose's wedding skulking around in the garden, he must have been afraid you'd come out and deck him,' I said thoughtfully.

Hamish laughed. 'That hadn't occurred to me. I thought I was suffering from delusions. I kept on thinking I'd caught a glimpse of Nigel, and then when I'd go and investigate he'd have disappeared. I like the idea of him playing hide and seek around the tent! I wonder why he was there,' he added thoughtfully.

'To cast a critical eye over who Rose was marrying, I expect,' I said. 'She gave him the push, which I gather makes her quite a rarity amongst his girlfriends.'

'Um, perhaps,' Hamish agreed, a shade doubtfully, and appearing to lose interest in the subject picked up his knife and fork again.

'What's happened to Bettina?' I asked quickly, before the opportunity was lost.

He shrugged. 'Don't know. Don't care.' He glanced at me with a glimpse of humour. 'You needn't worry that I'm still carrying a candle for her. Hearing someone tell lies about you in public is a bigger turn-off than any number of cold showers. You, however . . .' He looked at me meaningfully.

'In that case, finish your food. You need to keep your strength up!' I said severely, though my heart was lifting.

His eyes crinkled at the corners. 'Aye, aye, ma'am!' he said smartly.

I got the impression there weren't going to be many areas in which he'd obey me so readily.

CHAPTER 18

I often wondered in the days that followed what would have happened if I'd given into temptation and committed the one unpardonable offence against the sisterhood and put off my friend Tilly's visit to me for Thursday night while she was en route to Scotland. I was booked to go down to my parents' for the weekend the next day and I'd been given the impression it was the full disinheriting scenario if I cancelled without good cause – my father was having important business contacts to dinner on Saturday and required me to be present to stop my mother lobbing a couple of handfuls of tofu into the pheasant casserole or trying out one of her 'interesting' ideas for the pudding. Only death or complete immobilisation in hospital would have been accepted as excuses, merely being in love didn't even make it to the foothills of mitigating circumstances. It seemed intolerable to have to wait until Sunday to see Hamish again, so I was tempted to suggest to Tilly that she could just as easily come and see me on her way back. Only briefly tempted, mind you. Along with an absolute interdiction against speaking with your mouth full, one of my mother's precepts indelibly imprinted on my psyche is that you never, ever cancel a pre-existing arrangement with a girlfriend for the sake of a man. But I did think vaguely how nice it would be if Tilly rang to say that her holiday had been put off for a week or so. Needless to say, she didn't. She arrived at six with a large and wonderfully smelly jasmine in a pot as a housewarming present and what looked like half the contents of her local wine-merchant as a contribution to oiling along an extensive catching-up session.

Actually, as second-bests go, sitting up half the night with an old friend and drinking a lot of cheap red wine while you put the world to rights goes very well indeed. We hadn't seen each other for ages as she'd been working in a hotel in Cornwall for the last nine months, so there was plenty of material for serious gossip. Naturally, I made good use of the opportunity to eulogise about my own newly wonderful love life. Tilly was decent enough to listen and not let her eyes obviously glaze over.

It took me quite two minutes the next morning to realise that the sound reverberating through the house wasn't the alarm, but the doorbell. Groggily, I got out of bed, wondering how few hours I'd been there, and flung the window open, intending to say something extremely rude about people who ring bells before the milk's even arrived.

'Hi, Susie! Did we wake you up?' called Rose cheerfully, peering out from under the shelter of the porch where she'd taken refuge from the drizzling rain that had been falling fairly steadily most of the night.

'Yes!' I said grouchily. 'And as it's not May Day, I don't need to wash my face in dew at the crack of dawn, thank you very much!'

'It's not the crack of dawn and it's time you got up!' she retorted.

Unfortunately, she was right. When I rolled into bed sometime in the early hours of this morning I must have forgotten to set the alarm. So, instead of telling her exactly what she could do with herself at this unearthly hour, I struggled into my dressing-gown, waved a hairbrush vaguely in the direction of my head, and staggered downstairs, trying to unglue my eyelids and wondering if it was just a guilty conscience telling me I should hit the aspirin bottle, and soon.

Rose wasn't someone who enjoyed the fresh joys of the early morning – if she had to see the dawn she preferred to greet it on her way to bed – so what on earth had happened that necessitated visiting me before eight o'clock? I thought vaguely as I fumbled to open the locks with sleep-stupid hands. I blinked as I opened the door. She certainly hadn't got up looking like *that*. She was leaning against the door frame looking sheepish, wearing a scarlet skirt about the width of a Girl Guide's belt in length, a strappy little top, a blouson jacket and high-heeled 'follow me' shoes. Definitely not the usual outfit for a morning's shopping in Frampton. Both her knees had smears of mud on them, there was more dirt on her face and top, and her high-top ponytail hung limp and bedraggled in mousse-heavy hanks, as if it had got soaked and dried out again.

'What's happened?' I asked, appalled, imagining car crashes etc., then saw who was behind her. It was Luke, even dirtier than her, in a damp tee-shirt that must have been white originally and black jeans with heavily mud-stained knees.

'Oh, God!' I said, jerking into full wakefulness. 'What've you done now, Rose?'

'Nothing!' she said indignantly, while Luke chimed in with, 'We had a flat tyre.'

Rose sighed heavily. 'And it took *three* hours to change it. The garage had done the nuts up so tightly they were virtually impossible to undo, and I had to stand in the rain holding the torch so Luke could see what he was doing, then the torch

333

battery ran out, so we had to wait until daylight to finish.' I gathered from her tone that one way and another she hadn't been too impressed by Luke's performance. She looked down at the ground, and I could almost have sworn she was shuffling her feet uneasily. 'The thing is, Susie, can I come in and clean up? I've got something to change into. If I go home like this everyone'll think I've been in an accident.'

'Doing a bit of mud-wrestling, more like, but I see your point,' I said, stepping back to let her in. 'Do you want to ring Jeremy to let him know what's happened?'

She glanced at me quickly. 'It's all right, I've already rung him.' To tell him what? I wondered. You didn't need to be Miss Marple to know that something smelt very bad indeed here.

'You'd better come in too, Luke,' I said without warmth. He glanced at me with slight surprise, obviously wondering what had changed from the last time he'd been here, when I'd probably been behaving with only marginally more discretion than the two teenagers the other night. 'Would you both like some coffee?'

'I'd kill for some!' Rose said in a heartfelt tone and looked back at her companion. 'Dear me, you're so filthy you'll leave a stain on the chairs. Perhaps you'd better borrow something clean off Susie.'

'Frocks aren't really *me*, if you know what I mean,' he said, adopting an outrageously camp accent. At least he was decent enough not to have pointed out that his hip size was probably smaller than mine, I acknowledged grudgingly. 'But I wouldn't mind a chance to wash, if that's OK?'

'Go ahead, take a bath if you want,' I said. This'd give me a precious few minutes with Rose, to threaten to throttle her and do various other unpleasant things unless she explained exactly what she'd been doing spending the whole night out with someone who wasn't her husband. 'Bathroom's straight ahead at the top of the stairs and there are towels in the cupboard.'

'You're a doll, Susie!' he said kissing my cheek. Involuntarily I stiffened slightly and he looked at me queryingly before loping off up the stairs two at a time like a child.

'Perhaps I should go and change too,' Rose said uneasily, no doubt reading my mind and eager to escape from the question-and-answer session she knew was coming.

I fixed her with a stern look. 'Since you got me out of bed the least you can do is help get the coffee ready.' I left her to deal with grinding the beans – I didn't think I could cope with being so close to the vibrations – and looked for the aspirin. If what was rattling around in my head wasn't already a headache, I had a nasty feeling that what I was about to drag out of Rose would convert it into one.

'Well?' I demanded as I switched the machine on. 'What's this about?'

She jumped, almost dropping the mugs she was getting out of the cupboard. 'I don't know what you mean,' she said, blatantly untruthfully.

'Come on, Rose!' I said wearily. 'I'm not that stupid! You've got "guilt" written all over you in six-foot-high letters!' I looked at her with sudden suspicion; the brain was working really slowly this morning. 'Just where did Jeremy think you were going last night?' I asked pointedly.

'Oh, don't go *on* at me!' she said petulantly, pulling out a chair and sitting down. 'I've had a really tiring night and I'm just not up to being cross-questioned!'

If she thought this was 'going on' at her she had quite a surprise in store, I thought with grim wryness. I leant back against the kitchen units, arms folded, looking at her steadily.

'He thinks you were here, doesn't he?' I asked. She said nothing but the little toss of her head gave her away. 'Oh, Rose, how could you? I told you I wouldn't cover up for you again—'

Her head whipped around, and she stared at me with something very akin to fear in her face. 'What are you going to do about it?' she demanded aggressively. 'Be all high-minded and tell him I was economical with the truth?'

I sighed. 'You know I won't,' I said wearily. There was a flicker of relief in her eyes. So the aggression was bravado. The coffee machine burbled and burped its last few drops into the pot and I poured us both a mug, pushing milk and sugar across the table to her, then took up my place against the unit again. 'But I wouldn't mind knowing exactly what we were supposed to be doing, so I don't tell the wrong story if I happen to bump into Jeremy,' I said mildly. 'Line-dancing, poetry-reading at the library, advanced cake-making classes? And how often have we met up since we went to the cinema in Leicester?'

She flinched at the sarcasm in my voice. 'It's not like *that*!' she said defensively.

'Isn't it?' I asked derisively. 'What's spending the *whole night* out with Luke like then? A man, about whom, incidentally, you've already had one serious row with your husband! And who, also, you've had the major hots for and, judging from the way you were acting the other night, still do!' She began ladling sugar into her mug as if she was trying to see how quickly it would make the liquid overflow and said nothing. 'What's the matter with you, Rose?' I said in an exasperated voice, as she started to stir mechanically, apparently not even bothering to listen to what I was saying. 'Two months ago you were swearing undying fidelity to Jeremy and you're *already* playing around with another man!' Her head shot up as I said, 'We've all heard of a seven-year itch, but a seven-*week* itch must be something of a record!'

She started, eyes widening. 'It's not like that at all!' she whispered. 'Really it isn't! You've got to believe me!'

'I'm not the one you've got to convince,' I pointed out.

'Jeremy'll believe me about last night if you back me up,' she said. 'And I wouldn't go back to Luke's house to clean up like he suggested, so that proves I wasn't up to anything, doesn't it?' she asked, with what seemed in my opinion like a quite unreasonable amount of pride in her own common sense. And a considerable degree of naiveté too. 'He was a bit shirty about that, said it was miles out of the way to come via you.'

'And of course you needed to get your story straight with me,' I added dryly. She flushed and nodded. 'Have you got *any* idea what risks you're running?' I asked. 'This is the second time in three days you've used me to give you an alibi. Hamish dropped in the other night to return a book –' I looked away so she couldn't see my self-conscious expression – 'so he knows perfectly well that you weren't having supper with me.'

'But I really was at the cinema then!' she said earnestly. 'I can even show you the ticket if you like. Well, I think I've still got the stub somewhere,' she added doubtfully.

'I don't need to see it,' I said.

She glanced up. 'And I promise I wasn't meeting Luke there either!' She took a sip of coffee and made a face. 'Yuk! Who put all this sugar in here? I suppose I'll have to tell you all,' she said with a heavy sigh, as if I was being totally unreasonable, 'but if I'm going in for the full confession bit I'm going to need a fag.'

I can't say I appreciate second-hand smoke before I've had breakfast, but this was a special case. I fished a saucer out of the cupboard and pushed it over. She lit her cigarette and drew in thankfully. 'I wish Luke had never come to the wedding!' she said in a heartfelt voice. 'I'd honestly, well, if not exactly forgotten him, pushed him right away to some unimportant corner. And then he has to turn up on a day when I'm making the biggest change I'm ever going to make in my life, and I couldn't help it, I tried not to, but I couldn't help wondering if I was really ready to settle down. Then I thought it'd be all right if he went out with you, because your best friend's man is rather like a brother, he's off limits, isn't he?' I looked at her in some surprise, wondering if she really believed this rather ingenuous reasoning. What about a husband? Didn't he put someone off limits as well? 'Then after your car accident, when he came to visit you, he . . .' She hesitated, taking two nervous drags before continuing. 'Oh Susie, I'm sorry, but he made it quite clear that he fancied me.' She looked up with big guilty eyes.

'Oh, that's all right,' I said cheerfully. She glanced at me with soulful eyes and bit her lip, obviously not believing me.

'I know Jeremy loves me, but sometimes he gives the impression he's as keen on the lines of his new tractor as he is on mine. Luke made me feel, well, *gorgeous* all the time. I think I lost my head a bit,' she said quietly. 'I couldn't believe that what I wanted for so long was falling in my lap. But I didn't *mean* anything by it, honestly. Then Jeremy said he wouldn't have Luke in the house, he didn't want me seeing him. You should have heard him. He went on and on, like the complete domestic tyrant!' My mind boggled slightly, it was difficult to imagine Jeremy being tyrannical, he seemed much too good-natured. Either he had hidden depths, or Rose had provoked him to degrees she wasn't revealing. Judging by the look she gave me from under her lashes as she smiled wryly, it was the latter. 'You know I'm not very good at being told what to do, so when Luke rang me to suggest we go clubbing in Manchester—'

'*Manchester?*' I echoed.

'It's where the best clubs are, and it doesn't take long up the motorway,' she said casually. She inhaled deeply. 'I couldn't let Jeremy order me around, could I?' she asked, a tad defensively. 'So I agreed to go.'

She paused while I filled in, 'But you still thought it'd be wiser to tell your domestic tyrant that you were having a girls' night out.'

She nodded, shamefaced. 'I must have been mad! All I could think was that it was my last opportunity to go anywhere with Luke. You'd already broken up with Arnaud so you were free for him, hadn't you? And I'd already told you he was all yours, so I was going to have to step back. Luke said we'd be back by two – Jeremy would have just thought the girls' gossip session overran a bit – but we stayed later than we were supposed to and then he got this slow flat in the middle of *nowhere*. Then it was dawn and I'd been out all night and I knew Jeremy was never going to believe that I hadn't even kissed Luke!'

'Hadn't you, really?' I asked curiously.

'No!' she said indignantly. I watched with interest as a very untypical blush rose up her neck. 'He tried though,' she said quietly. 'I think that was why he was so annoyed I wouldn't go back to change at his house. He was hoping for . . .' Her voice trembled slightly and she swallowed hard. 'But it never crossed my mind,' she said earnestly. 'I thought we were just having fun. I mean, I've just got *married*!' I believed her. She can be remarkably simplistic at times. 'Jeremy mustn't ever find out, he'd never forgive me!'

I didn't know whether to laugh or cry, or give into the

impulse to grab Rose by the shoulders and shake her. She looked at me with tear-filled eyes. 'I'll never do it again, I promise, if only you'll back me up and say I was here all night!'

'You know I will,' I assured her, praying that she'd given herself a serious enough fright to make her promise of reformed behaviour stick. She still looked worryingly moist-eyed and droopy-lipped, so I said, 'I swear not even the Inquisition's torturers could drag your dreadful secret out of me! Don't worry, my lips are firmly sealed!'

She smiled at me in a slightly watery manner. 'You're a real friend. I knew I could trust you! Actually,' she confessed, 'I rang Jeremy last night when we got the flat to say I was spending the night . . .' She looked up as the sound of water rushing down the drainpipe announced that Luke had finished what must have been a liberal bath. I hoped he hadn't nicked my good bath essence. I didn't have much left. 'I suppose I'd better go and clean myself up.'

'If Luke's left us any hot water,' I said, adding idly as the gate on to the green gave its familiar protesting screech, indicating someone was coming up the path, 'I wonder who that is.'

Rose went ashen. 'It's Jeremy! Come to check up on me!' she exclaimed, with supreme illogicality. I would have thought he would have been more inclined to use the telephone, especially at this hour. She jumped up and rushed to the little window by the side of the door, peering through it cautiously to see who it was, and came running back into the kitchen, face, if possible, even paler. 'It's Hamish! What's he *doing* here?' she demanded in panic. 'He can't see me like this, he'll know I haven't been staying the night!' Unfortunately, she was right, even the most unobservant man would start to smell a rat over gold-dusted eyebrows and sparkling purple eyeshadow first

340

thing in the morning. And Hamish wasn't unobservant. Rose clutched at my sleeve. 'He'll tell Jeremy!'

It wasn't the time to tell her that Hamish wasn't the trouble-making type. 'He won't see you,' I said soothingly. 'Quick, up the stairs to my bedroom! And don't thump around,' I hissed. 'Tell Luke to be quiet as well!'

I went nervously to the door as her footsteps retreated upstairs. Oh God, at any other time it would have completely made my day to have Hamish paying me an unexpected visit, now I was afraid it was going to give me a nervous breakdown. Fortunately, he didn't appear to notice my rather strained smile as I opened the door, as he was concentrating on giving me a very satisfactory good-morning kiss. Thank goodness another of my mother's rules had been brush your teeth as soon as you got up, I thought, wrapping my arms around his waist and hugging him. 'Why aren't you dressed yet, lazybones?' he asked, looking quizzically at my dressing-gown and nightie.

'New style for the office,' I said, regarding him with pleasure. 'It was a late night and we overslept. To what do I owe this?'

He smiled down lazily at me, sending my blood racing and almost making me forget that I had three visitors upstairs, two of them uninvited. 'I thought I might drop in for a cup of coffee.'

'What!' I exclaimed. With a cottage as small as this there was no way anyone could be in it for more than a few minutes and not be aware that it was heavily overpopulated. 'No, you can't! You're due in court, aren't you? It'll make you late, my machine takes ages to brew, and Tilly's got a face pack on. She'd be mortified if you were to see her like that!' I gabbled.

He looked at me with a slight frown, as well he might. 'I was only joking,' he said slightly stiffly, as if he was offended by my reluctance to let him in. 'I think I must have left my diary here the other night and it's got a couple of numbers in it I need for today. Have you seen it?'

I felt my stomach contract with apprehension at a creak from the top of the stairs. Maybe it was only Tilly. 'Er, yes, I think so,' I said vaguely.

'I'll come in and see if I can find it.'

'No, I'll do it!' I said quickly, remembering with horror that Rose's bomber jacket in her favourite hot-pink was lying on the sofa. Combine that with the smell of cigarette smoke and he'd be bound to realise she was here. He knew me well enough by now to be pretty sure I was unlikely to offer to share my own bed with her, and it was apparent to the most casual eye that the sofa bed hadn't been used. It still had the plates from last night on it. I gave a silly nervous laugh. 'You'll only bang your head on the lintel again and you can't appear in court with a sticking plaster on your forehead!'

'I think I can remember to duck this time,' he said.

'Well, um, Tilly forgot her dressing-gown and is wandering around half dressed. She'll be terribly embarrassed if a strange man sees her in her undies,' I improvised rapidly, putting my hand on his chest to physically stop him coming in. 'You stay there, I won't be a tic.'

He was looking at me very strangely. Maybe Tilly in a face pack *and* her underwear was overkill, I thought, as I raced around the sitting room, searching down the sides of the sofa and chairs for his slim black leather diary, but I'd square it with him later. 'Here it is!' I said in a bright voice when I found the diary on a side table, and held it up for him to see.

'Thanks,' he called, coming in a couple of steps. The stairs creaked behind me. I spun around, heart falling through the pit of my stomach as I saw Luke, wet hair slicked back, coming downstairs wearing nothing more than my best towel. For a moment I was so stunned with horror that I literally couldn't move. What the hell was he up to? I thought frantically, turning towards Hamish, who was staring at Luke in disbelief.

'Hamish, it's not—' I said desperately, and then I felt two hands on my shoulders and before I could get my wits together enough to react was spun around into Luke's arms.

'Good morning, sweetheart!' he carolled, pressing me to him and silencing anything I had to say with his mouth. One hand was pressed to the back of my neck so I couldn't pull away, the other had grabbed one wrist and held it behind my back, while my other arm was trapped between our bodies. I couldn't even pull away enough to kick him. Hamish cast me a repelled look so scorching I could almost feel my soul shrivel, and said in a tight voice, 'I seem to have come at an inappropriate time. I apologise for disturbing you, Susie.' He turned on his heel and left, just as I managed to grind my heel on Luke's toe. Unfortunately, bare feet couldn't do much damage even though he winced, and he didn't let up on his effective silencing technique until the sound of the slammed door had stopped reverberating throughout the house.

'Let me go!' I grunted, trying to struggle free, but he still had me in too firm a grip.

'No!' he said with a very self-satisfied smile. 'Not yet! You've been telling me little porkies about you and Hamish Laing, haven't you?' he asked. 'He must be *really* keen on you to pop round and see you on his way to work!'

'You bastard!' I hissed, trying to knee him, but he moved smoothly out of the way, muttering, 'Naughty, naughty, Susie!' I don't think I've ever hated and despised anyone as I did Luke at that point, or been so overwhelmed with a sheer need for retaliation. I drew back as far as I could and looked at him

343

with narrowed eyes, then lunged for his shoulder. The last time I'd tried biting someone was when I was aged three at playgroup and I had a go at Marianne Carter's leg because she wouldn't let me have the saucepan from the Wendy House. The reaction this time was even more deeply satisfying. Luke shrieked, letting me go and clasping his hand to his arm. Rose and Tilly poked their heads around from the bottom of the stairs just in time to see me reach back with my freed hand and slap his face as hard as I could.

I tore myself away and ran towards the door, calling, 'Hamish! Don't go! I can explain!'

Rose raced after me and caught my arm as I was opening the door. I turned a savage face towards her and she let go of me, prudently backing away a step, no doubt remembering the strength of my right hook. 'It's too late, Susie,' she said placatingly. 'Look, he's getting in his car. Even if you don't mind making a spectacle of yourself, running across the green in your nightie, you won't get to him in time.'

That was the bit that convinced me. I couldn't have given a damn about making a spectacle of myself. My shoulders slumped in despair. Oh God, what was I going to do now? She shut the door, saying in a soothing voice, 'You can always ring Hamish later and tell him that he got the wrong end of the stick.' The wrong end of the stick? He'd just had the sharp end of the whole ruddy caber landing on his head, I thought desolately. I knew what I'd think if I walked in on a scene like that. 'I expect he was just embarrassed about barging in on what he thought was something intimate,' she continued, and laughed slightly. 'Honestly, what on earth did Luke think he was doing?' I had only too good an idea, I thought grimly, my fists balling up. 'He's such a prankster!' The 'prankster' was looking in disbelief at a livid mark on the fleshy part of his arm. I hoped it hurt, really hurt. Rose frowned slightly. 'But what was Hamish here for anyway? Did he have something for you to give Stephen?'

I looked at her incredulously, unable to believe that she was so wrapped up in her own problems she hadn't twigged exactly why Hamish had hit the roof on seeing Luke kissing me. But since she appeared to firmly believe I'd dumped Arnaud for Luke, despite everything I'd said, perhaps it wasn't so surprising she didn't appear to have a clue that her 'staid' friend had thrown her cap over every windmill in the flaming country for a third man, I thought, trying to be fair. It was very difficult to be fair. Impossible for anyone who wasn't a saint. And I'm not. She had eyes, didn't she? I thought, whipping up a good bit of rage as an antidote to the sick fear that was threatening to overcome me. I wanted to kill both her and bloody, bloody Luke Dillon. If she hadn't been playing at being a single girl instead of the married woman she was, none of this would have happened, I thought, hardly able to breathe past the lump in my throat. What if Hamish didn't believe me?

I struggled to get a grip on myself. 'I'm sorry, you must think this is a complete madhouse,' I said to Tilly, who was coming out of the kitchen, belatedly remembering that I was a hostess.

Her eyebrows went up at my oversocial manner. 'Life in the country sure is eventful!' she said thoughtfully. 'You don't get excitement like this in Brixton. Here.' She shoved a bundled-up tea towel towards Luke, who was slumped in a chair, holding his hand to his face. 'Ice cubes. Put them on that bruise.'

He put the bundle gingerly against his cheekbone and looked at me reproachfully. 'I think you've given me a black eye, Susie.'

'Good!' I retorted vindictively. It looked like it was going to be a nice big one too, the large silver ring my brother gave me for Christmas must have just clipped him on the edge of his cheekbone. I put my hands on my hips, glaring at him. 'Let me tell you this, Luke Dillon, if you ever *dare* lay one finger on me again, I won't only give you another black eye to match this one, I'll kick you so hard you'll be singing soprano for the rest of your life, understand?'

I noted with some pleasure that he instinctively crossed his legs protectively. 'Come on, Susie, you can't blame me for getting a bit carried away,' he said, smiling at me with a sugary charm that made my stomach curdle. 'But that nightie of yours gives a man ideas and the last time we kissed was so passionate, I thought you'd be happy . . .'

His effrontery was so immense that I almost laughed. 'Balls! You didn't give a damn what I thought!' I said succinctly. 'Why should I want a reprise when the last time we kissed held all the passion of eating a cold fried egg? Your technique doesn't match up to your looks, Luke. Personally, I prefer a bit more expertise.' His mouth settled into a mulish line. That hit home. One small point to me, I thought grimly.

Rose was looking at us both in a bewildered fashion. 'I don't understand,' she said plaintively. 'Aren't you going a bit over the top, Susie? Luke was just having a joke, I know it wasn't very funny, but all the same—'

'That was no joke, it was concentrated malice!' I interrupted. 'Just get this, Rose, your pin-up boy here was prepared to throw you to the wolves and risk letting Jeremy discover *everything* just so he could have a chance to get at Hamish. And why? Not because he's got the hots for me and was jealous of Hamish, but because it might gratify Nigel if he thought Hamish had the impression his girlfriend had been nicked off

346

him by Luke. And you'll do almost *anything* if it pleases your paymaster, won't you, Luke?' I asked, staring at him with contempt.

'What's Nigel got to do with this?' asked Rose, sounding even more confused.

'Hamish had an affair with his wife,' I said flatly. Her mouth opened in a horrified 'O'. 'Quite,' I said grimly. 'Nigel did his best to destroy him. He didn't succeed, but you told me yourself what Nigel's like. Didn't you ever wonder what sort of person Luke must be to hang around with him? And Luke thought Nigel would want the boot put into Hamish one more time, and you like to keep Nigel happy, don't you Luke?' I asked witheringly. 'Because what you manage to squeeze out of your doting grandmother can't possibly pay for that nice lifestyle you have, or all that white powder everyone says goes up your nose.'

Rose was staring at Luke as if she'd never really seen him before. 'That was a foul thing to do,' she said severely, 'and a complete waste of time as well.' Luke looked up at her blearily out of the one eye that wasn't closing up. 'Hamish won't particularly care if he thinks Susie's having an affair with you, Luke, though he might question her taste. He's already got a girlfriend, that gorgeous woman he was with the other night.'

'That can't be true!' Luke said instantly, then doubt began to overshadow his face. 'What was he doing here then?'

He can't have been able to see Hamish kissing me, I realised as I said, 'He came to pick up something he'd left behind when returning a book. As Rose said, it was a waste of effort on your behalf.' I looked pointedly at Tilly as she opened her mouth to speak. God knows she'd heard me banging on for long enough last night to know that wasn't true, but it was some small compensation to know that Hamish wasn't going to have to

347

bear the indignity of Nigel and Luke rubbing their hands together in delight at having aimed yet another broadside at him. I'd have to work out how to cope with the rest of it later, I thought tiredly.

The next hour or so was a complete blur. I was concentrating so hard on not giving way to the terror gnawing away inside me that I can't remember much, apart from Tilly being a complete trooper and taking charge. She got rid of Luke in under five minutes, sent Rose up to wash and change, rang for a taxi to take her to where she'd left her car last night, and made me a coffee with a very large slug of something alcoholic in it, saying firmly that I needed it. It tasted horrible, but after a stern look from her when I protested I drank it. At one time she was matron in a boys' boarding school. Despite the fact she's five foot one inch and weights about six stone, they were apparently all terrified of her. I wasn't surprised.

She despatched me upstairs to get dressed and I moved around like an automaton, choosing a dress at random, yanking my unruly hair into something like neatness and splashing make-up in the direction of my face as if I was dressing a dummy in a shop window. All I could think was, What if Hamish didn't believe me when I said I hadn't been kissing Luke by choice? Any man is going to smell a very large barrel of rotten haddock when he finds a near-naked rival in his girlfriend's house at eight in the morning, isn't he? I thought, chewing distractedly at my newly applied lipstick. Even if I completely ignored my promise to Rose, there was a very good chance he'd think the two of us had conspired together to cook up a good story. He knew perfectly well she owed me one over the drink in the cocktail bar and this was going to sound uncommonly like the sort of alibi dreamed up by his more dubious clients – much too unlikely to possibly be

348

true. Tilly offered to spend another night so we could both go to Hamish and, partially at least, explain what had happened, but I sent her on her way with many thanks, though I did take the precaution of getting her contact number in Scotland, just in case I needed verification of my story.

In the event, I needn't have bothered. He wouldn't speak to me. I must have tried telephoning him about thirty times, each time to be put off by the same smooth-voiced assistant, who informed me first that Mr Laing was in court, then he was in a meeting, finally simply he was unavailable to take my calls. There was a disturbing amount of sympathy in her voice when she gave me this last message. I put the telephone down with a shaking hand, unable to believe that Hamish wasn't even going to give me the *chance* to explain, a band of misery tightening around my chest so hard I thought I was going to suffocate. Martin came over with some pointless correction to something I'd done for him and I turned and gave him such a stare of loathing that he backed away, muttering something about he'd realised it wasn't so essential after all.

I started about twenty letters, but they all hit the bin, one after the other. My normal ability with words had left me completely, besides, if he wouldn't talk to me would he bother to read anything I'd written? I felt so desperate I'd have gone and camped outside his gates, for he had to come home sometime. But I was committed to going to my parents' and I really couldn't face explaining why I was bunking off yet again. I'll never know how I got down there without having an accident. The M1 and the M25 aren't the best places to drive when you can't even think about the other cars on the road, your mind is so occupied with what ifs.

I'd got to my parents' village and was passing by the telephone box outside the post office when I remembered the

349

phone card in my purse. I slewed to a halt at an angle to the pavement – luckily it's still one of those places where only two cars and a haycart go by every hour – and jammed the thing in the slot with trembling hands. I'd been planning to ring him from Mum and Dad's and had been chanting his number like some mantra that could act like a charm to make sure he'd pick up and listen. This'd be more private. His phone seemed to ring for ages before he picked it up.

'Hamish, I must speak to you—' I began.

'Susie, one day I'll feel up to hearing your excuses about what was going on this morning, but frankly, I don't want to just now,' he said, his voice sounding infinitely tired, and put the phone down.

My eyes blinded with tears, I misjudged the corner to my parents' driveway and clipped the side of the car on the gatepost. I was lucky, I only dented the front wing and I knew the local garage would be able to knock it out tomorrow, but it still gave me a good excuse for falling into my mother's arms in floods of tears when she opened the door.

CHAPTER 19

'Did you have a good weekend?' asked Jenny cheerily as I arrived at the office on Monday morning.

'No!' I said in heartfelt tones.

She dunked a chocolate doughnut in her coffee and took a large bite, looking at me critically. 'I must say you look a bit peaky,' she commented. 'You aren't coming down with this flu thing, are you? I hope not.'

It couldn't make me feel much worse, I thought as I took my place. It might even make me feel better. It would be a relief to have an excuse to drop my brave face and go to bed with extra quantities of Lemsip to hibernate for a while.

''Cause I don't want to have to run the office entirely on my own,' Jenny continued. 'Stephen's still off in Paris and both Amanda and Martin have rung in to say they're sick with it.' She sniffed contemptuously. 'Martin sounded like he only had a bit of a cold to me. Typical man, sneezes once and imagines he's got pneumonia!'

I assured Jenny that though I might be sick at heart, I wasn't harbouring any germs. Well, I didn't put it exactly like that, I just included the no germs bit. She smiled in relief. 'Good, I know Mondays are usually fairly quiet, but I hate it when you're alone and you have to lock the door to the street every time you want to go to the loo, and you have to rush because you're afraid there's going to be an impatient queue waiting outside when you've finished.'

Amazingly enough, her rash statement didn't immediately give our chances of a peaceful day the kiss of death, conjuring up queues of people beating a path to our door and demanding to see all our house details immediately. Mind you, it would have been better for me if they had, I needed something to occupy my mind. At least being with my parents over the weekend had meant I had to keep myself functioning, doing the cooking, putting on a decent face in front of Dad's business contacts, who were actually rather nice, and soothing various parental fears about the exact reason why I'd arrived on the doorstep doing a good imitation of a lawn sprinkler. It had taken them only about five minutes to work out it was unlikely to be about a minor prang with the car. My father instantly leapt to the conclusion I was afraid to tell them they were about to become grandparents (apparently, much the same situation had happened with his sister, my Aunt Fiona), and started to mutter dire threats about 'that bloody Frog' and what he'd do to him when he got his hands on him, though it wasn't clear whether this was going to be before or after Arnaud had been marched forcibly up the aisle at the point of Dad's duck gun. Mum's diagnosis was more accurate, though she tends to the dramatic, and I had a hard job convincing her I wasn't about to throw myself in the brook at the bottom of the garden like some latter-day Ophelia, which wouldn't have achieved much even if I'd felt like it. It's only about six inches deep in summer. Finally I snapped, 'Don't worry. I wouldn't give bloody Luke Dillon the satisfaction of thinking he'd driven me to top myself!'

She stopped the maternal fussing and looked at me consideringly. 'I believe you,' she said. 'I can remember saying much the same thing myself once, though *I* said it out of love, not loathing . . .'

'About whom?' I asked curiously.

'Dad of course!' she said matter-of-factly. 'He couldn't get it into his head that "make love not war" meant he made love to *me* and not anyone else! I got him licked into shape eventually,' she said reminiscently.

That really made me forget my own woes for a bit. It had been surprising enough to hear about Aunt Fiona, whom I'd always thought to be a pillar of rectitude – she certainly liked to behave as if she was the next in line for canonisation – but *Dad*? I'd sort of assumed, seeing photographs of him with shoulder-length hair and wearing trousers so tight you wondered he could move, let alone father children, that he'd been briefly indulging in a bit of fancy dress before returning to his true métier in insurance. But, now I really thought about it, even if he was now thinning on top and thickening around the middle, he can't always have been conventional or he wouldn't have ended up with my mother. And he must still have some sort of, if not exactly a wild streak, one that wasn't entirely tame, for they wouldn't have stayed together otherwise. Mum isn't your usual sort of lifelong partner for a Captain of Insurance.

Mum had the bright idea of plying me with drink so that I'd Tell All. What actually happened was that she happily worked her way down a bottle of wine herself and after a certain amount of prompting told me some very interesting stories about when she and Dad were first going out. I'd certainly never heard the one about the tarot reader, the tie-dyed shirt and the tent at the Glastonbury festival before. It made me look at Dad in a whole new light. It also made me wonder if he objects to my younger brother's behaviour so much on the 'been there, done that, know what can go wrong' principle rather than due to sheer middle-aged prejudice as we'd always assumed.

Needless to say, once Mum had softened me up with a few risqué parental stories she homed in with the maternal searchlights on full beam, and under a lot of expert probing I told her about the whole damned mess. She was justifiably confused; the last time we'd discussed my love life in any depth at all I had one amoral, part-time boyfriend and in the last week or so I had, she complained with some exaggeration, been picking up and discarding men like confetti. 'But you can't go on like this, you're going to have to make him talk to you,' she said firmly.

'I think it's quite difficult to *make* Hamish do anything,' I said.

'One of those, is he?' she asked with interest. 'Then you'll have to trick him into seeing you and then tell him the truth.'

'Do you think he'll believe it?' I asked dolefully. 'Come on, Mum, as an excuse for why his half-dressed girlfriend was being kissed by a man in a towel it's fairly high in the implausibility stakes, isn't it?'

'Mm, but I've heard worse. You should have heard your father . . . but we're discussing you, not him,' she said, abandoning this promising non sequitur to my disappointment. She looked at me, eyes serious. 'But don't let false pride stand in your way. If he doesn't believe you the first time, just go on telling him. He'll hear you in the end.' She reached over and patted my hand. 'You never know, he might be there when you get back on Sunday evening.'

When I'd got in last night the light was winking on the answer machine. For a moment I'd felt almost sick with relief, I was so convinced that there had to be a message from

354

Hamish, telling me he was prepared to hear me out at least. But not one of the messages was from anyone I wanted to hear from. Which was a bit unfair on my mother, who was checking that I'd arrived safely (and successfully evaded the police of three counties, who if they'd had any inkling of the number of consolatory gins she'd been pouring down my throat all weekend would have been following me in convoy waving breathalysers out of their windows), Tilly seeing if I was OK, and Claire, wanting to tell me about her new Mr Gorgeous (in the circumstances, I think it was quite reasonable of me not to instantly ring her back). But I was surprised there was silence from Rose. And not a little miffed too. Surely she must have twigged by now that I didn't dole out black eyes, not to mention bite marks, to men for simply having a crude and cruel joke? Was she refusing to face up to the truth because she was afraid it meant she'd have to explain all to Hamish? I wondered uneasily. I really didn't want to believe she could be so self-centred. I didn't believe it, but it still left a nasty taste in my mouth.

I tapped my tooth with my nail thoughtfully, glanced up to check that Jenny was suitably occupied in the back room sorting out some brochures, and gathering up my courage dialled Hamish's office number yet again. I was quite surprised the number pads hadn't worn out under their recent usage. My mother's words about tricking him into seeing me came back. It might make him even angrier with me, I thought doubtfully as the number began to ring but, frankly, at the moment what did I have to lose? I tensed as the call was answered. If it was the smooth-voiced woman who'd taken all my increasingly frantic calls on Friday I'd simply ask if I could speak to Hamish. There was no point in trying anything on, she must know my voice almost as well as she knew her own by now. But it was another woman, one with a warm and motherly tone who sounded rather like someone's grandmother, so the die was cast. I took a deep breath and explained that I wanted to make an appointment with Mr Laing to discuss a boundary dispute with a neighbour.

'Excuse my asking, but have you really talked this over with your neighbour?' asked the receptionist in a friendly voice. 'Because once you start consulting solicitors tempers start to rise and it gets more and more difficult to withdraw from the dispute. Before you know where you are, you can be locked into a court dispute that goes on for years!'

Oh God, surely most firms of solicitors were keen to rake in as many clients and as much money as possible, weren't they? Why did Hamish have to work for one that apparently had a social conscience? I thought bitterly. 'No, it's gone beyond the stage of talking,' I said.

'You wouldn't like to try just one more time?' she persisted. 'And I could pencil you in to see Mr Laing next week if it doesn't work.'

Next week? I thought in horror. I couldn't last that long! 'Er, no, he's . . .' I floundered, trying to think of something that held the necessary urgency. 'He's threatened to poison my cat!' I said triumphantly. 'I think I need to take immediate action.'

'Well, you can't have him doing that!' she said, sounding properly scandalised. 'It's really Mr Laing you want to see, because he's very tied up at the moment . . .? Mr Cathcart could fit you in this afternoon . . .'

'Mr Laing was especially recommended to me. I was told he's very sympathetic to people's problems,' I said quickly, hoping that she wouldn't ask me who'd made the recommendation.

'He's very good,' she confirmed. 'But he's terribly busy. Let me see, if you can manage first thing tomorrow morning I can squeeze you in for half an hour. I know it's not very long, but—'

'That'll do fine,' I cut in hastily. The chances were that Hamish was going to throw me out after half a minute, so there wasn't much point in taking up an hour of his time. Nor in paying for the whole hour, I decided quickly, after the receptionist kindly told me his truly eye-watering charges, if I ended up getting landed with the bill.

'And can I take your name?' she asked.

Name? Name? Someone would probably smell a rat with 'Jane Brown'. 'Tradescant,' I said with sudden inspiration. 'Miss Lily Tradescant.'

As I put the phone down with a flush of exultation that I'd at least done *something* Jenny poked her head around the back-room door. 'Susie, I've got a Mrs Murray on the other line.' She made an expressive face. 'She's really in a state about something, wouldn't tell *me*, because I'm just a secretary, and wanted to speak to Stephen or someone in charge. I, er, told her you were his second in command. Will you deal with it?'

She looked at me pleadingly and slightly guiltily too. It meant I was probably in for an ear-bashing of some sort or another, most likely about the agency's failure to find a buyer for Mrs Murray's house immediately it went on the market, despite the quite *enormous* fees she was paying us, etc. But to my surprise she wasn't in the least aggressive, she was very hesitant and kept on apologising profusely for making a fuss, but she really thought it was a point that needed to be cleared up. Of course she knew what a good agency this was, and she was sure it was only a mistake, but people in her position couldn't afford to spend money unnecessarily . . .

'Yes, I quite agree, Mrs Murray. Perhaps you could tell me what the matter is,' I said, cradling the phone under my chin and trying to bring up her details as she spoke. I blinked in slight surprise as they flashed up on the screen. She lived next door to Jeremy and Rose, in fact, as she went on, I recalled seeing her cottage; it was on the other side of the proposed new development to the piece of land Jeremy was being asked to sell. Her cottage was under offer and she was one of Martin's clients, which presumably meant when he came back I was in for a carpeting for even daring to speak to her.

I got the impression Mrs Murray didn't have a lot of people to talk to and she was making the most of the opportunity. I got her full history. She'd moved into her cottage as a young married woman when her husband had been a cowman on the neighbouring farm to Jeremy's, she'd brought up four children who'd grown up into fine young people, grew all she needed in her garden and never bought vegetables from the shops, and now that the peace of her cottage was going to be ruined by that horrid new development she'd decided to go and live near her daughter in Worthing. I waited patiently for her to get to the point, my mind wandering slightly under the relentless onslaught of unnecessary details. 'I've taken me time deciding, I can tell you. I wasn't at all sure I could abide being near our Joan, I'm still not, to tell you the truth. She's terribly bossy. And I'm not keen on that sea either. Can't see the point of it. Or the town. Full of old people, it is. But when Mr Prescott said the development was definitely going ahead I made up my mind I didn't want to be bothered with all that noise from the building work and it won't be the same any more with all them posh people next to me, so I accepted the offer from Mr Jenkins. It seems quite fair really and it's enough for me, though frankly I'd much rather stay where I am. I like my cottage, I always thought I'd die there.' She paused to take a breath. 'Now I got a letter this morning saying there's a planning application gone in for houses in my garden. It's that Mr Jenkins who did it, not me. That's not right is it? How can he do it when it doesn't belong to him? And the council don't do nothing for free these days, so are they going to send the bill to me? And do I have to do anything?' she demanded.

I assured her that, strangely enough, it was quite legal to apply for planning permission on someone else's land, she needn't worry about being sent the bill, whether it was granted or not, and they'd informed her of the application so she could object if she wanted to.

She cackled. 'There's no point! We were told years ago the council'd never give permission to build houses on our land, and Mr Prescott says they haven't changed their minds, even with the development next door. I asked him. I may be old, but I'm not senile yet!' she said triumphantly. 'So Mr Jenkins is wasting his money, but that's his look out, not mine. Thank you, dear, I'm glad to have had that sorted.'

'It's a pleasure, ring me if there's anything else you'd like cleared up,' I said automatically, still shell-shocked from the sheer amount of speech directed at me in the last five minutes.

How funny that Martin should be so convinced she'd never get planning permission, I thought idly, it seemed quite a logical place to grant it since it was bang next door to the new development. Mrs Murray had a big garden with road access and no ponds that might hold rare toads either. Maybe the planning department had decided enough was enough, they were often a law unto themselves, after all, but Martin should know. I'd probably have left a note on his desk to say she'd rung and gone back to have a good wallow in my own problems without ever giving it another thought if I hadn't happened to idly register as I was wiping the details off the screen that Mr Jenkins was a local man. My hand jerked above the keys and with trembling fingers I brought the details back up again. I wasn't mistaken. Mr Jenkins lived in Wickham. In fact Mr Jenkins lived in Luke's house.

I stared at the address incredulously. Luke didn't take lodgers. Luke and Martin were friends. Luke was apparently buying Mrs Murray's house. Martin had told her she wouldn't get planning permission. Luke had put in for it. Only the most olfactory-deprived idiot would have failed to smell a very large rat. I dialled our contact in the local planning department, thinking that if I was wrong all hell was going to descend on my head when Martin discovered I'd been checking up on him. But Frances, sounding overworked and harassed as usual, had no hesitation in saying she'd told Martin a couple of weeks ago that planning permission for building in the garden of Rosewood Cottage would almost certainly go through on the nod. 'I mean, it's not as if there's anything we could object to, is there?' she said practically. 'It's a real headache finding sites for all the houses the county plan says have to be built in the next ten years, so we aren't going to turn down anything as obviously suitable as this.' She sounded curious as to why I was bothering her, so I quickly said that Martin had been laid low by a killer dose of flu and I hadn't been able to find his files. She sounded as if it was the sort of thing that happened to her all the time.

I put the phone down and stared at my blank computer screen, feeling slightly sick. I might not like Martin, no, let's be honest, I detested him, but it had never occurred to me that he might be dishonest. But there could be no other answer. He and Luke had entered into a scam to defraud an old lady of what, a hundred thousand pounds? That was the very minimum difference between the with-and without-planning-consent value of her cottage. And what was this about the development definitely going ahead? As far as I knew, nothing had been decided, yet the offer had been put in two weeks ago . . . A super-large, steroid-enhanced rat emerged from its hole as I remembered Luke banging on to Rose about the future of the countryside. God, he'd even walked down to the site with her and pointed out it wasn't nearly as bad as she'd thought it was going to be! If Mrs Murray hadn't decided to sell her cottage would he be giving a toss about rural development? And pigs might fly. How soon after Rose had persuaded Jeremy to accept the developers' offer would Luke have just faded from her life? And had Martin and Luke tried this on anyone else?

'Jenny, how do I get into Martin's closed files?' I asked.

She swivelled around to stare at me. 'You don't!' she said flatly.

'But what happens if he's in hospital or something and there's an urgent problem that can't wait?'

'Stephen deals with it,' she said firmly, 'not us. I'm not kidding, Susie. If Martin discovers you've been in his files you'll be out of here so fast your feet won't touch the ground, no matter how much Stephen likes you. He can't afford to ignore Martin if he really digs his heels in. Martin brings in too much money to the firm.'

'Actually what Martin's about to bring in are the regulators and the police,' I muttered and told her about Mrs Murray.

Jenny proved to be someone who believed in making a thorough drama out of a crisis. She started scrabbling through her papers like a demented hen. 'We've got to tell Stephen!' she wailed. 'He's taken his mobile with him, said we could contact him in an emergency. I've got his number here somewhere, now where is it? This is an emergency, isn't it?'

'Oh, come on! It's really going to enhance his romantic long-weekend away with Liddy if we ring up and tell him his senior negotiator is on the take, isn't it?' I demanded. 'And what can he do from Paris except tell us to sit tight and do nothing? Let's tell him tomorrow when he's back and in a work mood.' I looked at her, wondering how I could get her to do what I wanted. Common sense said to leave this for Stephen to deal with, but I don't always bother with common sense. Besides, I fancied playing detective, it was a welcome diversion from thinking about Hamish. 'Look, we really ought to discover if Martin's done this with anyone else before it's too late,' I said cunningly. 'If he has, and they haven't yet exchanged contracts we might be able to save the situation.'

To my relief, Jenny stopped her frantic hand-wringing and nodded solemnly. 'Stephen's always telling me to work on my own initiative, I reckon this counts as that,' she said surprisingly. 'All the passwords are in one of Stephen's files. That's password protected too, but I should be able to work out what it is. Most people's passwords are pretty simple or they'd forget them.'

'Which means that Stephen's are even more obvious than most!' I said.

She grinned up at me. 'Dead right! When we first installed this system he chose passwords from the dictionary and then forgot what they were. It took me several days to crack them with a special programme, so I don't reckon he'll have made that mistake again.' Her fingers flew over the keys. 'Ah! I was right, there you are. Everyone's passwords.'

I glanced over her shoulder, seriously impressed at her speed. 'How on earth did you work that one out?'

'Easy,' she said, in a slightly disappointed voice, as if she'd

362

have liked a greater challenge. 'It's the passwords file, so the password is . . .'

'Password,' I supplied.

She nodded. 'Even Stephen couldn't forget that! There's Martin's. Enormous.'

We looked at each other and snorted with laughter. 'Wishful thinking, if you ask me!' she said.

We divided the list between us and began to work steadily through it, though neither of us were quite sure what we were looking for. It was staggeringly boring. Not only did Martin have a mania for secrecy, he also had the natural soul of a bureaucrat, so every meeting, every telephone conversation was noted in detail, including, I saw with disbelief, the 'no answers', but there wasn't a single thing that suggested he was indulging in crooked deals. Even the file on Mrs Murray's cottage looked completely above board. I hadn't been expecting it, but it would have been nice to find something along the lines of, '2 May, in partnership with nasty piece of work, Luke Dillon, decided to rook Mrs Murray. Like taking candy off a baby.'

'There's nothing in this lot,' said Jenny. I nodded gloomily, thinking I was going to have to hand it over to Stephen tomorrow and let him see what he could find after all, when she added surprisingly, 'I wonder if he's still got that floppy in his desk . . .'

'What floppy?' I demanded.

'He's been using our computers for his personal stuff, because his screen's broken and he hasn't got round to mending it, and a couple of weeks ago I had to come back for something after hours and he was saving something on a disk which he put in his desk like lightning when he saw me. It might still be here.'

363

Typically, Martin's desk was locked, which I should have expected really. 'I don't suppose you're as good at picking locks as you are at cracking passwords, are you?' I asked Jenny without much hope.

'Never tried,' she said. My heart plummeted with disappointment, we really wouldn't be able to get away with jemmying open his desk. It was just too obvious. 'I prefer to use the key,' she said, holding one in the air. 'This one should do it, it opens mine, Amanda's and yours, so I don't see why it won't work on his too. They're all the same model.'

A couple of minutes of judicious jiggling later, Martin's top drawer slid open to reveal a floppy disk with 'info' written across it. I put it in the machine and tapped in 'enormous'. No dice. 'Can you do anything?' I asked the office's resident computer genius.

She looked at the screen with an expression of pure joy, at last getting a decent challenge. 'Let's have a go. It's probably either based on his name or connected to his office password in some way, to make it easier to remember.' Her fingers flew over the keys. 'No, that one doesn't work.' Neither did several versions of 'Prescott'. She sat staring thoughtfully at the screen, then said suddenly. 'I wonder! Hand us the thesaurus, Susie.' I retrieved the company thesaurus from Stephen's office, wondering why she needed to look up synonyms for 'superb location' or 'charming villa'. 'Look up "enormous" will you?' We struck gold with 'gigantic'.

'How on earth did you think of that?' I asked in awe.

She shrugged casually. 'Just a bit of lateral thinking,' she said modestly, though she looked pretty pleased with herself. 'Be quick, won't you?' she said nervously. 'I don't want anyone to come in and see us going through Martin's private affairs.'

Neither did I, for that matter, and I wouldn't have put it

past the sneaky bastard to rise from his sick bed to check up on what we were doing either. I began to flick down all the file names quickly. Most were self-explanatory names like 'Pension', 'Insurance' or 'Tax rebate' which I ignored, stopping to open and glance through 'SageCott', which seemed to be a legitimate attempt to buy a house last year. Jenny was almost hopping from foot to foot in nervous apprehension so I printed anything which had a vaguely non-utilitarian name, about five in all, and handed the disk back to her. She put it back and relocked the drawer with an audible sigh of relief.

I settled down to leaf through what I'd got and struck pay dirt almost immediately. Here was the real story on Mrs Murray's cottage. He'd recorded everything; the date he and Luke agreed to go for it, their shares of the purchase price and the profit, the date the planning application went in on behalf of 'Mr Jenkins', Martin's conversation with Frances, and his negotiation with Mrs Murray about dropping the price by five thousand pounds. I was so angry at this last bit of petty skulduggery, when they were already conspiring to cheat her out of a fortune, that I had to go off and have a reviving cup of coffee before I could go on reading.

It seemed Rosewood Cottage was an opportunistic one-off, the other files didn't have anything to do with property transactions. I skimmed through them quickly, but found nothing of interest and was about to dump them in my waste-paper basket when it occurred to me it wasn't very sensible to put them where someone, i.e. Martin, might come in and see them and suss what I'd been up to. I stuffed the sheaf of papers in my tote bag, planning to put them in the bin at home.

I had to tell Rose about this, I thought uneasily, not looking forward to it. But first there was something I needed to settle with Martin. I'd been putting two and two together to come up with another unsavoury four. He could, was going to, tell me if I was right.

CHAPTER 20

Martin lived about twenty miles away, in a large village that was just beginning to merge into a bigger town. Within ten years it would no longer be able to call itself rural and would have become urban. To my relief there was only his convertible Golf GTi parked outside his anonymous little house; even I had enough sense to have done a runner if Luke's BMW had been there as well. Even so, I still spent a minute or two sitting in the car and looking around before I walked up the short path to his door and rang the bell.

He opened the door, wearing a red synthetic-silk dressing-gown that had seen better days, starting slightly when he saw who it was on the doorstep. 'What are you doing here?' he demanded aggressively. 'Can't you see I'm ill?'

Truly, it did seem as if Jenny had been unfair when she'd suggested he was blowing up a mere sniffle. In my opinion, he was not an attractive sight in general, but today the fox-like features of his face had the texture and colour of old goat's cheese and the point of his sharp nose was a lurid glowing red. He was sniffing too. I recoiled for a moment, wondering if even the causes of justice, information-gathering and general nosiness were worth the risk of being exposed to germs that had been in Martin Prescott. Oh well, I'd better stop off for an extra-large tube of effervescent vitamin C tablets when I left.

'Something's come up which I need to talk to you about,' I said. 'Can I come in?'

At first he seemed quite prepared to discuss whatever it was on the doorstep, but when I said I was sure he didn't want to run the risk of catching an even deeper chill by standing around outside he looked at me suspiciously, as if checking for sarcasm, and let me in. I was treated to a display of his usual ungracious manner, as he muttered under his breath about incompetents who needed their hands holding all the time and couldn't leave a man in peace for as much as a day. I had more important matters to discuss, so I didn't give into the temptation to score a cheap point by saying that, personally, I'd rather have root-canal work (whatever that is, it sounds horrible) than hold *his* hand. His little sitting room, full of heavy furniture of a style that had long gone out of fashion, rightly never to return, was one of the most dismal rooms I'd ever seen. Either his interior-design skills were on a par with his sexual attractiveness, or he'd gone to one of those house-clearance junk shops and done his furnishing for the minimum possible. It didn't go with the image he so carefully cultivated (not always with complete success) of the suave man about town with the nippy little car. Probably he was saving all the money he didn't need for image-building so that he could buy cottages off old ladies for a fraction of what they were worth.

'So what is this about?' he demanded, sitting down on an elderly sofa with a suspiciously greasy mark all along the back at head level. My chair had one too, I noticed, and I perched myself as close to the edge as possible without actually sitting on the floor. That wasn't any more appetising than the back of my chair. Also, Martin must belong to that male school of thought that only believes in washing socks when they get too stiff to put on, I thought, wrinkling my nose slightly, and wished I could suggest we sat outside in the garden.

'There's a query about the planning application for Rosewood Cottage,' I said flatly, watching him closely.

He was already so pale that it wasn't possible to see if he lost any more colour, and if he was shocked he recovered with admirable speed, putting his nose up in his usual supercilious fashion. 'That's absolutely nothing to do with you, Susie, and frankly I've warned you enough times about mucking around with my clients. Maybe you ought to think whether you want to start looking for another job. Since I strongly doubt you'll find anyone who'll want to employ someone of your poor skills I advise you to start doing what you're told!' I might have been a little more impressed with this speech if it had been delivered by someone properly dressed, and not in a tired dressing-gown, who didn't have to stop speaking to noisily blow his nose before he could go on. Martin rose to his feet, gesturing towards the door. 'Rosewood Cottage is none of your affair, and I advise you to keep that very large nose of yours out of this!'

My nose isn't that big, I thought indignantly. So it isn't exactly small, but it's in proportion and someone of my height would look ridiculous with a tiny little button in the middle of their face. Martin was looking at me expectantly with an increasingly annoyed expression. I gathered that I'd been given my marching orders and had failed to respond properly. As he started to splutter I smiled affably and said, 'Fine, if you want I'll go and have a word with Stephen. I'm sure he'll be very interested to hear how you assured Mrs Murray she wouldn't get planning permission, even though Frances told you she would, and how you're putting up some of the purchase money yourself.'

He froze into immobility. 'You bitch!' he exclaimed,

advancing towards me, fists bunched at his sides, face an unattractive shade of red with rage. With a little pang of fear, I remembered that he worked out quite seriously in an attempt to rectify what nature hadn't given him. Maybe it hadn't been quite so clever after all to come here on my own with the intention of provoking him into telling all. I might be taller, but my muscles have got the tensile strength of a squeegee mop. And, unlike with Luke, I wouldn't have the advantage of surprise. With an effort I stopped myself shrinking backwards as he stood over me and looked upwards with a questioning expression, praying it wasn't revealing the sheer funk raging away inside me, which was rapidly passing through the colour spectrum, from pale blue to the deepest indigo. My assumed calmness seemed to work for he took a deep breath and said, 'You're just guessing.'

'About Rosewood Cottage?' I asked. 'I *know* a lot – certainly enough to convince Stephen. It'll be you, not me, who'll be down the jobshop.' He took a step forward, hands lifting slightly. Had I gone too far? I wondered wildly. I cleared my throat and, gathering what little courage I had left, added, 'Unless . . .' leaving the word hanging on the air.

He stared at me and my heart fell into my sandals. He wasn't going to take the bait, I thought in fear, bracing myself for retaliation. Then he scratched his chin slowly. 'So you want a share of the action?' he demanded. To my immense relief he stepped back, rocking back on his heels and looking down at me. He thought for a moment. 'I'm not sure I can do that. Luke's putting up most of the purchase price, though I get an equal share of the profits, because it's my expertise that's got us the place,' he said, his voice inviting me to share his pride in having been so clever. 'I doubt he's going to agree to you having any part of it. He's not very keen on you just now.'

370

I smothered a laugh and forbore to say the feeling was entirely returned. 'For the moment you can just give me some information,' I said.

'What sort of information?' he asked warily.

I wasn't going to ask the most important question straight out, so I hesitated, then said, 'How can you be so sure the development's going ahead? You might be left with an expensive speculation on your hands if Luke can't persuade Rose to get Jeremy to sell.'

He shrugged theatrically. I looked away, the action had made his dressing-gown fall open a little, showing a lot more of his chest than I cared to see. 'Luke's never failed yet,' he said confidently.

'I think he just has,' I said. 'Rose isn't too impressed with him any more.'

Martin sniffed, whether from superciliousness or cold was hard to tell. Either way it wasn't pleasant. 'Thanks to you and your big mouth! But it doesn't matter anyway. Nigel's taken it in hand now.'

'*Nigel?*' I said blankly. 'What's he got to do with this?'

'Nigel's behind Champion of course!' said Martin impatiently. 'You know, Champion Developments, the company that's going to build the new estate.' His eyes narrowed. 'You *didn't* know, did you?'

He stared at me with such animosity that I began to think of those films in which the heroine discovers too much and the baddies begin to look meaningfully at bits of rope and the railway tracks conveniently outside the window. I wondered if I should start gabbling a list of all the people I'd just happened to inform I was coming here, but instead I said vaguely, 'It'd slipped my mind.' Well, of course, it's the sort of thing that does.

As a face-saving exercise it got me precisely nowhere. Martin reverted to his normal manner when faced by me, that of the master in the presence of a simpleton. Frankly, for once I didn't mind it. It was preferable to the aggression that had preceded it. He laughed shortly. 'I don't suppose it matters you knowing, there's nothing you can do about it now, even if you do go running to Jeremy Ashton. Nigel's fixed it, says the sale's definitely going ahead.'

'What do you mean?' I asked, a cold shiver of apprehension running down my spine. I didn't fancy the idea of Nigel 'fixing' anything. 'What's he fixed? And how?'

Martin shrugged again. It was no more pleasing to the eye second time around. 'Dunno. All I know is Luke told me not to worry about the little hitch he had, it's all sewn up.'

Had Luke disclosed everything about his 'little hitch' or was he claiming he'd walked into a door? I wondered with a flash of amusement, before I got down to the serious business of berating myself for being a complete and utterly unobservant idiot. Just how stupid was I? Of course I'd heard the name of the company behind the development before, I'd even seen 'Champion' in Martin's files and had passed straight over it because I was only looking for property details. This called for some revision of my conclusions. I badly needed some time to think, but I wasn't going to get it. I also wouldn't have minded resting my tense muscles by sitting back, but in this chair I wasn't going to be able to do that either unless I went off for some inoculations the moment I left. 'Let's see if I've got this right,' I said slowly. 'Nigel knew Jeremy was lukewarm about selling, so he set Luke on to Rose, to get her to persuade Jeremy it was a good idea.' Martin nodded slightly. 'And since even Luke could hardly move in on a newly married woman the day she came back from honeymoon I was targeted as the way in?' I asked, getting to the point that really interested me. I could guess the rest of it well enough, but I'd like to know if all Luke's keenness on me was a put-up job. It'd help me decide whether to black his other eye if I ever saw him again.

Martin's lip curled. 'You don't think Luke was ever interested in *you*, do you?' he asked contemptuously. 'He only asked you out because Nigel told him to. It was pathetic seeing you fawning over him, thinking he fancied you. Some chance! He prefers his women to displace less bath-water!'

Ouch. My eyes narrowed. 'At least I take baths!' I snapped, sniffing pointedly.

He stiffened angrily. 'I warned Nigel and Luke that you were the sort of nosy little cow who pokes her nose in where it isn't wanted, but they wouldn't listen. And look what's happened. The whole deal nearly fell apart because of you! They should have stuck to the original plan and let me be the one to go in and soften up Rose.'

'*You?*' I asked incredulously. The mind boggled. There was no way Rose would ever have done anything more than pass the time of day with someone as unattractive as Martin, which might be a lookist statement, but Rose has never been politically correct.

At that he lost his temper. He sprang up and started pacing around the room, mouthing abuse at me. I was afraid for a moment he might lay his filthy hands on me, but he kept a safe distance. Then I realised he was so angry he'd lost all sense of discretion, and I began to concentrate on what he was saying, wishing desperately I'd thought to slip one of those little tape recorders in my handbag. But even if I had, I probably wouldn't have remembered to switch it on. I didn't think I'd better try and take notes either. That might get me throttled.

Martin was striding around with his back to the window facing on to the village street. I stood up, thinking it was time to make my exit before he calmed down enough to catch on to exactly how much he'd told me about Nigel's financial difficulties or worked out how I knew so much about his financial involvement with the scheme for Rosewood Cottage, when out of the corner of my eye I saw a familiar dark-blue BMW slowing down in the road outside. Oh boy! Was I in trouble. Real trouble.

Martin ground to a halt as the doorbell went. I smiled at him, trying to look completely unconcerned. 'You do seem to have a lot of visitors,' I remarked. 'Will whoever it is want to come in, do you think? There are still a couple of things I'd like to go over with you.'

He looked at me with loathing. 'Stay there, out of sight,' he said brusquely.

I nodded obediently, but as soon as he was out of the room I slipped my shoes off and shot off through the door at the back of the room that led to the kitchen. As I'd prayed, there was a door leading to the garden, and someone really must have been looking after me, for it wasn't in direct line of sight of the front door either. I peered down the passageway cautiously. Martin had his back to me, and I tiptoed gingerly over a none too clean floor and tried the door handle. For a moment I thought my heart would stop in fear. It seemed to be locked and I couldn't see a key, but it opened on the second tug to a background crescendo of male voices, one of them sounding distinctly displeased.

I put my shoes on, walked around the side of the house, and nipped out of the side gate to the pavement, stopping to say a loud and cheery, 'Good afternoon, it's a good drying day, isn't it?' to a middle-aged woman taking down washing in the

374

next-door garden. She nodded at me through a mouthful of pegs.

Luke spun around so quickly at the sound of my voice he almost fell off the doorstep. I walked as fast as I could to my car without actually breaking into a panic-stricken run. 'Susie! I want to talk to you!' he called menacingly, bounding towards me.

'Afraid I haven't got time!' I said cheerily, hoping the quaver in my voice wasn't audible, unlocking the door and getting in.

He put his hand on the door frame, holding it open. I eyed it wondering if I had the guts to slam the door and see if he took his hand away before his fingers got mangled. Regretfully, I decided I didn't, but I still started the car up, letting the engine run while he bent down to eyeball me. His black eye was healing up nicely, though I can't say the yellow bruises were a particularly good colour for him. I leant forward slightly, hoping to block his view of my tote bag lying in the back, its bin-fodder contents half spilled out over the seat. A corner of a page stuck up in the air, with 'ampion' clearly visible. If he saw that he'd know at once I'd got at Martin's files, I thought fearfully, and despite the presence of the woman with the washing, who'd given up all pretence of folding sheets and was watching us with naked curiosity, he'd have no hesitation in hauling me out of the car and carrying me back to the house in a fireman's lift. I licked dry lips. 'If you want to make a public scene, go ahead,' I said affably, looking at the woman, 'but I don't think Martin'll thank you.'

He glanced over his shoulder, indecision written all over his face, then to my infinite relief he straightened up and slammed the door. 'Stay out of my business, Susie!' he growled.

'Nothing would give me greater pleasure,' I replied truthfully and made my escape.

I was quivering so much from reaction that I had to pull into a lay-by and have a cup of tea from one of those mobile stalls that serve lorry drivers. It was the exact opposite to what I usually have, being incredibly strong and very sweet, but it was just what I needed. After I'd had a second and a certain amount of discussion with the woman behind the urn about whether you really used to get a better class of lorry driver twenty years ago I was calm enough to sort through my bag and fish out the stuff about Champion.

How could I have missed this? I thought crossly. My only defence was that I hadn't been looking for it, and frankly that didn't go very far in the history of brilliant excuses. My mouth pursed in a silent whistle when I saw how much profit Martin estimated Nigel was going to make, and this was an area in which I knew I could trust his judgement. This made Martin and Luke's tacky little scam look like pocket money in comparison, we were talking *millions* here. Nigel must have been having kittens when he realised Jeremy wasn't necessarily going to sell, especially if he really had the sort of cash-flow problems Martin had been spouting on about. So it wasn't surprising he'd called in his troubleshooter and instructed him to use his charm in whatever way he could to get a result – and quickly. And now the charm offensive had failed? I shivered slightly as I folded the papers and put them in my handbag, wondering what Nigel's next steps were.

Rose was catching the last of the sun on a lounger by the edge of a small stone pool which Jeremy assured me was perfect for swimming. It looked disconcertingly cold to me. Certainly Rose's minute gold bikini didn't look as if it had been anywhere near water during the whole of its life, so I gathered she shared my opinion.

376

'Darling, could you go and sunbathe somewhere else tomorrow; say, the vegetable garden?' asked Jeremy plaintively. 'That way Roy might get around to doing the weeding there. He must have dead-headed this rosebed fifteen times this afternoon.'

She smiled from behind her dark glasses without opening her eyes until Dexter licked one of her bare feet. She sat up with a shriek and saw me. 'Susie! I'm so glad to see you!' She bounded up, hugging me. 'Are you skiving off, you lazy thing? I was hoping you'd ring, but this is even better. Let's go and have a drink, the sun must be over the yard-arm, or it will be once I've got my clothes on. I was getting cold anyway, so you arrived at a perfect time . . .'

She rattled on in a breathless, brittle staccato while she pulled on a tee shirt and white shorts that would have given Roy the gardener almost as much to look at as her bikini. A couple of days' hard work lying motionless in the sun had given her skin a wonderful hen's egg brown, no more. Rose might not care about the risks of skin cancer, but she was very aware that mahogany brown was passé. But even the glowing sun-kissed colour of her face couldn't hide the shadows under her eyes or, now I was alerted to it, the tight strain around her jaw and mouth.

'A drink's a good idea,' said Jeremy enthusiastically, 'I certainly feel as if I could do with one.'

Her face fell. 'Have you finished for the day?' she asked. 'If you're busy you don't have to feel you've got to stay and entertain Susie.'

'I'm never too busy to talk to Susie,' he said gallantly. I'd noticed before that Jeremy wasn't always sensitive to hints. 'I'll meet you on the terrace with the bottle.'

'Thanks,' Rose called after him, then gripped my wrist.

'I've got to talk to you! It's so horrible, I don't know what to do . . .' Her eyes filled with tears. 'But I can't tell you now. Jeremy might hear, and he mustn't find out!' She sniffed loudly in an inelegant fashion. 'You won't go before we've had a chance to be alone, will you? If Jeremy won't go back to doing some honest toil you can always come up to my bedroom to discuss shades of eyeshadow. I can guarantee he'll leave us in peace!'

'Of course I will – providing you don't make me up,' I said, remembering the time Rose had decided bronze make-up would suit me. I'd looked like a southern-European clown.

She smiled faintly as Jeremy appeared on the terrace above us, waving a bunch of glasses and a chilled bottle of white Burgundy. 'You were saying on the way in about having discovered something interesting,' he said in a curious voice as he poured out a glass of wine for each of us. Rose turned a horrified face towards me.

The telephone went inside the house and she jumped visibly and pushed her chair back. 'I'll answer that,' she quavered.

'No, you stay here, chat to Susie, I won't be a moment,' said Jeremy, pushing her back gently into her seat.

Rose looked after him, lower lip trembling slightly, then pulling herself together turned back to me and said with an almost palpable effort, 'What's the big news?'

'Something I reckon you might already know,' I said slowly. 'Who's behind your property development.'

The colour drained from her face. 'Oh God!' she moaned, clutching her glass so tightly that the tips of her fingers went white. 'Please, Susie, don't say anything to Jeremy until I've had a chance to speak to you alone! But it's probably already too late, I bet that's Hamish on the phone.' She lit a cigarette, inhaling in jerky puffs. She wasn't a particularly heavy smoker, being one of those people who like to hold a cigarette almost as much as smoke it, but since I'd been here she'd been virtually lighting one from another and smoking them right down to the filter. She cast a fearful glance towards the house. 'I was praying that he wouldn't get the confirmation until tomorrow, it would have given me a bit more time to think of what to do, but—'

She ground to a halt as Jeremy came towards us, her face rigid with apprehension. 'Sorry, darling,' he called, 'that was Matt. There's a problem with the new tractor, he wants me to come and look at it now, see if we can fix it ourselves tonight.'

'Oh, what a shame, we'll have to keep your drink for you,' said Rose with a disappointed pout and put her face up for a kiss, showing that she had really missed her calling when she decided not to become an actress. 'Don't be too long, will you?'

'I won't be more than an hour, promise,' he said, giving her a kiss that looked like it would have become something a lot more ardent if his eyes hadn't slid sideways and he hadn't recalled he had an audience. He stood up, giving me a rueful grin, and walked off whistling slightly self-consciously.

'You are lucky,' I said idly, watching him saunter off. 'He's a really nice man and he adores you too.'

She pushed the sunglasses she'd been wearing like protective armour on to the top of her head, revealing red-rimmed, scared eyes. 'He's not going to adore me for much longer!' she declared tragically, reaching out for the wine bottle and refilling her glass with a nervy hand. She drained it in a gulp. 'Susie, I don't know what I'm going to do!' she wailed and burst into tears.

I got up and sat next to her, patting her hand in a rather helpless manner and muttering platitudes about how she could rely on me.

'There's nothing you can do!' she declared, between gulping

sobs, reaching blindly for her cigarettes and lighting yet another. 'You must tell me how you found out it was Nigel behind this property thing sometime,' she said dully, staring blindly out over the garden. 'It'd be all right if it was just you, I know you'd keep quiet for my sake, but Hamish knows too, or if he doesn't he's about to. He's always thought there was something fishy about the company and he put an investigator on it. He rang this afternoon to say he'd let us know for sure tomorrow. He'll tell Jeremy, I know he will, and then it'll all be over.'

'What will be over?' I asked. I'd lost track of this somewhere.

'My marriage!' she wailed.

I must admit that at first I thought this was a typical piece of Rose exaggeration. I said something to the effect, but not quite so bluntly. She looked up, hands writhing in her lap. 'You don't understand. Nigel's given me until the end of this week to get Jeremy to agree to his offer.' She gulped. 'I had to agree, what else could I do? As Nigel said, we only gain by accepting, and I lose everything if we don't!' She sniffed loudly. 'But once Jeremy knows it's Nigel, he'll never agree to sell. He's got something against him . . .'

'That he's a crook?' I suggested. 'Or that he tried to frame Hamish for fraud?'

'Did he? I didn't know that,' Rose said with a flicker of interest. 'Maybe. Whatever. It doesn't matter. Jeremy's going to refuse to sell and even if he doesn't chuck me straight out our marriage is going to be finished for all intents and purposes!' Her face crumpled again. 'I don't know what I'll do! I think I'll kill myself if I lose Jeremy!'

'I'm sure it won't come to that,' I said soothingly, patting her hand in a particularly ineffectual manner, and wondering when she'd get around to actually saying what it was that

Nigel was threatening her about. What on earth was bad enough to break up her marriage to Jeremy entirely? So he wouldn't have been too pleased, in fact absolutely livid, if he'd found out about her lying to him and going out with Luke, but as I pointed out to her, Luke had put the kibosh on any suggestion that they'd spent the night together by draping himself all over me in front of Hamish. He might fondly think that he had a reputation as a lady killer, but there was no way Jeremy was going to believe that Luke would have had both Rose and myself during one night.

'Oh God! If it were only that!' Rose declared dramatically. 'This is much, much worse!'

What could be worse than Jeremy thinking his wife had had a fling less than two months after the wedding? I thought, delving in my handbag and finding a clean tissue. I handed it over and waited with mounting impatience while Rose dabbed at her eyes and blew her nose noisily. She gulped, swallowed hard and said tonelessly, 'Nigel's got a dossier on me. If he doesn't have a written acceptance of his offer on his desk by Friday morning he's going to send it to Jeremy.'

'What can be so bad in it that it's a marriage breaker?' I asked lightly. 'You didn't tell Jeremy you led a nun-like existence before you met him or anything, did you?' I saw the expression on her face and exclaimed, 'Oh Rose! You didn't!'

'You didn't think I was going to tell him about *all* of them, did you?' she asked indignantly. I could see her point. On the whole, men don't take anything like as indulgent a view of wild oats sown by their wives as they do of their own (quite natural and necessary to get it out of the masculine system), and Rose, who had regarded sex as a leisure activity to be indulged in as frequently as Dime bars and shopping, had sown more oats than most.

'Perhaps he doesn't have the full list,' I said hopefully.

'God! I hope not!' she exclaimed, looking shocked. 'Even half would be bad enough,' she added gloomily, 'but I might have been able to swing it past Jeremy, though he'd be furious with me for . . . well, gliding over a few of the names . . .' she hesitated, chewing on her thumbnail, 'but even the most tolerant husband gets narked when he discovers his marriage isn't valid!'

It took a few moments for this to sink in. Of all the things I'd been imagining that Nigel Flaxman might be able to use to pressurise Rose, this hadn't even made it on to the end of the list. 'That can't be true!' I said.

'It is!' she said miserably. 'I made a false declaration on the register, I said I was a spinster.'

'Well, that just means unmarried, doesn't it? I don't think you have to worry that it means "maid" in the old-fashioned sense. If it did, half the marriages in this country would be invalid!' I said.

'It's not that. "Spinster" means you haven't been married *before*. And I have.'

CHAPTER 21

I spluttered into my glass of wine. While I was still coughing and choking all I could think of was this had to be some sort of weird joke. Rose did have an oblique sense of humour sometimes. But this was June, not April the first, and she didn't look as if she thought there was anything funny about this. 'When?' I croaked, once I was able to speak again. 'Who to?'

'While you were in Montpellier, of course. If you'd been in the country you'd have stopped me from doing it,' she said flatly.

'You mean you think it's my fault?' I asked, startled.

Rose looked at me over the smoke of a newly lit cigarette. 'I wish I could, it'd be nice to be able to blame someone else,' she said frankly. 'But not even I can say it's anyone's fault except mine – and Nigel's. Do you remember what I said about him not liking to let his possessions go, well, not for nothing anyway? I know that from experience.' She sighed deeply. 'Going out with him was incredibly expensive. We used to go out to all these lovely places where, of course, he paid for everything, but he expected me to dress the part, and he didn't mean little numbers from chain stores either. I ended up having to borrow money from him, quite a lot actually, to buy clothes and things.' She smiled at me bravely. 'Don't get me wrong, at the time I loved it! It was so glamorous and the clothes were fabulous! I've still got some of them.'

'I think I can guess what happened next,' I said.

She nodded. 'When I broke it off he demanded his money back, with interest, at once, or else. He threatened to go to my father. He didn't expect to get anything out of him, of course, it was just to show me the sort of trouble he could make for me if I didn't do what he wanted. Of course I couldn't pay him back, and he knew it. He probably even planned it that way. Then he said I could repay him in kind,' she said dully, 'by marrying a Russian business acquaintance of his who wanted a permanent right of residence in this country. Apparently he wasn't likely to get it through the normal channels – I didn't think it would be a good idea to ask why not,' she added dryly. 'It didn't seem like any big deal at the time, I'd trot off to Kensington Register Office, meet my groom, marry him, say goodbye on the steps and then the divorce would follow through later. And I was let off the hook about repaying several thousand pounds. Besides, I didn't see I had much choice. So I did it.'

She reached out for her glass and drained it while I tried to absorb this incredible information. Eventually I said, 'But if you're properly divorced?'

'I am.'

'Then does it matter that you told a little white lie on your marriage certificate? It's not as if you've committed bigamy, is it? Surely it's on the same level as saying you were twenty-five not twenty-eight. You'd get a slap on the wrist, but that's all.'

'What I did was illegal, Susie,' she said flatly, 'and I could go to prison for it! Nigel read out the relevant bit of the act for me. He had it off pat, of course,' she added bitterly. 'I aided and abetted an illegal entry into the United Kingdom by entering into a false marriage, and if I don't do what Nigel wants he'll make sure the authorities find out about it. He's got the receipt I signed for the money he lent me. It's proof I was paid for the marriage.' Her eyes filled with tears again. 'Even if I didn't get sent to prison, there'd still be a trial and lots of publicity, you can bet your bottom dollar Nigel would make sure of that,' she said bitterly. 'Jeremy'd be a laughing stock, he'd never be able to lift his head up again!' She sniffed. 'And bang would go his chances of being a magistrate too.'

'I'm sure it wouldn't be that bad,' I said soothingly.

'It'd be worse!' she said with certainty. 'He'd be going through all of that for a woman he wouldn't believe he was married to.'

'He doesn't believe he's married to you?' I echoed, wondering if Jeremy was an imminent candidate for the funny farm. 'What does he think he was doing two months ago in front of three hundred and fifty people? Acting in his end-of-term play?'

'He does at the moment, of course,' she said impatiently. 'But he's Catholic!' When I didn't respond with instant illumination she said in a tragic voice, 'Catholics don't believe in divorce, I'm divorced, therefore in the eyes of the Church I wasn't eligible to marry Jeremy.'

Jeremy didn't strike me as someone who'd be particularly dogmatic about anything, especially a registry-office wedding which she'd virtually been forced into, but when I said this Rose tossed her head and said that I didn't know Jeremy like she did. 'You see, he thinks I've told him everything,' she said. 'He can't stand deceit. He's a terribly straightforward person.' She sniffed. 'That's one of his best traits, but it means he's not going to forgive me for lying to him.'

'But did you?' I asked. She looked at me blankly. 'What I

mean is, did he ever ask you if you'd been married before?'

'Of course not!' she said. 'But somehow I don't think he'll accept that as an excuse.'

'It's a good start.'

She looked at me reproachfully as if I wasn't taking this seriously enough. 'I can't tell you how frightened I was when I saw Nigel outside the church, I thought he was going to stand up with a just cause and impediment!' she said with wide eyes. 'Then he said he'd simply come to wish me well and he hoped bygones could be bygones, and I thought I could forget about it. But he was just softening me up!'

Actually, I thought he was waiting to see if Hamish had a business connection with Jeremy as well as being best man, and of course he found that out soon enough. Luke Dillon, master manipulator, wormed it out of me, didn't he? 'Can't you just tell him Jeremy's found out who owns Champion and it's impossible to get him to agree.'

'I tried that when I spoke to him this afternoon. He rings me at least twice a day to check on my progress.' There was nothing like keeping the pressure up. 'He said he doesn't accept excuses, and if I fail I have to accept what ever happens to me. Oh God, Susie! What am I going to *do?*

'Hire a hit man?' I said hopefully. 'Even if you got found out Jeremy'd think you were doing a public service! In that case, he probably wouldn't mind missing out on being a magistrate because his wife was doing time.'

She gave a weak smile. 'I wish! Unfortunately, hit men are in short supply in this part of the world.'

'In that case you should tell someone,' I said.

'Who? The police? You must be joking!' she exclaimed in horror. 'You can bet your bottom dollar that Nigel's covered his tracks and there'd be no trace of his trying to blackmail me. And the next thing you'd know would be the dossier would go to one of the tabloids and there'd be a banner headline of "Society wedding shock!" or something.' This appalling vision silenced both of us for a minute. 'He used to be quite fond of me at one time. If I keep quiet I might be able to persuade him not to carry out his threats,' she added hopefully.

She had about as much chance of that as a tethered goat has of the tiger undoing its rope and letting it wander away uneaten. But she was adamant that she wasn't going to talk to anyone, not even Hamish. Her mouth set into a thin line, 'I couldn't possibly, he'd tell Jeremy!'

'He wouldn't!' I said, affronted on Hamish's behalf. 'Solicitors are like doctors. They can't reveal what's been told to them in confidence!'

'Whatever,' she said, shrugging, 'I still can't speak to him. Nigel told me not to talk to *anyone* about this, and he might find out. Then what would he do to me?'

Her logic seemed slightly askew here, as she didn't seem to be worried about having told me, but maybe the all-powerful Nigel was such a dyed-in-the-wool misogynist that he didn't reckon a woman counted. What was undoubtedly true was that he'd scared her so much she wasn't capable of rational thought any longer, for she couldn't see that if she didn't tell Hamish enough to persuade him not to reveal to Jeremy who was behind the Champion bid the game was up anyway. 'I still might be able to sweet talk Jeremy into accepting it,' she said hopefully, in direct contradiction of what she'd said earlier. 'Anyway, how did you find out about Nigel and Champion?'

I was pleased to see that indignation over the line that'd been fed to both of us had replaced at least part of her dull despair, so that by the time Jeremy reappeared, asking

387

plaintively if we'd finished the whole bottle, she was able to smile lazily at him as if she didn't have a care in the world and say he had no need to complain since she knew perfectly well after he'd finished playing with the tractor he'd slipped down to the pub for a quick half with Matt and Derick.

'Why do you think that?' he asked self-consciously.

She sniffed the air pointedly. 'Fee, fi, fo, fum, I smell the beer in an Englishman!'

He grinned and wisely changed the subject. 'Is Susie going to stay for supper?'

'Help! I didn't realise it was so late!' Rose cried, looking at her watch and springing to her feet. 'You'll stay, won't you?' she asked with a pleading look.

I was only too glad to accept, in fact, I was hoping I could wheedle a bed for the night too. I might well have read too many thrillers, but somehow I didn't fancy spending the night alone in my cottage. There might be a few irritated beasties hanging around outside tonight and I'd rather stay away.

We pottered around the kitchen making a salad while a chicken something from Marks and Sparks heated up in the Aga. Maybe it was having at least talked through her fears or simply the influence of a second bottle of wine that made Rose begin to relax, but gradually the lines of strain began to blur on her face, though not disappear altogether. 'It's so good to be able to talk to someone about this, I haven't been able to think of anything else since Nigel rang,' she said as we laid the table.

'I don't blame you,' I said, remembering in a rather shamefaced way the snit I'd got into last night because she hadn't rung me. OK, so I wasn't psychic, but that doesn't stop you feeling sometimes that you ought to be.

She stopped, with a bundle of serving spoons held in mid-air over a peacefully sleeping Phuket on his chair. 'One of the worst things is the humiliation, isn't it? Being taken for a sucker like this. I know it's small potatoes compared to the rest of it, but I can't bear thinking all Luke wanted from me was to manipulate my husband. I thought he was after me, not that I was going to do anything, of course!'

'Well, I thought he was after *me* and I was quite prepared to do something!' I retorted. 'And at least you only got to help change a tyre, I got put in a ditch.'

Rose stared at me, wide-eyed. 'Surely that wasn't deliberate,' she said in a shocked voice. 'He's very proud of that car, he wouldn't have wanted to damage it!'

'And I'm entirely disposable, I suppose?' I asked sarcastically.

She met my eyes and we both began to giggle. 'Tell me,' she said confidentially, once we'd both subsided, 'is he really as bad as you said he was?'

'Rose!' I exclaimed. 'And you a married woman! Let's just say, on the evidence of his kissing you haven't missed anything.'

'Nothing at all?' she asked thoughtfully, as if the last remaining vestiges of her infatuation with him had at last been dumped and torn up into tiny little pieces. I might have been ladling it on a bit, he wasn't *that* bad, but it was in a good cause. Rose could, would, forgive someone for being bad, for being weak, easily led, all the sorts of excuses that someone could make for Luke, but she'd never forgive a man being useless between the sheets.

Jeremy came in, with Dexter bounding around behind him as usual, and glanced towards Phuket's chair. 'That cat was in that position this morning when I left to check the barley. Darling, if he doesn't move soon you'll have to check him for bed sores!'

Rose made a face at him, saying cats needed plenty of rest.

Not according to Dexter they didn't. He went up and dobbed Phuket in the stomach with the end of his nose until the cat gave an enraged growl and lashed out with one dark-chocolate paw. He didn't bother to open his eyes. With an expertise born of practice, Dexter leapt backwards and the unsheathed claws met thin air.

'You mustn't do that! Bad dog!' Jeremy said to Dexter in an insincere voice. I noticed that the hand that surreptitiously slipped him a cheese biscuit bore two long scratch marks down it. 'So what's your interesting news, Susie?' he asked as he pulled out a chair and sat down.

Rose clattered the dish she was getting out of the Aga and looked at me with acute alarm. I'd forgotten entirely about my leading remark. I thought frantically for a moment and mumbled something about Amanda thinking she was pregnant, hoping desperately that by the time Jeremy next saw her he'd have forgotten it. Fortunately, it didn't seem to occur to him this wasn't exactly the sort of hot news that would have brought me rushing over without warning.

As I'd hoped, sometime around when Jeremy was being sent off to find another bottle of wine, Rose decided that she'd never forgive herself if I got breathalysed on the way home and insisted I spend the night. Despite my safe haven I still refused to drink any of the third bottle, to her surprise. The prospect of seeing Hamish tomorrow was alarming enough without adding the spectre of coping with a crippling hangover while trying to stop him marching me straight back out of the door.

I might just as well not have bothered to be such a good girl, for I seemed to spend half the night tossing and turning, planning what I was going to say to Hamish. I fell asleep at last as light was beginning to creep across the sky, with the result that when the little alarm I'd borrowed off Rose went off at six o'clock I couldn't wake up and felt completely drugged with sleep as I stumbled my way down the stairs. Fortunately, I was alert enough by the time I rounded the corner on to the green at Little Dearsley to notice a dark-blue sports car parked unobtrusively in the lee of a leylandii hedge and with an excellent view of the front of my row of cottages. I started so much with shock that I crunched the gears and the noise seemed to echo across the silent green for ages, but the golden head tipped back against the headrest in the blue car didn't move. Like me, he must have spent half the night awake and needed more than a protesting gear box to wake him up. Uncharitably I hoped that when he finally did wake he'd have a stiff neck.

With meticulous care, and changing gear according to driving-test standards, I eased the car as quietly as possible past the sleeping Luke and parked it out of sight in the pub car-park. I walked the long way, around the edge of the green and in front of the row of cottages, to get to number three. My guardian angel must have been on duty for once – he rarely is, I find – for just before I pushed the gate open I stopped and glanced over the top. There, neatly stacked just behind it, was a pile of tins, positioned to crash over when the gate was swung into them.

'The crafty sod!' I breathed, reminding myself that Luke was by no means a dumb blond. By dint of sucking my tummy in so much I felt dizzy I managed to squeeze through the few inches the gate would open without setting the tins tumbling. As I opened my front door without being seen I had a pleased feeling, as if I'd already conquered Everest and it wasn't even seven in the morning yet.

I wasn't quite so lucky on leaving. Luke must have already been awake, for he was out of his car and striding purposefully towards me before I'd even locked the door. But I didn't really care if I had to meet him now, though I didn't want to be delayed too much – two cups of coffee, a bath, washed hair, loads of concealer cream to cover the bags under my eyes, a lengthy polishing and primping session, and one of my nicer dresses had done a lot to restore my strength of spirit. And everything was much easier in the daylight too, it was the idea of not being able to see him if he was creeping around outside the cottage that had given me such technicolour heeby-jeebies last night.

I picked up all the tins and put them to one side, wondering where he'd got them from. They weren't the usual sort of thing a man carries around in the boot of his car, and I couldn't imagine the immaculate Luke rootling around in people's dustbins for a bit of improvised alarm material. He got to me just as I opened the gate and stood there, with his hands on his hips, blocking my way. 'Where have you been?' he demanded angrily, for all the world as if he was my father (though my father learnt not to ask that sort of question some years ago).

'On a dirty stop-out, if that's any of your business!' I retorted flippantly.

His mouth tightened for an instant, then he widened his eyes and looked at me reproachfully. 'Susie, how can you say that?' he asked in a hurt voice, the picture of injured innocence. Natural injustice being what it is, sleeping in the car had done remarkably little to dent the sheer impact of his looks, despite the garishly yellow bruising around his eye. He might look a little worn and crumpled around the edges, seedy almost to the really stern critic, but he was still good-looking enough to cause a flutter in most maidenly, and non-maidenly, bosoms. Not mine though, I was pleased to note. 'I know I made a mistake last week, it was stupid of me, but I was jealous. Won't you forgive me?'

He gazed at me with limpid eyes while I shook my head in disbelief. He couldn't really think I'd fall for this one, could he? But perhaps he was so used to the knock-out effect of his looks that he couldn't believe that anyone would be immune to them. 'No,' I said in a pleasant voice and saw him start with shock.

'Please, Susie,' he went on gamely. 'I know you're angry with me about Rose, but that was just . . . business, it's you I'm really fond of. Can't we start all over again?'

I didn't even need to say anything this time, for his face changed from that of the polished charmer who was having one last try at soft-soaping the female to that of an extremely fed-up man who'd spent an uncomfortable night in a car and blamed me for every painful minute. 'We've got some things to talk about,' he said in a hard voice and grabbed my arm. 'Shall we go inside?'

Just how stupid did he think I was? If I could help it there was no way I was going anywhere with Luke Dillon in future without a whole gaggle of witnesses to monitor my every step. I was a lot happier out here. I was pretty certain Mrs Tanner would already be on net-curtain duty. I knew she was an early riser, heaven knows she'd told me often enough how she got up with the lark. 'I've got an appointment in Leicester,' I said politely, 'I can't.'

His grip tightened. 'Cancel it,' he said flatly.

'No.'

We eyeballed each other. I think he was wondering what to do next. I shook his hand off and stepped back a pace. 'What's this about, Luke? Rosewood Cottage?'

He shifted from one foot to the other. 'You don't want to

make trouble, do you, Susie?' He must have seen from my face that I wouldn't mind doing so in the least, for his eyes narrowed. 'All right then,' he said with a heavy sigh. 'Martin and I have been talking it over, and we're prepared to offer you—'

'If you're intending to offer me a share, forget it!' I interrupted. 'I'm not interested in cheating old ladies.'

Luke glared at me with intense dislike. 'Not interested in cheating old ladies,' he imitated in a contemptuous falsetto. 'You're so bloody pious you make me want to vomit!' I saw his hands flex reflectively, and I began to wonder if I was really quite so safe after all. 'Martin said you'd take this attitude,' he said in a resigned voice. 'So what do you propose we do?'

'We do?' I echoed. 'It's quite simple, Luke. Mr Jenkins is withdrawing his offer, unless of course he'd like to make one for the full value of the property with planning permission – ' a quick glance at 'Mr Jenkins' showed he wouldn't like at all – 'and meeting any of the costs involved in making his planning application. Incidentally,' I asked curiously, 'you took an incredible risk in making that application. Why didn't you wait until after you'd completed before you put it in?'

His face clouded with anger. 'That's bloody Martin's fault!' he spat. 'He was worried that if we couldn't start building at the same time as the rest of the development Nigel might think it wasn't worth doing. He said it would take at least three weeks to notify Mrs Murray, and the cottage would have been ours by then. It seems to have been done by return of ruddy post, and he wasn't even there to take her call!' he said in disgust. 'I could wring his bloody neck!' he declared vehemently. 'If it hadn't been for his stupid mistake we'd have had an easy seventy thou apiece. And thanks to your nosing around, of course,' he added, throwing me a vicious look, as if my neck was next in line for wringing. I stepped backwards a pace just in case.

'And what's Miss Goody Two Shoes intending to do now?' he sneered. 'Report us to the police?'

I shrugged. 'What's the point? I'll have to tell Stephen, of course, but neither of you have committed an actual crime yet and I don't want the agency to be damaged by loads of scurrilous rumours. I like working there.'

Tension seemed to drain out of the rigid line of his shoulders. I wondered suddenly if the two of them had hatched this little plot without Nigel's knowledge. If what I'd heard about him wasn't grossly exaggerated Luke was probably worrying, quite justifiably, that his position as favoured acolyte might be in severe danger if Nigel ever got to hear he had endangered the whole scheme by a bit of money-making on the side.

'You must be feeling very pleased with yourself,' I said coldly. 'You really managed to pull the wool over our eyes, didn't you? As a matter of interest,' I added casually, 'did you talk to me at Rose's wedding only because you saw me as a way of getting to her?'

'Oh, no,' he said blithely. 'Nigel hadn't made up his mind what to do then. I just thought you were rather pretty – ' well that was a small amount of balm to my injured self-worth – 'and of course it wasn't going to do any harm to chat up Rose's best mate.' No wonder he was so useful to Nigel if he was always on the look out for contacts like this. Did he ever do anything without an ulterior motive?

'And the car accident. *Did* you put us in the ditch on purpose?' I asked curiously.

'Of course not!' he exclaimed, looking shocked. It was his first reaction I believed was genuine. 'I wouldn't injure you,

Susie, I like you, really I do. That was a complete accident, but I won't pretend it wasn't useful. It advanced the whole thing by weeks. I had Rose eating out of the palm of my hand. Nigel promised me a bonus if I got the signature by the twenty-fifth of this month.' He scowled savagely. 'I would have too, if Rose hadn't turned out to be such a prudish little bitch. You wouldn't think it from the way she behaves. I had it all fixed, keep her out all night, a bit of snogging, maybe more, a few timed and dated photos and Bob's your uncle. But,' he said in disgust, 'she wouldn't go to my house and insisted on going to yours.'

I swallowed hard, feeling a chill wind go down my arms and spine despite the warmth of the morning. Rose had no idea how lucky she was. Luke glared at me. 'Don't look like that!' he said sharply. 'It's business and between the two of you you've lost me an absolute packet!'

'But you didn't waste much money on me, did you?' I asked derisively. 'You're such a cheapskate you wouldn't even take me out for a decent meal until you'd made sure I could be useful and there might be some profit in it!' Call me small-minded, but I was almost more annoyed about that than anything else. He was still looking like he was the one with the justified grievance so goaded, I added, 'But look on the bright side –' he didn't appear to want to – 'at least you haven't already spent someone else's money, unlike Nigel! No wonder he's so desperate for a result!'

Luke stiffened. 'How come you know about that?' he asked, suddenly suspicious. Oh brilliant, Susie! I thought. You've just made one smart-arse remark too many and really landed yourself in it! 'Martin said you must have stolen one of his disks to know so much about Rosewood Cottage. Did that prat also record a whole lot of stuff about Champion on it?'

'I didn't steal it!' I said indignantly. 'And it was Martin who told me about Nigel!' I shifted my bag on my shoulder, unconsciously putting the print-out of the Champion file under the protective cover of my arm.

He shook his head. 'Martin wouldn't do that,' he said, with misplaced confidence as it happened, and held out his hand. His eyes were fixed on my handbag. 'Are you going to give it to me, or shall I take it?'

I swallowed hard, wondering what to do. I was under no illusions about who would win in a fight, he could easily snatch my bag, extract the file and leg it to his car before the first person even got to a window in answer to my cry for help. Then, with wonderful timing, Eddie from number two emerged from his door. 'Morning, Susie,' he called, giving Luke a nakedly curious look. 'Don't usually see you leaving this early. I didn't think fat-cat estate agents ever bothered to roll in before ten o'clock, unlike us real workers, of course!'

'It's the first time I've ever heard advertising called "real work"!' I retorted.

He grinned. 'There was someone trying to get hold of you last night. Came and bashed on your door several times.' He glanced at Luke again.

'I wonder who it was,' I said blandly. 'I was spending the night with a friend, but I daresay he or she'll come back. Now, I must dash or I'll be late.' I looked hopefully at Eddie and said, 'Do you want to come and collect that tape I promised to lend you from the car?'

'Tape?' he asked, puzzled, then his face cleared. 'Yes, of course.'

We walked in a stiff threesome across the green, while Luke muttered quietly in my ear about what would happen if I started making trouble for him. Luckily, I couldn't hear most of it, but he looked so unlike the polished charmer I'd first

397

met that I had no difficulty in promising to keep my mouth shut. Naturally, I didn't tell him I had no intention at all of keeping my promise.

Hamish's offices were in a large Victorian house that must have been built for some industrialist to show off how much money he'd earned, and appeared to be serving much the same purpose for the firm of Harrison and Cartwright, solicitors. The pictures were real paintings, not prints, the pile of the carpet in the reception area was deep enough to lose a chihuahua in, the magazines were new, and brass gleamed all over the place, from the plaque outside with the firm's name on it, the lion's head knocker and letter box, to the decorative rail around the receptionist's desk. They probably needed to keep one person on the payroll permanently going around with a can of Brasso. No wonder they charged so much, I thought, as I took a seat on a sinfully deep sofa, and tried to calm my nerves by flicking through the legal notices in the *London Gazette*.

'I'm not sure Mr Laing is in yet,' the motherly receptionist who'd spoken to me yesterday informed me. My heart promptly sank to my freshly varnished toenails (out of sight, but a confidence booster, and I needed all the help I could get in that department right now), my little scheme was going to be scuppered before it even cast off if Hamish saw me waiting for him in reception. She rang through to check and turned back with a smile. 'He must have come in before I got here. He works so hard,' she added with faint disapproval. She looked just like her voice, a smiling woman in late middle-age with a well-rounded figure and a comfy lap that was probably used by several grandchildren. 'Mr Laing's secretary will be coming for you in a minute, dear,' she said. 'I do hope you can sort your problems out quickly. I can't abide cruelty to animals. He is all right, isn't he?' she asked anxiously.

I stared at her blankly for a moment, unable to think what she was talking about. Then, just as she was beginning to look as if she thought I was either mad or callous, I remembered my fictitious cat. So much had happened since I made that call it had entirely slipped my mind. 'Yes, he's fine,' I said quickly.

'Oh good, I was so worried for you. I adore cats. I've got three of them, two Persians and a Burmese. What kind is yours?'

'Um, just a moggy,' I faltered, praying that Hamish's secretary would come along and rescue me from this well-meaning woman before I put my foot in it and betrayed that I don't know that much about cats; my father is allergic to them, so we never had them at home.

'But even non-pedigrees are beautiful, aren't they?' she asked, in the indulgent voice of someone who knows that her own are infinitely superior. 'Ah, here we are, dear. Jessica's here to take you to Mr Laing.'

Jessica turned out to be about twenty-two, looked fearsomely efficient, and had probably turned to being a top-class legal secretary when she decided to give up being a supermodel. The very sight of her inflated my collywobbles to super-giant size. How could Hamish possibly be pleased to see me when he had that to look at every day? I thought despairingly as I followed her super-slim figure to an office on the first floor. She didn't even have the decency to be witheringly superior and imply I probably wasn't rich, important or good-looking enough for her to bother with so I could boost my flagging nerves with some spine-stiffening dislike and resentment. Instead, she asked me with absolute courtesy if I would mind taking a seat for a moment, since Mr Laing was taking a call. 'He knows that you're here and will come out for you as soon as he's finished. I'm just going to fetch him a coffee, would you like one too?' She glided off down the passageway as if it was a catwalk leaving me staring blankly at a painting on the wall and victim to a whole host of butterflies. I must be completely mad! I thought, tempted to get to my feet and run out, but I probably wouldn't be able to make my exit unobserved, and the actual humiliation of Hamish knowing I'd bottled out of seeing him was even worse than the potential humiliation of his refusing to hear me out.

His laugh sounded so clear and close that I almost jumped out of my skin. I looked up and saw Jessica hadn't closed his door properly and a draught must have inched it open a little more, so his voice was quite audible. Instead of politely burying myself in a magazine and pretending I couldn't hear, I pricked up my ears. I was burning with curiosity to know what – and who – could make him laugh like that at eight-thirty in the morning. 'Yes, it was great fun. We must do it again. Look, I've got a new client waiting so I'd better go. See you soon.'

Do what again? And with whom? I thought with sudden despair. It hadn't taken him long to find someone else to amuse himself with, had it? That had to have been a woman, he wouldn't laugh like that, not in that intimate way, with a man. Was it Merial? Had he decided to take her up on those lures she'd been casting his way? What remained of my confidence, so nicely boosted by outfacing Luke earlier this morning, was seeping steadily into the floor under my feet. The door opened and Hamish, wearing one of his ultra-conservative suits and a stupefyingly discreet tie, appeared saying, 'Miss Tradescant? Won't you come in?'

His welcoming expression froze into immobility as I rose slowly to my feet, knees shaking. I longed to ruffle his hair, loosen the immaculate knot of his tie, pull his shirt out a little, mess him up a bit, make him look more human. He was at his most formal, most solicitorish, most unlike the person I knew he was. All the words dried on my tongue in front of this unapproachable waxen image. Heart thumping, I waited for some reaction, a smile, a scowl, anything would be better than this damning indifference. 'Well, well, Miss Tradescant,' he said after a pause. 'A famous gardener, I presume? And Lily? Your second name?'

I found my tongue at last. 'Mum wanted to call me after her favourite aunt Lily, but my father refused to have a child called Lily Gardener, so they chose Susanna, which means the same thing,' I rattled off. He didn't look particularly interested and I couldn't blame him, frankly. He was standing with one hand on a polished brass doorknob, eyeing me from under heavy brows. I had the distinct feeling that whether or not I was going to be allowed to enter his office hung in the balance, and the scales were inexorably tipping up against me.

I was saved by Jessica sashaying back with a laden tray, carrying it as if it was a diamond necklace resting on a velvet cushion. I'd bet she could even make cleaning the windows look elegant, I thought jealously. She apologised for taking so long, and Hamish smiled at her in a way that made my stomach crease up with longing that I might have one of those too. 'It doesn't matter. We've been introducing ourselves.' He stepped back from the door and then I got my smile, except mine was so glacial that it sent shivers down my spine. 'Won't you come in, Miss . . .' He hesitated. 'Tradescant,' he finished, with what seemed like mocking emphasis.

I was so conscious of him that the hair on the back of my

neck prickled as I walked past him into a spartan and immaculate office. I wondered if it was always like this or got progressively more untidy during the course of the day. Hamish waved me to a chair in front of his desk as Jessica followed us in. 'You wouldn't prefer to be over there, Mr Laing?' she asked in a slightly surprised voice, with a look at a low table and three chairs set up in one corner of the office as an informal discussion area.

'I think Miss Tradescant will be more comfortable here,' he said.

Jessica looked as if she was wondering why I'd be more comfortable with the width of his large desk between us. I knew; but it was his comfort he was thinking of, not mine. She set the tray down on the edge of the desk without comment, handing out the coffee, in bone-china cups too, and placing a plate of biscuits within reach of both of us. 'Will that be all, Mr Laing?'

'Yes, thank you,' he said with another of those smiles. It faded from his face as he turned back towards me. 'So, Miss *Tradescant*, you have a property dispute, I understand,' he said as the door closed behind his secretary.

I'd practised what I was going to say endlessly on the journey here, but at the sight of his impassive face, I forgot the lot. He looked more like a hanging judge than a sympathetic and receptive listener to initially implausible excuses. As my tongue-tied silence lengthened he shifted restlessly and I blurted out the first thing that came to my mind. 'In a way. Except it's not my dispute. It's Rose's. She's being blackmailed by Nigel Flaxman.'

Whatever he was expecting to hear, it certainly wasn't that. He put down his coffee cup with a resounding clink, looked at me with narrowed eyes and said, 'Let me guess. He wants her

402

to get Jeremy to agree to the land sale.' I nodded. 'And he's got something on her?'

I nodded again.

'And of course she confided in her best friend.' He linked his fingers together, eyeing me with polite interest. 'But as a matter of interest, why has she deputised you to act for her and not come to see me herself?'

I could feel myself flush at the derisive tone in his voice. 'She's too frightened to talk to anyone. In fact, she doesn't even know I'm here, and I thought . . . I thought that you were, well, the person most likely to take an active interest in thwarting Nigel.'

'What impeccable logic,' he said mildly.

My hands clenched in my lap. I was not going to squirm under his sarcasm. I forced myself to keep still and look at him while I said, 'It certainly seemed better than the other option.'

'Which is?'

'Do nothing.'

'It didn't occur to you to go to the police?' he asked.

'Of course not! Why do blackmailers usually succeed? Because it's something that the victim wants kept secret! And Rose is desperate that Jeremy won't find out . . .'

'I really can't imagine what little peccadilloes Rose has in her past that she's so desperate to keep from Jeremy,' Hamish said, leaning back in his chair and looking at me as if he suspected I was playing an elaborate practical joke. 'Over-ran her Barclaycard limit? Had a few more boyfriends than she's admitted? I think he knows that already.' He didn't know quite how many more, though. 'Is there a naughty picture or two in existence?'

It wouldn't have surprised me, she had a photographer boyfriend at one time, but Nigel didn't seem to have got hold of them if there were any. 'Nigel has got a dossier in which he has gathered as much dirt about her as he can. The serious bit is that she's been married before, and Nigel says he can provide proof that she was paid for the marriage.'

Hamish's pencil dropped out of his fingers on to the desk. 'Oh,' he said slowly. 'I can see why she might not want Jeremy to know about that. What happened?'

'You won't tell Jeremy, will you?' I asked cautiously.

'Of course I won't!' he said impatiently. 'At the very least, you might have the decency to realise I'm not going to do Nigel's dirty work for him!'

'Sorry,' I muttered, and began to tell him everything Rose had told me.

'What a bastard!' he said softly once I'd finished. He frowned abstractedly, tapping the end of his pencil on the polished wood of his desk. 'I don't really see what I can do. Technically speaking, Nigel committed a crime himself by arranging for Rose to marry this Russian, but frankly it'll do Rose much more harm than him if all this gets out, which is what he will be banking on.'

'Oh,' I said in dismay. Unrealistically, I'd been hoping that Hamish would come up with some magic legal formula by which he could impose a gagging order on Nigel – at the very least – a hang, draw and quartering order would be even better, in my opinion. 'But there must be *something* he doesn't want coming out about it, otherwise he could have rung Rose and given her the order as soon as she came back from honeymoon, rather than go through all this elaborate palaver with Luke.'

Hamish's frown deepened. 'Luke?' he said sharply. 'What's he got to do with it?'

If I'd hoped that Hamish would feel for my humiliation in

discovering that his supposed rival had only been interested in me for the short cut I could offer him to a lot of money, I was disappointed. He did crack a smile about Nigel and Luke turning up at the wedding though. 'Nigel must have nearly had a heart attack when he saw me.'

'His original plan was to suggest to Rose at the reception she help an old friend by persuading Jeremy to sign on the dotted, presumably with the hint that it'd be better for her if she did. That went out of the window when he realised Jeremy probably knew a good many unpleasant things about him via you, then when he found out you're the estate solicitor they decided to go for the subtle approach with Luke.'

'And that's where you came in,' Hamish said flatly. 'I'm sorry for you that it had to turn out that way.'

The detached sympathy in his voice was like a hammer blow in the stomach, winding me so I couldn't speak. I couldn't get the breath to tell him it was wasted, I didn't give a damn, and he went on thoughtfully, 'You're right, there must be something he's risking by threatening to expose Rose, but what? The problem's time. I doubt the man I'm using can discover much concrete in three days.' He drummed his fingers on the desk. 'I might be able to buy a couple of days or so by asking a few legal questions, but I've already covered most of those. And from what you say Rose'll have a nervous breakdown if this is spun out for much longer.'

'Might this help to speed things up a bit?' I asked, opening my bag and handing over the print-out of the file on Champion properties.

Hamish took it and his eyebrows rose as he scanned it rapidly. 'Is this genuine?' he asked.

'As far as I know. When Luke gets fed up of toadying to his grandmother he goes around to Martin's and gets stoned. I think Martin's always been a bit worried Nigel and Luke might do the dirty on him, so he's been collecting as much information about the project as he can as protection, and since Luke gets loquacious when stoned there's been a lot to collect.'

'And how did you come by this?' asked Hamish, giving me a very old-fashioned look.

'It's all right,' I assured him. 'I didn't burgle Martin's house to get it. We – er – opened a drawer in his desk, found a floppy and looked through it just in case it had stuff to do with the agency on it. It was just luck that all that stuff about Champion was on there as well. I put it back after I copied it,' I added virtuously.

'You still appear to have broken into Martin's desk and helped yourself to a piece of his private property,' Hamish said in a resigned voice, and sighed faintly. 'I suppose it was in a good cause.'

'I had no idea you had such a refreshingly liberal attitude to the law,' I said admiringly. He glared at me down his nose. 'What it doesn't say in there though,' I went on, 'is Nigel's already used some of the money he got from his backers to fund his venture in America. He was counting on being able to get the banks to put up some more to cover the actual building costs once the contracts were signed. That's why he's so desperate to get this going ahead and quickly, otherwise he'll have to repay the money and that's going to be extremely difficult. According to Martin, his backers aren't the sort of people you want to have thinking you've embezzled their money.' They must be seriously nasty if Nigel was afraid of them, I thought with satisfaction.

'According to Martin . . .' Hamish echoed. 'What did you do, feed him a truth drug or something?'

'No, I just went round to clear up one or two things. He

406

must have overdosed on the Benylin, because when he lost his temper and started shouting he got very indiscreet.'

'You went to *see* a man whose files you'd just hacked into—'

'That was Jenny, not me,' I interrupted.

He threw me a withering glance. 'When you were preparing to blow the whistle on a nice little scam he had going, and when presumably you didn't know if he was alone or had his accomplice with him . . .' He saw my involuntary shudder as I remembered my panic when I realised Luke was turning up and his face hardened. 'Are you completely mad?' he demanded. 'Have you got no idea what happens to women in your position? How bloody irresponsible can you get?'

For a moment, I basked in the pure bliss of Hamish getting all hot under the collar and protective about me. It must mean he hadn't given up on me entirely, mustn't it? I thought hopefully, and then my raised spirits came crashing back down to earth as I realised it was probably no more than the general concern he'd show towards any woman. Apart from his initial surprise at seeing me, he'd behaved with complete professional detachment. Hardly the behaviour of a man who was eating his heart out, I thought, feeling more depressed by the second.

He was looking at me enquiringly, probably wondering why I'd apparently been struck dumb. I swallowed hard to get rid of the lump in my throat and said, 'I won't do it again, I promise you, but it did get results.'

'It could have been at too high a cost,' he retorted grimly. 'Did you find out anything else useful from Martin?'

'Only how much he dislikes me, which I'd gathered already,' I said ruefully.

'Are you surprised?' he asked, a distinctly oblique comment, in my opinion. He began to tap the end of his pencil on the

407

desk again, thinking. 'Rose really is caught in a cleft stick here. I can easily see why she doesn't want Jeremy to know about this Russian, but it would probably be almost as bad if he were to believe she'd colluded with Nigel over the land deal. He'd never trust her again, especially since Luke Dillon is involved too.' He glanced at me quickly with half-closed eyes. 'Jeremy's much more observant than you think,' he said with emphasis. 'I'll get another couple of men digging around and we'll see if they can discover anything concrete which we can throw back at Nigel to get him to back off.' He smiled in a distinctly malicious manner at the thought.

There was a knock on the door and Jessica's head poked around. 'I'm sorry to disturb you, Mr Laing, but Mr Pierce has arrived and is waiting for you in the boardroom.'

'Hell!' Hamish swore softly, and looked over at me. 'Is that all? He can wait another few minutes if it isn't.'

I opened my mouth to speak. Then closed it again. What was the point? He was hardly going to be concentrating on what I had to say while he was clock-watching, was he? He might even think I'd been softening him up first by telling him all this to demonstrate how terribly I'd been misled by Luke. Oh, why had I bottled out at the beginning? It was too late now. Too late. The most bitter words in the English language. With leaden legs I rose to my feet, smiling mechanically, and said, 'I won't keep you.'

Jessica hurried forward with what sounded like a small sigh of relief and handed Hamish a buff-coloured file. 'This is what you need, Mr Laing. I'll show Miss Tradescant out.'

'You're incredibly bossy, Jessica!' he said with a smile as he took the file and turned to me, his face not showing any regret that we hadn't moved to matters personal. 'Thank you for coming to see me, and ring me if there's anything else you can think of,' he said in a politely bored voice that seemed to intimate 'please don't bother'.

'Shall I make you another appointment to see Mr Laing?' Jessica asked.

'No, I don't think so,' I said sadly.

CHAPTER 22

In a thoroughly melodramatic manner, I contemplated throwing myself off the top level of the multi-storey car-park for being such a fool as to mess things up quite so comprehensively, then realised I hadn't yet handed over the proof of Martin's nasty little scam to Stephen. I certainly couldn't let him get away with it. Suicide would have to wait for the moment. And then I'd have to check I'd remembered to clean the bath this morning and get rid of the shaming remains of the giant bar of Fruit and Nut chocolate from beside my bed . . . I sighed gloomily. It looked like life would have to go on.

Stephen was already in his office when I got in, and called me straight in to see him, looking unusually solemn and worried. 'Susie, Martin's been making some very serious accusations against you,' he began as I sat down.

Why hadn't I expected him to try and fight back? I sighed heavily. 'What a slime ball he is! What's he been saying?' I asked with interest.

Stephen shifted uncomfortably and took off his glasses, polishing them industriously and playing for time. 'Basically, that you've been conducting a vendetta against him. You've been altering his files, interfering with his clients, bad-mouthing him to everyone, even manufacturing evidence to make it look like he's ripping off our clients,' he said in the general direction of his handkerchief, not meeting my eyes. 'He says you've even copied some of his files and inserted damning bits in them.'

Nice one, Martin, I thought with grudging admiration. Quick thinking for someone who was half doped with flu remedies. 'And did he say why I might be doing this?' I enquired.

The polishing went up a couple of degrees in intensity. 'Um . . . er . . . because you feel rejected,' Stephen mumbled.

'What!' I exclaimed in disbelief, gawping at him. 'Let me get this right. Martin claims *I* made advances to *him*? And he turned me down?' Stephen nodded. 'In his dreams!' I snorted with laughter. 'I'd rather neck a cockroach than lay a finger on Martin Prescott! Couldn't he have come up with a more plausible scenario?'

'I thought it was a bit unlikely,' Stephen murmured.

'More than unlikely, downright flaming impossible!' I retorted. 'And what about Jenny? Has she also been panting with unrequited love for Martin?'

His eyebrows shot upwards and he stared at me. 'Er, I don't think so,' he said, looking puzzled. 'What's she got to do with it?'

'She was with me yesterday when I took the call from Mrs Murray . . .'

It took a bit of time for the full import of what I was saying to sink in, which wasn't really surprising. Stephen simply didn't want to believe his second in command had been on the take and at first tried to insist that Jenny and I had to be mistaken, we'd taken a whole lot of circumstantial evidence and drawn the wrong conclusion, on the face of it a reasonable conclusion, but a wrong one nevertheless. Eventually, even he had to admit that the circumstances added up just too well.

412

He sat there, face grey with shock, trying to come to terms with it. 'I *trusted* him,' he said at last. 'And I expect he's been doing this on a regular basis ever since I employed him, and laughing at me all the time behind my back for being a soft, gullible touch,' he added bitterly.

I'd been thinking about this myself. 'Surely if he'd done it before he'd have known enough not to have made the mistake with the planning permission?' I asked. 'I think Martin saw what looked like a golden opportunity to make a lot of easy bucks and took it, but honestly, Stephen, how often does a cottage with a big garden come up for sale on the edge of a development, and its elderly owner is so convinced she won't get planning permission that she doesn't even bother to apply?'

'Hardly ever,' he said, looking slightly more cheerful.

'I reckon you can assume this was a one-off and we can put Rosewood Cottage back on the market with "planning permission applied for" and no one will ever be any the wiser.'

The colour began to come back into Stephen's face as the spectre of the regulators and the law descending on the agency and ruining its reputation began to recede. 'Funny thing, Liddy never liked Martin, said he was a sleazy toad, even if he was good at his job,' he said, pushing his glasses back up his nose and frowning thoughtfully. 'I should have listened to her.' I hoped he wouldn't listen to her too much, I dreaded to think what Liddy's opinion of me was. 'As of now Martin has resigned due to ill health, which will become much worse if I ever lay eyes on him again,' he added grimly. 'Amanda can take over as senior negotiator, she's more than capable of it, but I'd better get on with finding someone to replace her. Can you get on with drafting an advertisement . . . Though Maurice was saying the other day he knew of a bright young man who's unhappy where he is.' He looked up, eyes alert. 'Unless of course, you, Susie . . .?'

'Me?' I asked, startled.

'I'm well aware that you're capable of doing a lot more than finding my misplaced filing,' he said dryly. 'I don't want to lose you as a PA altogether, but I was thinking that perhaps if we got a junior in to do all the really routine stuff it would free you up for at least half your time. You'd be really good as a negotiator, it'd suit you down to the ground.' He looked at me hopefully, waiting for my acceptance.

I could see he was about to launch into his persuasive spiel, and what with one thing and another I wasn't feeling strong enough to resist. If I didn't stop him now I'd find myself as an estate agent (trainee, part-time) before I'd had time to think. I probably would anyway, Stephen had that deadly persistent look in his eye that brooked no argument, but I wanted to feel that the decision was at least partially mine. 'Can I think about it?' I asked.

'Of course,' he said promptly, with a satisfied air. As far as he was concerned, it was already as good as confirmed. I escaped before he could start listing all the benefits I should consider and sank into my chair with a sigh of relief to have got off so lightly.

Too soon. My behind had barely hit the fabric before Rose was on the line and she wasn't in a good mood. In fact, she was incandescent. 'How *dare* you go running to Hamish?' she hissed. 'You *promised* you wouldn't tell anyone!'

It didn't seem like a good idea to point out that in fact I'd only promised not to tell Jeremy, she wouldn't have appreciated it. I felt like beating my head against my computer screen. I'd been intending to warn her as soon as I got into the office, but what with Stephen immediately landing me with Martin's

414

accusations and my potential new career I'd forgotten all about it. Hamish must have got his meeting with Mr Pierce through in good order, for he'd already been on to her, checking up on the name of the Russian she'd married. I wondered if she'd given him the earful she was giving me. I doubted it somehow. 'How can I ever trust you again?' she demanded. 'You might have thought you were doing it for the best, but you've laid me wide open to Nigel. If he finds out he'll go straight to Jeremy and it'll all be your fault . . .'

I was tired, this morning seemed to have been made up of one stressful encounter after another. I knew perfectly well Rose was so wound up she couldn't think straight, but this was just too much. It's not true that redheads have worse tempers than other people, lots of brunettes and blondes have tempers just as filthy as mine when roused. So I've been told. Luckily, it's impossible to really lose your rag when you're having to speak in a hushed tone so the rest of the office, not to mention a client, can't hear, so what I said about spoilt princesses who think only of themselves didn't slip from offensive right into the never to be forgiven, downright abusive. As it was, the call ended rather abruptly and when I'd calmed down, about half an hour later, I realised there was now probably another name on the ever-lengthening list of people who didn't want to speak to me ever again.

I really thought my cup was finally going to run over completely when Jenny called across to say Gina was on the phone. Remembering her distinctly cool attitude when I last saw her, I braced myself for a rough passage. She'd probably asked Hamish how I was and he'd answered along the lines of 'enjoying Luke Dillon in a bath towel' and was ringing me full of sisterly wrath. I almost fell off my chair with surprise when I heard her tone. It couldn't have been friendlier. 'I'm at the

Stable Gallery hanging the pictures and I thought how nice it'd be to see you again. Shall we have lunch?'

'I can't, we're so short-staffed because of illness – and things – I'm not going to be able to get out,' I stammered, glad to have a genuine excuse for avoiding her. I liked Gina, in other circumstances I could see myself becoming good friends with her, but I couldn't think of anything more akin to a nightmare than skirting around the topic of Hamish with his sister over a gossipy lunch. It would be like tap dancing over a minefield. Sooner or later I'd be bound to give something away.

'What a shame,' she said, sounding genuinely disappointed. 'And I know I can't do tomorrow. Still, you are coming to the opening shindig, aren't you? I'll never forgive you if you don't,' she threatened as I hesitated.

'Of course, I wouldn't miss it,' I assured her. Hamish was bound to be there, but if I got there right at the start and made some excuse to leave early I should be able to avoid any embarrassing encounters. 'Friday, isn't it?'

'Thursday,' she corrected, 'so we can get the photos to the local paper for the weekend edition. Just think of it, you might make the social pages of the *Frampton Gazette*!'

'What a joy for everyone!' I said.

It might not have been for the others, but for me Martin's precipitate departure was a blessing in disguise, as it threw us into such hectic chaos I hardly had any time to sit and brood over the next couple of days. A slimeball he might have been, but as it turned out no one could have accused him of being lazy, he had the most incredible amount of work on the go, with, as we all noticed, a quite disproportionate number of the most profitable jobs. We didn't think it was by chance. Amanda answered the emergency call and returned to work, still looking fragile around the edges and with a long-suffering martyred expression, claiming she needed to spend at least another two days in bed. She came out after half an hour with Stephen, a promotion and a payrise looking as if she'd just spent a week at a health farm. 'And I hear you're on the way up too,' she said, sitting on the edge of my desk in a manner distinctly unlike that of the former senior-negotiator.

'Nothing's definite yet,' I said firmly. I could feel this hole being inexorably dug for me. Stephen was in high-octane persuasive mode, never letting a chance go by to tell me why I should become his latest trainee, and it was becoming more and more difficult to explain why I wasn't leaping at what on the face of it seemed like a golden opportunity. It really was one too; a job I thought I'd enjoy, a decent salary, workmates I liked, a nice place to live. Except there were several very large pitfalls. Namely that I'd bust up with my lover, given the local golden boy a black eye and was on non-speaks with my best friend, who was rapidly turning into the local hostess with the mostess. What sort of social life was I going to be able to have? At any gathering of more than about three I was bound to run into one of them with all the awkward consequences. It was daunting enough to make me contemplate being one of those pathetic women who throw in the towel the moment they've been crossed in 'lurve' and bolt for cover, except the prospect of explaining to everyone I knew how I'd managed to completely muck up my new life in under two months was even more appalling.

Stephen solved the problem of what he considered my quite unreasonable shilly-shallying (taking longer than five minutes to agree to do what he wanted) in his own inimitable way. He simply announced that as we were so shorthanded I was going to have to start showing houses, whether I cared to call myself a PA or a negotiator. Virtually before I had time to marshal the first word of protest I was sent off by this genial dictator to show a couple a mews development in a nearby town. As I pointed out when I came back, since I'd had to take them in my car it was a good thing I'd happened to clear the sweet papers off the floor the day before, wasn't it?

'My father used to take clients around in the car he used for transporting pigs. Once, it even still had a couple of piglets in it,' Stephen said laconically. 'So what are a few sweet papers by comparison?'

He was in a blindingly good mood, dispensing a degree of bonhomie to all, which was amazing considering the brouhaha over Martin. Amanda and I were having a good speculate about it over a quick lunch in the wine bar on Thursday and decided that things had to be going right with Liddy and he was lucky in love.

'Nice to know someone is,' I said in a depressed voice as I picked at my salad.

Amanda glanced at me sharply. 'Oh, is that why you're going around like a month of wet Sundays? Not mourning that nice Arnaud?'

'I've hardly thought of him,' I said truthfully, and a bit guiltily too, though I didn't know why. I daredsay he wasn't spending hours thinking wistfully of me either.

'Problems with Luke then?' Amanda asked with a suggestive smile.

'No,' I said equally truthfully. 'No problems at all—'

I was about to expand on this, explain why, when I stopped in sudden embarrassment. In the mirror along the wall behind Amanda I could see the reflection of the table to our rear. And there, just finishing a cup of coffee, was the unmistakable shape of Gina in a paint-stained tee shirt, hair dragged back off her face and held in place with a rubber band. She caught my eye so, face flaming, for I was sure she'd heard every word, I had to turn around and say hello.

'Just in case you're worried, I'm not intending to turn up like this tonight,' she said smiling and with a rueful gesture at her dishevelled apparel. 'One of the pictures got dropped so I had to dash over for a bit of emergency repair work. I hope the paint dries in time,' she added, not looking too convinced about it. 'You aren't going to forget about coming, are you?' she asked pointedly.

I'd been thinking that I might, but judging from her expression I wasn't going to get away with having a sudden amnesia attack during the afternoon. 'Yes, of course I am. I'm looking forward to it,' I assured her untruthfully.

'Good,' she said firmly. 'See you then.'

The party was in full swing by the time I arrived. My plans for an early arrival and departure had been scuppered by a delightful young couple who were so enchanted with the house I'd shown them they virtually started measuring up for curtains on the spot. At long last I managed to hustle them out and they left with stars in their eyes to go and ring up everyone they knew to tell them they'd found The House, while I dashed home to have a quick bath and put on the amount of make-up needed for a brave face.

The Stable Gallery was one of those terrifyingly chic places full of exquisite craftsman-made pieces, none of which had a price tag, presumably on the basis that if you needed to know how much something cost you weren't going to be able to afford it anyway. I'd lingered in front of the large windows on several occasions, admiring the displays which changed every week. Once it had been heavy, hand-beaten silver jewellery in archaic shapes, the next time driftwood sculptures in such wonderfully fluid lines it was impossible to tell what was due to the hand of man and what came from the motion of the sea. Today, agate and carnelian necklaces and bracelets were scattered, seemingly at random, over a swathe of dark-green velvet, like pebbles seen through water, while one of Gina's paintings, a long, long riverscape, hung suspended in mid-air above the display. Behind the painting I could see loads of people chatting and drinking wine, while the occasional flash lit their faces – presumably the reporter from the *Frampton Gazette* was getting his pictures in nice and early for the press deadline. I hesitated, momentarily daunted by all these unknown faces, then Gina, now quite transformed from the scruffy object at lunchtime into svelte glamour by a loose chignon and a wonderful slim-fitting golden dress that looked as if it had been made out of a sari, looked up and saw me peering through the window. She smiled and waved so, smiling rather nervously, I went in.

'I wouldn't have recognised you!' I said.

'I hardly recognise myself!' she said wryly, looking down at her elegantly shod feet. 'I was still in trainers and jeans twenty minutes before the photographer was due to take pictures of Sally and myself before the rush started. As it is, I'm having to walk around with my hands in fists so no one can see I didn't have time to get the paint out from under my nails! I can't believe the number of people that have turned up. It's packed already.'

'Take it as a compliment to your talent,' I said.

'Thanks, but I think it's probably more of a compliment to Sally's caterer. The crispy prawn things are *delicious*,' she said cynically. 'You should try them before they run out. There must be lots of people here that you know. Hamish is around

420

somewhere,' she informed me casually, 'and Jeremy and Rose are already here.'

Oh, great! Were they going to cut me dead or be stiffly polite? I wondered gloomily. 'That's nice,' I said woodenly, my eyes scanning the room for them. Jeremy was walking slowly down one cream-painted stone wall, examining the paintings with frowning attention, but I couldn't see the other two. At least it was unlikely that Luke was here too, also giving me filthy looks and confirming me as the local pariah.

'And Stephen and Liddy, of course. Isn't it great—? Oh bother!' Gina said as her eye was caught by the owner of the gallery. 'Sally wants me to talk to Harry Filbert, and he's *such* a bore, even if he does spend a fortune on art! I suppose I'd better. But there's Rose. She's just coming over.'

I tensed, wondering if I could cope with recriminations when I'd barely got my feet in the door, but it was too late to pretend I hadn't seen her. She was incredible, I thought with grudging admiration, no one who didn't know her well would think there was anything the matter at all. She was as pretty as usual, hair hanging glossy and thick to her shoulders, hand motions full of their normal lively energy, except her dress hung loose on a figure that was slipping from slimness to downright thinness and no amount of eye drops could have put a sparkle in her eyes. She was also looking uncharacteristically nervous. We said rather formal hellos to each other and muttered a few platitudes about Gina's pictures, quite unlike the normal way we carry on. I was about to make an excuse and move away, this was too depressing, when Rose shuffled her feet and smiled cautiously. 'Susie, I'm sorry,' she said in a rush. 'You were trying to help me, I shouldn't have said what I did.'

I gaped at her. Rose doesn't apologise. Not normally. She

421

went on rapidly, 'I was completely out of line. I don't know what came over me, in fact—'

'Come on, if you go on in that soapy manner I'll start thinking there's something seriously wrong with you!' I interrupted before the breast-beating could get too excruciating. 'I seem to remember that I said the odd thing best forgotten too.' She nodded in wry agreement. 'What's much more important is, do you have any news?'

She made a worried face. 'Not yet. But Hamish says if the worst comes to the worst he'll persuade Jeremy to accept Nigel's offer.'

'Will he be able to do that?' I asked, startled.

She sighed gloomily. 'He thinks he can. He says he'll tell Jeremy he hates to admit it but he thinks it would be the best thing for the estate – in truth it's not going to do us any harm even if the thought of Nigel making a packet from our land leaves a very nasty taste in the mouth,' she said practically. 'He says the important thing is to put it up as his idea so Jeremy doesn't think I – or Luke – had anything to do with it . . . I . . . I never realised before how *nice* Hamish is,' she said in a rush. He was a lot more than just that, I thought sadly. 'But I'm trying not to think about Nigel – or Luke – it's bad for my blood pressure,' she said firmly, looking around. 'Oh, there's Stephen. Yummy! Shame he's got Liddy with him. They do look pleased with themselves,' she added, glancing over to where they were the centre of an animated group. 'I wonder why.'

Stephen was standing with his arm around Liddy, looking particularly self-satisfied. No wonder he's been in such a good mood! I thought. He must have had a result in Paris. 'I think I can guess why,' I said, 'but let's go over and see.'

But before I could even ask any pertinent questions he

422

demanded in a single-minded fashion, 'How did you do?'

I couldn't help preening myself and saying slightly smugly, 'They're putting in an offer for the asking price in the morning.'

'There, what did I tell you?' he asked with a broad smile. 'It's only the second time you've done it and you've already made a sale. You're a natural, Susie!'

'Yes, of course I am, and it had nothing to do with the fact that you already knew the Davidsons would adore Old Forge House?' I asked.

He grinned at me in acknowledgement. 'You need to get your confidence up.'

'And you want to get your own way!' I retorted. I glanced at Liddy's left hand, which was resting possessively on Stephen's arm. A large diamond-and-sapphire ring winked as it caught the light. Stephen had got his own way in something else too. 'So that was what Gina was about to tell me!' I exclaimed. 'No wonder you were so keen to take the afternoon off, Stephen. Doing a bit of jewellery shopping, I daresay!' His pleased smirk confirmed my guess. I kissed him heartily on both cheeks. 'Congratulations! I'm so pleased for you both.'

Liddy gave Stephen a long considering look, but showed she wasn't completely devoid of a sense of humour by giggling when he glanced at her fearfully and said hastily, 'It's the first time Susie's *ever* kissed me! Isn't it, Susie?'

'Mm,' she said, 'and the first time with *Rose* too?' as Rose reached up to deliver him a couple of smackers.

'You needn't expect *me* to kiss you, Stephen, first time or not!' said a deep voice from behind me. I felt my heart miss a beat and stood rooted to the spot as Hamish moved around me with a murmured, 'Excuse me,' and gave Liddy a hug, saying, 'It's about time you made an honest man of him! It's great news, well done!'

He'd barely acknowledged my existence, I thought with a lump in my throat, as I watched Liddy return his embrace with considerably more vigour than Stephen had done with Rose or me. I could understand, even if I didn't appreciate, that Hamish might not want to be all kissy-kissy with me, but a brief smile would have done. A big smile would have been better. But not ignoring me altogether. I turned away, deciding to do one tour of the pictures so as not to offend Gina, and then I could decently leave with dignity and spend the rest of the evening in front of a non-weepy video, comfort-eating my way through a bar of chocolate. I'd never have thought there were advantages to heartbreak, but that was one. For the first time in my life I could eat as much chocolate as I liked and still lose weight.

I went down one wall, seeing everything and taking in nothing other than a vague impression of colour, sipping mechanically from an already empty glass, senses constantly on the alert just in case Hamish wanted to come and talk to me. But he seemed quite content to stay in the congratulatory group around Stephen and Liddy. 'Hey, Susie, here a minute!' hissed Rose, dragging me into a corner. It was a completely different Rose to the one I'd spoken to a quarter of an hour ago. This one was fizzing with energy and high spirits, cheeks glowing without the aid of blusher, eyes gleaming, smile stretching from ear to ear. 'He's done it! He's *done* it!' she hissed.

'Who?' I asked rather stupidly.

'Hamish! He's warned Nigel off. I can't believe it!' she said, looking as if she was about to start doing a victory dance on the spot. 'You know the Russian I er . . .' she looked around quickly to see if anyone was in earshot, but Jeremy was safely on the other side of the room '. . . erhummed?'

I nodded.

'It turns out Nigel owes him a *fortune*, really a fortune, millions, I believe, much more than he was ever going to get from the development. As Hamish told Nigel, if my Russian were to discover that he was in danger of losing his permit to stay here because Nigel had informed the authorities our . . . erhum . . . was a put-up job, he *wouldn't* be pleased. At the very least he'd demand to be repaid and Nigel'd go bankrupt as opposed to being merely severely dented in the pocket area by this project not going ahead. So it isn't!' she added happily. 'This whole nightmare's over. I can't believe it! Hamish says Nigel's promised never to say anything about the . . . erhum, but he thinks that I ought to tell Jeremy myself sometime, just in case. I think he's right,' she said seriously. 'He said to pick the moment when Jeremy's feeling at his most indulgent, something like just after we've had our first baby. What do you think?'

'Good idea,' I said, 'but doesn't that mean you're going to have to wait rather a long time? You did say Flavia was going to have to move or pop her clogs first.'

'That's the icing on the cake! Flavia's had her stay in Yorkshire extended by another week!' She gurgled with laughter. 'The colonel wasn't being keen enough in her opinion so I suggested she told him Arnaud was coming to stay with you again! The invite came out at the speed of light! Isn't that great? I can just about cope with her being the doting granny if she's a hundred miles away, rather than down the passage!' She shuffled her feet restlessly. 'You see, I've started to think how nice it would be to have a small Jeremy,' she confessed in a rather shamefaced way, probably remembering the number of times she'd banged on over a bottle or two about the inconceivability of ever wanting to muck up her life with children. 'And if you have your first baby over thirty they call you an elderly something or other and that'd be so embarrassing! So I'd better get a move on, hadn't I? And we can have such fun trying. I can have an excuse for calling Jeremy back in the middle of the day . . .'

'*Rose!*' I hissed. The gallery wasn't big, but it had excellent acoustics and her voice was very clear. 'And have you thought that the baby might not take after its father, but its grandmother?' I asked.

She stared at me in horror. 'God wouldn't be so unkind!' she exclaimed. 'Really, he wouldn't, would he?' she added doubtfully. 'And with my genes it couldn't be like Flavia!' she said firmly, as if that settled it. She hugged herself in sheer pleasure. 'I'm so happy I don't know what to do with myself! Hamish is *brilliant!*' He is, he is, I agreed. 'I could just go over and kiss him right now,' she declared with sparkling eyes. Oh, so could I, I thought, following her gaze to where he was in the middle of the room, head bent, listening attentively to something Tony was saying, if only I could. But I'd get brushed off like a troublesome mosquito. Rose turned back to me, frowning slightly as she saw my face. I quickly rearranged my expression. 'If it hadn't been for you telling Hamish about Nigel I'd still have his threats hanging over me.' She hesitated for a moment and then said with a rueful smile, 'I did apologise to you before I knew about this, didn't I?'

I didn't feel I was up to garment-rending remorse from Rose, she's never moderate in her emotions, so I said, 'OK, if you insist then. I'm owed one session of being thoroughly unreasonable when I'm beside myself about something and you aren't allowed to complain. Agreed?'

'You've got a deal,' she said with a smile. 'Look, here's Hamish. I've just been telling Susie how brilliant you are,' she added with a glowing look upwards. If she went on casting looks like that at him she was going to make Jeremy extremely jealous, I thought with not a small pang of the green-eyed monster myself as he smiled at her.

'Go on, go on, I love hearing nice things about myself.' At last he turned his head my way, though he didn't meet my eyes. 'Hello, Susie. I didn't have a chance to speak to you earlier. I wanted to tell Rose the news as soon as possible.'

'I understand,' I said through stiff lips, watching him covertly from under my eyelashes. He looked tired. I'd have liked to have believed it was because of me, but it was much more likely he'd been burning the midnight oil trying to find a way around Rose's problems.

She was virtually dancing up and down in her impatience to get his attention back. 'You didn't finish telling me what's going to happen to the development. Does it just peter out now?'

Hamish shrugged. 'Who knows? I imagine eventually something modest will go up there, nothing like Nigel's grandiose plans, since Jeremy won't give him access, and with all the land that has to be set aside for the toad park there just isn't room for his ideas. He's going to make an enormous loss.' He smiled in a distinctly shark-like way. 'Of course, we really mind about that, don't we?'

Gina bustled her way through the crowd towards us and laid a hand on Rose's arm. 'You've just hit the big time, you're about to star in the social pages of the next issue of the *Frampton Gazette*! Come and get your picture taken, I'll take you over.' A minute later, Rose was preening slightly self-consciously in front of one of Gina's bigger pictures, practising in-front-of-the-camera expressions while Hamish and I stood rooted to the spot where we'd been left, each of us, so I imagined, determined not to be the one to lose face by making a break for it first.

The silence was getting increasingly awkward. Eventually I said, simply to break it, 'It's a good thing the photographer decided to take his picture after you told Rose the good news. She looked like a death's head before. I can't believe you did it so quickly. You are clever.'

I got a smile that was far brighter than my inane little comment warranted. I wished he wouldn't do that to me, make my insides churn with pleasure when it wasn't going to lead anywhere, but at least it was better than ignoring me altogether. 'You deserve lots of the credit too,' he said. 'If it hadn't been for you and your computer-raiding we'd never have realised how much Nigel was in debt to Andrenov.'

This was completely unfair. If he started paying me compliments I was going to stop being able to think straight altogether. 'Was it really as easy as Rose made it sound?' I asked, more to keep him talking than because I thought I'd be able to concentrate on the answer.

'I edited out a bit to spare her feelings,' he said with a slightly grim smile. 'I had to convince Nigel I'm as big a bastard as he is and I was quite prepared for Rose to lose everything, reputation, marriage, the lot, if it meant I'd get my revenge for what he did to me. A task made easier as Nigel tends to judge people by himself and he understands only too well the burning desire to get even – and what you'll do to achieve it. He'd certainly have thrown Rose on the scrap heap in the same circumstances. In fact, I think he believes I'm rather a sad act for not letting her marriage come out, then I could have really finished him – or so he imagines.' He smiled

428

tightly. 'Luckily, being the sort of person he is, he's equally unable to see how Jeremy would have overridden anything I had to say and agreed to sell the whole of Moor End if it meant Rose's name wouldn't be publicly blackened.'

'She was a bit unsure of that herself,' I said, twiddling my empty glass round and round in my fingers.

'She shouldn't be. It'd be obvious to a blind man how much Jeremy adores her,' he said in a slightly terse voice. I looked up, wondering why he was sounding so impatient. He drew his breath in sharply. 'Can we stop talking about Nigel or Rose or Jeremy?' he asked in a weary voice. 'She's going to be back any minute.'

My heart began to pound. 'What do you want to talk about?' I mumbled.

'What do you think? Gina's paintings?' he asked. 'You. Me. Luke Dillon. *What happened*, Susie?' he demanded urgently.

His demand came from so far out of the blue that initially I couldn't get my words in the right order and they came out in a jumble, falling over themselves as I tried to begin my complicated story. His face clouded, as if he was interpreting my muddled speech as an attempt to dodge the issue, and he cut across me. 'I know I don't have any right to expect you to speak to me now, when I wouldn't let you explain before, but try to understand how I felt when I saw you with him,' he said in an intent voice. 'I was so shocked I couldn't think straight. I was afraid I'd say something unforgivable, something that'd mean I'd *never* get you back.' He put out his hand and gripped my arm lightly, as if he was trying to force my attention. He had it anyway. 'You mean so much to me I'll do almost anything to have you back – except share you with Luke Dillon, that would be too much,' he added judiciously. 'I can't pretend I like what happened, in fact I hate it, but if you just needed to get him out of your system—'

'Hang on!' I interrupted, holding up my hand to cut him off. 'Let's make one or two things absolutely clear. I didn't, nor will I, *need* to get Luke Dillon out of my system, because he's never been in there! I do wish everyone would stop presuming I'm nurturing some desperate passion for him. I'm not! I never did either. Yes, I was taken in for a bit by a pretty face. Well, it is quite something, isn't it?' Obviously Hamish didn't think so. I went on. 'And if Rose hadn't banged on about him being my particular piece of forbidden fruit, making him seem unwarrantably exciting, I might have seen the light even earlier. He was a trophy boyfriend, wonderful to be seen with and have on your arm, but it was like dating a poster, all height and breadth, no depth! I'd gone off him even before I knew what he was really like – round about the time I realised there was probably a good reason why everyone called him a cokehead. It was either that or he had a weak bladder.' I wasn't getting any response from my audience so I looked up and, making sure I had his full attention, added, 'I kissed him *once* and frankly that didn't score very high on the passionometer, so I was hardly going to be desperately tempted to let him run his boring hands over me again, was I? Especially when I'm in love with someone else.' Hamish was staring at me as if he couldn't believe what he was hearing, so I said, 'Shall I repeat it slowly so it can sink in? Luke Dillon Is A Jerk And I Have Absolutely No Interest In Him.'

I was enunciating Rose-style, with her faultlessly clear diction. Hamish heard. Unfortunately, so did about thirty people around us. A couple of people covered their mouths to hide their smiles and Liddy, who was squeezing past, murmured a most surprising, 'Atta girl!'

I could feel myself going crimson with embarrassment,

while Hamish, face pale, gripped my arm tighter. My little speech didn't seem to have had the comforting effect on him I'd hoped it would. 'What did you say?' he asked urgently.

'That Luke's –' I began.

'Not that!' he interrupted roughly, and groaned with open displeasure as, picture-taking session over, Rose cut a swathe through the crowd towards us. 'Why does that bloody woman have to keep butting in at the worst possible moments?' he demanded.

'Shush!' I commanded, cheeks burning even brighter as I realised what he was talking about. I'd just declared myself in front of a roomful of people. He didn't really want me to do it again, did he? Yes, from the look of him, he probably did, I decided nervously.

'What are you two discussing so seriously?' Rose asked brightly as she reached us.

'Luke,' I said quickly.

'I'm not interested in him any more,' Hamish murmured in my ear. 'He's history.'

'Not ancient enough though,' I murmured back. 'Rose can tell you how long Luke was in the cottage before you arrived, can't you, Rose?'

'*You* were there too?' he exclaimed, as her eyes widened in alarm.

'And so was Tilly,' I said hastily, before he got any ideas about threesomes. Or foursomes. 'I told you it was girls' sleepover night,' I added breezily.

Rose breathed out with relief and flipped me a tremulous smile. 'He'd been there about ten minutes, I think. Maybe a quarter of an hour. Just about enough time for Susie and me to get the coffee going and have a cup ourselves anyway.'

'He'd only just arrived?' asked Hamish incredulously. 'At

431

eight o'clock? Who goes visiting at that hour in the morning?'

'Well, you did. Susie's a popular girl,' she said flippantly. I could have slaughtered her. Hamish's mouth was tightening, as if he suspected he was being taken for the most almighty ride. I sent her a poisonous glare and she smiled, slightly apologetically. 'What happened was, Luke's car had a flat tyre, he got covered in mud changing it and was on his way to an appointment, so he called in at Susie's to ask if he could clean up,' she rattled off rapidly. 'He must have just got out of the bath when you turned up. Honestly, Hamish, they weren't alone long enough for even a *Guinness Book of Records*-style quickie.' I frowned at her awfully, but she took no notice. 'And if you thought she was enjoying it you should have seen the way she belted him!' she added gleefully. 'I'm surprised you didn't hear him scream on the other side of the green.'

Hamish was looking as if he was having a lot of difficulty taking all this in. I couldn't blame him, especially given Rose's style of delivery. 'But why?' he asked eventually.

'Why did Susie punch him?' she asked brightly. 'That's obvious, isn't it?'

'Rose!' I said warningly. I was going to throttle her in a minute if she didn't stop treating this like a joke. I looked upwards, trying to ignore my gleefully smirking friend, but Hamish had already begun to answer his own question.

'He was simply making trouble, wasn't he? And like a jealous fool I swallowed it . . .'

Rose stopped sniggering, her eyes growing round like saucers. 'So there *is* something going on between you two!' she breathed, eyes darting from Hamish to me and back to Hamish again. 'You sneaky thing, Susie! I didn't have a clue! No wonder you were so furious with Luke! How long's this been going on then? I can't *believe* you didn't tell me about it!' she added reproachfully.

'It was right in front of your nose if you'd cared to notice,' I said a touch tartly.

Her eyes widened. 'It was, wasn't it?' she asked slowly. 'I should have realised you wouldn't have laid Luke out like that if it was merely a case of an unwelcome grope! Oh, I'm so sorry! All I did was go on about my own problems—'

'Rose, could you save your self-recriminations for another time?' Hamish asked in an exasperated voice. 'I've got some grovelling of my own to do with Susie and, frankly, I'd rather do it in private!'

'Oh yes, I'm sorry, I'll leave you alone,' she said hastily, still watching us with fascinated eyes and apparently rooted to the spot. 'I can't believe this, it's great! You two really suit each other. You've shown some good taste at last, Susie, *and* he's taller than you are too!'

Hamish almost visibly ground his teeth and sighing heavily beckoned Jeremy over from a nearby group. 'No offence, Jeremy, but will you please take your wife *away*?'

'Of course,' said Jeremy amiably, putting his arm around Rose's waist. 'Come on, darling, you're a bit de trop here.' He grinned at her. 'And that's a tenner you owe me.'

'It's not fair!' she protested. 'You must have had inside information. I thought he only liked them dark and small.'

'He likes them female,' he corrected. 'And why do you think he always used to find an excuse to drop in every time Susie was at our house?' He caught Hamish's eye and said hastily, 'OK, we're going!'

Hamish turned back to me with a relieved smile. 'Peace at last – for who knows how long?' He looked down at me and shrugged helplessly. 'What can I say? I jumped to a conclusion,

I behaved abominably. I should have known that you wouldn't do that—'

'I doubt I'd have hung around for explanations either if I'd discovered you and Merial rolling around half clad,' I said, putting my hand up across his mouth to silence him.

'Don't do that!' he hissed, seizing my hand and taking it away. Had I got it all wrong? I thought with sudden fear. Was this a formal apology and a goodbye situation? Still holding my hand he said, 'If you tempt me like that the headline in tomorrow's *Frampton Gazette* won't be "Gina Laing's Stunning Show" but "Sex Romp in Art Gallery".'

'Oh,' I said. Actually, it didn't sound such a bad idea, well, not the newspaper headlines, the other bit. 'There's a nice big pillar over there, we could continue our talk behind it in private,' I said hopefully.

Hamish eyed it up with a very un-solicitorish expression. 'Not big enough,' he pronounced finally to my regret. 'Now, to get back to what you were saying to me — Oh, bloody hell! What now?' he exclaimed in irritation as Gina approached us with a friendly smile and a nakedly curious look.

'Hamish, sorry to disturb you, but Mr Parry wants to speak to you about something. I think it's business.'

'Apologise to Mr Parry and say I'll ring him tomorrow,' he said, grabbing my wrist and beginning to head for the door, towing me behind him.

'Where are you going?' Gina called after us.

'Susie's feeling faint. Yes, you are,' he informed me as I began to protest, 'and you need to be taken outside for some fresh air. No, we *don't* need any help, thank you!' he said over his shoulder to his sister. I doubt she could have matched our speed anyway, though she tried gamely, pursuing us with calls that Hamish must remember he'd promised to come out with

434

them later on. He waved his free hand at her in reply, but didn't slacken his pace.

'This should do,' he murmured, pulling me out of sight of the gallery's large windows and down a small pedestrian alleyway running between the High Street and the back of the church. 'With any luck I should be able to speak to you for more than five seconds without someone butting in!' He stopped by the doorway of a little terraced house and drew me towards him, wrapping his arms around me. 'I was afraid I'd never be able to do this again,' he murmured against the top of my head, echoing my thoughts exactly. 'Have you got any idea what it did to me when I realised you'd only come to see me because of Rose?' he demanded. 'It was worse in a way than seeing you wrapped around Luke Dillon, because my hopes were raised and then dashed—'

'But I didn't! I came to tell you everything about Luke,' I protested against his shoulder, 'except you were looking so unapproachable—'

'Me? Unapproachable?' he interrupted, at that moment looking very approachable indeed.

'Very!' I said firmly. 'And not at all pleased to see me either.'

'Not pleased? I was beside myself with hope,' he said quietly. 'I was sure that if you'd come to see me there *had* to be some explanation why Luke was— Hang on!' he exclaimed suddenly, drawing back and looking at me with an intent expression. 'Since when did Luke Dillon ever have an appointment that early in the morning?' he asked suspiciously. My heart did a nasty little skip of fear. 'Let me guess,' he said slowly. 'You were giving Rose an alibi? And she definitely wasn't in a face pack or a nightie.' I nodded unhappily. 'No wonder you didn't want me to come in!'

'The bit about the flat tyre is completely true, though I

think Luke must have staged it, it would have been easy enough to do, all he had to do was ram a nail into his tyre. He even went cross-country so they'd get stranded miles from any help,' I said quickly, 'and Rose never meant to spend the night out with him.'

'I'm sure she didn't and frankly I don't care right now either way. You bother too much about your friends, you silly idiot,' he said indulgently, with a look on his face that made my spine tingle, 'you'll have to tell me about it sometime, but not now, we've got more important things to talk about.'

'Like what?' I asked, a bit indistinctly.

'You know very well,' he said severely. 'What you said to me earlier, and *not* your opinion of Luke Dillon, much as I enjoyed hearing it!' I looked away, suddenly shy. 'Would you like me to go first?' he asked gently.

'Yes, please!' I mumbled.

He rumbled with laughter. 'You weren't supposed to take me up on that!' He cupped my face in both hands and gently tipped it upwards so I had to look at him. 'I love you,' he said softly. 'I didn't realise how much until I thought I'd lost you . . .' I waited expectantly for him to go on with this very satisfactory topic, then I heard him swear under his breath. 'I do not *believe* this!' I wriggled around to see a tall, slim figure in a gold dress standing around at the top of the alleyway, looking this way and that.

'You shouldn't have said I was feeling faint. She's probably imagining I need cold compresses and loosened clothing,' I murmured, as he pulled me completely into the lee of the doorway so we were hidden from sight.

'I'll go the full distance with the loosened clothing!' he said against my ear. 'But perhaps a little later. And she knows perfectly well you're absolutely fine. She's just eaten up with

436

nosiness and can't wait to find out if she should start measuring up Benjy for a page boy's outfit!' He sighed in a resigned fashion. 'After the way I'd refused to speak to you I was afraid I'd get repaid in my own coin if I tried to see you alone, and I thought if we met in public I was at least safe from you physically attacking me. That was before I knew what you'd done to Luke,' he added reflectively, the corners of his mouth turned up with pleasure. 'I want the full details on that! Gina's already had several digging sessions to try and find out what's been going on between us since I took you to lunch with her, so when I asked her to make sure you were coming tonight I should have known she'd immediately jump to several, perfectly correct, conclusions about what I felt about you. And why I wasn't doing it myself. I wonder if she's already been on the blower to the parents, probably has.' It didn't sound as if he minded too much.

'Oh, Hamish!' I said, infinitely moved that such an intensely private person had been prepared to lay himself open to the family gossip train for my sake. It meant much more than any number of flowery declarations, though I was pretty keen on having those too.

He slipped an arm around my waist, fingers playing idly up my back. 'What about going somewhere we won't be interrupted all the time?' he murmured. His fingers had reached the bare skin where my dress dipped low down my spine and I shivered with pleasure, thinking there was nothing I felt like more, but some vestige of conscience made me remind him he'd promised to go out with Gina later on.

'Damn,' he muttered, 'there'll be all hell to pay if I bunk off that, but we're leaving early.' I certainly had no objection that. 'In the meantime –' his arms tightened around me – 'she can jolly well go on with her curiosity unsatisfied for a while longer.

It's years since I did any snogging in a stranger's doorway, but I don't expect I've lost the knack . . .'

'I've *never* snogged in a stranger's doorway,' I said rather breathlessly, wondering how on earth I had ever thought Hamish was stuffy, and what other surprises this supposedly conventional solicitor had in store for me.

'Haven't you?' he asked with raised eyebrows as I wriggled pleasurably against him, seeing a lot of fun ahead. 'It's an experience you shouldn't miss out on.'

I didn't. And he certainly hadn't lost the knack either.